The
BONE
ORCHARD

Center Point
Large Print

Also by Paul Doiron and available from
Center Point Large Print:

Mike Bowditch Mysteries
   Trespasser
   Bad Little Falls
   Massacre Pond

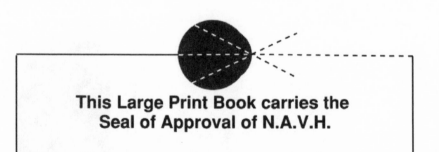

The
BONE
ORCHARD

Paul Doiron

CENTER POINT LARGE PRINT
THORNDIKE, MAINE

This Center Point Large Print edition
is published in the year 2015 by arrangement with
St. Martin's Press.

The text of this Large Print edition is unabridged.
In other aspects, this book may vary
from the original edition.
Printed in the United States of America
on permanent paper.
Set in 16-point Times New Roman type.

ISBN: 978-1-62899-431-5

Library of Congress Cataloging-in-Publication Data

Doiron, Paul.
  The bone orchard / Paul Doiron. — Center Point Large Print edition.
  pages ; cm
  Summary: "Mike Bowditch has left the Maine Warden Service and is
working as a fishing guide in the North Woods. When his mentor Sgt.
Kathy Frost is shot outside her farmhouse, Mike joins the hunt to find the
man responsible and is forced to confront past choices and determine the
kind of man he truly is"—Provided by publisher.
  ISBN 978-1-62899-431-5 (library binding : alk. paper)
  1. Game wardens—Fiction. 2. Wilderness areas—Maine—Fiction.
   3. Large type books. I. Title.
PS3604.O37B66 2015
813'.6—dc23
                                                        2014044044

For my brother Roger

Let him lose all companions, and return under strange sail to bitter days at home.

—HOMER, the *Odyssey*

MAINE DEPARTMENT OF PUBLIC SAFETY

BUREAU OF CONSOLIDATED EMERGENCY COMMUNICATIONS TRANSCRIPT

REGIONAL COMMUNICATIONS CENTER: KNOX COUNTY

*** NOTICE ***

KEY
ECS1: Emergency Communications Specialist
C1: Caller / Lyla Gammon

ECS1: 911. What is your emergency?
C1: I'm afraid my son is going to hurt himself.
ECS1: OK, what is your address?

C1:   12 Farrier Lane. In Camden.

ECS1: And what is your name?

C1:   Lyla Gammon. My son is James Gammon—Jimmy.

ECS1: What is Jimmy doing?

C1:   He's been drinking all day. And he's on pain medication for his injuries. He's not supposed to have any alcohol.

ECS1: What meds is he on?

C1:   I'm not sure. Vicodin maybe. Or oxycodone. He's on all sorts of drugs. He gets them from the pharmacy at Togus.

ECS1: Togus? The VA hospital?

C1:   His father goes with him to his appointments, so I don't know what drugs he takes.

ECS1: Your son is a veteran?

C1:   He was in Afghanistan, yes. He was . . . injured. Jimmy's in a great deal of pain.

ECS1: So he is intoxicated now?

C1:   Yes.

ECS1: Has he threatened you?

C1:   No, never. Jimmy never threatens us. I'm worried he's going to hurt himself. He says he can't take it anymore.

ECS1: Can't take what, Lyla?

C1:   The pain.

ECS1: Has he threatened to hurt himself before?

C1:   [Inaudible]

ECS1: Where is Jimmy now?

C1:   The barn. He locked himself in with the horses, and he won't come out.

ECS1: Is anyone else there with you?

C1:   No, my husband is coming home from Washington. He's due back any minute.

ECS1: I'm going to send an officer out there.

C1:   OK.

ECS1: Someone should be there very soon.

C1:   Please tell them to hurry.

ECS1: I'm going to stay on the line with you.

C1:   [Inaudible]

ECS1: Lyla?

C1:   You need to tell the officer something before he gets here. It's very important.

ECS1: What is it, Lyla?

C1:   Jimmy was a military policeman. And he has a gun.

1

When I think of Jimmy Gammon now, I remember the way he was before the war: a redheaded, freckled-faced kid with a body like a greyhound, all arms and legs, with a jutting rib cage he'd gotten running up and down the hills of midcoast Maine.

Jimmy had just graduated from Dartmouth, the alma mater of his father, James Sr., and, like his father, he was planning to make a career in the law and politics. The elder Gammon had been decorated for bravery as an infantry lieutenant in Vietnam and belonged to a generation that believed military service was a necessary prerequisite to holding higher office. Maybe it still was. In a state with the highest percentage of Afghanistan war veterans in the nation, having worn a uniform overseas carried an undeniable political advantage.

On his father's advice, Jimmy had joined the Maine Army National Guard. He chose the 488th Military Police Company, which I find odd, considering what I came to know about his gentle temperament. I was the new game warden in the district, less than six months on the job, and I met the father and son one autumn day in the field. The Gammons were hunting for grouse and woodcock in a pocket of woods outside their estate and both had bagged their limits when I came upon them. We spent a few minutes comparing notes. I marveled at their handmade European shotguns and the sleek springer spaniel that James Sr. had brought over from the UK: honestly the best-trained hunting dog I'd ever seen.

Their estate occupied something like a hundred acres of rolling fields and broadleaf forests in the Camden Hills. There were birch groves and fast-flowing streams, apple orchards and hard granite ridges like the fossilized spines of dinosaurs protruding through the turf. From the hilltop above the Gammons' palatial farmhouse, you could watch the sun rise over the ink blue waters of Penobscot Bay.

To his credit, Jimmy knew how wealthy his family was. You might even say he possessed an overdeveloped sense of noblesse oblige, or he never would have volunteered to go to Afghanistan as an E4 enlisted man. He could have avoided the conflict entirely, the way most men of my generation had. As I myself had done.

In college, I had decided that the best way for me to serve my country, given my own interests and abilities, was by becoming a cop. More precisely, I chose to become a game warden, which in the state of Maine is pretty much the same thing.

Game wardens here are full law-enforcement officers, with all the powers of state troopers. They are the "off-road police," in the language the service uses to market itself to new recruits. This special status comes as news to many urban and suburban people who mistakenly equate the job with that of a forest or park ranger. While wardens are charged primarily with enforcing hunting and fishing laws, the rural nature of the state means that a warden is often the nearest officer to any given crime scene. Call a cop in Maine, and you just might get a game warden.

It was just as well that I'd steered clear of the military. In the years since I'd joined the Warden Service I'd learned a number of uncomfortable truths about myself, the first of which was that I am a malcontent by nature. I was certain I would have been a troublemaker as a soldier, even more than I was as a warden, and it was unlikely I would have had as forgiving a field training officer as Sgt. Kathy Frost to save me from the stockade.

I admired Jimmy Gammon for his readiness to put himself at risk for the good of the country, though.

My last memory of him was shortly before he shipped out for six months of basic and police corps training at Fort Leonard Wood in Missouri. The Gammons had invited me to the private pheasant club they'd helped create on some scrubland over near Sebago Lake. Consisting of twenty acres of trails and coverts, it was a place designed to hold birds whose sole purpose in life was to be spooked into the sky and shot with twenty-gauge shotgun pellets.

On the hunt, Jimmy let me borrow his over-and-under. He told me that a British gun maker had handcrafted it out of walnut and steel. I had never handled such an exquisite firearm. I was hesitant to hold the gun after Jimmy told me the price his father had paid for it—more than three times my yearly salary—but when the springer flushed a pheasant out of the alders, instinct took over. I brought the butt up to my shoulder, squeezed the first trigger, and watched as the bird fell, limp and lifeless, from the air.

"Great shot!" said Jimmy in a high voice that would intimidate none of the Taliban or al-Qaeda prisoners being held at the Bagram prison.

As a prospective military policeman, he viewed me as a colleague of sorts, a fellow officer only a little older than himself—and potentially a friend. It was a time in my life when I wasn't making friends, and so I was willing to put in the effort, although I had my doubts about the Gammons.

"You should join our pheasant club, Mike," he said.

The idea was ridiculous. As a rookie warden, I was hard-pressed to pay my college loans and the rent on the ramshackle house I was sharing with my girlfriend at the time. "It's a little rich for me."

"What if I told you we have a special rate for law-enforcement officers, Warden Bowditch?" said his father, studying me through yellow shooting glasses.

I found James Sr. to be an imposing presence. He was a lobbyist now but had served in two Republican administrations in mysterious positions that seemed to come with basement offices in the Pentagon. He had the bushiest red eyebrows I had ever seen and a foxlike grin that suggested he could read my thoughts at will.

"We're serious, Mike," Jimmy said.

"I'll save my pennies for when you get home."

"Jimmy's going to Harvard Law after his deployment," James Sr. pronounced, as if his son's admission was a foregone conclusion, which it was probably was.

"You're going to have lots of stories to tell there," I said.

"He certainly will," said his father.

The truth was, I was worried about Jimmy Gammon. It wasn't just his voice, a boyish tenor that seemed ill-suited to breaking up riots in a war zone; it was his absolute inability to gain muscle no matter how many barbells he lifted. His resemblance to Howdy Doody didn't help matters, either. I had just gotten to know the family, but I'd already begun wondering if joining the MPs had been the father's idea of toughening him up for a future in bare-knuckle politics.

That evening, Jimmy and I exchanged e-mail addresses over glasses of Macallan on the south-facing porch of their home back in Camden. We watched his mother train a Morgan horse in the darkening field below. When the sun had finally set behind Bald Mountain, we went inside to eat the pheasants we had shot, prepared by a woman the Gammons hired to cook for special occasions.

Jimmy later sent me a few messages from Bagram. I still have one of his first e-mails, telling me that he had been stationed at Camp Sabalu-Harrison and his duties were different from what he'd imagined:

Hey, Mike:

Thirty days in-country and I haven't set foot in the prison! I figured I'd be guarding terrorists. To be honest I'm glad I'm not.

I'm part of a Quick Reaction Force, or QRF. We're in charge of perimeter security around the prison. There are three of us in the M-ATV. Donato is the CO, Smith is the gunner, and I'm the driver. The truck weighs 40,000 pounds! It makes a Humvee look like a frigging Matchbox toy. Some days it's like driving an eighteen-wheeler through a maze with all the T-walls and Jersey barriers, and there's basically nothing between us and the Afghans.

The guys in my truck are all first-class. Donato is a correctional officer at the Maine State Prison. Smith is a potato farmer up in The County. The guy's the size of André the Giant. Our interpreter calls him "Monster." He's an E4 like me.

We just had a missile attack, and I'm kind of on edge. Also, my back is all fucked-up from the weight of my kit. Helmet, Kevlar vest, plus ceramic plates, M4, full combat rounds (210), Beretta M9 with three clips, boots, etc., etc. Even with all the armor, you feel exposed out there. There's this garbage pile across from one of our battle positions. Every day we have to go out there and break up a riot because the people fight over whatever we throw out. Not just food, but bits of plastic—anything they can use.

The best part of the day is the time we get to spend with the dogs. We use them at the entry-control posts and some-times for crowd control. I envy the dog handlers, wish I could be one, but they're all contractors. The Afghans are terrified of dogs, for some reason. My favorite is Lucille. She's a Belgian Malinois.

Playing with the dogs is the only "normal" thing we do here at the camp.

I miss all the normal stuff.

You don't know what you've got till it's gone, right?

Take care, bro.

Jim

I remember thinking that it was meaningful that he'd signed his name "Jim" instead of "Jimmy." The war was already turning him into a different person.

I wrote him back a few times, telling him about the ten-point buck I had shot on my day off, the five night hunters I'd arrested in a single evening, the lost child whose body we searched for but were unable to find because we believed the abusive father had expertly dismembered and hidden it. My then girlfriend, Sarah Harris, encouraged me to keep sending Jimmy messages "to keep his spirits up." But they failed to have the desired effect. His e-mails in reply became shorter and edgier—laced with profanity he had never used in my presence—and then, finally, he stopped responding altogether.

We lost touch six months after he deployed, and I never heard about the explosion that left him without a nose, scarred across his face and shoulders, and half-blind in one eye.

2

The truth was, I was too busy circling my own drain.

While Jimmy was busy patrolling the twenty-foot walls outside the Bagram prison, the Maine Warden Service saw fit to redeploy me as well. After two years stationed in Sennebec, my supervisors politely encouraged me to swap my pleasant coastal district for a rugged outland on the border with the Canadian Maritimes. It was a transfer that I viewed (correctly) as a punishment for various insubordinate acts, not the least of which was going AWOL after my father was accused of committing a double homicide.

The reassignment was painful, since it meant leaving a landscape I had grown to know and love, as well as a supervisor who was a friend and mentor to me. I owed my career—such as it was— to Kathy Frost, who had been my first sergeant and defended my habitual misbehavior for reasons that baffled both of us. My supervisors had long viewed me as a know-it-all and a meddler. They had pushed me to rethink my choice of professions, and after nearly four years of being resented and criticized, I got tired of pushing back. I had made the decision they'd always hoped I would make.

And so, on the night in question, I was nearly two hundred miles away, making a halfhearted attempt to study for the LSATs while raindrops ricocheted like BBs off the hard metal roof of my cabin.

At the time, I experienced no premonitions. When the people we love are in danger, we like to think psychic powers will kick in and that we will somehow sense their peril. Maybe this is true of mothers and children—my own mom claimed she'd felt a jabbing pain in her chest the day I was shot in the line of duty—but Kathy Frost wasn't a blood relative. In some ways, she was as close to me as a family member, though, which is why I can imagine so clearly how events must have unfolded on the night of the shooting.

The Gammons' farm, for instance.

On that rainy evening in late May, a curtain of falling water must have hung between the road and the distant farmhouse as Kathy's patrol truck turned onto the quarter-mile drive. The long stretch of wet weather had brought with it a plague of frogs, which hopped every which way through the blurred beams of the head-lights. Earlier, Kathy and her passenger, Warden Danielle Tate, would have slowed to avoid the amphibians—I can imagine Kathy making biblical jokes—but the mood in the truck would have turned serious after the wardens received the call from the Knox County dispatcher:

An Afghan war veteran, a former military police-man, had barricaded himself inside a horse barn and was threatening to blow his head off with a shotgun.

Frost and Tate were the first to respond.

The two wardens were soaked to the skin from having spent a bug-bitten day checking turkey hunters who were either too determined or too dumb to let the rain keep them from setting up their blinds and decoys, often illegally on posted property. They'd had a bad encounter with a man from Maryland—a military contractor—who had claimed any criminal conviction would jeopardize his government clearances. They had written half a dozen summonses and been on duty for close to twelve hours.

Physically, the women were a study in contrasts. Kathy was past fifty, although she looked ten years younger, and was tall enough to have played college basketball. She wore her sandy hair cut in a shoulder-length bob and was considered attractive by male wardens, not because she was good-looking in any conventional sense, but because of her good humor and sheer likability.

Danielle "Dani" Tate was newly graduated from the Advanced Warden Academy, and she was half Kathy's age. At five-four she was also the shortest warden in the service. Her body was solid and square, and her shoulders were as wide as her hips. It was rumored that she held a black belt in

Brazilian jiu jitsu. She had flat gray eyes and a flat face that rarely displayed any emotion except seriousness of purpose. Every morning, she shined her patrol boots before zipping them up and pulled her blond ponytail through the hole in the back of the brimmed service cap all wardens are required to wear.

In the rain, the lighted windows of the farmhouse must have looked fuzzy, as if seen through smudged eyeglasses. The clapboard building had been erected in the mid-nineteenth century, but the original structure was unrecognizable beneath the extensive renovations and additions that James Gammon had made when he'd purchased the property. The four-car garage was entirely new, as was the barn where Lyla Gammon kept her Morgan horses and taught riding lessons to the wealthy children of Knox and Lincoln counties.

She was waiting for the wardens behind the misted glass door, a skeleton-thin silhouette around which the interior light had gathered like an angelic aura. As the patrol truck pulled up, Lyla Gammon stepped outside, wearing a waxed-cotton Barbour raincoat, riding pants, and knee-high wellies. Despite the rain gear, the wardens could see that she was thoroughly drenched.

Kathy checked the time on the clock and radioed in that they had arrived at the scene. Then both wardens pulled up the hoods of their olive jackets and climbed out of the truck for the hundredth time that day into a raging downpour.

"Thank God you're here!" Lyla Gammon said. She'd come from Virginia originally, and she spoke with a Tidewater accent that was as out of place in midcoast Maine as the Chanel cosmetics smeared across her face.

"You're Mrs. Gammon?" Kathy asked.

"I'm Jimmy's mom. Yes."

"We received a report that your son was threatening to harm himself," Kathy said. "Where is he now?"

"Still in the barn." Lyla stretched out her arm to indicate the long red structure behind the house. Its external floodlights had been turned off, and there was no glimmer visible through the windows. The double doors in front were both shut. "He locked himself in with the horses."

The two wardens exchanged glances. The bitumen smell of rain falling on asphalt hung in the air. The night was neither particularly warm nor particularly cold—just unrelentingly wet.

"We understand that he is armed," Danielle Tate said.

"I believe so."

Kathy wiped her forehead. "You don't know for certain?"

"I found the case he keeps his shotgun in open on the dining room table. It was empty."

"Do you know what kind of shotgun it is?"

Kathy wanted to know if they were dealing with

a single-shot firearm or a tactical weapon capable of firing nine shells without being reloaded.

"It's a Royal," said Lyla.

The pouring rain made it hard for the wardens to hear; it must have been like trying to have a conversation while standing under a shower-head.

Danielle Tate blinked water from her eyes. "A what?"

"A British model—an over-and-under twenty-gauge made by Holland & Holland."

Meaning that the gun held two shells. But a person needs only one shell to blow his brains out—or those of somebody else.

"Is it possible he has another gun with him?" Kathy asked.

The mother gathered her raincoat at the throat and clutched the waxed cotton tightly. "I checked the safe, and the Royal was the only one missing."

"Why do you think Jimmy might be suicidal?" Danielle Tate asked.

It was an important question, but Kathy would have known not to phrase it bluntly when his mother was already so distraught.

"He was badly injured in the war. He's been drinking all day. And he's on pain medications. He's not supposed to mix them."

"Is anyone else at home?" Kathy asked.

"My husband is driving back from the airport. He should be here soon."

Kathy studied the darkened building. "How many doors does the barn have?"

"Three," Lyla said. "There's another set of doors at the far end and a smaller door around the corner on the right that we use to enter the building."

"How do you know Jimmy is in there now?" Kathy asked.

"Because that's where he goes when he is sad," his mother said. "Jimmy loves the horses."

In the statement she made to the state police, and in subsequent interviews she gave to the media and the attorney general, Lyla Gammon recounted what (according to her) happened after the wardens arrived.

The two women conferred for a minute or two, and then the taller one—the sergeant, Kathy Frost—told the mother to wait inside the house. Lyla wanted to go with them to the barn. She thought she could help calm her son down, but Sergeant Frost said that they needed to assess the situation first.

Lyla believed the wardens had her son's best interest at heart, or she never would have returned to the house. Sergeant Frost appeared to be a competent and experienced officer. The younger one, Tate, seemed nervous, although she didn't say or do anything to confirm that impression; it was just a vague feeling Lyla had as a mother.

She went into the house, where the dog—

Winston Churchill, or "Winnie"—was whining anxiously at the door. Jimmy usually took the springer with him everywhere he went on the property. The two had been inseparable since her son was released from the hospital. But on this night, the young man had locked the brown-and-white spaniel in the house when he made his way through the torrential rain to the barn. That act alone had frightened his mother.

Lyla didn't pause to remove her raincoat or boots. She left a trail of water from the foyer, through the dining room and kitchen, to the mudroom, where a row of windows faced the barn.

Through the rain, Lyla watched two silhouettes approach the darkened building. She couldn't tell if the wardens had drawn their service weapons. She tried wiping the fogged glass with her sweater sleeve, but the condensation re-formed almost instantly. One of them went to the side door, while the other disappeared around the back. The sense of panic she'd felt before returned, as if her lungs were folding like black wings around her heart.

It was then the cell phone rang. Her husband was on the line, driving home from the airport in Portland. He had just turned off the numbered rural route and onto the country road that led through the green hay fields that were the last remaining evidence of Camden's agricultural past.

"What's happening?" he demanded.

"The game wardens are here."

"Game wardens? Where the hell are the Camden cops?"

"I don't know," she said. "The wardens were the first to arrive. There are two of them—two women."

"Who are they? Do you know them?"

"No."

"Fucking hell." James tended to curse more after his visits to D.C., and Lyla assumed it was something he picked up there: a way people had of establishing their hierarchies in the halls of power. "Is Jimmy still in the barn?"

"I think so."

"What does that mean?"

"The wardens wanted me to wait in the house while they tried to talk with Jimmy."

"I need you to do something for me, Lyla," James said. She always took comfort in her husband's absolute confidence, the quick way he arrived at decisions. "I need you to go out there and call them back from the barn. I don't want them talking to Jimmy until I get home. Tell them I'm only five minutes away."

"But what if they—"

"Tell them he'll listen to me. They just need to wait. Everyone just needs to wait."

"But James—"

"Just do what I say. I can take care of this."

Lyla opened the mudroom door, and the springer

tried to push past her leg, until she shoved his head down. The sound of the rain was a constant roar. The water gushing from the house's roof drains was louder than if she'd been standing beside a rushing stream.

She took several steps toward the barn, crossed half the distance from the house to the double doors, when a scream brought her up short. It was one of the Morgans. Lyla had grown up with horses and recognized when an animal was terrified.

The next thing she remembered were the shots: two of them, back-to-back. And then all the horses were screaming, panicked by the echoes, and she was running to the side door, which was standing open now, the rain slanting in.

An arm caught her as she stepped inside, holding her fast. It was the young warden, Danielle Tate. Their eyes met for a moment, and Lyla saw the other woman's surprise and fear. The barn smelled of gunpowder in addition to the usual hay and manure. Tate was gripping a pistol.

Sergeant Frost loomed over Jimmy's fallen body. She was holding a pistol in one hand and a flashlight in the other. The tiny blue beam was the only illumination in that huge space, and it shone straight down on the disfigured face of her son: a face that had once seemed beautiful to Lyla because of its resemblance to his father's, but which was now the texture and color of melted tallow, as fake-looking as the red wig the young man had worn in public after he returned from the war.

Blood pumped from the hole in his neck and flowed across the rubber mat between the stalls. Even from the doorway, Lyla saw that his eyes were open, but they were fluttering, losing focus. In horror, she watched Kathy Frost kick the shotgun away from Jimmy's clawlike hand, as if her dying son could possibly pose a danger to anyone now.

It was only when the sergeant raised her eyes to Lyla that the mother found her voice. "What have you done?" she cried, louder than the horses. "What have you done to my boy?"

3

On the morning after the shooting, while the medical examiner was zipping up the body bag and the detectives were beginning their interviews with everyone involved—including James Gammon Sr., who had arrived home five minutes after his son was shot through the carotid artery—I was sitting in the stern of a Grand Laker canoe, many miles to the north and east.

Two people were seated in front of me in the boat. One was a smooth-faced, bespectacled young man with a slight paunch and the weary air of middle age coming on way too fast; the other was his attractive girlfriend, who seemed to be compensating for her own long hours at a desk with militant dieting and exercise. Both were investment bankers from New York City who had paused in Freeport on their drive to Down East Maine to equip themselves from head to toe in outdoor clothing and fly-fishing gear from L.L.Bean.

Before setting out from the lodge, I'd given them both casting lessons on the dew-beaded lawn. The man, Mason, claimed to have been a lifelong angler, but he threw awful loops that kept twisting his tippet into wind knots. The young woman, a button-nosed blonde named Maddie, had never held a fly rod before. Within fifteen minutes of instruction, she was shooting line forty-five feet with pinpoint accuracy. Her success just made her boyfriend red-faced, and the harder he tried, the worse he cast.

I'd found it generally true that women were the best fly-casting students, since the secret to success is acquiring the smoothest form, which generates greater line speed. Men believe that the only way to prevail is to muscle their way through things, which is exactly the wrong lesson to draw from fly-fishing (and life). Too often I'd tried to use brute strength to solve my own problems, and I'd failed miserably. So I could sympathize with Mason.

A week of steady rain had raised the surface waters of West Grand Lake to the point where it was nearly swamping the boathouses, and the dam keeper who watched over the gate at the south end had been forced to increase the flow to levels few of the locals remembered. Most of the fishermen who came to the North Woods village of Grand Lake Stream—a nine-hour drive from Manhattan—came for the landlocked salmon that gathered in the river below the dam. They came to wade in the gin-clear water and cast to fish whose movements showed as darting shadows on the gravel and sandbanks along the bottom. But only a suicidal fool would have attempted to wade the stream at a flow of three thousand cubic feet of water per second.

In an effort to salvage some business, the local guides had switched to bass fishing on the surrounding lakes and ponds. The conditions weren't much better, given the high, cold water. The bass hadn't yet moved to their spawning beds and were hanging deep around the submerged boulders that dot the landscape of Washington County. If you wanted to catch anything, you'd be best off dunking a golden shiner down into the depths, something alive and wriggling, and even then you'd need some luck to catch a trophy.

But Mason and Maddie wanted to fly-cast for smallmouth using streamers and poppers. I warned them to lower their expectations. I was a

31

guide, not a magician who could produce fish from murky lake bottoms.

"We don't care if we catch anything," Mason said. "We just want to be outside."

Those are the magic words every fishing guide hopes to hear.

We dubbed around for a few hours, trying various rock clusters I knew to be fishy, as well as some hidden ledges and bars that the lodge owner, Jeff Jordan, had recommended. Maddie even managed to catch a decent-size pickerel. Mostly, though, I did my best to inform and entertain the couple. The mist made it difficult to take in the views, but occasionally a breeze would open a curtain in the fog and the pea-green hills would sharpen into focus, and you'd feel as if you were standing in a museum in front of the greatest landscape painting you'd ever seen.

I pointed out the distinctive songs of the migrating warblers we heard along the shore, nineteen species in all that morning, including Blackburnian, Cape May, mourning, bay-breasted, and northern waterthrush—birds that serious bird-watchers paid money to add to their life lists.

Coming around a bend, slowly because I was afraid of wrecking us on rocks that even in good conditions were hard to spot, we surprised a moose feeding in the shallows. It was a bull who had lost his antlers over the winter, and his shedding coat was mottled gray in patches across his shoulders. To me, he looked shopworn, but he was the first moose Maddie had ever seen and therefore something special.

"Oh, wow, he's beautiful," she said, trying to take a picture with her cell phone while I paddled in close. The animal lifted his dripping camel nose and squinted at the unfamiliar shape approaching across the gray water. As excited as I was for Maddie, a sadness enveloped me as we drew near the shore. I had seen many dead moose as a game warden and had killed more than a few myself, but the ones that haunted me were the five I'd found along a logging road the previous autumn: slaughtered out of pure evil by men who'd left the corpses to rot. It was one of the experiences that had shaken my commitment to my chosen profession. I had discovered there were limits to the cruelty I could bear witnessing.

I tried to shrug off the ghost images and nudged the canoe closer. But the bull decided he'd had enough of the paparazzi and shook his enormous head before splashing away into the forest.

Maddie turned to me in her high-backed chair. Her face was flushed. "That was awesome!"

"Thank you," Mason said.

"My pleasure." I scratched my chin. It was a new experience, touching my face and finding whiskers there.

Maddie had been looking at me strangely all morning. There was something about her face that seemed familiar, too. We must have been thinking the same thing.

"Mike, what did you say your last name was again?" she asked.

"Bowditch."

"Did you go to Colby?"

"Yes."

"I knew I'd met you before! I'm Maddie Lawson! Sarah's friend from Choate."

I barely remembered my ex-girlfriend's roommate from prep school. Maddie had come to visit Sarah a couple of times in Waterville. The picture I had in my memory was of a homely brown-haired girl who had struggled unsuccessfully to keep off weight.

"You're . . . blond," I said.

"Yeah, and I have a new nose, too. I can't believe we've spent the whole morning together and I didn't even recognize you. Sarah told me you were some sort of forest ranger."

"A game warden," I said. "I used to be."

"I was so sure you two were going to get married someday."

I had thought so myself. "Sarah and I realized we were going in different directions."

"Did you know she was back in Maine?"

The news took a while to settle in my gut. "The last I heard, she was in D.C., working for Head Start."

"She's living in Portland now," Maddie said,

"doing development work for a new charter school. We talked about meeting for a drink on the drive home. She's going to be so freaked-out to hear that you were our fishing guide!"

We were drifting closer to shore than I had intended, and suddenly I heard a scraping sound under the boat and quickly pushed the paddle over the side to keep from running aground.

"You should have dinner with us at the lodge and catch up," Mason said.

"You should!" said Maddie. "It would be our treat. Are you allowed to do that?"

"Yes, I am." I kept my head down and back-paddled the canoe away from a looming rock. The mention of food made me check my wristwatch. "I should make you two a shore lunch before it gets any later or it starts to pour again. There's an island up ahead with a picnic table. The guides have set up a tarp, so we can get out of the rain for a while."

"It's not raining now," said Mason.

"We've been so lucky today," said Maddie.

"We haven't caught as many fish as I would have liked," I said.

"Oh, we don't care about that," she said. "We're just grateful for the experience."

Magic words, as I said.

Mason gazed out at the blurred shoreline and breathed in the pine-sweet air. "I can't believe you get to come out here every day and see all this beauty," he said. "You probably hear this all the time, Mike, but I think you must have the best job in the world."

Coming from a guy who pulled down a seven-figure salary, it seemed like a funny comment. But Mason was right that guides heard similar remarks from men who lived their lives utterly detached from the natural world. There was almost a physical shock that came from breathing air heavily scented with balsam and hearing the cries of a loon across a mirror-smooth lake. To the extent I believed in epiphanies, it was from watching people venture out to the edge of the wilderness and realize how hollow their souls were. Whether being a low-paid fishing guide was the "best job in the world" was another matter.

Now that we were no longer strangers, some of the pleasure had seeped out of the morning for me. Maddie and Mason seemed perfectly nice, among the friendliest and least demanding "sports" I had met. But I had been enjoying the anonymity that came from being just another fishing guide in a town with dozens of them.

I wasn't sure about dinner, but it seemed rude to refuse their invitation. After I'd left the Warden Service, I'd made a resolution that I was going to put aside my regrets and direct my attention to the days ahead of me. Rehashing the past with Sarah's friend might not be my idea of a good time, but it wasn't like I had other plans.

• • •

Once we were clear of the shoreline boulders, I cranked the engine on the Evinrude outboard and pointed the bow in the direction of Bump Island. The canoe took off, and it felt like we were traveling along a corrugated surface. Every few seconds, the bow of the boat would hit a wave, and we would be momentarily jolted into the air before gravity pulled us back into our ladder-backed seats. I tried not to go so fast as to soak my clients or collide with one of the half-submerged trees that the winter storms had knocked into the lake.

As we approached Bump Island—an almost perfectly dome-shaped rock just large enough for a cluster of spruce trees to have taken root—I spotted a boat floating offshore. Another fisherman was using our communal picnic site.

The boat was a wedge-shaped Champion—the kind you see on Saturday-morning fishing shows. It had a flat deck for standing, a ruby red paint job that seemed to include a liberal amount of girlish glitter, and a huge black Mercury outboard. Eastern Maine has some of the best smallmouth fishing in the country, but it was unusual to see these tournament-style bass boats on our icy lakes.

"Looks like it's occupied," said Mason.

"I'm going to say hello, if you don't mind," I said.

I didn't recognize the boat and wanted to have a look at its owner. The impulse to investigate any unusual occurrence in the woods was one aspect of the warden's mind-set I was having trouble letting go.

As we drew nearer to the island, I saw blue smoke drifting sideways from under the spruce boughs, pressed down by the low-pressure system that had descended on the Northeast for the past week. Beside the picnic table, with its overhanging canvas tarp, stood an enormous electric-blue tent. Its owners had pitched it no more than ten yards from the NO CAMPING sign.

The campers had heard my engine, because the tent flap opened and two men crawled out. They were both middle-aged, with big bellies, and were wearing relaxed-fit jeans, sweatshirts, and sneakers ill-suited to the woods or the wet weather. One guy had a mustache and was holding a can of Coors in his hand; the clean-shaven one was eating a sandwich.

I maneuvered the Grand Laker so that it was parallel to the shore, not so close that the waves would push us aground, but near enough to have a conversation without shouting. I switched off the engine.

The two men looked at us with the silent disinterest of steers.

"Good morning," I said.

The mustached one touched his forelock in

some form of salute. The other took a bite of his sandwich.

"You guys must have missed the 'No Camping' sign on that tree beside the picnic table."

"No, we saw it," Mr. Mustache said. The accent wasn't southern, but it wasn't recognizably from Maine, either. "We just figured that in this crappy weather, no one was going to care if we camped here."

"It's still illegal, though."

"Is this your island?"

"No."

The sandwich eater spoke with his mouth open. "Then why is it any of your business?"

"I'm one of the fishing guides on the lake, and we maintain these picnic sites for everyone to use. If you're camped here, it means none of us can come ashore with our sports for lunch. Basically, you're hogging the place."

The guy with the mustache took a swig of beer. "So go find someplace else to eat."

Out of my peripheral vision, I saw Mason and Maddie fidgeting. I'd always had a low tolerance for assholes, but I had the safety of my clients to consider.

"Look, guys," I said, "there are lots of legal campsites along these lakes. You're welcome to any of them."

"Fuck off," said Mr. Mustache.

I tried to keep the rising anger out of my voice.

"If you don't pack up, I'm going to have to call the game warden. He's kind of a hard-ass. He's going to give you a court summons. And if he's really pissed off—which he usually is—he's probably going to arrest you, too."

The mustached man pulled up his shirt, revealing both an abnormally white and hairy gut and the grip of a semiautomatic pistol tucked into the waistband of his boxers.

"I said, 'Fuck off.' "

When I was a game warden, I had traveled everywhere with a firearm. My SIG Sauer .357 was my constant companion in life. Even when I was off duty, I carried a Walther .380 in a holster hidden inside the waistband of my jeans. But when I'd resigned from the service, I'd decided that going around armed would just be a way of clinging to an identity I was desperate to shed. I'd kept my concealed carry license for future use, but at this particular place in my life, it didn't feel right to pack a pistol everywhere I went.

The naïveté of that decision announced itself as a pain in my spleen.

The clean-shaven one pushed the last of his sandwich into his mouth and rubbed the crumbs from his hands. He smiled wide to show his teeth.

"We don't want any trouble," Mason said, his voice cracking.

Mr. Mustache let his shirt drape over his beer

belly. "Then stop bothering us, assholes, and go find your own fucking island."

I was clenching my back molars so hard, I was surprised they didn't crack. I pulled the cord on the engine and turned the tiller so that the spray arced upward in a rooster tail behind the stern. I wanted to get clear of the island as quickly as possible so that I could make the phone call to the local warden, Jeremy Bard.

For the past few months, I'd told myself that giving up the powers that came with wearing a badge was a fair trade for not being responsible for the safety and welfare of every single human being I came into contact with. I was deep inside my head, trying to tamp down my doubts and anger. It took me a long time to realize that Maddie had turned in the boat to face me. She was repeating my name, trying to get my attention, concerned that something was wrong with me.

4

W hen I'd told Kathy Frost that I had decided to leave the Warden Service, she'd responded with silence. The phone had gone quiet for the better part of a minute. It was an unusually cold day in early March, with the sky spitting snow showers outside the windows of my rented cabin.

"Kathy?"

41

"I understand," she said at last.

I had expected her to try to talk me out of leaving. I had even prepared a point-by-point counterargument, assuming that she was actually going to argue with me.

"I've done a lot of thinking, and I'm trying to be honest with myself," I said. "I became a warden for the wrong reasons. I was young and wanted to show my father what a tough guy I was, which was stupid and pointless."

Silence.

"The only reason I held on as long as I did was because of the faith you had in me," I said. "But I was never a good fit for the service. I was always disregarding regulations because I thought I knew better, and then when I tried following the rules, that didn't work for me, either."

More silence.

"I know this must come as a shock," I said. "You probably figured I'd finally turned a corner, and we'd been talking about me moving back down south again. But I'm tired of fighting against my own nature all the time. I appreciate everything you've done for me."

I waited a long time for her to speak. "Kathy?"

"I understand," she said again.

In the time I had been a game warden, I had been investigated or disciplined for numerous infractions, from interfering in the homicide investigation of a young woman back in Sennebec to pursuing a sexual relationship with the sister of a murder suspect here in Washington County. I had been the subject of not one but two use-of-force inquiries. In both cases, the attorney general's office had ruled that I had discharged my weapon in self-defense, but the fact remained that I had shot and killed two men.

The warden colonel himself had called me an "embarrassment to the service," and I had been hard-pressed to disagree. His plan, in exiling me to the wilds of eastern Maine, was to make my life so miserable that I was forced to quit. Instead, I had begun to transform myself into a semi-competent officer, which was why I had expected Kathy to insist that I stay.

On the other hand, she knew better than anyone what kind of a year I'd just endured. I had recently buried my mother after a short, devastating illness. The suddenness of her death had left me feeling punch-drunk. Every time the phone rang, I expected to hear my mom's voice calling from the great beyond.

Over the winter, I'd also testified for the prosecution in a trial against one of my best friends, who had killed two men who had deserved killing, in my opinion, and I had watched him go to prison for manslaughter. Out of guilt, I had taken to doing chores around Billy Cronk's house: chopping firewood, replacing the short-circuited bathroom fan, changing the oil in the family Tahoe. But my penance seemed incommensurate with the problems I had brought on his wife and children. If Billy managed to stay out of trouble in the joint, which was unlikely given his violent temper, he would return to them in seven or eight years.

So maybe Kathy just looked at me and saw a person who needed to become someone else for a while, and that was why she understood.

After we got back to the ramp and I had winched the boat onto its trailer and returned my clients to the lodge, I walked down to the Pine Tree Store for a bottle of something. I didn't drink wine normally. Bourbon and beer were my particular vices. But if Mason and Maddie were paying for my lobster dinner, it seemed the polite thing to take them. I stood in front of the wine display for several minutes with what must have been a dazed look in my eyes, because the kindly white-bearded owner finally came out from behind the counter, plucked a bottle from the cooler, and handed it to me with a sigh.

"Does this go with lobster?" I asked him.

"Rosé goes with anything."

There was no price sticker. "Can I afford it?"

"I'm not sure there's anything in here you can afford, based on the size of your tab." He was a jolly old elf of a man.

"I'm going to pay it off this month."

44

"That's what you said last month. Fortunately for you, I am an incurable optimist."

"In that case, can you give me a pint of Jim Beam, too?"

On the way back to the lodge, I made a stop at my Ford Bronco, parked in the wet grass behind the kitchen, and found a wrinkled but clean flannel shirt in the duffel bag I kept behind the passenger seat. I took it into the bathroom and used a bar of Lava soap to wash the fish smell from my heavily calloused hands. Having had a crew cut for years, I wasn't used to having shaggy hair or a beard. Not having a comb, I did the best I could with my fingers.

Looking at myself in a mirror had become an uncanny experience. It wasn't so much that I didn't recognize the reflected image. The blue eyes and scar on my forehead were still markers of my identity. But when I saw my bearded face now, I was reminded of someone else. I just couldn't tell you who it was.

I took a swig of the whiskey and felt the warm liquid slide down my throat all the way to my heart. My pulse was still thumping from the confrontation I'd had with the men on Bump Island. I tucked the bottle in my back pocket.

Mason and Maddie were waiting for me on the screen porch. They had both showered and changed. Mason was reading a dog-eared copy of *Fortune* magazine with a raised eyebrow.

"I wonder how many people lost their shirts buying that stock last year," he said.

"Hindsight is always twenty-twenty," Maddie said.

"Is it?" I asked.

Maddie glanced up with a chemically brightened smile. With her blond hair pinned back, I could finally recognize her as Sarah's former prep school roommate. It was like seeing a familiar portrait that had been heavily retouched.

She must have been experiencing a similar sensation looking at me.

"I still can't believe it's you," she said. "You were always so clean-cut at Colby."

I felt self-conscious in my grease-stained jeans and scuffed L.L.Bean boots. "And now I look like a lumberjack?"

"You wear it well, though."

There was a shine in her eyes that made me think the cocktail hour had already started back at their cabin.

I offered her the bottle of wine. "I brought this."

She glanced briefly at the label. "We already have a couple of bottles of Pinot Grigio chilling in the fridge. But we can drink this one tomorrow." It was my understanding they were leaving in the morning. She set the bottle down on the lacquered table beside her chair as if it was something she planned on leaving behind. "Did you ever reach the game warden about those scary guys?"

"I left another message."

It didn't surprise me that Jeremy Bard was ignoring my calls, given our mutual dislike for each other. I'd probably made a mistake not contacting the state police dispatcher directly and reporting the men for criminal threatening.

"I've never had anyone pull a gun on me," Mason said from his armchair. "It felt like something out of the Wild, Wild West."

"More like the Wild, Wild East," Maddie said.

Mason removed a neatly folded handkerchief from his chino pockets and used one of the corners to clean his tortoiseshell glasses. "You must have seen stuff like that all the time. How long were you a game warden, Mike?"

"Three years, more or less."

"What made you decide to change careers?"

His girlfriend scowled at him. "Mason!"

"It's all right," I said. "I realized that being outdoors was what I loved most about the work and that there were other jobs where I could be in the woods without having people shoot at me."

He leaned forward. "You were actually shot at?"

"From time to time."

I wasn't going to tell him that one of the bullets had found its mark. Mason would just want me to roll up my shirt so he could see the scar on my chest—more like an indelible bruise really— where my ballistic vest had stopped a 9mm round from a Glock 19.

"I'm fascinated by police work," he said. "I think it's because I could never imagine going into such a dangerous profession myself. I prefer to take risks with my client's money rather than with my own life." He had a disarming smile. "Did I just call myself a coward?"

I admired the sense of humor he had about himself.

"Most cowards I've met won't admit to being afraid, so I doubt you really are one."

"You haven't seen him around spiders," Maddie said.

"Some of them are poisonous! Have you ever heard of the brown recluse?"

The door opened behind me, and I heard fast-paced female voices raised in conversation. A group of four young women dressed in bright-colored Patagonia rainwear and muddy hiking boots hurried in out of the mist. As I stepped out of their way, I found myself unexpectedly face-to-face with the woman I considered the love of my life.

Stacey Stevens had long brown hair tied in a ponytail, light green eyes, and the lean body of an Olympic pole-vaulter. Her chin was probably a little too prominent, a genetic inheritance from her father, who had a jaw like the toe of a boot. The high cheekbones came from her stunningly attractive mother. I knew men who didn't find Stacey particularly good-looking—"too bony," they said—but to me, she was the most beautiful human being on the planet.

She'd been avoiding me for months, ever since I'd made public some unpleasant information about her then fiancé, Matt Skillen, while I was still a game warden. My discovery had precipitated the end of their relationship. Stacey seemed to be taking out her humiliation on me.

"Hello, Stacey," I said.

"Oh, hello." She continued with her friends into the dining room.

When I returned to my clients, I saw that Maddie was looking at me with a quizzical smile.

5

At dinner I took a chair that gave me a view of the table where Stacey was eating with her friends. She had positioned herself so that her back was to me. The seating arrangements seemed deliberate.

The women all looked to be in their late twenties and projected that aura of vitality that people who pursue lots of outdoor activities always seem to radiate. I had the sense that they might have been college classmates, maybe members of the same ski team. I'd seen a couple of Subaru wagons with Vermont plates and kayaks strapped to the roof racks out in front of one of the cabins. The lodge was often the launching spot for kayakers beginning a camping trip through the chain of lakes north and west of Grand Lake Stream—although most people wisely waited until the end of the blackfly season.

Their table was too far away for me to eavesdrop, but they seemed to be having a rowdy good time. Three of them were sharing bottles of wine. The fourth, who had ink-black hair and a nose ring, stuck to beer.

"What are these green things?" Mason asked as our plates arrived.

"Fiddleheads, silly," said Maddie. "Haven't you eaten them before?"

I speared one with a fork. "They're ostrich ferns. We consider them a Maine delicacy."

He bit his in half. "Tastes like spinach."

As promised, Mason interrogated me on my former career as a law-enforcement officer with a terrierlike persistence. I kept trying to divert the conversation to anything else—fishing, politics, their banking jobs in New York. But Mason's curiosity would not be denied. He waited until his girlfriend got up to use the bathroom and then launched a fusillade across the table.

"So here's what I'm wondering." His speech had grown a little sloppy from the wine. "How did you go to work each day knowing that someone might try to kill you?"

"Most days, no one tried to kill me."

"Yeah, but you didn't *know* that. There was no way of anticipating what you might encounter in the woods. Like those guys on the island. How would you have dealt with them? If you'd been all alone, I mean."

"I would've told them to get the hell off the island before I busted them for trespassing."

"But they were carrying guns," Mason said.

"That's not unusual," I said. "Just about everyone a warden meets in the woods is armed." I poured whiskey from the pint bottle onto the melting cubes in my water glass. "These days, you also have to assume that anyone might be carrying a concealed weapon."

Mason leaned his elbows on the table, his fingers clasped, almost as if in prayer. "What if they'd threatened you?"

"I would have done everything in my power to keep the situation from escalating before I started acting tough," I said. "But sometimes they don't give you a choice. People react to your overall presence, so it's important to show them you're the alpha dog. You do that through your posture and the tone of your voice. You try to come across as someone not to be fucked with."

"So what would you have done if that guy with the mustache had pulled his pistol? Would you have tried to shoot it out of his hand?"

"That's just something from the movies," I said. "Cops don't shoot to wound. You shoot to kill."

51

"How do they train you for that?"

"Repetition. Role playing. But no matter how much you train, it doesn't prepare you for having somebody point a gun at you in real life. You're a human being, and you're afraid."

"So you would have killed him?" Mason asked.

"I would have done what I needed to do to protect myself."

Mason leaned back in his chair, nodding, as if a problem that had been puzzling him all evening finally made sense. "That must have been what happened with those two cops," he said.

"Which two cops?"

"The two cops who shot that crazy vet last night. There was a thing on the radio about it before dinner."

The muscles in my neck and back tightened. "Where did this happen?"

"Somewhere south of here."

"Did you get the names of the officers?"

"The police spokesman said they weren't giving out that information yet. It sounded like a real shit show, though. To use a term from the hood."

At that moment, Maddie returned. She sat down and fluffed out her napkin and laid it across her knees. "What did I miss?"

As the cute Latvian waitress cleared our dinner plates, Maddie began musing aloud about the possibility of buying a vacation home in Maine. I

52

found myself unable to focus on the conversation.

There was a decent chance that I knew one or both of the cops involved in the shooting, either from the Criminal Justice Academy or from having worked a search or a drug bust with them. And Mason's mention of a "crazy vet" had left the back of my neck tingling, for some reason. I was eager to ask Jeff Jordan if I could borrow his computer to find out what had happened, but politeness kept me in my chair.

Dessert was blueberry pie made with blueberries that Jeff's kids had picked the previous summer.

One of Washington County's few claims to fame—aside from being the easternmost county in the United States—was that it was the wild blueberry capital of the world. Grand Lake Stream sat on the edge of the big woods, but south and west of us there were miles of open fields where migrant workers from Latin American countries came each year to rake berries. They'd set up their gypsy camps for a few months and then move south again in the fall. The sight of the barrens in autumn, blazing like a red carpet thrown over the hills, always made me think of my first district. There were blueberry fields along the Midcoast, too.

I'd been living Down East for more than a year, but I still felt homesick for the fishing villages and hardscrabble farms where I'd learned to be a game warden. I'd done a lot of growing up since I first joined the service, but sometimes I experienced painful feelings of nostalgia when I remembered my youthful enthusiasm and naive desire to do good in the world. I missed that kid. Where the hell had he gone?

Without meaning to, I found myself staring at the back of Stacey's head. I wasn't sure why. My gaze just locked onto her as if pulled there by a magnetic force.

Her friend, the one with the nose ring, was watching me with a sour expression. She leaned across the table, nearly upsetting one of several beer bottles in front of her, and muttered something. Stacey half-turned her head in my direction, then thought better of it.

Stacey worked as a field biologist for my former employer, the Maine Department of Inland Fisheries and Wildlife. She was the only woman I'd ever met who loved the woods with the same intensity I did. Her parents, Charley and Ora Stevens, were among my best friends in the world. The rift between us was stupid and unnecessary, I decided, even if she was never going to reciprocate my feelings.

I excused myself from the table.

The friend with the nose ring gave me the evil eye when she saw me crossing the dining room. I stopped beside Stacey's chair and said, "Good evening."

I had the sense from their forced smiles that they all knew who I was.

"Sorry to interrupt your dinner," I said. "Stacey, could I have a word with you?"

She narrowed her eyes. "What is it, Mike?"

"Maybe we could talk out on the porch."

I wasn't sure she would agree, but she did. The chair made a screeching noise as it slid back across the pine floorboards. Out on the porch, an older couple was playing gin rummy. I glanced around for a private alcove, but the library was also occupied by guests. Stacey just pushed past me, going through the front door and out into the lightly falling rain. I followed her outside. Neither of us was wearing a jacket.

Rain spun in the light above the lodge entrance. Stacey was dressed in a green zip-neck shirt that clung to her small breasts. She had on blue jeans tucked into rubber-soled Bogs boots.

She crossed her arms and cocked her head. "What is it?"

"Did your parents get off on their trip all right?"

Charley was taking Ora on a flying vacation to Newfoundland to see the vast colonies of seabirds—gannets, puffins, and kittiwakes—that nested along the cliffs there. He was a retired warden pilot and a legend in the service. He had also been the closest thing I'd had in my life to a father figure.

"That's what you wanted to talk with me about? My parents' vacation? How much have you had to drink?"

Not enough, I thought. "I want to apologize."

"Apologize? For what?"

"I know you blame me for what happened between you and Matt."

The suggestion seemed to annoy her. "I don't blame you. Why would I blame you? I was the one who got engaged to a scumbag."

If she didn't hold me responsible for ending her engagement, why did she always make herself scarce when I visited the home she shared with her parents on Little Wabassus Lake?

"Jeff told me Matt is running for the state legislature," I said.

"He'll probably win, too. Don't criminals always win elections? Why are we having this urgent conversation again?"

"I want our relationship to be better."

"We don't have a relationship."

"That's what I mean. I'm friends with your parents. I'd like it if you and I could be friends, too."

"What are you, sixteen?" She wiped her wet face with both hands. "Can I go back to my dinner now?"

I rubbed the water from my own face. "The women you're with don't seem to like me, for some reason."

"Maybe they didn't like having their dinner interrupted."

"The one with the short hair and the ring in her nose—"

"Kendra."

"She's been glaring at me for the past hour."

"Kendra never likes it when men look at me. It's always pissed her off."

"Why would it piss her off?"

"She and I used to date when I was in college. I'm surprised my dad never shared that juicy tidbit with you."

She'd intended the words to land like a punch, and they did. "I guess he didn't think it was any of my business."

"It's not any of your business. Are we finished, Matt? Because I'd like to go back inside." She closed her eyes, shook her head, and took another stab at it. "I meant 'Mike.'"

After she had returned to the dining room, I stood in the rain, feeling more like a fool than I had before. I wouldn't have imagined that was possible.

6

The rain began to fall more heavily as I drove west out of the village on my way home. I flipped the wipers into high-speed mode. The rhythmic clacking made my head hurt. Drinking half a pint of whiskey might have had something to do with it.

Just as likely, I was suffering the side effects

of my conversation with Stacey. When she'd first come to work for the department, I'd heard whispers about her sexual orientation, but I'd dismissed them as the self-serving stories men tell themselves to explain why attractive women show no interest in their crude advances. The gossip had ended after she'd gotten engaged to Matt Skillen. I expected the rumor mill would start churning again. Not that it was any of my business. Stacey had been right about that part.

I rounded a corner, where someone had set up a memorial to a girl killed in a car crash the previous year. It was a simple wreath of white flowers nailed against the shattered stump of an oak tree. Local jerks kept taking down the display, but the unidentified mourner kept arranging for replacements. Just as soon as one memorial was stolen, another took its place. The back-and-forth contest struck me as symbolic: the eternal struggle we undergo, trying to hold on to a memory when others have a stake in forgetfulness.

After a while, I turned down a darkened dirt road. The steady rain was carving new channels into the packed earth. I felt the emergent potholes through the worn shock absorbers of my Bronco.

A steel gate loomed in my headlights. It was a simple metal bar that pivoted on a pillar. With the engine idling, I pulled the hood of my jacket over my ears and climbed out into the mud and mist. Wood frogs were quacking in the darkness. I bent over to turn the combination lock, shining a flashlight on the dial, then pushed open the heavy, groaning gate. There were hidden night-vision cameras on me the whole time. Only I and a handful of other people—the owner and her new security team—knew about the surveillance equipment.

I drove down the shore of Sixth Machias Lake to the compound at the far end, passing through a stand of ancient hemlocks that the landscape architects had left standing when they built Moosehorn Lodge. The main building was an enormous log mansion constructed atop a field-stone foundation. Motion-sensing lights snapped on as my vehicle approached, and I knew that more video cameras were recording my arrival, sending the images to a digital feed, which the security company could review at its leisure.

Although the buildings were all new, a forsaken air hung over the place. Everything was well maintained—there was no flaking paint or loose roof shingles—and yet even a casual observer could tell that no one had lived here for a while and maybe never would again. This place would always be haunted by bad memories.

It felt like returning to my own personal fortress of solitude. I pulled up in front of one of the guest cabins but kept the headlights focused on the door. Steam rose from the hood. I reached into the pocket of my jacket and took another pull from the whiskey bottle, warming myself before I started my nightly rounds. I turned off the ignition and listened to the engine ticking.

My arrangement with Elizabeth "Betty" Morse was this: In exchange for free rent and a thousand dollars a month, deposited electronically into my bank account in Machias, I was to lend a human presence to her property. I wasn't officially the caretaker, because that title would have suggested Ms. Morse cared for this collection of buildings in any meaningful sense of the word. Her plans to create an ecological preserve on the estate hadn't worked out as she'd hoped, and sometimes I wondered if she wouldn't have been happier walking away from her Maine holdings with a multimillion-dollar insurance check.

The last I'd heard, she had turned her attention to a valley in northern Montana and was making a project of buying up her own private glacier. After the initial phone conversation we'd had—word had gotten to her that I had left the Warden Service, and she thought I might be right for the job—she had stopped answering my e-mails. Betty Morse was famous for her wandering attention. When you are worth nearly half a billion dollars, you can afford to follow your whims.

My responsibilities started at occupying one of the guest cabins and stopped at letting people in the area know that a former law-enforcement officer was in residence at Moosehorn Lodge. I didn't feel right about taking her money for living rent-free in the most luxurious cabin in the world, so I made a point of poking around the grounds with a flashlight. I was sure that Mrs. Morse would have found my unwarranted devotion to duty endearing.

I spent fifteen minutes taking a tour of the property, which included a visit to the end of the dock, where I watched raindrops stipple the surface of the lake. There wasn't another building on Sixth Machias. It always astonished me to gaze across such an enormous expanse of water without seeing so much as a single lighted window.

The irony of my living situation was not lost on me. Morse's last caretaker had been my friend Billy Cronk, the one currently doing seven years in the Maine State Prison for manslaughter. Prior to working at Moosehorn, Billy had been a hunting and fishing guide—my other newly chosen profession.

When I'd told him over the phone that I'd accepted the job with his former employer, he'd said, "What are you, nuts?"

"I know she can be difficult."

"That's not what I meant. I'm just wondering why you think it's a smart move, following in my footsteps. You planning on getting sent to prison, too? What the hell's wrong with your head, Mike?"

"There's nothing wrong with my head."

"So why'd you quit being a cop? You were one of the best I ever met."

"You have low standards," I'd said, trying to make a joke out of it.

"I guess I do."

I'd put off visiting Billy in prison for too long. Part of me was reluctant to revisit the Midcoast, where I'd once been a warden. The other part was afraid of seeing my friend in an orange jumpsuit, knowing I'd helped put him in it.

By the time I stepped inside my cabin, the front of my jeans was soaked through, and I needed another sip of Jim Beam to shake off the chill. I hoped that Mr. Mustache and his friend were getting thoroughly drenched out on Bump Island. I took another swig of whiskey, then another. When the bottle was empty, I went back outside to the Bronco and retrieved my Walther PPK/S from the locked glove compartment.

I found my gun-cleaning kit in one of the cardboard boxes I had piled in the corner. I took a yellowed newspaper from the wood box and spread the pages out across the granite bar that separated the kitchenette from the living area. The PPK series is an old-fashioned design, originally favored by the Nazis—a holdover from the days when firearms were made of steel and not high-tech polymers. It weighs more than it should. If you grip it the wrong way, the slide bites viciously into the webbing of your hand between your thumb and index finger every time you fire a shot. I disassembled the gun, poured bore solvent on a rag, then pushed an oiled patch inside the barrel to remove the carbon buildup.

It bugged me that Jeremy Bard hadn't returned my calls. We had worked together as wardens in adjoining districts for more than a year. I had come to his assistance when he'd needed me in emergencies. What the hell was his problem?

I decided to phone his house from the landline in the cabin, knowing he wouldn't recognize the number if he was screening his calls.

Sure enough, he picked up. "Game warden," he said, not even bothering to give his name.

"Bard. It's Bowditch."

He reacted with the same friendliness he might have shown a telemarketer. "What's going on?"

"I left you two messages today." I wasn't going to go through the charade of asking if he'd received them. "I wondered what you did about those two guys camping on Bump Island?"

"I didn't have a chance to get out there."

That figured. "One of them flashed a pistol at me and my clients. Displaying a firearm in a reckless manner is criminal threatening. You didn't think that was worth following up on?"

"Fuck you and your attitude, Bowditch."

"Excuse me?"

"You heard what I said. I am not at your beck

63

and call anytime you see somebody breaking a law. You think being an ex-warden gives you special privileges? You should have thought of that before you quit."

Bard had been one of the wardens who couldn't resist telling me how ill-suited I was for the job, so his giving me a lecture on resigning from the service was pretty rich.

"My sports are staying at Weatherby's," I said with as much calmness as I could muster. "Can you meet us there in the morning to take our statements, or should I call the sheriff's office instead?"

He paused, and I could practically hear the sound of cogs laboring to turn in his rusty brain. "Did the guy actually wave his gun in your face?"

"No."

"Then what the fuck, Bowditch? You know the DA isn't going to bring a criminal-threatening case, especially if I go out there tomorrow and find they've cleared off the island."

Bard's argument had the virtue of being the truth. The police in Washington County were too thinly stretched to chase down every third-rate complaint. But I was too fired up with alcohol to back down.

"If someone had called me last year to report this," I said, "I would have taken a boat out there ASAP."

"That's why you're a civilian now."

"Go to hell."

"What's got you so wound up tonight?" he asked. "Is it that thing with Frost?"

I sat up straight on my barstool. "What thing with Frost?"

"She was the one who shot that guy last night. I thought you'd heard."

In my self-absorbed outrage, I'd forgotten about the shooting Mason had mentioned earlier. The whiskey I'd been swigging all night surged back up into my throat.

"Frost and Tate shot a guy who just got back from Afghanistan," Bard said. "Everyone's saying it was a suicide-by-cop scenario. I guess the kid was wounded pretty bad over there. I can't believe you didn't hear about it."

"I was guiding," I said.

"The guy was a decorated vet, and his old man is well connected, from what I heard."

My palm had grown sweaty from holding the phone to my ear. My tongue stuck to the bottom of my mouth.

"So, is that it?" Bard asked.

"Are you going out to Bump Island tomorrow?"

"You really are a piece of work, Bowditch," he said, and hung up.

I sat at the counter, looking down at my newly cleaned pistol resting on its bed of newspaper. In my short career as a law-enforcement officer, I had killed two men. On each occasion, I had been subjected to a government inquisition that stopped just short of tooth pliers and red-hot pokers.

I sat down at the desk where Elizabeth Morse had arranged for a computer to be installed for the use of her guests. She wanted them to be able to check their stock portfolios every day.

The shooting was the top story on all the Maine news sites. The headline on the *Portland Press Herald* page confirmed my worst fears: POLICE KILL ARMED VETERAN.

Beneath the words was a photograph of the dead man in his dress uniform. With his low-slung beret and stern expression, I had a hard time recognizing Jimmy Gammon.

7

Law dictionaries define the term *suicide by cop* as an incident where an individual engages in consciously life-threatening behavior to such a degree that a police officer has no choice but to respond with deadly force. Other terms for this phenomenon are *police-assisted suicide* and *victim-precipitated homicide.*

The Jimmy Gammon I had known was a young man who loved life. He took pleasure in expensive scotch, in wing shooting alongside his dog, in the private half marathons he ran on summer mornings before the heat began to rise off the cracked roadways. What had the war done to make him want to snuff out his own candle?

The news reports were vague on this point. They said that he had been wounded in Afghanistan, but they didn't say how severely. They mentioned that he had been receiving treatment at the Veterans Affairs Medical Center in Togus, but they didn't explain what he was being treated for. They reported that there had been a previous call by his family to 911, but they didn't detail what precipitated the prior emergency or how it had been resolved.

Christ, I hadn't even heard Jimmy was home from Afghanistan. I felt sick to my stomach just thinking about what had happened to him.

I stared into the digitized eyes of the photograph. The picture had been taken after he completed his live-fire training at Fort Bliss, in Texas, but before he shipped out for the Afghan war. At first, I was inclined to see his grim expression as an affectation: the mask of a tough guy headed into battle. But the more I studied it, the more I realized that he hadn't been acting. Even before he'd been deployed to a war zone, he had already changed from the goofy kid I'd known. His own death had ceased to be an abstraction for him. In the lens of the camera, he was seeing a reflection of his own mortality.

Experience had made me an expert on the subject of police shootings. In Maine, the Office of the Attorney General reviews all such incidents. The investigators start by asking two questions: Did the officer reasonably believe that deadly force was about to be used against him or someone else? And did the officer reasonably believe that deadly force was needed to prevent that?

If the answer to either question is yes, the shooting is deemed to have been justified. If the answer is no, then the officer is terminated and liable for criminal prosecution. But even if a cop is cleared of criminal negligence, he or she can still face a civil charge from the dead person's relatives. I'd been fortunate in my two shootings. The men I'd killed had no family members with the resources to hire a lawyer to take a pound of my flesh.

Not so with Kathy. The Gammons were not people I'd want as enemies. It was late, and on the nights when she wasn't working, she tended to hit the sack early. I felt an overpowering urge to call her, but I didn't know how welcome my words of support would be. We hadn't spoken since my resignation two months earlier.

The Warden Service puts all officers involved in shootings where deadly force has been used on paid leave until their reviews are completed. Regulations would prohibit her from discussing the incident. Her union-appointed lawyer would say that she shouldn't even talk to her friends about it, not unless she wanted them to be subpoenaed.

Was I still her friend? There was only one way to find out. I picked up the phone.

As I'd expected, I got a machine. My words came out with a stammer. "Kathy, it's—it's Mike. I just heard the news. How are you doing? I know you're not supposed to talk about it, and you're probably still pissed at me for dropping off the face of the earth. But if there's anything I can do, please let me know."

I didn't expect her to call me back that night, but I left my cell on the bedside table.

Last fall, Kathy had talked about getting me reassigned to my old district in the Midcoast, but I had dragged my feet. If I had taken her offer, it would have been me in the truck with her that night instead of Dani Tate. I should have been there.

I awoke before dawn to the sound of rain drumming its long fingers on the roof. The bedsheets felt damp from the humid air blowing in through the window screen. With all the wet weather we'd been having, I expected one morning to find my skin growing a coat of moss.

No word from Kathy.

I checked the Maine news sites, but there were no significant updates from anything I'd read the night before. The whole idea of Jimmy Gammon's being in such physical and emotional pain that he'd forced another cop to end his life amazed me. As a former MP, he must have known the scars that would leave on the psyches of the responding officers.

To combat my own feelings of despair, I did my morning workout: push-ups, pull-ups, and planks. I was trying to maintain the muscle mass I'd needed as a cop, since you never know when you might be called upon to wrestle a drunken Goliath to the ground. Now that I was a civilian, I could have let myself go to pot. Instead, I found myself pushing my body harder, as if I wanted to punish it for some betrayal.

After I'd finished my exercises, I took a hot shower in the ridiculously luxurious bathroom Elizabeth Morse had installed for her guests—a round vessel sink made of polished granite, bronze fixtures, a heated toilet seat—then wrapped a hundred-dollar towel around my waist and padded out to the kitchenette.

I sat down with a glass of orange juice at the computer. The weather forecast showed that the low-pressure system currently drenching the Northeast was settling in for an extended stay. I couldn't imagine Jeff Jordan would have any clients for me to guide once Mason and Maddie headed back to the Big Apple.

Charley and Ora Stevens were off on their Canadian adventure, so I couldn't even swing by their cottage on Little Wabassus for a bottomless cup of coffee and tall tales. Stacey had never liked me hanging around the place anyway. I wondered if she and her friends were still planning to undertake their camping trip up West Grand Lake and over to Pocumcus and points north. I hope they'd packed plenty of bug dope and firewater.

For more than a year, I'd drawn sustenance from my unrequited love for Stacey Stevens—not unlike the way a vampire bat draws sustenance from its sleeping host. But as the murky light of day filled the cabin windows, I found my self-pity turning to anger. Who needed her?

The new librarian in Machias was single and had pretty legs, and I was willing to bet she didn't walk around with her nerves pulled as tight as rubber bands. With the exception of Sarah, every woman I'd ever been attracted to should have come with a warning label attached to her forehead. Given my luck, that librarian had a box of strap-ons and anal plugs stashed under her bed.

The phone rang as I was making my artery-clogging breakfast: eggs and smelts fried in bacon grease.

It was the wife of my incarcerated friend, Billy Cronk.

"Hi, Aimee," I said.

"Hey, Mike. I didn't wake you, did I?"

She was a cheerful, big-bosomed mother of four with ginger hair she wore pulled back in a scrunchie and an outfit made up entirely of flannel shirts, T-shirts, and jeans she'd purchased on sale at the bargain store in Calais.

"I was just making breakfast."

"Smelts again?"

I removed the cast-iron pan from the burner. "How in the world did you know that?"

"The last time you were over here, I saw a five-gallon bucket in the back of your truck, along with a slimy smelt net. I figured you'd been out dipping and ran into a few fish."

Aimee Cronk seemed to have an intuition that bordered on the uncanny, but, in fact, her mind worked entirely through deductive reasoning. She'd never graduated from high school, but I'd always said she would have made an excellent psychologist—or detective.

"I have three bags of smelts in the freezer," I said. "Do you want some?"

"I've been doing Weight Watchers, so I can't be eating all that bacon fat."

She paused, and I heard a child scream in the background. Visiting the Cronk house, filled with four kids all under the age of seven, always reinforced my conviction that small children are essentially insane little people.

"Is there any way you could come over here and give me a jump? I need one wicked bad."

I thought I'd misheard her. "What do you need?"

"The Tahoe won't start, and I ain't sure if the

battery's dead or the alternator's shot. What did you think I meant? That I wanted a quick lay or something?"

I ignored the question. "It could be your distributor cap is wet, with all this humid weather we've been having."

"Whatever it is, I can't afford to be stranded here in the boonies. I only got the Tahoe now that the bank's repossessed Billy's truck. I'm working lunch and dinner at the Bluebird Ranch and can't miss another shift."

"I'll be right over," I said. "If worse comes to worst, I'll be your personal chauffeur today."

"That's the least you can do if you ain't going to screw me."

I nearly dropped the phone.

She laughed out loud. "I'm joking! Billy always said you was the most uptight individual he'd ever met. You're a worse prude than my aunt Lillian, and she's a Baptist."

8

There was a dusky-looking Swainson's thrush hopping around in the pine needles outside my cabin. It was hunting for ants and beetles. Like all thrushes, it had those big black eyes that looked like they'd been drawn by Walt Disney.

Sarah had taught me a lot about birds during our

years together, first at Colby and then in that on-again-off-again period after I'd become a game warden. She enjoyed the outdoors, but only as a playground. Cabin living was never her thing. It hadn't surprised me when she announced she was leaving our backwoods shack to take a prestigious fellowship in D.C. The prep-school girl from the Connecticut suburbs had never been cut out for a life that involved splitting and stacking wood for the stove.

Maddie had said that Sarah was back in Maine, working at some new school in Portland. I'd never believed that our destinies are predetermined. If you look back on your life, you might see what looks like a meaningful progression, but it's no different from gazing at the moon and seeing a man's face. Just because you perceive a pattern doesn't mean it's really there. I tried not to dwell too much on the circumstances that were drawing these people from my past into my life again.

The forest road crossed a number of quick-flowing streams whose beauty disguised the fact that they were the breeding grounds for blood-thirsty insects. Unlike mosquitoes—which seek out stagnant pools to lay their wriggling larvae—blackflies only breed in swift, clean water. As the day warmed, the voracious bugs would rise from the streambeds in clouds so thick I was afraid to take a deep breath for fear of inhaling them.

Spring is a season of pure misery in the Maine woods.

When I arrived at the Cronk house, I checked my phone again for a message from Kathy, but there was nothing. It bothered me not having heard from her. I typed a text message and hit SEND. *Please let me know how you're doing,* it read.

In the meantime, I had plenty of chores to keep me occupied. The Cronks lived in a too-small shack of a place in a clearing in the woods down around Whitney. Looking through my bug-smashed windshield, I noticed that the pile of firewood Billy had furiously cut before he went to prison was a quarter of its former size. There also seemed to be a crack in one of the upstairs windows that was new since my last visit. And a roof gutter was dangling free and needed to be reattached.

As I climbed out of the Bronco with my toolbox in hand, Aimee Cronk appeared in the doorway, holding their youngest child, a daughter, under her arm, while a snotty-nosed boy peeked at me from behind her leg. Billy called his blond brood of four "the Cronklets." I could never keep them straight.

Aimee was a big woman, but shapely; she carried her weight in places men found attractive. She had just washed her hair, and loose red strands hung around her open, freckled face.

Watching her husband head off to jail for close to the next decade or so would have crushed lots of women, but not Aimee Cronk. "I always figured it was more a question of when and not if," she'd told me. "You can't break the law as much as Billy did without it breaking *you* sooner or later."

"There's the man of the house," she said.

"I wish you wouldn't call me that."

She showed the gap between her front teeth when she smiled. "You're still thinking about that joke, ain't you?"

How did she know these things? I couldn't imagine a single secret Billy had managed to keep hidden from his wife. It would have been like being married to Hercule Poirot.

"So I guess I should have a look at your engine," I said.

She gestured with her free hand at the faded blue Tahoe parked beside the picnic table. "Keys are under the seat," she said. "I got to get changed for work."

A damp gust blew the smell of blossoming apple trees down the hill while I worked, and a chestnut-sided warbler harangued me from the roadside willows. In my ears, the call sounded like words: *Hey! Hey! Hey! What's with you?*

I poked around under the hood, checked the electrical wires for loose connections, found none, then tried using my jumper cables. I ran the engine for a solid fifteen minutes, but the Tahoe failed to start. I was despairing of fixing it and figured I'd have to remove the air-intake system in order to get at the distributor, when an odd thought occurred to me. I used a screwdriver to pry loose the battery port covers.

When I knocked at the front door again, I saw that Aimee had changed into her pale blue waitress uniform and was slipping barrettes into her newly dried hair. "What's the bad news?" she asked.

"I don't suppose you have any distilled water."

"Billy might have a jug in his shed. What for?"

"Your battery has no water in it."

"In all this wet weather?"

"The battery is sealed," I said, rubbing my blackened hands together. "The good news is that if we refill it, we can probably get you on the road, but you should have your battery changed in Machias while you're at work."

She smiled. "Ain't you the handy one, though."

"Not like Billy," I said.

Her smile went away like the sun behind a cloud. "So when are you gonna visit him in the penitentiary, anyway? He thinks you're punishing him by not going down there."

"I'm the one who testified for the prosecution!"

"It don't matter," she said. "Billy did what he did, and now he has too much time to think on things. I don't want him obsessing over the past. It's unhealthful. He can't change it anyhow, and I

77

need him to start writing letters to his kids and not getting into fights that add years to his sentence or other stupid shit like that. Just tell him whatever he wants to hear so he can start living for today again." She removed a dirty Kleenex from her skirt pocket and rubbed my nose with it. "You've got grease all over your face."

"Thanks," I said.

"Will you promise to go down there tomorrow? I know you filled out that visitor application, because I made you do it at dinner that time."

She had put the sheet of paper in front of me at her kitchen table and refused to serve any of us until I'd completed the form.

"Aimee," I said.

"Promise me you'll go see him," she said. "It's more important than cutting firewood or any of this other shit. You're his only real friend in the world, Mike."

"What about his army buddies?" Billy had served in both Iraq and Afghanistan.

"The band of brothers? Don't get me started on those misfits. Will you go see Billy tomorrow or won't you? I need you to promise."

The chestnut-sided warbler started up again in a rosebush across the yard.

"I promise," I said.

"Good, because I'm late for work. Can you stay and watch the rug rats until my sister gets here?"

I looked past her into the monster's lair. I had

close to zero experience caring for small children. Even baby-sitting the Cronklets for fifteen minutes was a frightening prospect. "What do I do?"

"Just listen," she said. "If they're crying and fighting, everything's OK. But if it goes quiet all of a sudden, then you know all hell has broken loose."

The text arrived a few minutes before Aimee's sister did. I had taken up my post in the doorway of the living room, holding the sleeping eighteen-month-old in my arms, terrified she would wake up while two of the kids threw Legos at each other or put them in their mouths. There was one Cronklet missing, I realized. The question was whether to hunt that one down or risk having the other two choke to death on pieces of plastic due to my negligence.

Like many parents, the Cronks viewed child care as a rudimentary human skill, while to me it seemed like managing a sophisticated series of no-win situations. When the two children on the floor in front of me suddenly rushed off in different directions, one toward a kitchen full of sharp knives, another down a darkened basement stairwell, I found myself paralyzed with indecision.

My cell phone vibrated in my jeans pocket and I managed to fish it out without waking the little girl. It was a text from Kathy: *I killed a guy. It sucks. Thanks for your concern.*

When I was just out of the academy and Kathy was my field-training officer, she used to call me "Grasshopper," after the old *Kung Fu* television show. It was the nickname the blind Shaolin monk gave to his naive young student. Even when I was no longer one of her district wardens, it had remained Kathy's pet name for me. Its absence here affected me even more than the sarcasm in the text itself.

The Maine State Prison was located twenty minutes from the Gammons' horse farm and not much farther from the hilltop where Kathy lived at the edge of a rolling field of blueberries. My promise to Aimee had committed me to revisiting at least one landmark from my past. I was still trying to decide about the others when Aimee's sister burst through the door and rescued me from a house that had grown alarmingly quiet.

9

I spent the rest of that day reattaching the gutter and taking down a dead spruce that was threatening the Cronks' roof. I used a chain saw to split the tree into lengths I could drag into the bushes. It was a white spruce: a species Mainers call "cat spruce" because the crushed needles have the ammonia odor of cat piss. Aimee wouldn't want to put these fast-burning, smelly logs into her woodstove, not unless she was trying to clear the house of unwanted guests.

By the time I was done, I was coated in perspiration and sawdust. I'd applied a layer of bug repellent to every inch of exposed skin but had managed to sweat away the powerful chemicals, so my neck and ears were swollen with bites from the blackflies that follow you everywhere in the woods in May. I drank a gallon of rusty-tasting water from the hose, packed up my tools, and headed to Day's General Store for a cheeseburger and a cup of coffee.

The store had been one of my regular stops when I was a game warden, and it wasn't unusual to find other wardens, state troopers, and sheriff's deputies sitting at the lunch counter. My friend Cody Devoe once explained to me why Day's was popular among the law-enforcement crowd. "It's the only place around where I know the guy in the kitchen doesn't spit in my food," he'd said.

The screen door snapped shut behind me on its too-tight spring as I stepped inside. Day's was always dim—the fluorescent bulbs hadn't been dusted in years—and the first odor to hit your nose was inevitably the oily starch of the deep fryer. I hated to contemplate the last time Bill Day had changed the grease in that contraption. Ratty taxidermy mounts—stuffed raccoons and fishers—stared down at you from the shelf above the register with glass eyes. The display of dead animals was Bill Day's idea of interior decoration.

A state trooper was alone at one end of the counter, separated by two open stools from a redneck in the corner. I had to make up my mind where to sit. I chose the stool beside the cop.

His name was Belanger. We had worked together on a few occasions, but I couldn't say that we were well acquainted. Like many troopers, he was an impressive physical specimen: a Greek statue in a powder-blue uniform. His eyes flicked sideways as I took a seat and then returned to watching the television mounted to the wall.

I had the feeling he didn't know who I was. "Belanger? It's Mike Bowditch."

He put a paper napkin to his mouth and swallowed what he'd been chewing. "Didn't recognize you under all that hair," he said.

I rubbed my scruffy chin with my knuckles. "Sometimes I don't recognize myself."

"That's a tough break you got," he said.

"What's a tough break?"

"I heard you were fired."

"Actually, I resigned. I'm guiding up around Grand Lake Stream now."

He nodded and took a sip of water. "Enjoying it?"

"Mostly," I said. "You know, the grass is always greener."

He nodded again and turned back to the TV.

Now that I was no longer a cop, he had nothing to say to me.

The local news station was running a segment on the diluvial rain we had received. The weather-man was standing with an umbrella in a puddle while cars drove by, splashing his pants.

I studied Bill Day's slope-shouldered back as he flipped burgers on the grill. He was a soft guy, bigger on the bottom than the top, and his body always gave me the impression of melting even when he wasn't standing in front of a burner.

"Afternoon, Bill!" I said.

He glanced over his shoulder, his face red and streaming, and waved a metal spatula. "Hold your horses. Hold your horses."

Day's wasn't known for its customer service.

I settled back on my stool. The television anchor was introducing a new story—the volume was too low to hear anything—but there was a picture of Jimmy Gammon floating beside the newscaster's handsome head.

"Hey, Bill," I said. "Can you turn up the TV?"

The cook refused to look up from his grill. "Remote's on the counter."

I glanced along the Formica and saw the remote control beside a ketchup bottle in front of the redneck.

"Can you turn that up?" I asked.

The man had a bird's nest beard and a drawn face from a lifetime's worth of booze and cigarettes.

He was wearing an olive green sweatshirt, from which he had scissored the sleeves, revealing skinny arms patterned with tattoos. He peered at me from beneath the frayed brim of his baseball cap.

I pointed at the television. "Increase. The. Volume."

With a grunt, he slid the remote down the counter, but it caromed off a napkin dispenser and landed on the floor behind me. I glared at the red-neck, then hopped off the stool to retrieve it. By the time I got it aimed at the set and boosted the volume, the scene had changed to some sort of protest outside the headquarters of the Maine Warden Service in Augusta. There were a dozen or so people with signs, some bearing photos of Jimmy.

A female reporter had the microphone in the face of a fierce-looking young man with a crew cut and the shadowy suggestion of a goatee. He wore a navy suit and a striped tie, but the jacket seemed too tight; his shoulders looked ready to burst through the seams. Words along the bottom of the screen identified him as Sgt. Angelo Donato, Maine National Guard (Ret.).

"Jimmy Gammon was a hero," he was saying. "What happened to him over there in Afghanistan I wouldn't wish on my worst enemy. He had his share of problems, no doubt about it, but no way did he want to kill himself. Jimmy was one of the happiest guys I ever met. Those cops' stories just don't add up. And you know they're going to get off with a slap on the wrist." He stepped back and shouted "Justice for Jimmy!" to the people behind him.

The camera cut back to the studio, where the anchor began a new story: Domestic violence reports were up in Maine. I muted the sound and set the remote on the counter. Belanger arose from his stool and towered over me. He didn't have the most expressive face in the world, but I sensed that the story about Jimmy Gammon had gotten to him. After a moment, his features hardened again into the stony expression he wore while on duty. He adjusted the chin strap on his blue Smokey the Bear–style hat. Then he reached into his wallet for a ten-dollar bill to leave beside his empty plate on the counter.

"Have a good day," he said to me, as if I were a driver he'd just handed a ticket.

After the trooper left, I swiveled around on my stool to address the redneck on my right. The front of his sweatshirt proclaimed his manly virtues: WOMEN WANT ME. FISH FEAR ME.

"What's your problem?" I said.

He used his thumbnail to remove a piece of gristle from between his front teeth. "Huh?"

"The remote control. You couldn't have just handed it to me?"

There was no white in his eyes at all, only pink. "You don't recognize me, do you?"

"Should I?"

The man flared his nostrils. "You pinched me for night hunting last year. You and that other warden had that robot set up by the side of the road, and you entrapped me into taking a shot at it, when I was just driving home, minding my own business. I got a five-hundred-dollar fine and lost my hunting license for a year on account of you."

The memory came back to me as if illuminated by a magnesium flash. I'd been working night hunters with Cody Devoe. Poachers began to get itchy in September, with legal deer season so close. They started driving into fields of goldenrod, illuminating the edges of the trees, hoping to jacklight a buck. Wardens know where to wait for poachers by following tire tracks in the weeds. Cody and I had been hiding in the puckerbrush, using a remote control to manipulate a mechanical decoy shaped like a deer. With the push of a button, we could move its extremely realistic head.

This loser had been half in the bag when he'd come cruising past. He'd stopped, backed up, and then stuck a .22 rifle out the window to take a shot at Robby the Robo-Deer. He'd missed the decoy by a country mile. When Cody and I had sprung from the bushes, shouting "Police!" he had stomped on the gas, running his Chevrolet Monte Carlo off the logging road and into a stump.

"We also arrested you for operating under the influence, I seem to recall."

He slid off the stool and stood face-to-face with

me. His breath stank of coffee, cigarettes, and incipient gum disease. "I heard you ain't a warden no more."

"That doesn't mean I can't kick your ass."

"We'll have to see about that some time." He lowered his voice an octave to sound menacing.

"Why wait?"

"I know where you live, asshole."

The local scofflaws had all heard that I'd left the Warden Service, but they probably didn't know that I'd moved out of my rented cabin. I was hardly going to give this one driving directions to Moosehorn Lodge.

"Bring some beer when you come over," I said.

After he left, I found myself alone at the lunch counter. Bill Day wiped a dishrag over his red skull, trying to soak up some of the beaded sweat. "What'll you have?"

"Cheeseburger deluxe. And some coffee."

While Bill filled my cup, I leaned my elbows on the edge of the counter and reflected on the two conversations I'd just had. The trooper had been frosty with me because I was no longer a law-enforcement officer. The poacher had been pissed because, in his twisted thinking, I would always be a game warden.

A man just couldn't win.

The fry cook gave me a baffled expression. "What are you laughing at?"

"Nothing," I said.

10

The next morning, I made an early start for the Midcoast. The drive to the Maine State Prison in Warren usually took a solid three hours, longer in the rain. Aimee had told me that Billy was being housed in the Medium Custody Unit and had "contact visit status," meaning that he was permitted walk-in visits with anyone who had filled out the required form, as I had, and received prior approval.

I filled a thermos with coffee for the road and turned the dial to a classic-rock station in Bangor. In northern Maine, the listening choices broke down into roughly four categories (not counting the broadcasts from Canada): classic rock, country, Christian, and right-wing yelling. You only had to listen to the radio for ten minutes to guess that Maine was the whitest state in the nation.

I decided to take the northern route, skirting Elizabeth Morse's extensive land holdings, by driving from Topsfield to Lincoln and then south along Interstate 95 through Bangor. It was a slippery ride. A wet white fog rose like steam from the asphalt, and the logging trucks, barreling down the highway at eighty miles per hour, threw behind them blinding curtains of water.

By the time I finally saw the Camden Hills, the knuckles in my hands were sore from gripping the steering wheel. I passed a series of familiar landmarks: the lobster pound at Lincolnville Beach, the terminal where the Islesboro ferry docked, the road up the side of Mount Battie. Everything looked just as I remembered it, and yet something seemed profoundly different.

Not much had changed in Camden's picture-perfect downtown. Some of the boutiques and restaurants had been replaced by other boutiques and restaurants, and the nonfunctional smokestack at the mill-turned-condo complex still needed a fresh coat of paint. The same schooners were docked in the harbor, their masts rising into the mist. I had always been prone to nostalgia, but I hadn't expected to feel such an overwhelming sense of homecoming.

I resisted the urge to take the turn that would have brought me to the rolling farm country where the Gammons lived. I had no idea what I would have said to them anyway. Jimmy's parents had been generous and caring people. They had recognized that their son, for all his intelligence and good cheer, had trouble making close friends. They had hopes for me that I had probably dashed. The Gammons couldn't have known that, for complicated reasons of my own, I wasn't interested in forming close relationships when I was twenty-four. A stubborn desire to inflict loneliness on myself had kept me from forming a meaningful bond with Jimmy Gammon.

Leaving Camden for the considerably less picturesque quarry land to the south, I realized it wasn't the Midcoast that had changed. It was me.

The road to the prison led me through the western reaches of the city of Rockland. A century earlier, miners had dug deep pits into the fields and forests to excavate limestone. There was still a working cement factory—an enormous industrial complex with smoking chimneys you could see from miles out to sea—in the middle of this pockmarked landscape. Dump trucks still carried smashed stone out of the gravel pits, but most of the old quarries had been abandoned. Decades of rain had filled the man-made chasms with water. And over the years, people had thrown trash into these deep, dark lakes—not just bags of dirty diapers and chicken bones but also broken refrigerators and derelict cars. The city itself used one of the quarries for its municipal dump.

The Old County Road threaded its way between the flooded pits. Occasionally, a vehicle would crash through the guardrails and plummet hundreds of feet into the black water below. Sometimes the driver would even survive. A sulfurous odor hung over the quarry land. Rounding one of the many sharp corners, it was as if you'd just missed seeing the devil disappear in a puff of smoke.

I passed through the pretty Colonial-era town of Thomaston and crossed the tidal St. George River into Warren. The river was high from the week of rain we'd received, but I could tell that the alewives were running because of the huge flocks of birds perched on rocks and in trees along the shore. In the spring, schools of sea-run fish return to the lakes and streams where they were spawned to reenact their primeval mating rituals. Most die before they can reproduce. Snake-necked cormorants dive for them. Ospreys plunge from the sky with talons outstretched to carry them back to their nests. Lobstermen net the fish by the truckload to use as bait. But still the alewives return.

So I wasn't the only fool coming home.

I'd visited the Maine State Prison a few times while I was stationed in the area. It was an enormous cream-colored fortress, hidden from the major roads by thick stands of oaks and pines, but visible at night from a distance by the ocher glow that radiated into the sky above the brightly illuminated buildings. Nearer to the jail, the trees had been cleared so that the guards in the towers would have a clean shot at any fugitive who managed to get past the razor wire.

I parked in the paved guest lot and turned off the engine. Visiting hours began at nine o'clock, so I had to wait inside the Bronco for a while, listening to the rain tap-tapping against the truck's steel roof. I desperately needed to piss, but this was hardly the place to sneak into the bushes. I wondered how many video cameras were already watching my suspicious, lonely vehicle.

One of Jimmy's buddies from Afghanistan was a guard at the prison. Many of the guys with the 488th worked in law enforcement or corrections; it was why they'd joined the police corps. What was his name? Donato. He was the angry guy I'd seen on the television news. I wondered what I would say to him if we ran into each other inside. Offer condolences for the loss of our mutual friend? Or defend my other friend against his unfair accusations?

At nine sharp, I made my way to the door, my shoulders hunched against the rain. To my dismay, the bathroom in the lobby had an out of order sign taped to the door. The guard behind the armored admissions desk was a stern-faced man with the elongated torso of a weasel. He wore reading glasses balanced at the tip of his pointed nose. His nameplate said TOLMAN.

"I'm here to see William Cronk."

He looked me up and down, and I realized how sketchy I must appear to someone who judged a person's moral character by the cleanliness of his clothes or the length of his hair. Tolman pushed a clipboard at me through a slot. There was a pen attached to it by a little chain. "You need to fill out a visitor application."

"I already did. My name's Michael Bowditch. I should be in your system."

He grunted and swiveled his chair around to a computer terminal. "Spell your name, please."

I did so, trying to ignore the swelling pressure in my bladder. What had made me drink an entire thermos of coffee?

After a minute, the guard stared at me over his reading glasses. "You'll need to schedule an appointment."

"I thought I could just walk in if my name was on the list."

"That doesn't apply to prisoners in the SMU."

"Wait," I said. "Billy's in the Supermax?"

"He's in the Special Management Unit."

It was the same thing. "Since when?" I asked.

"I can't disclose that information."

"Why was he moved from Medium Custody?"

"I can't disclose that information."

I could only guess what my hot-tempered friend had done to earn a trip to solitary confinement. If his actions were deemed heinous enough by the Knox County district attorney, he might be facing a criminal charge that would result in a longer sentence. Aimee would be out for blood when she heard the news.

"I'd like to make an appointment to see him," I said.

Tolman removed his glasses and set them on the desk. "You need to do that by phone."

"But I'm right here."

"We have rules here, and they apply to everyone." He handed me a card with a phone number on it.

"Who's going to answer this number when I call?"

He ran his tongue along his lower lip. "I will."

"But you won't just schedule the appointment for me now—in person?"

"We have rules," he said again.

I removed the cell from the inside pocket of my rain jacket and used my thumb to tap in the number on the card. The phone on the desk beside Tolman rang loudly, and a light flashed on top of it. He let it ring for a long time.

Finally, he picked up the receiver. "Hello?"

"I'd like to make an appointment to visit an inmate in the SMU." I stared straight into his eyes.

"Don't be a wiseass," he said, actually speaking into the receiver, as if I were miles away.

"I'm just following the rules."

A woman with two loud young children came bustling in through the door behind me, followed by an embarrassed-looking older couple, both dressed in dark colors, probably there to see their misbegotten son. Visiting hours were fully under way at the prison.

Tolman continued to speak into the phone, so his voice came to me in stereo. "Prisoners assigned to the Special Management Unit are permitted a single one-hour visit per week."

I hung up my cell and addressed him over the desk. "Has Billy Cronk received his visitor this week?"

"No." He placed the receiver back down on the cradle.

"Then can I please schedule an appointment to see him?"

"Visitors are required to give twenty-four notice."

"Oh, for Christ's sake."

I drove halfway down the long wooded drive that connected the prison with Route 97 and then hopped out to relieve myself behind a tree. The Department of Corrections probably had hidden cameras in every bush within a mile of the jail, but I didn't care. Let them arrest me for public urination.

I was deeply worried for Billy. I'd seen the inside of the Supermax and knew something of its horrors.

An inmate in the Special Management Unit spent twenty-three hours a day in solitary confinement, living in a room measuring six and a half feet by fourteen. For the remaining hour, he might be given exercise in a dog run outdoors (provided the weather was good, which it rarely was). The lights in his cell burned brightly twenty-four hours a day. All food in the unit was served cold.

Guards slid the tray through a slot in a door that might have been contaminated by the blood, feces, and urine of other inmates. Prisoners had no access to computers, and all radios and televisions were prohibited. Instead of a toothbrush, the inmate was given a plastic nub to use on his fingertip. Billy would get to shower no more than three times per week.

There were men in the Maine State Prison who deserved death, in my opinion, but execution would have been a kindness compared to what inmates endured every day inside the Supermax. The facility existed not so much to protect society from dangerous individuals or even to punish them in the conventional sense of denying free men their liberty; instead, it had seemingly been designed to drive convicted criminals slowly insane. Billy Cronk had fought for his country in foreign lands with codes of justice Americans considered medieval. After he'd survived Iraq and Afghanistan, it enraged me to think that the first time he'd experienced torture was now, after he'd returned home.

I had felt anxious about seeing Billy before. Now I couldn't imagine leaving the area without making sure my friend was OK.

11

I called my boss from the parking lot outside the Square Deal Diner and Motel.

"I'm not going to be available for a couple of days," I told Jeff Jordan.

Technically speaking, Jeff wasn't my employer. As a Registered Maine Guide, I was the sole proprietor of my own little business. Jeff hired out twenty or so local guides at a time, each of whom had a different skill set. Some were masterful entertainers who could spin stories to distract clients when the bass refused to bite. Others had a sixth sense for finding birds to shoot, even during "bad grouse" years, when the hens had been flooded off their nests. A few guides, like me, earned our two hundred dollars a day by taking on whatever was thrown at us—last-minute jobs, bored teenagers, or world-class assholes who wouldn't be satisfied if they caught twenty salmon.

"I don't have work for you anyway," he said. "Two more parties canceled on me this morning. They saw the long-range forecast and backed out of their reservations. I swear, sometimes I think the Weather Channel is intent upon destroying my business."

"What about the IRS?" I knew Jeff had no

great love for the agency that had just audited him.

"They're in cahoots with the Weather Channel."

"I'll let you know my availability when I'm back."

"Stay dry."

The parking lot of the Square Deal was as packed as ever. A celebrity chef on the Food Network had decided it exemplified all the best qualities of a classic New England diner, and now the place was routinely overrun with tourists. I noticed a specialty license plate from Maryland with the Ducks Unlimited logo.

I raised the hood of my raincoat over my ears and prepared myself to venture inside. When I'd been a game warden in the district, I had stopped at the Square Deal nearly every day. The owner, an apple-faced woman named Dot Libby, would set a molasses doughnut on a plate and pour a cup of coffee the second she saw my patrol truck pull up outside the window.

The last I'd heard, Dot was receiving chemotherapy for skin cancer. She could conceivably have passed away in the interim, and the news might have eluded me. It was sobering to realize that another person who had been a regular fixture in my life could have died without my knowing about it.

When I walked inside the door, it was as if I'd never left. The crowd at the Square Deal tended toward the gray-haired and the blue-collared: older couples who considered a meal at the diner to be an integral routine in their married life, plus a regular gang of lobstermen, clammers, builders, linemen, and road workers. I recognized several of the weathered faces at the counter, and there was Dot behind the register, ringing up a bill, looking thinner than I'd ever seen before, but not unhealthy.

"Well, as I live and breathe," she said.

"Hi, Dot."

She came around the register and gave me a big soft hug. She had round cheeks that were pimple-red with rosacea and wrinkles around her eyes from a lifetime of laughing. She gripped my shoulders and appraised me from arm's length. "Look how hairy you are!"

"I need to get it cut."

"What are you doing back in town?"

"Just passing through." Under the circumstances, I decided not to mention my business with Billy at the Supermax. "I was hoping to get a room at the motel for the night. Do you have any vacancies?"

"We'll always have a room for you, Mike." She reached for the coffeepot and filled the ceramic mug in front of me. When she looked up again, there was an expression of concern in her eyes. "I was so sad to hear about your mom. Are you doing all right?"

The Square Deal had always been the hub of gossip around Sennebec, but I was surprised that word of my mother had reached Dot. I had been gone from the area for more than eighteen months. I figured Kathy must have told her.

"Thank you, but I'm fine," I said in a tone that probably didn't sound convincing.

She laid a hand on my forearm. "Just know that you are in my thoughts and prayers."

"Thank you."

"You know I've had cancer myself."

"How are you doing?"

Dot shrugged. "The docs cut some things off my back—it looks like the craters on the moon—and now they've got me on all sorts of experimental medications. So far so good. 'Any day above-ground is a good day,' Earl used to say."

There was a picture of her late husband on the wall. He had passed away a decade earlier, and had been underground a long time, but his weary hound-dog face remained a lugubrious presence at the restaurant.

I emptied two containers of cream into my coffee.

"It's so nice to see you again, Mike," Dot said. "We've been keeping tabs on you from afar." She removed a molasses doughnut from the display case and set it on a small plate. "So what's the story behind the beard? Are you working undercover?"

"Actually, I decided to leave the Warden Service. I'm working as a fishing guide up in Grand Lake Stream."

She appeared genuinely surprised. "I always thought you were in it for life."

"I needed a change."

She brought the nail of her little finger to her mouth and chewed on it. "Are you happy?"

"Yes."

"Well, then."

A road worker at the other end of the counter signaled for her attention, and she hurried off to attend to him. I spun around on the stool, looking for familiar faces. There was a new waitress, a thin young woman with frizzy hair and a pinched expression. Her name tag identified her as Destiny. Otherwise, the diner looked exactly the same as it had the last time I'd visited. When I thought of the hours I had spent here as a rookie warden talking up the locals, trying to gain a working knowledge of the area—finding out where the four-wheeler trails were or who might be tending a secret marijuana plot in the woods— I felt another knife stab of nostalgia.

Eventually, Dot returned. "I just realized you must be here on account of Kathy."

"Everybody's been talking about the shooting, I suppose," I said.

"That's the truth," said the new waitress, Destiny, passing by with dirty plates balanced on her forearms. "There was a Neanderthal in here yesterday who couldn't stop yakking about how cops can shoot anyone they please and call it self-defense."

"We have lots of vets who come into the diner,

and people know Kathy, of course," said Dot. "What a horrible thing! It sounds like that poor soldier was in a lot of pain from his injuries. It's too bad he couldn't have found comfort without resorting to such desperate measures. He is in a better place now at least. God rest his soul. But I can't imagine what Kathy and that new warden must be feeling."

I noticed that Dot hadn't used Dani Tate's name. "Does she come in here much? The new warden?"

"From time to time," Dot said. "But she's real quiet. Not that you were a chatterbox, but she just sits at a booth, alone. Won't even sit at the counter unless she's here with Kathy or another officer."

The job attracted plenty of loners, individuals who preferred their own company to that of other people. And yet one of the most important lessons I'd learned was that you couldn't be antisocial and succeed as a warden. Too much of your success depended on creating relationships with potential informants. A good police officer of any kind needs to be a diplomat. Danielle Tate might not be a natural people person—I certainly wasn't—but sooner or later she'd have to learn how to fake it.

"I guess I should throw my stuff in my room," I said.

"Let me call Destiny over to work the register, and I'll get your key," Dot said.

I reached for my wallet to pay for the coffee and doughnut, but Dot rested a hand on my forearm again. "Mornings here haven't been the same since you left us," she said.

The sincerity in her voice took me aback. I had gone through life with the conviction that I could disappear at any moment and never be missed. What else had I been wrong about?

Dot handed me a key attached to a lozenge-shaped piece of plastic with the number 6 on it. The motel was located across the parking lot from the diner and consisted of a string of small cabins painted white, orange, and green.

I kept a bug-out bag in the Bronco in case I ever decided to spend the night in the woods. The hours before dawn were the best for fishing, and I'd slept in my truck on many occasions to get an early start on a stream. I pulled the waxed canvas duffel from the backseat and threw it on the bed.

It was still early in the day, but I didn't know what to do with myself. I could have taken a drive around my old district, but I'd indulged my nostalgia enough for one day. I sat down in a chair in the curtained darkness, smelling the residual cigarette smoke in the carpet and listening to the hum of the combination heating and air-conditioning unit in the wall above my head.

When Sarah and I had lived in Sennebec, we rarely went out, at least as a couple. Over time, she'd made friends of her own, other women her age, whom she'd meet for a glass of wine in Rockland. At first, she'd invited me along on her girls' nights, but I was usually too exhausted, and not that interested in any case, and eventually she stopped asking. It always bothered Sarah that I had no social life—that I'd based my entire identity around being a Maine game warden.

"You're more than just your job, Mike," she'd said to me during one of our final arguments.

"I know that," I'd replied.

"You need to get a life!"

I wondered if Maddie Lawson had actually met Sarah for drinks in Portland after leaving Weatherby's. If so, I could only imagine the surprise with which Sarah had received the news that I had belatedly followed her advice.

It had been a long time since I'd thought about Sarah. Even now I was having trouble seeing her clearly in my mind's eye. The elements were all there—short blond hair, clear blue eyes, a killer smile—but they no longer came together to form a coherent memory. When I tried to imagine Sarah's face, I kept seeing Stacey Stevens's instead.

12

Somehow, despite having consumed a quart of coffee, I managed to fall asleep in the motel chair. It said something about the extent of my caffeine addiction that the stimulant had so little effect on me. The hum of the heater might have caused me to drift off, or maybe it was the steady rumble of tires on the wet pavement outside the window, but when I awoke, it was already late afternoon.

I got up and washed my face in the bathroom sink, and then I went back to the diner for the early bird special. I ordered the meat loaf and mashed potatoes. And another cup of coffee.

Dot had gone home, leaving the restaurant in the care of Destiny and an older woman, whom I also didn't know. There were a few people I recognized in the booths and at the counter, and some of them even recognized me as their former warden. I tried making small talk with a plumber named Pulkinnen, who had repaired a frozen pipe for me once, but all he wanted to do was bemoan the sad state of affairs that had descended on midcoast Maine since I had departed for my posting Down East.

"The poachers are running wild around here, Mike." He was a paunchy man with thinning sandy hair and a walrus mustache that was a darker shade of brown. He had slitted blue eyes and a broad face. He wore a pin shaped like the flag of Finland on the pocket of his blue coveralls. "Not a week goes by that I don't hear shots in the woods after dark."

"Have you tried talking with Warden Tate?"

He let out a whopper of a snort. "Oh, sure. She comes over when I call. She's good about that. Writes everything down in a little notebook. But does she ever catch a poacher? No."

"She's still new at the job. You should cut her some slack."

"The problem is, the poachers aren't afraid of her. People around here knew you'd catch them if they went out night hunting. And so they went up-country or wherever to jack their deer."

It was actually news to me that I'd been considered something of a badass. But I was glad Pulkinnen, at least, had a favorable opinion of me. "I don't know what to tell you."

"Can't you make some calls to Augusta and tell them we need a better warden? Maybe you could get yourself transferred back here."

"You should give Warden Tate a chance. Sometimes it takes a while to make a case the DA can take to court."

He ran his tongue along the broom bottom of his mustache. "She won't be around much longer anyway. Not after what happened over in Camden. I heard the dead guy's father is a politically connected lawyer. He's going to sue everyone involved."

Pulkinnen's characterization of James Gammon Sr. was in line with my own experience of the man. Even if the attorney general cleared the wardens of wrongdoing, there were ways for a vengeful attorney to inflict pain on Kathy Frost and Danielle Tate. He could hire investigators to drag skeletons out of the women's closets, spread malicious rumors about them to his friends who ran media companies, make phone calls to bureaucrats in Augusta with the authority to derail their careers. He could do all these things and still bring a wrongful-death suit.

Ever since I'd decided to visit the prison, I'd flirted with the idea of driving out to Kathy's house. I needed to speak with her for my own peace of mind, and I suspected that, despite the text she'd sent me, she might appreciate having someone to confide in who'd been through an investigation involving use of force recently.

Sitting at the diner, listening to Pulkinnen's dire prophecies, I decided to stop waiting for an invitation.

The rain let up while I was on the road. I didn't realize it at first because there was so much standing water. The tires of the car in front of me kept splashing my windshield, forcing me to use my wipers.

107

Kathy lived on Appleton Ridge, in a drafty old farmhouse that looked down a hillside at a field of blueberries. At the top of the ridge was a grove of red pines. On the other side of it was an orchard where deer came at dawn and dusk to eat the fallen apples the pickers had left behind after the harvest. Kathy called it "the bone orchard" because there was a family cemetery hidden among the roots of the trees. The mossy gravestones were so weathered, you could no longer read the names of the dead.

I turned off the rural road and onto the long driveway that led to her front door. I drove past a row of elm trees shaped like umbrellas, slowing as I approached the house, until I saw there was a dim light in the window, and I knew that Kathy was home. Her teal-colored patrol truck was parked beside her personal vehicle, a Nissan Xterra SUV. The dooryard was crowded with a game warden's many modes of transportation: two canoes, a sea kayak, a motorboat on its trailer, a snowmobile waiting out the warm weather beneath a tarp, and a still-shiny all-terrain vehicle that had replaced the machine one of her wardens had crashed. None of these things belonged to Kathy. If she lost her job, they would all go to the sergeant who replaced her.

A dog began to bay inside the house as I came to a stop beside her truck. Kathy was the head of the division K-9 team. Most of the wardens who worked with dogs used German shepherds or Labs, but Kathy's longtime companion was a black-and-tan coonhound named Pluto. At age twelve, he was more gray and tan than black and tan, but Kathy occasionally brought him out of retirement to search for a missing child. Pluto's nose was legendary in the annals of the Maine Warden Service. His specialty was finding the dead, not the living; Kathy had taken him to New Orleans after Hurricane Katrina to search for cadavers, and the experience had left her profoundly shaken. She often talked to me about finding another puppy to train, but she never seemed to get around to it. I doubted she would buy another dog until Pluto passed away.

Even before I could climb out of the Bronco, the front door opened and Pluto came waddling down the steps on his bad hips, yowling at the intruder. Kathy remained in the doorway. I could see her lanky outline but not much more than that.

We used to have a ritual that if either of us showed up at the other's house, the visitor was required to bring coffee. I'd forgotten all about the tradition until now. There were so many things from those days that had slipped my memory.

"Hey," I said.

The question of how she would receive my visit got a quick answer. "What are you supposed to be? The prodigal son?"

"I was in the neighborhood."

"Right."

I bent down to scratch Pluto's head between his heavy-hanging ears, but the dog kept on baying. "Actually, I was visiting a friend at the prison."

"Now, that I can believe. Nice beard, by the way."

I straightened up and took a step toward the open door. "Aren't you going to invite me inside?"

"Isn't that what vampires say?" She stepped onto the stoop and closed the door behind her. In the failing light, her face looked ashen, and she was dressed in dark colors—black jeans and a black fleece vest over a gray turtleneck—which seemed in keeping with a person in mourning. Her posture was stiff. Her hands were balled into fists. I'd forgotten how tall she was. "Why are you here, Mike?"

"I was hoping we could talk."

"About you or about me?"

"Both."

"No offense, but I don't think we have that kind of relationship anymore."

"I felt I owed you that after my mom died. You helped me get through it."

The muscles along her mouth relaxed and she closed her eyes. "You don't owe me anything."

"That's bullshit, and you know it. I thought you might want to tell me what happened at the Gammons'."

"You know I am not allowed to do that."

"I'm not afraid of being called to give a deposition if it goes to a civil trial."

She ran a hand through her bobbed hair. "Did you read the interview with the Gammons in the paper today?"

"I was on the road."

"If I'd known the kid was the son of one of the most powerful lawyers in the country, I would have let him blow his own brains out."

Kathy had a sarcastic side, but I knew she wasn't a coldhearted person. "You don't mean that."

"All right," she said. "I would have let the Camden cops take the call."

"You don't mean that, either."

She folded her arms under her breasts. "Why is it you think you know what I mean?"

"Because I know you, Kathy. You wouldn't have shot Jimmy Gammon unless you were certain that he was going to fire his gun at you or Tate."

"Maybe I screwed up," she said. "Have you thought of that? It was pretty dark in that barn."

"You wouldn't have screwed up. You're too good an officer."

"I appreciate the vote of confidence."

"I know something about use-of-force investigations. I've been through two of them."

"Now we're even."

I'd forgotten that Kathy had shot a man when she was my age. It had happened in her first district, way up north amid the potato and broccoli fields of Aroostook County, where she'd grown up. She'd confided only a few of the details to me, but I knew it had been a domestic violence call. A three-hundred-pound brute named Jacques Decoster had been beating his wife with the metal end of his belt while their son looked on in horror. Decoster had come after Kathy with a butcher's knife before she unloaded a .357 slug in his chest. The review board had ruled that the shooting was justified.

"The AG is going to clear you," I said.

"If you think that's what's bothering me, you should send your psychologist's license back to the dime store," she said. "Gammon survived a tour in Afghanistan. But instead of getting killed by the fucking Taliban, it ends up being me who shoots him."

"He wanted to die."

"Oh, really? You're one hundred percent sure of that?"

"I knew him, Kathy. I've been to his house."

She bit her lip, and I sensed that this came as news to her. I had never had reason to mention Jimmy Gammon to my former sergeant before.

"Did you see what they did to his face over there? His skin looked like it had melted."

"I knew him from before he went to war. I didn't even know that he had been wounded."

"Then you don't know shit, Mike."

"I know you shouldn't blame yourself for his

actions. If he wanted to end his life, he should have done it himself. No matter how fucked-up he was, he had no right to put you in that position."

"We're not suppose to stand by and let people commit suicide," she said. "Oh, that's right. You've absolved yourself of those responsibilities."

"That's what this is about, isn't it? You're pissed at me for resigning?"

Her face darkened with blood. "Of course I am! Do you know what I went through to keep you from being fired? Not just once but constantly for three years?"

"I have some sense of it."

"I don't think you do," she said. "Both Major Malcomb and I made promises to the colonel that you were worth saving. We went on bended knee to the commissioner when he was looking for ways to have you shitcanned. We said, 'Bowditch doesn't always make the best decisions, but the kid has the heart of a lion. You wait and see. He might seem like a fuckup now, but someday he's going to become a legendary warden.' "

I knew that they had often argued with the brass on my behalf, but I hadn't realized what a fight it had been.

"I didn't ask you to do that," I said.

"You forced us to put our own reputations on the line. And then you went and quit. The colonel and the commissioner said to us, 'We knew this guy couldn't hack it.' You made us look like fools, Mike."

"Would it help if I said I was sorry?"

"What would help is explaining why you screwed me over like that. I was pulling strings to get you transferred back to Division B. The next thing I know, you're calling to tell me you're quitting."

"I didn't quit. I resigned."

"Call it what you want. The fact remains it was a cowardly thing to do."

"It wasn't cowardly," I said. "It was just the opposite."

"Keep telling yourself that." She brought two fingers to her mouth and whistled sharply.

Pluto spun around and trotted back to her. She turned her broad back to me and climbed the stairs to the door and opened it without ever looking in my direction.

"That's it, then?" I called after her.

She paused without facing me and said, "Do you know who you look like with the beard and the long hair? Your old man. I'm sure he would be proud."

She stepped inside the house and closed the door.

13

Kathy's parting shot about my looking like my father hurt as much as she'd intended it to. My father had been a notorious poacher of deer, a wrecker of barrooms, and a seducer of other men's women. Then, in the last weeks of his life, he'd become something worse. Even before the bitter end, he'd been the kind of violent and self-dealing man I'd pledged never to become.

It's just a beard, I wanted to yell at the closed door. But what would be the point?

Even though we were approaching the longest days of the year, the low-hanging clouds made it seem later than it was. I stood beside the open door of my Bronco, staring at the house and trying to decide if I should knock. But the conversation was going to continue only when—and if—Kathy decided it should continue.

I climbed behind the wheel and restarted the engine. I reached my right arm across the passenger seat headrest so I could back out of the dooryard without hitting one of Kathy's sugar maples. Then I headed back to the motel.

As I passed the dented mailbox at the end of the drive, I glanced into the rearview mirror and saw headlights in the pine grove at the top of the ridge. There was a road that entered the orchard from the other side, and Kathy had told me that she occasionally chased teenagers out of the parking lot after dark. Most of the local kids knew that there were better spots to toke up and get laid than in the backyard of a law-enforcement officer, but word must not have reached the dumbbells in that vehicle. Given the foul mood Kathy was in, I feared for the teens' safety if she spotted those lights out her bedroom window.

An invisible mosquito had found its way inside the vehicle when I'd opened the door; I could hear it buzzing around my head. I waved my hand ineffectually in the air and waited for the mosquito to land and draw blood. It used to be that insect bites were just annoyances, the price you paid in Maine for the salt air and blooming lilacs, but that was before the creeping tropics unleashed their pestilences upon us: West Nile virus and eastern equine encephalitis. I knew wardens who'd never used bug dope in their lives—seasoned woodsmen who'd endured thousands of bites over their careers—who now slathered themselves in Deet. These days, you never knew what little thing might get you.

I'd been on the road for ten minutes when my cell phone vibrated in my pants pocket. Once again I had a momentary illusion that it was my mother calling from the afterlife. I reached into my jeans, trying not to swerve into a telephone pole, and looked at the lighted screen. It was Kathy's number.

I pulled over to the side of the road and put the truck into park.

"I shouldn't have called you a coward," she said.

"It's all right. I understand."

"That doesn't mean I'm not still mad at you. But this has been a pretty crappy week."

"The crappiest."

"You know I've been getting hate mail? Not just the usual anonymous stuff. I've gotten signed letters from guys who served in the Guard with Gammon, and from other vets, too. My e-mail address must have gotten posted to some military bulletin board. Do you know what that's like, having people you admire hate your guts? My own brother Kurt is a Vietnam vet."

"It must be hard."

"Don't patronize me, Mike. It was a rhetorical question. I just keep thinking . . ."

I waited. "What?"

"Dani Tate is a good kid. She's going to make a decent warden when she grows up. I've never had a rookie who's as gung ho about the job as she is."

I felt that she was making an unflattering comparison. "What about me?"

"You thought about everything too much. It wasn't enough for you just to enforce a fucking rule; you had to second-guess the people who wrote it. Tate does what she's told. I think she's memorized every regulation in the book."

I had met Dani Tate on only a handful of occasions, and she hadn't left me with a strong impression, other than that she seemed a lot younger than me despite there being only four years between us in age.

"How is she doing?" I asked.

"The union lawyer says we're not supposed to communicate. They don't want us getting our stories straight. She's not the most talkative person in the world anyway. Being in a truck with her on patrol is like being with my dog, conversationally speaking."

That had been my experience with Tate as well. When I'd tried to make small talk, I'd gotten a blank stare, which made me think she disapproved of me. At the time, I figured she'd heard about my misadventures and been brainwashed by the higher-ups into seeing me as unworthy to wear the red dress jacket of a Maine warden. Now I wondered if she'd just had nothing to say.

"The thing is, it should never have happened," Kathy said.

"You can't think that way."

"No," she said. "I mean it wouldn't have gone down the way it did if you had been there. Not just because you knew Gammon. It just wouldn't have happened at all. That's why I'm so pissed at you right now. I needed you that night, and where the fuck were you?"

House-sitting for a multimillionaire, studying

for a law school exam I'd never take, nursing a bottle of cheap whiskey—none of the answers I had to offer was worth a damn. I was trying to collect a few sentences that didn't sound pathetic, when somewhere in the background, Pluto let loose with both lungs.

"What's going on?" I asked.

"Probably a raccoon outside. Give me a minute, and I'll call you back."

I sat in the Bronco, listening to the engine belts whir while traffic passed in both directions along the country road. A few minutes passed without the phone ringing, and I glanced at my watch. I turned off the engine to save gas. The mosquito made its presence known again around my ears. I decided to give Kathy another two minutes.

The headlights from the passing cars would light up the inside of the cab for several seconds and then everything would fade again into darkness.

The cell phone rested in my open hand. I brought up her number from the favorites menu and tapped the button. The phone rang for half a minute and then went to voice mail.

"Kathy? It's Mike again. Give me a ring."

The mosquito finally landed on my neck. I didn't feel it at first, then reflexively I brought my hand up fast, dropping the phone to the floor. When I looked at my palm, there was a black stain on my life line that I knew was blood.

I had seen lights in the orchard above Kathy's

house and had assumed it was just teenagers parking. What if it wasn't?

"You know I've been getting hate mail?" Kathy had said. "I've gotten signed letters from guys who served in the Guard with Gammon, and from other veterans, too."

I had to unbuckle my shoulder belt to retrieve the cell phone from where it had landed on the floor mat. I left a message: "I'm headed back your way, Kathy. I'll be there in ten minutes or so."

I buckled myself in and restarted the engine, then pulled an abrupt U-turn in the road in front of a speeding pickup truck. He was going fast, but I was going faster.

The road to Kathy's house zigzagged up the side of the ridge through the blueberry barrens. Tumbled stone walls ran along the edges of the asphalt. I tried not to crash into them as I cornered the Bronco.

As I turned into the driveway, I leaned forward against the shoulder belt and saw the lights of the farmhouse on the hillside above me. Seeing the homey glow made me relax for a few seconds. There was something reassuring about the sight of the illuminated windows. Then I realized that one of the bright shapes I was looking at was a wide-open door.

I eased my foot off the gas pedal. The truck

slowed to a crawl as I approached Kathy's dooryard. The high beams searched ahead of me into the gathering darkness.

There was a black shape lying on the flattened grass where I had parked my vehicle a few minutes earlier. At first, I thought it was a bunched-up blanket or discarded coat. I braked hard as the headlights brought the object into view.

It was Pluto. He was lying in a pool of blood.

I shoved the shift into park with my right hand and reached for the door handle with my left. That was when the windshield exploded.

Everything happened in an instant. Broken glass filled the air. I felt the airborne shards tear at the side of my face and neck. Simultaneously, I heard the crash of the shattering windshield and the bang of a gun. Reflexively, I ducked down behind the steering wheel and dash.

My cheekbone stung. I clapped a hand to the side of my face, and it came away red with blood and glistening with powdered glass. The entire passenger side of the Bronco was coated with blue shards. The windshield was entirely gone except for a webbed section directly in front of me.

The second blast tore the rest of the windshield away.

This time I heard the distinctive pinging of shotgun pellets. Atomized glass rained down on my right arm. I had pulled the flap of my raincoat over my head to protect myself, the way a frightened child hides under a blanket during a thunderstorm.

My hair was matted and wet. Blood was pooling inside my ear and running into the corner of my eye. I hurled my body across the passenger seat, nearly impaling myself on the gearshift. I pawed at the glove compartment before realizing it was locked and that I needed to turn off the engine and remove the keys. I managed to drop the keys on the floor twice before I got the glove compartment open and saw my newly cleaned pistol inside.

My slick hand closed around the textured grip of the Walther. It was a .380. In the gravel pit where I practiced shooting, I could put all seven bullets in a tight cluster from a distance of fifteen yards. Beyond that, my aim got iffy. I pulled back the slide and chambered a round.

I stared at the heavy little pistol in my hand, trying to feel confident about it, telling myself that at least the Walther gave me a chance, while I waited for the next blast to come.

Rolling onto my side and looking up at the ceiling, I tried to make sense of the wreckage inside the vehicle. The first blast had angled toward the right side of the vehicle before the shooter had corrected his aim and taken out the rest of the windshield. The driver's side window was also shattered. My quick guess was that the shots had been fired from that direction: up the hill and to my left.

I managed to get my entire body on the right side of the vehicle, then popped the handle on the passenger door. Even before it had fully swung open, I lunged through the crack and dropped hard to the wet grass. I landed flat on my chest and stomach, a belly flop in the mud.

I wriggled away toward the rear of the Bronco, hoping that my estimate of the sniper's location was correct and that I wasn't completely exposed now. When I'd crawled around to the rear of the truck, I pushed myself up onto my knees and then my heels, making myself as small a target as possible.

Blood was oozing between my skin and my shirt collar. With my free hand, I rubbed my right eye and found that I could see better. The pain in my head and face was sharp and stinging. The phrase "death by a thousand cuts" came to my mind, but if I died, it wasn't going to be from these small wounds. It was going to be because the shooter got the drop on me for real and fired a load of heavy shot into my heart and lungs.

Where was Kathy? She had heard Pluto baying and had gone outside to see what had gotten him riled up. The front door was standing open.

I glanced around the yard, looking for better cover. There was an open stretch of unmowed grass and then a stone wall and a cluster of sugar maples. I hated to waste a bullet, but I didn't see much of a choice.

I sprang to my feet, extended my arms across the cold, wet roof of the Bronco, and squeezed off a shot in the direction of the pine grove. I didn't expect to hit anyone. In fact, I aimed at a tree, in the unlikely event that Kathy herself was up there, playing cat and mouse with our assailant. If I was lucky, the shot would catch the sniper off guard and the unexpected muzzle flash would cause him to duck behind whatever he was using for cover.

A second after I'd pulled the trigger, I took off across the yard. The sniper wasn't intimidated by my return fire, because he let loose with another blast from the shotgun. I must have been correct about his position—somewhere between the house and the pines—because he didn't have a clear line on me. I heard the blast and thought I felt the pellets ruffling the air behind my head, but the sensation might have been something I imagined.

I hurdled over the stone wall without breaking my neck and dived down behind the roots of the nearest maple. I had good cover here, and the sniper knew it. He also knew that I was armed. The question was, What would he choose to do with this knowledge? Would he try to reposition himself to take me down from a different angle— he obviously had some sort of night-vision scope—or would he cut and run, figuring that one of Kathy's neighbors would have already called the cops?

The nearest house was probably half a mile away, but the sound of gunshots travels a long distance, and the people at the bottom of the hill would've heard them. A single shot after dark would have been cause for concern, but this was a full-on firefight.

I couldn't wait for help, not knowing where Kathy was. I looked to my left for the next place where I could take cover and spotted Kathy's bronze Nissan, which was parked in front of the old hay barn. Filling my lungs with air again, I jumped to my feet and sprinted as fast as I could toward the humpbacked SUV. As I ran, I wondered if I would feel the shot that would kill me or if everything would go suddenly black and that would be the end of the picture.

When I found myself crouched against the damp metal of the Nissan, I experienced a feeling of surprise; I hadn't expected to make it. The gunman hadn't fired another shot. That meant he was probably on the move—but was he coming toward me or running away?

I decided to risk a peek at the dooryard. Light was spilling out onto the long grass from the front windows and open door. It reached as far as Pluto's unmoving body. The dog had never had any particular affection for me, despite the hours we'd spent together, but he had rescued lost children and located the bodies of frozen Alzheimer's sufferers so their relatives would have something to bury. The heroic animal had deserved a better end than this.

It was hard to see past the illuminated patch. I began calculating if I could make it through the door without getting winged. That was when I noticed the dark liquid on the front steps. It didn't look red. The tricky light made it appear more like spilled motor oil. But I knew that it was blood, and I knew that it belonged to Kathy.

Without another thought, I leaped out from behind the SUV, firing a random shot back toward the pine grove and the orchard beyond. I might even have yelled something. I went leaping up the front steps, taking them two at a time, leaving my boot prints in the streaked blood.

I found her lying facedown in the hallway in a spreading pool of blood. One of her arms was outstretched; the other was at her side. Her right knee was drawn up. The position of her body was that of a swimmer doing the crawl.

"Kathy?"

The sniper must have caught her as she stepped out the door and onto the front steps. She had let Pluto outside to chase his raccoon. Then came the shot that ended the dog's life. I could only imagine the horror she'd experienced in that moment, watching her life's companion slaughtered before her eyes.

The second shot must have come soon after. As shocked as she was, Kathy's muscle memory would have kicked in and sent her diving for cover. She had too much training and experience to have remained frozen and upright when a gun was going off nearby.

The shotgun blast had struck her in the torso as she was turning back toward the house. Her fleece vest was shredded in the back and bloodstained along the side.

"Kathy?"

I dropped to my knees beside her and turned her over as gently as I could. I was more terrified than I'd ever been in my life. Her face was an unnatural color: a gray that was almost the color of bone. Her eyes were closed and sunken deep into their sockets. Her lips were a bruised shade of blue.

The front of her vest and turtleneck, from her left lung down across the abdomen, had been ripped by the pellets, but it was hard for me to tell how bad the damage was because her entire torso was painted with blood. I pressed two slick fingers beneath her jawline but felt no pulse. I tried again with a wrist. I thought I could detect a faint flutter.

"Kathy?"

I pulled up her shirt and saw the horrible patterned wounds below her bra and rib cage. The pellets had driven threads from her clothing into the ragged holes. Blood was still pumping from them. Her heart was laboring to beat.

As I tore off my own shirt, the buttons went

popping everywhere. I wadded the flannel into a ball and pressed it hard against the multiple wounds. My eyes lost focus as they flooded with tears. I felt the warmth of my friend's blood soaking through the knees of my jeans.

To this day, I can't remember hearing the siren. The wail of the approaching ambulance was drowned out by my strangled cries for help.

14

What I didn't see in my rush down the hall was the cell phone lying a few feet from Kathy's outstretched hand. What I didn't hear was the voice of the 911 dispatcher, who was still on the line, repeating with practiced calmness that help was on the way.

How had Kathy even managed to key in those three numbers? While losing that much blood?

The deputy sheriff and the EMTs arrived within seconds of one another.

The cop, whose name was Skip Morrison, had been more than an acquaintance but less than a friend when I'd lived in the district; we'd gone out for beers a few times. He was a long-limbed guy who bounced around like a marionette on strings and had freckles that multiplied when he spent more than an hour in the sun.

Seeing the dead dog and the blood smeared like

a slug's trail leading into the house, Deputy Morrison radioed for backup, then ordered the paramedics to stay put while he scoped out the situation. He unholstered his service weapon and darted across the yard. He flattened himself against the peeling clapboards of the house and edged into position so that if he craned his long neck, he could peek inside the building.

He saw me shirtless and covered with blood, crouched over the prone body of Kathy Frost, whose house he knew this was. From the back, he couldn't identify the half-naked man. Nor would he have recognized me beneath my shaggy hair and stubbled beard. It was unclear from his vantage point what I was doing to the motionless warden. In his report, he said he'd heard me sobbing.

Deputy Morrison identified himself as a police officer and shouted at me to stand clear. I have no memory of him doing so. Evidently, it took me quite a long time to respond. Not knowing whether I was the attacker, Morrison considered shooting me. He would have been justified if he had, given my gore-splattered appearance and refusal to comply with a direct order. For all he knew, I was a homicidal madman still at work snuffing out a human life.

But something stayed his hand. Deputy Morrison had been with the Knox County Sheriff's Department for ten years, and he had been the first officer to respond to many horrific events: babies dropped to their deaths by drunken fathers, car crashes in which not one of the unbuckled teenagers packed inside the station wagon had survived, boyfriends standing like exhausted boxers over the women they had just beaten to death. He had seen violence in all its shapes and sizes. When he looked upon my gore-spattered body, he might have reasonably concluded that I was the assailant. Instead, he chose to interpret the uncertain evidence of his eyes and ears with caution and compassion. He heard my sobbing and decided that I was also a victim of whatever shocking thing had just happened.

Morrison let his arm fall by his side and padded carefully up the steps to avoid the blood.

"Sir?" he said in a soft voice. "Sir?"

I moved my head. One eye was squeezed shut to keep out the blood; the other was bright with tears.

"Sir, I am a police officer," Morrison said. "There are paramedics out in the yard. We're here to help you. You and Warden Frost. Will you let us do that?"

"She's been shot," I said, my voice scarcely more than a mumble. "She's lost a lot of blood."

"Is she still alive?"

"I think so."

"Then let me call in the EMTs so they can take it from here."

"I can't take my hand away. I need to apply pressure to the wound."

"OK," Morrison said. "You keep doing that while I get the EMTs."

He turned and waved in the paramedics, a man and a woman, dressed identically in white shirts, tan slacks, and blue jackets with medical-looking insignias on the front. They were both wearing latex gloves and carrying boxes with lifesaving equipment. The man gripped my arm by the wrist and replaced my hand—the one I was using to clamp the blood-soaked shirt to Kathy's side—with his own.

"Sir?" the female EMT said. "Can you tell me your name?"

"Mike."

"Were you shot, too, Mike?"

"Yeah. But I'm OK."

"I don't think you are," she said.

There is a period when you awake from a particularly vivid dream and your mind is afloat between sleep and consciousness. You're not sure what is real and what is imagined. You might have memories of the dream that are so detailed and persuasive, you can't believe they were only mirages. In those same moments, the physical world that you are reentering can seem unsettling and out of focus, everything blurred around the edges, as if it is not to be fully trusted, either.

My experience of the hour after I discovered Kathy's body was like that. I place greater faith in what Skip Morrison told me about that time period than I do in my own recollections.

The first trustworthy memory I have is of sitting alone in the back of the ambulance with a blanket wrapped around my naked and shivering shoulders, pressing an enormous cotton bandage against the side of my head because the EMTs were in the house, doing everything in their power to save the life of my former sergeant. I must have said something to Skip about the shots coming from the direction of the pine grove, because he was gone, too, standing guard outside the farmhouse until other units could respond.

The lights inside the ambulance were as bright as those on a movie set. I was sitting on a gray vinyl seat opposite the rectangular place where the stretcher would be secured for the ride to the hospital. But the stretcher was not there. The EMTs had rolled it off the vehicle and taken it into the house. The ambulance door was open, and the overhead lights were drawing swarms of moths and mayflies inside the vehicle.

One of them landed on my wet knee. It was an *Ephemerella subvaria*. I hadn't realized that Hendricksons were hatching. Soon all the guides in Grand Lake Stream would be swapping out their fly boxes.

I was a fishing guide now, no longer a warden.

And Kathy had been shot. The idea was having trouble taking hold. I raised my free hand, red and tacky with blood, to my eyes, and still I couldn't accept it as reality. Then I remembered the peculiar grayness of Kathy's face, and I had to clench my teeth together to keep from vomiting. I expected the EMTs to return at any moment and tell me that my friend was dead.

"Bowditch?"

A man in a warden's uniform was standing in the lighted aura of the ambulance door. Even through my tears, I saw the major's oak leaf on his collar. He was in his late fifties and in extraordinary physical condition: flat-stomached, back straight as a fence post, with oversize forearms like Popeye the Sailor Man.

"How are you doing?"

"Some glass hit me when the guy shot out my windshield. How is Kathy?"

"A LifeFlight helicopter is on the way."

When the first responders call in a medevac team, you know everything's gone to shit. As a warden, I'd been required to train each year in emergency medicine. I knew that the EMTs would be doing everything possible to stabilize Kathy for the chopper ride. They would be applying clotting agents and pressure bandages to her wounds. They would have jammed an IV needle into her arm to replace some of the blood that she had lost. A woman's body Kathy's size holds eight pints of blood. If she'd lost 40 percent of that—three to four pints—she would probably die. How much had I seen spilling across the floor?

"I want to see her."

I stood up and then found my head going empty. The next thing I knew, I was sitting down again.

"I don't think that's a good idea," said the major.

When I'd first become a game warden, Timothy Malcomb had been my division lieutenant, but he'd recently received a promotion after the retirement of the service's second in command. His former job was still vacant. I'd been hoping that Kathy might apply for it. If anyone deserved to be rewarded for years of dedication, it was my former sergeant. But now she lay at the gates of death.

"Someone needs to call her parents," I said. "They live in New Sweden, in Aroostook County."

"I'll take care of it."

Malcomb was famous, or infamous, for his lack of expression. In my time, I'd heard him compared to a Roman statue, a cigar store Indian, and a wax museum replica. But in this awful moment, his agony was engraved upon his face. Like me, he cared deeply for Kathy Frost, although his relation to her was different from mine. He had been her mentor, just as she had been mine.

"Did you get a look at the shooter?" he asked.

"No," I said, trying to gather my wits. "I think

he was hiding in the blueberry bushes between the house and the trees. He would have had to come down from the top of the ridge to get a clear shot at the front of the house. He was probably hoping to get closer, but Kathy let Pluto out." In my mind's eye, I saw the hound lying dead in the grass and felt a surge of acid coming back up my throat. "Pluto must have been barking, and when Kathy came outside to check on him, the shooter fired from the bushes and caught her broadside."

"I'm surprised he didn't pursue her into the house."

"He must have seen my headlights approaching," I said. "From the hillside, you can see down to the bottom of the valley. He didn't want any witnesses."

"You saved her life, Bowditch."

"For now."

I heard car doors slamming and men's voices shouting and, over it all, the unmistakable chittering of a distant helicopter. The noise got louder and louder, until I could make out the distinctive sounds of the two rotors over the airplanelike roar of its engine. The LifeFlight chopper was landing in the leafy blueberry barrens below the farmhouse. Without a word, the major stepped out of view around the ambulance door.

The bandage made a sticky sound as I peeled it away from my blood-matted head. There were red polka dots all over the batting, and a few hairs I'd torn loose. With my fingertips, I felt my injured cheek and removed a tiny shard of glass that had been driven into the flesh. Exposed to the open air, the wounds began to smart and bleed again.

Kathy's blood had been dark red, not bright red. It had pumped from the wounds when she breathed, rather than spurted through my fingers. She was bleeding internally, but there was a chance that the shotgun pellets had missed the major organs and arteries and had severed veins instead.

I pushed myself to a standing position and grabbed the edge of the compartment over my head. My head went woozy, and I thought I might faint, but after wobbling like a toddler for the better part of a minute, I felt my head clear and strength returning to my legs. I threw the blanket off my shoulders and stepped carefully down onto the packed gravel of the driveway. A misty rain was starting to fall again.

The helicopter had landed on a flat patch of land to my right. The chopper was white and green, with gold swooshes along the side. The crew wore matching green jumpsuits. With all the rain and fog, it was a miracle LifeFlight had been given clearance to take off. Leaning against the side of the ambulance, I watched as a mob of paramedics, cops, and wardens carried the litter out of the house and across the field to the waiting helicopter.

Few cops will ever admit that they consider the

life of a fellow officer to be more valuable than anyone else's. But when you watch a spectacle like the one I was witnessing—officers elbowing one another aside to be litter bearers—it becomes hard not to draw that conclusion. And why not? If you put your life on the line for strangers each day, wouldn't you hope that someone would honor your sacrifice?

After they'd secured the stretcher inside, the men backed away and the chopper lifted off with surprising suddenness. Its rear end tilted up first and then the whole enormous contraption came off the ground. The whirling blades sent loose leaves flying. A few of the guys standing closer to the landing site actually threw their bodies flat on the ground.

I watched the loud, blinking machine shoot south across the sky until it was smaller than a meteor.

Malcomb was kneeling beside the sprawled corpse of Pluto.

I walked unsteadily toward him. "Major?"

He had approached the dead dog as close as he deemed wise, given that this was an active crime scene. The animal that had been his colleague on so many missing-person investigations was gone. Now there was just a dog-shaped piece of evidence that was not to be touched.

He looked up at me from the ground, his face hard again.

"I need to get down to Maine Med," he said. "Lieutenant Soctomah wants you to walk him around the scene while your memory is fresh. Maybe someone can drive you to the hospital after the detective is done with you. You'll want to get those cuts looked at. I expect you'll survive a few more hours."

"Yes, sir," I said to the man who was no longer my commanding officer. "I'll survive."

15

The state police detective who had taken charge of the investigation was a lieutenant named Wayne Soctomah, whom I'd first met when my father was a fugitive in the North Woods. My dad had been accused of having ambushed and killed two men with a high-powered rifle. There were certain similarities to the present case.

Soctomah was a member of the Passamaquoddy Nation, having grown up near my current home outside Grand Lake Stream, in the Indian village on Peter Dana Point. He had become a Maine state trooper during a time when Native Americans were not automatically welcomed into the state police's ranks. Later, he took night classes to get a master's in criminal justice from Boston University and had risen quickly through the ranks to a senior position as a detective in the Major Crimes

Unit. He was a muscular man with a thick silver crew cut and closely set eyes that reminded me of those of a bird of prey.

I must have looked to Soctomah like one of the intoxicated rednecks Maine game wardens routinely arrest: bearded, shirtless, with blood of indefinite origin smeared all over my torso.

"We need to get a bandage on your head" were the first words he spoke to me.

"I wouldn't mind a jacket, either."

"I've got one in the cruiser." He had a faint accent I'd heard on the Passamaquoddy rez. I wondered if he'd worked his whole life to rid himself of that singsong cadence.

The navy blue polyester jacket he gave me had POLICE stenciled on the back. The fabric felt slippery on my bare skin, and my wrists poked out of the too-short arms. I felt like an impostor wearing it.

Soctomah had called over one of the EMTs to tape a fresh bandage to my bleeding skull. It was the size of a sponge you might use to wash a car.

"Better?" he asked.

I still felt like my knees might buckle. "Yeah."

"Good, because I need to know what happened here. Give me as much detail as you can."

Despite the ringing in my skull, I did my best to recount the entire sequence of events. Soctomah took notes the whole time. I told him about my earlier visit to the house, the argument I'd had with Kathy, and then her call to apologize. I told him how Pluto had begun barking and how we'd ended our conversation abruptly. I demonstrated where I'd stopped the Bronco when I'd first seen the dead dog, then pointed out the route I'd taken to seek cover behind the stone wall, showing him exactly where I'd pressed my body into the weeds. After that, we walked toward the house—avoiding the evidence techs at work—and I showed him how I'd entered the hall.

"It seems like you might have surprised the shooter before he could finish the job." Soctomah glanced at my pockmarked Bronco. "How long do you think you kept him occupied?"

"Long enough for the ambulance to get here."

"It's lucky the station is just down the hill in Union," he said.

I felt the mist beginning to shift to something with a heavier, downward trajectory. I wondered if the helicopter could beat the rain to Portland.

"Will they call you if Kathy dies en route to the hospital?" I asked him.

He laid a hand on my shoulder in a friendly way. "Do you know the Serenity Prayer?"

"God, grant me the serenity to accept the things I cannot change, the power to change the things I can, and wisdom to know the difference."

"It's not 'power,'" he said. "It's 'courage.' Why don't we focus on what we can change here? I've got evidence techs searching the blueberry fields for spent shells. The major has loaned me a K-9 team to backtrack up the hill to those trees. Is that where you saw the headlights when you were leaving?"

"There's a parking lot on the far side of those pines. It's the entrance to an old apple orchard. Kids sometimes park there to smoke pot and fool around."

"Does it seem like the vehicle was parked there?"

"I think so." I tried to retrieve the memory, but it was eluding me. "The headlights seemed high off the ground, so I would say it was a pickup or a Jeep, maybe even with a raised suspension. Like a truck someone had altered to go mudding."

He jotted something in his notebook. "She didn't say anything else before she hung up on you—something specific?"

My head and face still felt like fire ants were crawling around under the cotton batting, but my leg muscles had regained some of their sturdiness. I'd come to the conclusion that I didn't have circulatory shock.

"She was getting death threats. I'm sure you'll find them on her computer. Hopefully, the guy who did this e-mailed her first, because then you'll have an electronic trail to follow. But I wouldn't count on it."

"Why?"

"This all feels too deliberate and careful.

141

Whoever shot Kathy had been scouting her house awhile. He's going to be hard to catch."

The detective wasn't about to divulge any of his suspicions, least of all to me. "I'm going to need to borrow your Walther. I'll give it back to you after we do a ballistics test."

I reached around to the back of my jeans, where I'd tucked the pistol. Then I cleared a round out of the action and ejected the magazine. I handed him the gun in pieces.

A state trooper wearing a long, dark raincoat and hat with the plastic wrap they use to cover their brimmed headgear strode up toward us. He was holding a Baggie with a single crimped shotgun shell in it. The plastic was burnt-orange and as long as my finger: HEVI-Shot Magnum Blend.

"What kind of sniper uses a turkey gun?" I asked.

"I have a red-dot scope on my boy's Ithaca at home," the trooper said. "He doesn't miss a bird with it."

"If our guy is a turkey hunter, he'd be on the list of people who tagged one," I said.

The detective nodded. "That's a pretty long list."

The drizzle was falling more heavily now, hard enough that I could see individual drops bounce off the trooper's hat.

"Has anyone called Danielle Tate and told her what happened to Kathy?" I asked.

"Major Malcomb did, I believe."

"Because whoever shot Kathy might be going for a twofer tonight."

Soctomah's head snapped around toward the trooper, and without either of them saying a word, the tall policeman waded through the weeds toward his cruiser. He would be paying Warden Tate a visit.

"I can't think of anything I haven't told you," I said. "If you don't mind, I'd like to go see Kathy now."

"We can take him!"

It was the female EMT. I hadn't realized she'd been eavesdropping on our conversation. She'd changed out of her own blood-soaked clothes and was sipping what looked like hot coffee from the lid of a thermos. The ambulance could have left after the LifeFlight helicopter had taken off, but the paramedics had spent nearly half an hour fighting to keep Kathy alive. They probably even knew her, given that their lines of work often intersected. After a night like this one had been, it's not so easy to pack up your gear and go home.

I walked halfway toward the waiting ambulance; then I remembered I was still wearing Soctomah's jacket. I pulled my arms loose and was preparing to hurl it back to him, but the detective held up his hand.

"Hang on to it," he said. "I don't want you to freeze to death."

I put the jacket back on over my naked shoulders and snapped the buttons to keep some of the damp out.

Portland was more than an hour south of Appleton. It was a long detour for the paramedics to make for the sole purpose of giving me a taxi ride.

"You're not going to charge me for this?" I asked, climbing again into the back of the ambulance and sitting down on the familiar gray vinyl seat.

"That depends," said the EMT with a smile and a wink. "Do you have insurance?"

16

We arrived at Maine Medical Center close to midnight. I'd asked the EMTs to let me know if they got word of Kathy's condition, but nothing had come over the airwaves. They'd given me a T-shirt to wear under Soctomah's borrowed police jacket.

The ambulance had clearance to use one of the hospital's emergency bays. The wounds on my scalp had stopped bleeding, which was a promising sign, but the EMTs said I still might need stitches. The woman whispered something to an attendant at the door and then waved me forward.

"Marcus is going to take you to triage," she said.

"Thanks for the lift."

"We'll be praying for her."

My own prayers didn't have the best track record. They certainly hadn't helped my mother. The last time I'd visited this hospital was the night of her death.

Marcus, the admitting nurse, or whatever he was, escorted me to a room the size of a phone booth and took my blood pressure, measured my pulse rate, shined a light in my pupils, and peeked under my bandages. He must have determined that my death was not imminent, because the next thing I knew, I was being escorted back to the waiting room of the ER.

I checked in with the receptionist, who had me fill out a form and take a seat. She didn't need to give me instructions. For an otherwise-healthy young man, I'd spent a fair amount of my life in hospitals.

"I don't suppose you can tell me the condition of a friend of mine who was brought in by LifeFlight?" I asked the clerk, already knowing the answer.

"Are you a relative?"

"No."

She had a sad, understanding smile. "I'm afraid I'm not allowed to release private information."

The wardens, my former colleagues, began to

appear before my name was called. The local guys arrived first, the ones from Division A, which patrols the southernmost part of the state. Kathy was a Division B sergeant from central Maine. But the Warden Service is a small, tight-knit corps—a hundred field officers, more or less—and everyone knows everyone.

I recognized each anguished face. There was Sergeant Ouelette and Tommy Volk; David DiPietro and John Taylor; Patrick Flynn, who had been in my class at the Academy. They passed through admitting on their way to the waiting room outside the surgery unit. Not one of them glanced in my direction; not one of them recognized me under my bandaged, bearded face.

Eventually, my name was called.

I followed another guy in nurse's scrubs through the door into the examination room. I must have waited forty-five minutes for the doctor to appear. He was a lean man with a salt-and-pepper beard and the smallest hands I'd ever seen on an adult. He glanced at the chart the nurse had left and then began asking me questions about my medical history. I rattled off my life's injuries: seven broken bones, some from childhood, others from a more recent ATV crash; eighteen stitches in three places incurred over twenty-seven years; two concussions, including one caused by a crowbar to the back of the skull; residual frostbite damage to my fingers, toes, and both ears; a nonpenetrating gunshot wound to the chest; and now these lacerations from a windshield that had exploded in my face.

He waited to make sure I had finished with my list. "You've lived a dangerous life."

I couldn't disagree.

The doctor used his tiny hands to pick shards of glass out of my face and skull with tweezers, remarking twice how lucky I'd been that they'd missed my eye, as if to make a broader point about my general indebtedness to good fortune in light of the many abuses my body had suffered. He placed three stitches above my ear, bringing my life's total of sutures to twenty-one. And then he bandaged me up again. He worked with such speed and precision that I almost missed my chance to ask him the only question that was on my mind.

"Doctor?"

"Yes."

"A game warden named Kathy Frost was brought in here by helicopter. She was shot by the same person who shot me. Please tell me: Is she alive?"

"You're not a member of her family?"

"No, but she's my friend."

"I'm really not supposed to say, you know." He stuck his hands into his pockets and looked at the floor. "But what I heard wasn't good."

"Thank you," I said.

147

• • •

Now that I was stitched up, I was free to leave, but I had no intention of going anywhere until I heard how Kathy was doing.

I returned to the ER waiting room and took a seat. Once again I had a clear view of the doors leading to the parking garage. A woman entered the building, dressed in brown cords and an orange turtleneck sweater. I recognized her immediately. She had gray hair cut in a short and spiky style, and she was wearing blue-framed eyeglasses. The Reverend Deborah Davies never looked much like a warden chaplain even when she was wearing a clerical collar under her uniform.

She gave a brief glance at the waiting room, started forward, then stopped, looking me straight in the eyes.

"Mike?"

I rose stiffly from the chair. We met at the edge of the carpet.

"It is you," she said.

"Hello, Reverend."

She reached out her arms and gripped my shoulders. "How is Kathy? Have you heard anything?"

"Only that she's in surgery. She lost a lot of blood."

She brought her fingers up to touch my bandages. "How are *you*?"

"A few stitches."

She surveyed the room. "Where is everyone?"

"Waiting down the hall, I think, in the room outside surgery."

"Why are you out here by yourself?"

"I'm not a warden anymore."

"Poppycock."

I had forgotten what a natural goofball Deb Davies was.

"Come with me," she said.

She didn't give me a choice.

There were close to twenty wardens, half in uniform, the rest in street clothes, gathered outside surgery. The guys in jeans and T-shirts had been off duty, at home with their families, maybe even on vacation. But from the first day at the Academy, you pledge yourself to an unwritten, unspoken oath: When a fellow warden is in trouble, you put aside whatever you are doing and you go.

Deb Davies pulled me into their midst, as if I were a shy child. Major Malcomb was in the center of the group. The wardens fell silent at their chaplain's arrival.

"Anything?" she asked.

"She's in surgery now," Malcomb said.

The chaplain addressed the group. "I'm going to say a silent prayer for her, if anyone would like to join me."

She could have spoken the words out loud and

no one would have objected, but Deb Davies was a politically correct twenty-first-century minister. She was sensitive about her role as a religious officer in a secular governmental institution. Overly sensitive, some said. She closed her eyes and bowed her head, and we all did the same. In the silence that followed—not really silence, because the hospital was very noisy—I tried to conjure up something like a coherent prayer.

"Please, God, let her live" was the best I could do.

The sentiment seemed inarticulate, the exercise ineffectual. I felt no stirring of the supernatural in my heart. Kathy would live because her body was strong enough to resist the damage caused by losing so much blood, or she would die because help hadn't come in time to save her.

I opened my eyes and saw other wardens still praying, a few moving their lips.

"Amen," said Deb Davies.

"Amen," replied the wardens.

There was an awkward minute where no one seemed ready to talk. Then Deb Davies broke the silence. "Do the state police have any suspects?" she asked the group.

"It's got to be one of Gammon's buddies," Tommy Volk said. He was a big, blunt guy who never had a problem sharing his opinions. "Or just some crazy vet pissed off about the shooting, looking for revenge."

"Let's not make assumptions," said his sergeant, a man named Ouelette.

"I'm a Marine." Volk tapped his own sternum hard. "If a buddy of mine got shot, I wouldn't care if they called it 'suicide by cop.' I would go looking for payback. Whoever shot Kathy was trained to take out targets from a distance. What does that tell you?"

"Come on, Volk," someone behind me said.

"You don't think it's a vet?"

"I just hope I'm there when they corner the fucking son of a bitch," John Taylor said.

He was one of the six district wardens whom Kathy supervised. When he spoke those angry words, it felt like a spark jumped from him and ignited something inside me, the way a wildfire moves from treetop to treetop. Until that moment, I had been so preoccupied by guilt and fear that I hadn't acknowledged the rage I was feeling. I also wanted to find the person who had shot Kathy—and I wanted to kill him.

"Enough," said Malcomb, raising his hands. "Enough."

"Keep your shit together," said Sergeant Ouelette.

"It's not helping Kathy," added Deb Davies.

Volk turned his back, mumbling, and the crowd spontaneously seemed to fall apart into smaller groups.

"Hey, Bowditch," DiPietro whispered, waving me away from the major and the sergeant. A

151

few other wardens joined us in a corner. "What happened out there? What did you see?"

I was no longer a warden and didn't feel bound to obey the major's order to refrain from voicing my opinions. "The guy was in the blueberry barrens above the house. I think he'd been waiting in that pine grove along the ridgetop, waiting for dark, and then he went down the hill. I don't know if he was planning on setting up there, or if Pluto's barking made him stop, but he had a clear shot at the steps when Kathy came out. And then when Kathy came out onto the steps, he shot her in the side. I don't know how she managed to crawl back inside, but she did. That's when I pulled up, and he took a couple of shots at my truck."

"What happened?"

"Shattered the windshield. I had my Walther in the glove compartment and managed to squeeze off a few rounds."

"You didn't hit anything?" DiPietro asked.

"I never even saw muzzle flashes. But my shots must have been enough to spook him, because he took off. There was blood on the steps. I followed the trail into the house, and that's when I found her."

"How did she look? Tell the truth."

The image of Kathy lying in the hallway with blood pooling away from her like spreading red wings flashed through my mind. "Not good."

"Hey, Bowditch, I have a question."

I turned around at the sound of the coarse female voice and found myself looking down into the fierce gray eyes of Danielle Tate.

17

Warden Dani Tate was wearing carpenter's pants and a loose flannel shirt that made her body look like that of a short, stocky man. She hadn't bothered to comb her straw-colored hair. I couldn't remember ever seeing her in civilian clothes before.

Kathy Frost had been a trailblazer in the Maine Warden Service back when it was arguably the most chauvinistic agency in state government. Yet she still showed moments of vulnerability that I associated, rightly or wrongly, with being a woman. The same could not be said of Danielle Tate. She had a gruff voice, and she always stood with her legs braced as if to steady herself against a heavy wind. Maybe she was insecure about her gender and felt a need to overcompensate for it by projecting an outsized machismo. The other alternative was that Danielle Tate was a genuine hard-ass.

There were spots of red on her cheeks that looked like they'd be hot to the touch. "I want to know what you were doing at the sergeant's house. Why were you even there in the first place?"

"I'd gone over there to apologize," I said.

"For what?"

"For not being there the night of the Gammon shooting."

"Because he wouldn't have pulled a shotgun if you had been there instead of me?" she said. "You think I fucked up somehow."

"No, I don't."

"You're not even a warden anymore, so I don't know who you are to judge me."

Kathy herself had said Jimmy Gammon would still be alive if I had been present that night. But just because Dani Tate wanted to throw a hay-maker at me didn't mean I needed to throw one back.

"I'm not judging you, Tate."

"Go fuck yourself."

She turned her square shoulders and pushed past David DiPietro. She crossed the room, until she was standing toe-to-toe with Major Malcomb, interrogating him about Kathy's condition. I had to hand it to Dani Tate. She might be five-four and a rookie, I thought, but she doesn't seem intimidated by anyone.

"So, Bowditch," DiPietro said, "how's civilian life treating you?"

Earlier, he and the others had been chummy, but as I looked around the little circle, I sensed a sudden chill. With everything that had happened, my former colleagues had momentarily forgotten that I had left their fraternity. Dani Tate had reminded them of that fact.

I tried to break the tension with a joke. "If I'm still getting shot at, it doesn't feel any different from when I was a warden."

None of them laughed. After a minute, they all wandered off, leaving me alone in the corner. I decided to go to the cafeteria for a cup of coffee.

I was dreaming about Stacey. We were picking blueberries in a field on a glorious summer day. She was wearing tight jeans and a sleeveless white T-shirt that clung to her breasts and abdomen, and she was laughing as I had never seen her laugh before. She would pick a blueberry and pop it in her mouth or send it flying playfully at my head. There were blue stains on her lips and fingers.

This isn't real. This is just a dream, I thought.

At first I didn't mind because it was such a happy, sexy dream, but after a while I found myself growing nervous. There were trees at the edges of the blueberry barrens. The thought came to me that someone dangerous might be watching us. I was afraid to look away from her in case I turned back and she was gone.

Somewhere in the distance behind me, I heard an echoing gunshot. Reflexively, I turned my head.

A hand was shaking me by the shoulder. "Michael?"

The Reverend Deb Davies was bending over the booth in the cafeteria where I'd fallen asleep.

"What time is it?"

"Three o'clock."

I sat upright. "A.M. or P.M.?"

"P.M."

I couldn't remember falling asleep. I had gotten coffee and a plastic-wrapped sandwich, then wandered around for a while before checking in on Kathy's condition with the wardens. The last I'd heard, she'd still been in surgery. I must have returned for another cup of coffee.

I barely dared to ask the question. "Kathy?"

"The doctors are calling her condition serious but stable. They've put her in the SCU."

"Can I see her?"

"Not yet." The chair opposite me was empty, and she sat down in it. Behind those blue-framed glasses her eyes looked puffy. "The major has sent the others home. He left Ouelette as the family liaison officer and to organize a series of rotating vigils, so there will always be wardens outside her door. Malcomb told me you got a ride down here in an ambulance. I thought I might give you a lift somewhere. Where would you like me to take you?"

My duffel bag of clean clothes was on the bed at the Square Deal Motel. My shot-up Bronco was, presumably, still in the dooryard outside Kathy's farmhouse. Everything else I owned was stashed in cardboard boxes in Elizabeth Morse's guest cabin.

"I'm going to wait here to see Kathy," I said.

"She hasn't regained consciousness. It might be days before she does."

"Thanks, but I'd prefer to wait."

"I think some people in this room might appreciate it if you took a shower."

I couldn't resist turning my nose to my armpit. The experience was not pleasant. "Are you sure you want me in your car?"

"God calls upon all of us to make sacrifices."

"I don't want to leave Kathy again."

"That's understandable, but you need to take care of yourself, too."

I followed Deb Davies to the hospital garage, a cold, cavernous space that made me button up Soctomah's windbreaker. It felt weird walking around in public with POLICE emblazoned on my back, looking as battered as I did. It must have seemed to the people we passed that a homeless man had beaten up a cop and stolen his jacket.

Portland is an ocean city, and there was a fog hanging in the air that carried with it the briny smell of the sea. The hospital complex sits atop a steep hill called the Western Promenade. On clear days, you can see the summit of Mount Washington, ninety miles away in New Hampshire. But on this

157

afternoon, all I could see were the smeared lights of cars moving along the misty streets below.

Davies drove a lemon yellow Volkswagen Beetle with a vanity license plate reading REVDD. There was a flower vase inset in the dashboard. She had placed a cutting from a lilac bush in it, and the vehicle was filled with the blossom's rich perfume.

She exited the garage and turned in the direction of the expressway. We passed a series of fast-food restaurants and tire dealerships whose neon signs were blurry and hard to read in the fog. She pressed the gas pedal hard to accelerate into the speeding northbound traffic. For a second, I worried that the Beetle would be flattened like a bug against the grille of the eighteen-wheeler that came racing up behind us. The trucker let us know what he thought of her driving by blasting his air horn.

"So where am I taking you?" Davies asked, as if she hadn't nearly killed us both.

I needed a shower and a hot meal, but without a vehicle, I was effectively stranded. At the very least, I knew the Bronco required a new wind-shield. I hadn't checked to see what other damage the shotgun pellets had inflicted on my prized possession.

"Kathy Frost's house," I said. "My truck is there."

"So, I'm curious about your decision to leave

the Warden Service," Davies said, "but I don't want to pry."

"I appreciate that."

"Why did you leave the Warden Service?"

I hadn't had a real conversation with the chaplain in a couple of years. I'd forgotten she didn't have the same boundaries as other people. My mother had raised me as a Catholic, and the priests I'd known had been characterized by their aloof disinterest in my spiritual condition. They had waited, sometimes with visible boredom, to hear my acts of contrition. Deb Davies's pastoral approach seemed to be to aggressively pull confessions out of you.

"Politics," I said.

Her eyes flicked in my direction. "That's it?"

"I think it sums everything up."

"I've heard you're a hunting and fishing guide now. I suppose that job doesn't have a political element at all?"

"Not particularly."

"You're not in competition with other guides, in terms of fighting for business?"

An SUV went speeding past, its taillights vanishing into the fog. "I understand what you're getting at," I said. "Every job is political. But it's not like being a warden. Sometimes I used to think the first job requirement was kissing ass."

"You sound angrier than I remember."

"Why shouldn't I be? My friend was just shot. Her dog was killed. I think sometimes anger is justified."

She was quiet for a few minutes. "I can't disagree with you. I'm struggling with angry feelings myself." I saw the muscles beneath her jawbone working. "I'm not sure I should say anything. I want to, but I'm not sure I should."

"So now you're teasing me? Come on."

"The colonel is resigning."

"Harkavy?" I said. "Why?"

"There was an incident at his home between his wife and another woman who claimed to be a friend of the colonel. The police were called."

"Jesus."

Duane Harkavy had been the service's chief commanding officer for as long as I could remember and was one of the last of the old-school wardens. He had been with the department for close to thirty years. He'd served alongside Charley Stevens, who'd once described him to me as "a cocksure son of a Montreal courtesan." Not that I'd needed confirmation of this fact.

"How has this not been in the paper?" I asked.

"It will be soon," Davies said. "The *Bangor Daily News* has two reporters on the story. I've heard it could happen any day. Otherwise, I wouldn't have told you."

I wasn't sure what shocked me more: the prospect of Harkavy resigning in a public scandal or the idea of the self-righteous old bastard having a secret mistress.

"I didn't see him at the hospital."

"He wasn't there," she said, tightening her hands on the wheel. "I was appalled that he let Malcomb stand in for him last night. He's still the colonel until he resigns. He knew the story was going around today, and he was too embarrassed to show his face."

I couldn't imagine a greater violation of the warden code.

"I appreciate your telling me the news."

"Anger is sometimes justified," she said. "It's only wrath that's a sin."

"I'm not sure I know the difference."

"You'll know it when you feel it."

If the colonel resigned, Major Malcomb would likely be named the acting commander until the commissioner hired a permanent replacement. "Now what's going to happen?" I asked.

"I don't have the faintest clue."

Darkness had arrived prematurely with the fog.

18

We stopped at a gas station so that she could use the ladies' room and I could grab a snack. I bought a canned energy drink and two slices of undercooked pizza, which she asked me to eat outside the car, given how much they reeked of garlic. The puddles in the asphalt reflected the moving lights of the passing traffic.

When I'd thrown away my greasy paper plate and buckled myself back in the car, I found Davies staring at me intently. "It was wrong of me to tell you about the colonel," she said. "It's been a long two days, and I'm very tired. That's no excuse."

"I was bound to hear it anyway."

"Not from me, though. Ministers are supposed to keep secrets."

"Are you apologizing to me for being human?" I said. "Because I'm the last person who should hear anyone's confession on that score."

She gave a sudden laugh, as if she'd just now remembered the funniest joke that she'd ever heard. There was no doubt in my mind that, deep down, Davies was truly a bit of a kook. But if your job is getting people to drop their guard and open up to you, it might help to come across as a charming weirdo. It had worked on me.

"That pizza was disgusting," she said. "I hope you usually eat better than that."

"You don't want to know," I said.

As we turned past Kathy's dented mailbox and climbed the switchback up the ridge, the horror of the previous evening returned, and I found the muscles in my back and shoulders knotting up. There was yellow crime-scene tape strung between the maples. The mist was turning once again to rain. Up ahead on the hillside, the house seemed to be dissolving into the fog. From a distance, I could see the boxy green-and-white shape of my damaged Bronco.

"The police must have left a light on," Deb Davies said.

She pointed, and I saw a faint glow in a second-floor window—one of the upstairs bedrooms.

"Wait," I said. "Stop."

There was a car parked on the other side my Bronco. It was a sedan of some kind, painted a dark color. The outline didn't resemble that of any vehicle driven by law-enforcement officers. My first impression was that it was a very old and angular car.

"What's going on?" Davies asked.

"There's someone inside," I said. "Turn off the engine. Turn off the lights."

The chaplain had fast reflexes. When her headlights went dim, the darkness seemed to seep inside the Beetle. Then my eyes began to accommodate themselves to the night, and I noticed another light go on in the house, in a window adjacent to the first one.

"I don't suppose you have a gun with you?" I asked, not really serious.

"There's a revolver in the glove compartment."

I thought she was joking. She wasn't. It was a Smith & Wesson .38 Special. The handle was pink.

"I've been called to some pretty scary places over the years," she said by way of explanation.

The pistol-packing pastor, I thought.

I popped open the cylinder to check if the gun was fully loaded—it was—and snapped it shut again.

"What are you going to do?" Davies asked me.

"I'm going up to have a look inside the house while you call nine one one."

"I can't convince you to sit here and wait with me?"

She already knew my answer.

I turned the collar up on Soctomah's windbreaker and stepped out of the Beetle, closing the door quietly behind me until I heard the latch click shut. I crept to the side of the driveway so I could sneak up the road in the shadow of the maples. Why would someone be lurking in Kathy's house, especially so conspicuously?

As I crept closer to the dooryard, I could see that the car was a battered Oldsmobile Cutlass. It had probably rolled out of the factory with a midnight black paint job, but twenty years of sitting in the sun and being driven along salted roads had weathered the vehicle a lead gray. There were dents in the driver's door and the rear fender. The side mirror was bent back, as if it had recently clipped a telephone pole.

I didn't recognize the car, but it had a Maine license plate. It was one of those Purple Heart specialty designs with the words COMBAT WOUNDED at the bottom. I remembered hot-headed Tommy Volk's theory that the shooter might have been a crazy vet looking for revenge. I memorized the number in case it might prove important later. I saw a crumpled white Burger King bag on the passenger seat and a cardboard box full of recyclable booze bottles in the back. The car didn't fit at all with my impression of the sniper as a cautious, methodical person.

Whoever it was had broken the police tape that had been strung across the door and found his way inside the house. I tried to avoid looking at the dark stains on the front steps but found myself unable to resist the impulse.

Slowly, I swung the door open and waited. I wasn't sure if I expected shots to be fired from across the foyer, but the only sound I heard was the oil furnace humming a tune in the basement. Someone had turned on the heat.

The house smelled of dog. Pluto lived on after death in that distinctive canine odor that clung to every fabric surface. The hallway became pitch-dark when I closed the door behind me. I would have preferred to turn on a light, if only to avoid stepping in the blood that I had glimpsed on the carpet runner and the maple boards. I pressed my body against the wallpaper and slid along until I reached the staircase to the second floor.

When I peered up the stairs, I saw a bluish glow

coming from the direction of the bedrooms. I took a careful step onto the first riser. The wood gave out a painful-sounding creak, which made me clench my back teeth together. The second step seemed even louder. I pointed the barrel of the revolver at the top of the staircase.

There was light coming from two rooms: the bathroom and the bedroom beside Kathy's. I straightened up and drew in a deep breath. I took the remaining two stairs with one big step. Again, I pressed myself against the wall, keeping the pistol pointed in front of me in case the intruder leaped out of one of the rooms.

When I got to the bathroom, I paused to listen for the sound of running water or a toilet seat creaking, but I heard nothing. I poked my head inside. The shower curtain concealed the tub. I used my left hand to peel back the plastic liner. No one was there.

I moved on to the lighted bedroom. The door had been left open a crack. I gave it a gentle push. I saw an empty bed with rumpled sheets and an heirloom quilt in a heap on the floor. I had never been on this floor of Kathy's house. It seemed to be less a guest room than a space belonging to a specific person: a teenage boy, maybe. There were athletic trophies arrayed along a shelf and framed family photographs. A red-and-white sports pennant for the Caribou Vikings was tacked over the window.

I bent sideways to see if someone might be hiding under the bed and felt a disorienting head rush when I straightened up.

The closet?

Standing to one side and raising the gun, I eased the door open. Clothes hung from wire hangers, but they seemed more like the pants and shirts of a grown man. I had no idea whose room this was.

The basement furnace chose that moment to cease running, but the radiators continued to make a ticking sound. I heard something dripping and noticed a faded army fatigue jacket slung over a chair beside the window. Beside it were a pair of enormous work boots. The coat and the boots were still wet.

I became aware of another sound: snoring. It was coming from Kathy's darkened bedroom.

I stepped back into the hall and gave the door a tap with my boot so that it swung in on itself. Light from the hall leaked into the room around my head and shoulders.

A tall, fully dressed man was lying facedown on Kathy's bed, his right arm hanging over the side. He had a full head of sandy hair and was wearing a Nordic sweater and paint-splattered jeans. There were holes in the bottoms of his tube socks. On the rug beside the bed, an open bottle of vodka stood upright. The sweet scent of exhaled alcohol was cloying.

I pointed the revolver at the sleeping man. "Hey!"

He didn't budge or flinch.

I stepped forward and poked his sole with the pistol. He moved his foot lazily, the way a horse flicks its tail at a biting fly. His snoring continued without so much as a pause. He was so drunk, he'd gone to the bathroom and forgotten which bed he'd been sleeping in.

"Wake up!"

The man was either out cold or putting on a very convincing act.

I took a chance and picked up the bottle of vodka from the floor. It was Absolut, Kathy's brand of choice. The man had consumed the better part of the bottle. I dumped the rest on his face.

He awoke with a start, sputtering. He rolled onto his side and sat bolt upright, his legs thrashing.

"Motherfucker! Motherfucker! Motherfucker!"

"Police! Don't move," I said. The words came out so fast, I forgot they were untrue.

He had clapped a hand over one eye, and I saw that he was wearing a black patch over the other. It was like something a pirate might wear. I was sure the alcohol must have stung like acid.

"I can't fucking see!" he said.

"Who are you? What are you doing here?'

He worked his knuckle back and forth in his good eye. "I live here. This is my home."

"Bullshit. This is Kathy Frost's house."

168

"I'm her brother."

It took me a moment to connect the dots. "Kurt?"

"Yeah," he said, squinting at me with an eye as red as a crushed tomato.

I knew all about him.

19

Kurt Eklund was Kathy's one and only sibling. In the dark days when my father was accused of killing two men and had taken off into the woods to escape capture, Kathy had told me things about her brother. She saw certain similarities between Kurt and my dad. Both had come back from Vietnam physically and emotionally wounded and fundamentally changed from the good people they had been before; both used alcohol to numb the chronic pain that had infected their souls in the jungles of Southeast Asia; both had volatile tempers that blew up unpredictably, like the summer thunderstorms that come in over the mountains.

"He'll call me late at night when he's been drinking," she'd said. "Just ranting and raving about the Republicans, how they've become the party of the old Confederacy and want to reinstate the plantation system for the twenty-first century. He starts quoting Marx and calls himself 'the last American Communist.' He gets totally weird and paranoid when he's wasted, and I can't calm him down. When he sobers up, he has no memory of even calling me. You can have a normal conversation with him in the morning about politics—Kurt's really smart and well read—and you never hear any of that Communist stuff. I don't know where it comes from."

Kurt was older than Kathy by close to a decade—so somewhere in his early sixties. I had always understood that he worked as a carpenter and that he made his home up north in the town of New Sweden, where their aging parents still lived. She hadn't mentioned that he had moved in with her. He was a handsome man, or he had been in his youth. He had a full head of blond hair (dripping now with vodka) and he had made it well into middle age without acquiring even the hint of a potbelly. He was as lean and long-limbed as his sister.

If you looked closer, though, you could see that his body was on the verge of breaking down. The blood vessels in his cheeks and nose were in the process of turning from pink to purple. The effect made him look like he'd gone twelve rounds with a heavyweight prizefighter. His skin elsewhere had a lemonish cast, which I took to be the outward manifestation of an ailing liver.

"What did you do that for?" he said in a slurring nasal accent that sounded almost Midwestern.

"You wouldn't wake up."

He ran a hand through his mop, pushing the wet strands off his forehead. "You're a cop?"

"My name is Mike Bowditch. I'm a friend of your sister."

It didn't seem to mean anything to him.

"You have a pink gun," he observed.

I lowered the revolver. Kurt didn't strike me as dangerous—if only because he was so deeply drunk—but I remembered what Kathy had told me about his violent mood swings.

"Why're you in my house?" he said with sudden defiance.

"I saw a light on. Someone had torn down the crime-scene tape."

"What tape?"

The ramifications of the question took a moment to settle in. "You know what happened to your sister?"

"Course I do."

He seemed to make an effort to collect himself. He rubbed his face hard, as if his cheeks were frostbitten and he was trying to get the blood flowing. He readjusted his black eye patch, snapping the band.

"Kathy's in the hospital, Kurt. She's been shot."

"What?"

"You didn't notice all the blood downstairs?"

"You're nuts, man," he said. "Don't know what you're talking about."

I tucked the revolver into the pocket of my

jacket. "Your sister was shot outside, in the yard, but she managed to crawl inside and call for help. She's in the hospital."

His voice rose an octave. "I don't believe you."

"Stand up, and I'll show you the blood." I found myself resenting his pathetic drunkenness.

He swung his legs off the bed and planted his feet on the floor. He tried to stand, but just as quickly he lost strength in his legs and sat back down again. The bed bounced under him. He turned his discolored face to me with an expression that seemed to dissolve from one emotion to another while I watched.

"Gimme a minute," he said.

If I hadn't dealt with so many alcoholics in my career, I wouldn't have believed this display. But nothing drunks did surprised me anymore. Once, back in Machias, I'd seen a drunk girl leave a grocery store and drive off across the parking lot while her baby screamed in the shopping cart where she'd abandoned him. Another time, I'd responded to a report of an intoxicated motorist driving the wrong way on the interstate, dodging oncoming traffic, before she'd gone off the road and into a telephone pole, decapitating herself. On yet another occasion, I'd assisted the dive team in the retrieval of a man's body from the Penobscot River after one of his drinking buddies dared him to jump off a bridge into the frothing water—in October.

I heard the siren through the half-open window beside the bed. The wailing sound was faint at first but grew louder as the cruiser came speeding up the hill. Soon I saw the flashing blue lights of the Dodge Charger reflecting off the glass behind the curtains.

"Can you stay there on the bed, please?" I said.

"Sure." He seemed relieved to remain stationary.

I turned on lights as I went back down the hallway, until the entire house was ablaze. The stain on the floor downstairs seemed more brown than red now. In the brightness of the flush-mounted ceiling light, I noticed a man's big footprints in the middle of the drying pool. The sight of Kurt's boot marks made me sick and angry.

Deputy Skip Morrison peered in through the front door, his service weapon in hand. "Mike?"

"I'm OK," I said.

"What's going on?"

"It's Kathy's brother. I found him passed out on the bed upstairs."

"I called in the plate just now." Morrison holstered his pistol. "But I didn't recognize the name. The guy's a habitual offender. He just got his driver's license back last month, after the judge had suspended it for six years."

"He says he lives here," I said.

"Not according to the DMV. They have his address as New Sweden."

"We could ask him about it, but he happens to be drunk off his ass."

"If he lives here, where was he when his sister was shot?"

"Off on a bender." I gestured at the floor. "When he got home, he tore through the police tape and trampled through her blood on the way to find the liquor."

Morrison folded his arms and shook his head at the sadness of it all. "So what's the plan, then? I could take him back to the jail until he sobers up. Call it a B and E for now."

"She might have given him permission to stay here," I said. "I already feel bad about hitting him with the news about Kathy."

"The last thing we need is for him to get behind the wheel tonight."

That was true enough and a real possibility. "I can stay with him."

Morrison smiled. "Baby-sitting duty, huh?"

"I think Kathy would want me to look after him."

"Anything you want me to do?"

"If you happen to swing past the Square Deal, I left a duffel bag in room six." I gave him the key, reached into my back pocket for my scrawny wallet, and pulled out three twenty-dollar bills, leaving me with one. "Give this to Dot while you're at it. Tell her she can keep the change."

"You know Dot's not going to take your money."

"Give it to her just the same."

I followed Morrison outside and found Deb Davies standing in the wet weeds beside the cruiser. She'd opened an umbrella against the drizzle. It was child-size, with pink flowers and cats and the words *Hello Kitty* written all over it. Something about the sight of her with that little girl's umbrella made me laugh in spite of myself.

I explained to her about Kathy's brother and his condition. I told her that I intended to stay with him until he sobered up.

"Maybe I should talk with him." Her face was blue from the pulsing pursuit lights.

"He's pretty drunk."

"It's not the first time I've counseled someone who is intoxicated."

I reached into my pocket for the revolver. "Before I forget . . ."

"If you're going to stay here tonight, I'd prefer you keep it."

I shrugged and put the gun back in the jacket. We turned and headed together for the door.

"You know I could arrest you for impersonating a police officer," Skip Morrison said when he saw the logo on the back of the windbreaker. When he smiled, he showed a set of teeth that would have made a horse feel inadequate.

"Someone could do the same to you," I said.

"Stop the presses! Mike Bowditch told an actual joke. You really have changed, dude. I'll be back with your bag."

175

Inside the house, Davies paused in the entryway, staring at the trail of tacky blood and the smeared pattern where Kathy's body had been before the paramedics spirited her away. The sight seemed to send a shiver through her body. She gripped the handrail and physically pulled herself up the first riser the way you might use a sapling to help climb a hill. I followed her up the stairs.

Kurt Eklund was still sitting on the bed, where I had left him, leaning back on his outstretched arms to keep himself upright. His head was tilted back and his good eye was squeezed shut. In this posture, he resembled a sunbather taking in the rays.

"Kurt? I'm Reverend Davies. I'm a chaplain with the Warden Service."

He opened his good eye. It was still pink and painful-looking. "Reverend?" His tone was suspicious.

Davies plucked at her spiky gray hair to lift it up. The drizzle had flattened her do. "Your sister has been badly wounded. Someone shot her last night. She's in very serious condition at Maine Medical Center, but the doctors have managed to stabilize her."

"Is she going to die?"

"She is out of surgery. Your parents are with her now."

How had I missed seeing the Eklunds at the

176

hospital? I had always wanted to meet them. Kathy's parents were Swedes from the northernmost part of Maine: a flat farmland that had been colonized by Scandinavians who considered the climate to be balmy compared to the Nordic wastes from which they'd emigrated. Her father had been a minister before he retired.

Kurt Eklund pushed himself up suddenly from the bed, using his long, strong arms to give himself some leverage. He wobbled on his knees and reached out for the bureau. He nearly fell on his face.

"I'm gonna go see her," he said.

"I don't think that's a good idea," I said.

He staggered forward, his shoulders bent like Methuselah's. "I'm gonna go see her."

"You need a good night's sleep first, Kurt," said Davies. "In the morning, I can go with you if you'd like."

She touched his arm, but he shook it off.

"I'm fine! Just let me go."

I stepped between Kurt Eklund and the door and prepared to tackle him onto the bed if necessary.

"I can't do that, Kurt," I said.

He raised his head, and I saw tears streaming down his discolored cheeks, one from his open eye, the other leaking out from under the concave patch. "Where's Pluto?"

"He was shot, too," I said.

He tried to sniff up the liquid that was running from his nose. "Can I see him?"

As always, Deb Davies was more compassionate than I was. "The state police are investigating the shooting. They've taken Pluto's body to help find evidence to catch the person who did this. When they're done, you will have a chance to say good-bye to him."

Eklund reached his rough hand out and set it on my shoulder. The sudden weight caught me by surprise. There was no aggression in the motion, only a physical need for support. I took hold of his arm to lighten the load. His biceps and triceps reminded me of a twisted ship's rope.

"I'm sorry I'm such a mess," he said.

How many times has he said those words to his sister? I wondered.

"I'm so, so, so sorry." The tears were coming quickly now, and his lips were trembling.

"Let's get you into bed," Deb Davies said.

I wouldn't have known what to do without the chaplain.

20

After Kurt had fallen back to sleep, Deb Davies and I went downstairs to confer. Over the years, Kathy had transformed the formal sitting room into what she called her "woman cave." She had removed the rocking chairs and love seats and replaced them with a leather recliner, sectional couch, and wide-screen TV, on which she watched nothing but sports. She'd had me over for a Patriots game once, but she'd gotten so apoplectic, screaming at the television after every dropped pass and missed route, that I'd never dared return.

"You don't have to stay," I told Deb Davies.

"What are you going to do?"

"I'll grab my sleeping bag from the Bronco and camp out on the couch until he wakes up." There wasn't much else I could do for Kathy at the moment.

"You know," she said, "there's a good chance he won't remember anything that happened tonight. His blood-alcohol level is over the moon. You might have to break the news to him all over again," she said.

"Yippee."

"What if he wakes up with withdrawal symptoms?" she asked.

"You mean like the DT's?"

"If he's been on a bender, he could have a seizure while he's detoxing."

"I'll just have to watch over him."

Davies removed her trendy blue glasses, massaged her eyes, and then rearranged herself. "I wonder where he was all this time."

"I doubt he even knows." I shifted positions and

felt the revolver in the jacket pocket pressing against the arm of the sofa. "The state police will want to interview him."

"That's assuming he remembers anything."

"You sure you don't want your gun back?"

"Give it to me the next time you see me."

"If he sobers up, I was thinking of driving him to Maine Med," I said. "Unless you think that's a bad idea."

"I guess it depends on what he looks like in the morning. Watch him closely. He could have a seizure if he goes through alcohol withdrawal. The DT's can be fatal."

I showed Deb Davies to the door and then closed and locked it behind her. My recent experience as a caretaker prompted me to do a circuit of the house to check that all the windows and doors were securely fastened. I wondered what was happening back at Moosehorn Lodge now that it was essentially unguarded. The video cameras would have already recorded my extended, unexplained absence. My gig watching over Betty Morse's estate was the least of my concerns at the moment.

On my way through the kitchen, I passed the open pantry and noticed Kathy's shelf of liquor bottles. Her taste in booze always struck me as surprisingly girlie. She liked chocolate liqueurs, honey-sweet bourbons, cordials infused with melon and other artificial fruit flavors. I grabbed a bottle of rum and poured a splash into a coffee mug. It tasted like suntan lotion.

It said something about the frazzled state of my nerves that I took both the mug and the bottle back with me to the living room. I'd visited Kathy on a number of occasions, but I'd never gotten the full tour of the house.

She'd thrown exactly one get-together for her district wardens during my time under her command. We'd lighted a bonfire and dragged up lawn chairs and sawn-off stumps to sit on, and everyone passed around a gallon of Absolut in honor of the Swedish Midsommar. Kathy had always impressed me as a walking contradiction: a sociable hermit. She seemed extroverted and was capable of making small talk easily enough. But she seemed to consider no one in the Warden Service to be a close confidant, not even me. The Midsommar party was the only one she'd ever held here.

I tried to respect her privacy now. I didn't open any drawers or cabinets. My prurient curiosity had certain limits.

I half hoped to come across a picture of her first and only husband, Darren Frost, about whom I knew next to nothing, other than they'd split up ages ago. I didn't know why they'd divorced or where he lived now or what he did for work. Kathy's mysterious ex-husband had come to stand for everything I didn't know about my friend.

There were no photographs of him on any of the walls or shelves, of course. Who keeps pictures of their exes?

I found other photos, though: Kathy playing high school and college basketball; Kathy graduating from the University of Maine, with her hale-looking blond parents in attendance; Kathy in her warden's uniform, receiving an award; many pictures of Pluto. But none of Darren Frost.

The alcohol began dissolving the adrenaline in my bloodstream, and I found myself growing tired. Rather than waiting for the local news to come on television, I sat down at the desk in Kathy's study, planning to turn on her computer. The machine was gone, of course. Lieutenant Soctomah had taken the computer after I'd told him she'd received death threats. The computer forensics team would need to trace every e-mail she'd received. All that remained were dusty rectangles on the desk.

Her office was a mess. There were not one but three mugs of unfinished coffee, one with a grayish scrim floating on the surface. A leaning tower of hunting and fishing magazines was one good nudge from sliding onto the floor. Soctomah had left piles of paperwork untouched, concluding that Kathy's various personnel reports and duty logs were not the best starting points for his investigation. The vengeful veteran theory still seemed to offer the most promise.

I wondered, though. The short interval between the Gammon shooting and the sniper attack suggested the two incidents were linked, but every warden I knew had enemies, and what better time to settle an old grudge then when the detectives might be misdirected? Had anyone interviewed Danielle Tate about whether Kathy had had a dustup with one of the local dirtbags recently?

I leaned back in the squeaky desk chair and extended my feet under the desk. My toe caught a wastepaper basket that was hidden under there, overturning its contents onto the hardwood floor. I bumped my head on the sliding drawer while picking up the wadded pieces of paper.

Most of it was junk mail, opened envelopes that had contained bills, magazine-renewal cards, catalogs—the usual sorts of things. But there was a crumbled sheet of legal paper that caught my eye. It was a crudely drawn sketch of a rectangle. There were no words on the page, just three X's, each with a dotted line extending outward from it. The drawing had been done in pencil and I saw that one of the lines had been erased and redone at a slightly different angle. It looked like a schematic rendering done by a child.

There was also a neatly folded piece of paper that I couldn't keep from opening. It was a news story that Kathy had printed out from the computer. It was dated four days earlier:

POLICE BELIEVE
LYNDON, ME, WOMAN DIED
FROM FALL DOWN STAIRS

HOULTON, ME—Police say they believe a woman found dead in her Lyndon, ME, home Saturday died from a fall down her stairs.

The Major Crimes Unit suspended its investigation Sunday night after finding no evidence of a crime in the death of 67-year-old Marta Jepson.

A concerned neighbor found Jepson dead around 11:00 A.M. Sunday at the bottom of a staircase in her home on Svensson Road. Police became suspicious because of trauma to her body, a broken lamp in the living room, and items possibly missing from the home, said Aroostook County sheriff Alvin Cyr. The Sheriff's Department called the state police Major Crimes Unit to investigate.

Authorities said Jepson died of head injuries consistent with a fall. Cyr said Jepson's house was locked when police were called to check on her.

Jepson had last spoken to a friend by phone about 5:00 P.M. Friday, Cyr said. She apparently lived alone in her house and was home when she spoke to her friend by phone.

Cyr said investigators have found no evidence of a crime or that anyone was in her home at the time of her death. If police get additional information about her death or autopsy results indicate she did not die of an accident, police will resume an investigation at that point, Cyr said.

I wasn't sure what to make of the story. The town of New Sweden, where Kathy had grown up, was just down the road from Lyndon. It was possible that the dead woman was someone she had known, perhaps the mother of a friend. Jepson sounded like a Scandinavian name.

The woman had died on Saturday, the day after the Gammon shooting. Was there any significance in the timing? Probably not. She was an older woman who had lived alone. She had fallen down and died.

I took the article back to Kathy's woman cave and reread it, hoping it would open a door in my mind. I set the piece of paper on the coffee table to look at again later.

The rum might have been oily to the taste, but there was nothing wrong with its sedative properties. The nerve endings throughout my body seemed to be going numb, and my breathing was becoming shallow and more regular. My injured face and scalp stung a little less.

My mind had been lurching from crisis to crisis

for more than twenty-four hours. That sort of intense focus takes a toll. I couldn't imagine how men and women in combat managed to stay sane. I'd heard that soldiers were prescribed amphetamines. When you are under extreme stress, the first thing to go is your ability to regain perspective after traumatic events. Our brains are the tools we rely on to make sense of the world, but what happens when your brain is broken?

If you're Jimmy Gammon, you decide to die. The first emotion I had experienced when I heard the news of his death was anger at what he had forced the wardens to do. Perhaps if I'd visited him after he came back from Bagram and seen for myself the extent of his injuries, it would have been easier to reconcile myself to his suicide. People had described Jimmy's wounds as disfiguring; they'd said his pain was constant and unbearable. I was fairly certain that the grinning guy with whom I'd gone pheasant hunting hadn't existed for a long time. He had died years before his body bled to death in that barn.

I was half-drunk myself when I finally stretched out on the sectional sofa in Kathy's woman cave. I'd fetched the sleeping bag from my Bronco and rested my head on a throw pillow. Kurt was snoring so loudly, I could hear him downstairs.

I gave a thought to what Deb Davies had said: that Kurt might awaken with no memory of the previous night and might regard me as an unknown intruder. I removed her pink revolver from my jacket and tucked it under the pillow.

Over the years, the sofa fabric had become impregnated with the smell of Kathy's dog. I found myself blinking back tears. The horror that Kathy must have experienced in those few seconds between the time Pluto was gunned down and she was shot herself must have seemed like a nightmare come true.

When I closed my eyes, I saw a mutt lying at the bottom of a brackish swimming pool. The grotesque image grew more and more vivid as I tried to fall asleep, and I felt my wakeful mind returning to a time and place I'd almost forgotten. It was a memory that had the blurred edges of a dream.

21

On my first day as a game warden, I was called upon to shoot a rabid dog. The animal had just bitten a little girl in the face. Her name was Kaylee. The dog's name was Goofus.

I was twenty-four years old, a recent graduate of Colby College and the Maine Criminal Justice Academy. I'd just spent the previous eight weeks being taught the arcane tradecraft of my new career. I'd learned how to vanish into alder swamps to catch deer poachers, follow clues left by panicked people lost in the snow, disarm the trip wires used by marijuana growers to guard backwoods plantations. By most standards, I'd become an accomplished woodsman. In those early days of my occupation, I believed these specialized skills would automatically admit me to an ancient order of wardens—a brotherhood of trackers, detectives, and scouts. This arrogant assumption was the first of many misconceptions I would have about my job.

My reeducation began with Goofus.

It was true that being a game warden was an odd job relative to other law-enforcement specialties—we dealt with moose poachers and pirate rafters and other strange specimens of humanity. But in Maine, you never knew when you might wander into a firefight between two rival gangs of back-woods heroin dealers. That was the reason we wore bulletproof vests.

Sarah had arisen early that first day to mark the occasion. She was a gorgeous short-haired blond who was getting a master's in education while teaching at a private school to supplement our meager incomes. She had misgivings about my new profession—secretly she hoped it was just a phase I would pass through—but she was being a good sport about it. She photographed me as I buckled on my gun belt and laced-up my L.L.Bean boots. I'd dreamed of being a Maine game warden for years. This was supposed to be the most exciting day of my life.

Kathy arrived to pick me up at dawn. She'd brought us both tall cups of coffee from the store at the base of Appleton Ridge. Sarah made us pose in front of Kathy's green patrol truck.

"Say 'yoga,' " Sarah said.

"Why not 'cheese'?" Kathy asked.

" 'Yoga' makes your mouth smile more naturally."

Kathy and I set off on patrol. It was supposed to be a day of checking fishing licenses and boating registrations—nothing too serious.

Around ten o'clock, the radio crackled and Kathy's call numbers were recited. The dispatcher reported a 10-42. A possibly rabid dog had attacked a young girl playing in a trailer park nearby. The EMTs were on the scene. In my mind, the call properly belonged with an animal control officer, but we were the nearest unit. I was depressed to begin my new career as a glorified dogcatcher.

Kathy turned the wheel in the direction of the hamlet of double-wides. Some of the mobile homes were neat little residences with welcome mats and window boxes of chrysanthemums. Others looked liked derelict boxcars with plywood doors and barrels out front filled with empty beer bottles. The older people tended to live in the nice trailers; their sons and daughters inhabited the others, along with their chosen fuck buddies and assorted offspring.

As we entered the park, a skinny shirtless guy with a billy-goat beard waved us down. "It's at the pool, man! Cujo!"

The ambulance was parked near a chained-in rectangle of ragweed, under a bright and cloudless summer sky. Along the horizon stood the serrated treetops. It was the municipal center of the trailer park. There was a crowded cluster of bodies, young and old, but mostly young, inside a mesh fence that the local boys had nearly succeeded at kicking in. The mob had brought with it stones and bottles to throw.

I hopped out of the truck and nearly collided with a shiny-faced paramedic emerging from the rear of the ambulance.

"How is she?" I asked the EMT.

His expression was grim. "Depends on the plastic surgeon. We're gonna haul ass getting her to the hospital if it's all right by you."

"Go for it."

"By the way, some guy shot it for you with a crossbow."

"Is it dead?"

"No," he said. "Unfortunately."

Kathy appeared beside me. She had brought her shotgun from the truck. It was the old Mossberg 500—subsequently replaced by the combat-tested Mossberg 590A1 as the Warden Service has become more heavily militarized. She handed me the heavy weapon.

We shouldered through the mob. "Game wardens!" Kathy shouted.

When she wanted, she could make her voice as deep as man's, although it wasn't naturally that way.

The Red Sea parted. I angled my way through the pool gate and across the cracked tile of the patio, feeling the surging kids around my thighs. A heavy, sweaty man in cutoff cargo pants and an odiferous wifebeater T-shirt was trying to aim a crossbow into the pool bottom.

"Hey, Robin Hood," said Kathy. "Drop the bow."

He let fly another arrow.

"I said knock it off!"

I found myself staring into a concrete hole in the ground. A shallow green pond had formed at the bottom. Beer bottles and cans floated in the water, along with grass clippings and a yellow dusting of pine pollen. You could practically hear the sound of hatching mosquitoes rising in swarms from the stagnant reservoir.

As the crowd grew quiet, the dog's whining seemed to grow louder. Occasionally, it let out a yap and snarled up at us before turning in circles, trying to snap at the crossbow quarrel buried in its bloody haunches. Its brownish fur was coated with some sort of lather, maybe from having licked its ribs with its foaming mouth. The animal was starving, fleck-mouthed. No question it was rabid. I guessed it to be a rottweiler-Lab mix, although it no longer resembled anyone's pet.

The people of the park had been hurling stones and bottles down on its head before the flabby-armed joker thought to bring out the crossbow.

"Shoot it!" one of the adult women said.

"Would everyone back away!" I said. "It's for your own safety!"

Kathy leaned close to me and I smelled the Avon Skin So Soft that she used as her own personal bug repellent. "Do you want me to do this?"

"I've got to do it sometime."

"Doesn't have to be today, Grasshopper."

I hefted the twelve-gauge. "What have you got in this? A slug or buckshot?"

"Buckshot."

I fired directly at the poor suffering dog's head. My hands didn't flinch. It was, in fact, a fantastic shot. The dog's brains flew out, and it dropped dead.

The sound of the explosion deafened me for a moment; I should have inserted the foam earplugs I carried in my chest pocket.

When my ears cleared, I heard clapping. I looked around and saw that several of the youngish adults—overweight girls pushing strollers; whip-thin men with pants falling down—putting their hands together. Then the children imitated them. I was receiving applause.

I slung the shotgun over my shoulder. Somehow, I kept my feet as I slid down the slick sides of the pool. The water wasn't much more than a yard deep. I removed a pair of latex gloves from a pouch in my belt and snapped them on like a doctor preparing for surgery. Then I carefully lifted the dead animal in my arms—its bones might have been as hollow as a bird's—and waded through the muck to the steps at the shallow end.

I heard the jangling of dog tags on its collar and saw one shaped something like a bone with the name GOOFUS stamped into the blue metal. There was a phone number and address on it. I would need to call the owners and tell them what I'd been forced to do their family pet. How did the dog contract rabies? I wondered. Any mammal could carry the virus.

"Hey, Sergeant, can you bring me a tarp?" I shouted.

But Kathy was already there with one of the same body bags the state provided us for human corpses. I placed Goofus atop the plastic liner and zipped it up.

"Hydrophobia," I mumbled, shaking off my algae-green arms.

"That's the Latin name for rabies," Kathy said. "Fear of water."

"So we both studied Latin," I said. "*Cave canem.*"

" 'Beware of the dog.' For whatever it's worth,

the first month I was a warden, I had to shoot a person."

"What happened?"

She took a deep breath and looked me in the eyes. "This guy, Decoster, was beating his wife. She'd called the police about him a bunch of times before, but somehow he always talked himself out of being arrested. I guess he was drinking buddies with the local cops. But here I was, a rookie and a *woman*. I didn't know this asshole, and I wasn't going to give him another free pass on beating up his wife. He went apeshit when I tried to put him into cuffs. He grabbed a knife from the table and turned on me. I'd never been that scared in my life."

I steadied myself against the Mossberg. "Jesus."

"Afterward, the woman was a crying mess. She kept saying she didn't mean for me to kill him. And there's this fat little kid bawling his eyes out in the corner. Jason didn't know what the hell was going on. I thought I'd fucked up big time. Sometimes I still wonder if I did." Kathy reached down and touched the plastic bag, almost as if she was petting the dead dog inside of it. "I know you must be feeling like shit right now, Mike, but if this is as bad as it gets for a while, consider yourself fortunate."

I appreciated the confession, but more because my new sergeant had opened up to me than because it soothed my guilt.

· · ·

The alcohol dropped me down a well but didn't keep me asleep very long. I awoke after a few hours, dry-mouthed and unsure where I was because the room was so dark. I flopped onto my back and lay with my eyes open until the blackness of the room faded and I could make out the fuzzy shapes of the big-screen TV and the head of the eight-point buck Kathy had shot the first morning she'd ever gone bow hunting.

After a while, I heard floorboards creaking overhead; Kurt was awake and roaming around. The footsteps continued down the hall until they came to the top of the stairs. I reached for the gun under my pillow and sat up. There was no lamp within easy reach of the sofa, or I would have turned on a light.

The footsteps stopped midway down the stairs, and I thought I heard an in-drawn breath. The next sound was heavier. I had the impression Kurt Eklund had just collapsed on the staircase.

The next thing I knew, he was sobbing.

I swung my legs off the sofa and rose to my feet, tucking the revolver into my pants at the small of my back. I padded across the thick carpet until I came to the foyer and poked my head around the corner.

Kurt was indeed seated on one of the steps. He was holding onto a baluster as if for support and staring down at the dark stain on the floor.

I snapped on the overhead light.

"Kurt?"

He blinked down at me, half-blinded by both the sudden illumination and his own streaming tears. His hair was the color of a golden retriever, I realized.

"That's her blood?" he said.

"Yes."

"Then it wasn't just a nightmare."

"No."

"Is she going to be OK?"

"I honestly don't know."

He let loose of the baluster and buried his wet face in his hands. "It's all my fault."

I wasn't sure what he meant, but it seemed the wrong moment to press him to clarify himself. "Do you remember who I am?"

"A warden?"

"You can call me Mike." I was shocked that he had any memory of our conversation, given his off-the-charts blood-alcohol level. "Why don't you go back to bed, Kurt. Get some sleep. In the morning, I'll drive you down to Portland to see her."

"I don't think I can sleep."

"Do you want me to make us some coffee?"

"What I want is a drink."

"I don't think that's a great idea. Why don't you come with me out to the kitchen and we'll see what Kathy has in her refrigerator."

He rubbed his one good eye and puffed out his cheeks before sucking them back in. He didn't say another word but rose shakily and plodded down the narrow steps. The sour smell of alcohol drifted behind him.

There was a draft in the kitchen, coming from the direction of the mudroom. I made a fire in the woodstove, using newspaper flyers and fatwood from a pine box in the corner. Kurt settled himself at the antique table, which tilted in his direction when he rested a forearm on it. He bent down to look at the uneven legs.

"I need to fix this."

Kathy had told me he was a carpenter. I wondered how he'd pursued his vocation when he'd been without a driver's license for so long. According to Morrison, Eklund was a habitual motor vehicle offender. That hardly came as a surprise.

I made coffee in the fancy Bunn machine that had been Kathy's big splurge a few years back. Then when the woodstove began to steam, I fried eggs in a cast-iron griddle. I'd hoped for some toast, too, but the bread in the bread box had acquired a bad case of the blue splotches.

Kurt watched me quietly, sipping black coffee. He removed his dusty Nordic sweater. His long underwear was wet and yellow under the arms and in a stained crescent above his sternum. When he rolled up his sleeves, I saw that he had patches of rough red skin on his elbows.

"Do you mind if I open a window?" he croaked. "It's like a sauna in here."

I found the room chilly myself. "Go ahead."

He raised the window above the soapstone sink and stood there, his arms braced on the counter, staring down the hill. "Red sky at morning," he said.

There was a glow like a distant wildfire burning beyond the hills to the east, but elsewhere the sky was still dark and dense with clouds.

"How much do you remember about last night?" I asked him.

"There was a woman with you. She said someone shot my sister."

He still didn't seem entirely sober to me, but he seemed coherent enough to attempt a conversation. I set two plates on the table and sat down to eat. After a moment, he took the chair across from me and lifted a fork.

"Do the cops know who did it?" he asked.

"Not yet. I was wondering if you had any ideas."

"She's a warden. She's made a lot of enemies in twenty-eight years. Start at the beginning."

"She never mentioned a name to you? Someone in particular who had threatened her?"

He cocked his shaggy head and studied me with his one working eye. The retina was the same shade of hazel as his sister's, but the sclera was a sickly yellow. "Katarina and I don't have that kind of relationship."

Katarina? I'd always thought her first name was Katharine. "You know about the shooting she was involved with a few days ago?"

"Of course I know. I was here when she came home that night. She was very upset. She pretended not to be, but I could tell she was. This wasn't the first time she had to kill someone in the line of duty, you know?"

"She told me about the Decoster shooting."

"Then you know how it's haunted her. Most cops never shoot one person in their career. What do you think it's like killing two people?"

I had a good idea. "How long have you been living here, Kurt? Your driver's license says you live in New Sweden."

"A few weeks. What is this, an interrogation?"

I hadn't intended the conversation to go in that direction, but Eklund was such an ornery character, it was hard not to treat him with hostility.

"I don't think the detectives who are investigating your sister's case even knew you were living here."

"What does it matter to them?" He hadn't touched his eggs.

"They need a complete picture."

"Kathy's been putting me up until I get some steady work. I asked her for asylum, and she gave it to me."

My fork paused between the plate and my

mouth. "That's an interesting choice of words."

"What? *Asylum?*" he said. "I'm an expert on the subject. Ask me anything. 'Bedlam' was originally slang for the Bethlehem Royal Hospital in London. Bellevue Hospital in New York treated Eugene O'Neill and Norman Mailer. The blues legend Lead Belly died there. Psych wards are my specialty."

"Do you mind if I ask you a personal question?"

"Since I have no clue who you are, *Mike,* or what you're doing in my sister's house, it seems like it should be me interrogating you."

"I'm a friend of your sister. I used to be one of her district wardens."

"Used to be?"

"I was here the night she got shot. I arrived a few minutes after it happened. The shooter was still here, though. Whoever he was, he blew out the windshield of my Bronco. You probably missed it on the way in. It's the vehicle out there with all the holes in it."

He placed his hands flat on the table and made a smacking noise with his lips. "I'm sorry if I seem like I'm being a dick. I'm hungover and not feeling particularly good about myself in general this morning. The shrinks at the VA say I have a major depressive disorder. I always tell them, 'How happy would you be if you were a chronic alcoholic with one eye?'" He began to laugh in a way that reminded me of a comic book villain. He

200

held up both hands, palms outward. "These mitts of mine are going to start shaking soon if I don't get a drink."

"Maybe you should eat some of your eggs." The grease had already congealed around the whites.

"I have no stomach for it anymore."

"Maybe you should check into rehab."

"Interesting suggestion. Never heard that one before."

Without another word, he wandered down the hall to the nearest bathroom, leaving me alone in the dimly lit kitchen. I eyed his untouched plate of fried eggs, knowing he wouldn't eat them now. I decided to help myself.

When he came back, he headed straight for the pantry and emerged with a bottle of amaretto. He twisted the metal cap and kept pouring until his coffee mug was mostly booze. He raised the cup to his mouth, watched me the whole time like a kid deliberately hoping to provoke a scolding.

I remained quiet.

"I expected you to try to stop me," he said.

"It's not my house," I said. "I can't let you drive today, though. Where are your car keys?"

"Under the driver's seat."

Dawn was brightening the window above the sink, but the sun still hadn't risen. I'd need to fetch those keys if I didn't want him to sneak off while I was taking a shower. And I should check Kathy's patrol truck, too.

"You never answered my question," I said.

"Go ahead."

"You weren't here the night Kathy was shot, and you weren't here the next day when the house was crawling with state police detectives and evidence technicians. Then you come back shit-faced in the middle of the night? Where were you, Kurt?"

He took another swig from the mug and set it down on the tabletop. "I see you ate my eggs."

"Are you going to answer me?"

"I found a card game at the VFW in Sennebec."

"You were playing poker for two days?"

"You don't play, do you?"

"I learned a long time ago that I am a poor loser."

"Two days at a table is nothing for me if they keep the drinks coming." When he smiled, he showed stained teeth that looked unnaturally long, and I realized it was because the gums had pulled back from the roots.

I leaned back in my chair and crossed my arms. "Something's puzzling me. If someone told me that my sister was on her deathbed in the hospital, you couldn't stop me from rushing off to see her. I wouldn't be sitting here getting drunk and making wisecracks."

"You have a sister?" he asked.

"I have a stepsister."

"And when was the last time you saw her?" He

seemed to be playing a game with me—a game with rules only he understood.

"Last year, at the wake following my mother's funeral."

He'd expected a different reply from me, I could tell. "I don't like hospitals," he said.

"That's your answer?"

"When I was eighteen years old, I remember waking up in the Twelfth Medical Evacuation Hospital in Cu Chi, Vietnam. It was across Highway One from a petroleum dump and artillery battery. I had no idea how I'd gotten there, but when I woke up, I discovered that I was missing an eye. They had to tie me down, I heard. I've never trusted doctors since they plucked my eye out."

"Is that your all-purpose excuse?"

"For what?"

"For everything that's gone wrong in your life."

The smile vanished in an instant. If this had been a fencing match, I would have said that I'd scored a touch against him. He brought his fingers to his chin and ran the back sides of them along the stubbled hair beneath his jawline. The noise was loud and rasping, like sandpaper on a block of wood. "You're ex-military, right?"

"What makes you say that?"

"You have anger issues." The smile returned, more condescending than ever, and he pointed a finger at me. "And *that* is why you are no longer

203

a warden. Am I right? Because of your anger-management problems?"

"I have reasons to be angry," I said.

I stood up from the table with the two greasy plates and carried them to the soapstone sink. I squirted some dishwashing liquid on them and ran the water until it was scalding hot. Then I brushed the plates with a sponge until my hands were red. I cleaned the cast-iron griddle pan with a paper towel.

Kurt Eklund watched me with the patience of a cat. He'd managed to get under my skin with an ease that I found embarrassing. I was mad at him and mad at myself at being so easily provoked. I felt an urge to take his car for the day and leave him stranded here with his self-pity and his pantryful of booze.

As I was drying the inside of my coffee mug with a rag, I glanced out the window. The clouds had drifted to the eastern horizon, blotting out the newly risen sun. It was visible as a pale disk in the sky, shedding little in the way of heat or light. Below the blueberry barrens were a patchwork of hay fields with a river running through them and a distant pond that reflected the sun like a mirror.

A figure dressed in full camouflage was striding through the barrens less than a hundred feet from the house. He had a mesh bag filled with turkey decoys slung over his shoulder and was carrying a pump shotgun tucked under his arm. He was wearing a sheer green mask over his face, but when he looked up at the lighted window and saw me watching him from the house, I could have sworn that he gave me a smile.

"What the hell?" I said.

22

D o you know who that is?" I asked Kurt.
He pushed himself up from the oval table, causing it to groan and tilt again beneath the weight of his outstretched arms. He peered over my shoulder, through the window.

"Son of a bitch!"

Before I could ask another question, he'd taken off through the mudroom, pushing the back door open with such force, I thought it might fly off its hinges. Despite his sixty-something years and ill health, Eklund was a strong guy with muscles hardened from a lifetime of physical labor. Through the cracked window, I saw him striding in his stocking feet across the dooryard in pursuit of the turkey hunter.

"Hey! Hey!" he shouted.

I followed him out of the kitchen and down the back steps.

The morning was gloomy, but drier than it had been for a long time, and a wave of warblers was moving through the treetops, singing as they flitted from branch to branch. I heard a whistle of wing beats and looked up to see a pair of wood ducks rocketing against the overcast sky.

The hunter paused and lifted the barrel of his shotgun slightly, not enough to be threatening but definitely as if he was preparing himself for trouble. "Ahoy, matey! If it isn't Captain Kidd."

"What do you think you're doing, Littlefield?" Kurt said.

"Using my right of way."

"Kathy told you to stay off her land."

"She should post it, then." The man, Littlefield, was dressed from cap to boots in camouflage, making it impossible to see anything except his rheumy eyes, which were visible above the leaf-patterned veil that covered the bottom of his face. He was a big guy under all those hunting clothes, but he had the cracked, high-pitched voice of a very old man.

"What's going on here?" My tone was the same one I used to use as a warden to establish my command presence.

"Who are you supposed to be?" he asked. "Another of the lady warden's brothers?"

"My name is Mike Bowditch. And I'd like to know what you're doing here."

"His name is Littlefield," said Kurt. "He owns the farm on the other side of that stone wall."

"And I own the right-of-way through these fields, too."

206

"The hell you do," said Eklund.

"I got the deed that says so!"

I was already steaming at the "lady warden" comment, but I tried to keep the emotion out of my voice. "Do you mind removing your hunting mask, Mr. Littlefield, so we can have a polite conversation?"

"I ain't interested in having a conversation with either of you needle dicks. Stand aside and let me use my right-of-way."

"You know the woman who owns this property was shot the other night," I said.

"Of course I know. Cops trampled all over my place looking for clues."

"She was shot by someone with a turkey gun."

"You accusing me of something?"

"You don't think it's disrespectful to be hunting on her land under the circumstances?"

"I doubt she cares much one way or the other at the present time."

Eklund stooped down and grabbed an apple-size rock from the weeds. "Fuck you!"

Littlefield lifted the barrel of his shotgun. "Easy there, Cyclops!"

My right hand went around my side and found the grip of Davies's revolver where I'd tucked it into the back of my pants. "I suggest you move on, Mr. Littlefield."

"That's what I was doing before you clowns accosted me."

"Don't think I won't throw this!" Kurt said.

"And don't think I won't defend myself if you do."

"Go home, Mr. Littlefield," I said.

"I don't take orders from you, sonny. I do what I want on my land."

Kurt shook his arm, the one holding the stone. "It's not your fucking land!"

Littlefield chuckled. "Have another drink, alkie."

He hoisted the bag of turkey decoys over his shoulder and set off across the barrens to the south, in the direction of the stone wall that marked the edge of Kathy's property. Robert Frost had evidently been wrong about good fences making good neighbors.

Kurt and I watched him go, the camouflaged hunter becoming harder and harder to see as he receded across the green field.

"Can you tell me what the hell just happened?" I said.

Eklund smacked his lips again, as if to gather the saliva to form a string of sentences. "He claims the deed to his property gives him the right to ride his ATV and snowmobile across Kathy's land. She'd told him to knock it off, but the bastard keeps doing it because he likes to provoke her. Kathy went to see a lawyer in Augusta about it, and there are problems with the title that should have come out when she bought the place. She'd probably win in court—although it would cost her a few grand, the lawyer said. Meanwhile, old Littlefield took out a lien on Kathy's property just to be an even bigger dick than he already was."

I should tell Soctomah about the territorial dispute, I decided. It sounded as if he'd already spoken with Littlefield, but this morning's stunt with the turkey gun deserved to be reported. And at the very least, the detective would want to interview Kurt about his recent whereabouts, too. I wondered how the lieutenant would feel about my spontaneous decision to become the man's bunk mate.

"I need a drink," Kurt muttered, and headed back toward the house.

I had no idea what to do with the guy. His utter disinterest in seeing his sister continued to baffle me. Was he that afraid the doctors would take one whiff of his eighty-proof breath and lock him up in the detox ward? I wished Kathy had confided in me more about her troubled brother; I felt hobbled by a lack of insight.

At the very least, I wanted to visit her again at the hospital. I wandered over to my vintage Bronco, wincing as I ran my fingers over the punctures in the hood and side panel. The right front tire was flat. I tried the door and found it unlocked. The entire dashboard and front seat appeared blue from powdered windshield glass. The glove compartment was still open from when I'd grabbed my Walther.

Davies's .38 Special packed more of a punch, but I missed my James Bond gun. The pistol had been my eighteenth-birthday present to myself. It had even saved my life once. Maybe if I asked Soctomah nicely, he'd have the technicians expedite their ballistics tests.

It was obvious I would not be taking my Bronco onto the roads of midcoast Maine this week, this month, or maybe ever again. I had doubts the damage could even be repaired, let alone quickly, or at a cost I could afford. In other words, I was effectively stranded up here on Appleton Ridge.

Kurt Eklund's ash-gray Cutlass was parked in the shade of one of the big sugar maples. The car seemed even more battered than its owner. It was hard to find a place on it that Kurt hadn't scratched, dented, or chipped. I popped the driver's door and rummaged around beneath the seat, finding in the process an empty fifth of Five O'Clock vodka and three crushed cans of Milwaukee's Best. The keys were there, too, just as Kurt had said. Weighing them in my hand, I felt reassured that he'd told me one truthful thing.

I stuck the keys in my pants pocket and was turning back to the house, when I looked down the drive and noticed that Kathy had a plastic mailbox where she received the morning newspaper. I wandered down the hill to see if the deliveryman had arrived. When I opened the box, I discovered the previous two editions.

The older copy had nothing about Kathy's shooting, since it had happened only hours after the paper went to press. It did have a story on the front page about Jimmy Gammon, though.

TRAGEDY FOLLOWED GUARDSMAN FROM AFGHANISTAN HOME TO MAINE

They'd found a different picture of Jimmy for this one. It showed him posing like a bodybuilder with snow-covered mountains in the distance. The caption identified the other men in the picture as Sgt. Angelo Donato, of Thomaston, and Spc. Ethan Smith, of Presque Isle.

Donato, I recognized from the televised clip I'd seen on the news. He was wearing a crew cut but hadn't yet grown the debonair goatee he had sported recently on TV. Smith was a hulking dude who looked like he could bench-press a dairy cow.

This morning's edition had the story about Kathy.

GAME WARDEN SERGEANT SERIOUSLY INJURED IN SHOOTING

The editors had used the formal portrait of Kathy provided by the Warden Service. She was dressed in the unique dress uniform Maine game wardens wear: a red wool jacket, black leather bandolier, and olive green fedora. The retro outfit had the effect of making her look older and more mannish than she did in person.

Halfway up the driveway, I heard a car approaching along the road and then the single bleat of a pursuit siren going off. It was a silver-and-blue Knox County sheriff's cruiser. The Charger rolled to a stop, and Skip Morrison hung his head out the window.

"Special delivery for Bowditch."

He reached across his body and held out the duffel bag of clean clothes he'd retrieved from my room at the Square Deal.

I took the bag from him. "Thanks, man."

"How's life on the farm?"

"Eklund's inside getting hammered again. But I took his keys, so it's not like he's going any-where."

Morrison pointed at my blasted Bronco. "What about you? You need a lift today?"

"Not unless you're headed down to Portland."

"We only provide taxi service to Knox County."

"Oh, well." I hefted the duffel. "Thanks for getting this, Skip. I owe you one."

"I've got something else for you, too." In his hand appeared the three twenty-dollar bills I'd given him to pay my motel tab. "I told you Dot wouldn't take your money, dude."

23

W hen I returned to the kitchen, I found Kurt stuffing paper napkins under one of the legs of the table in an attempt to rebalance it. He sat down in his squeaky chair and pressed his scabrous elbows on the surface. Nothing moved. He smiled at me with his long, almost equine teeth.

"Success," he said.

I put the newspapers down on the tabletop.

"In case you're interested in reading what happened to your sister," I said, making no effort to be courteous.

He poured the rest of the amaretto into his coffee cup. "You really think I don't want to see her?"

"Based on the evidence in front of me, that would be an accurate conclusion."

"What if I told you I was bad luck? Not just bad luck but the worst luck. Cursed, snake-bit, and fundamentally fucked is what I am."

At certain dark hours, I occasionally viewed my life as the proverbial sequence of unfortunate events. But I didn't ascribe my misadventures to any occult forces. Most of the scrapes I'd gotten into had been the result of happenstance or my own piss-poor judgment. Then again, I wasn't an active alcoholic on the lam from his own conscience, so I had no need of supernatural explanations.

"You think that if you go visit Kathy, your bad luck is going to rub off on her?" I said.

He scratched at a flaky red elbow with fingernails overdue for a trim. "The best thing I can do for her is to stay away. It's no coincidence all this shit happened after I moved in."

Had this been what Kurt meant when he'd said the shooting was all his fault? Did he really think that by coming to live with his sister, he had infected her with some sort of bad juju?

"I'd say that sounds like another lame excuse," I said.

"Hang out with me long enough and see what happens. Don't be surprised if your car crashes off a bridge or you fall down a well."

"Maybe your luck would improve if you eased up on the sauce," I said.

"I'd been sober seven months when the docs told me I had cirrhosis. That's another reason I hate hospitals."

A rotting liver would explain the orange-yellow complexion.

"That must have been a tough diagnosis," I said. "You could still ease up."

"If you had six months to live, what would you do with it?"

"Is that how long they gave you?"

214

"Six months to a year."

I leaned against the soapstone sink and listened to the breeze blowing through the cracked window behind me. "I don't know what I would do in your situation."

"Then maybe you can cut me some fucking slack."

He glanced at the newspaper in front of him, smoothing the pages out across the tabletop, and began to read the story about his sister.

Every time I thought I'd gotten a handle on who Kurt Eklund was, he'd do or say something to slip from my grasp. He was a miserable mess of a person who deserved understanding or, at least, compassion. No, he was a cruel and manipulative asshole with no regard for others. I couldn't imagine how Kathy and her family had dealt with this mercurial man over the years, but I understood why she had barely mentioned him.

A phone began to ring somewhere down the hall. The tone sounded like my cell. I reached into my pocket, but it wasn't there.

I followed the noise into the woman cave. My mobile had fallen into a dusty crack between the sofa cushions.

"Hello?"

"Where the heck are you? Billy said you blew him off."

"Aimee?"

With everything that had happened since I'd

arrived on the Midcoast, I had completely forgotten about my scheduled visit with Billy Cronk at the Maine State Prison.

"He's wicked depressed about it," she said.

"I'm so sorry. I feel horrible."

She hesitated a few seconds, then said, "It has something to do with the game warden who got shot the other night."

Aimee Cronk—armchair psychiatrist, amateur detective, unschooled mind reader. Her insights into human behavior were uncanny at times.

"Kathy Frost used to be my sergeant. I've been at the hospital a lot."

"Jeezum. Is she going to be all right?"

"The doctors don't know. She lost a lot of blood and hasn't regained consciousness, the last I heard."

"Do the cops know who did it?" she asked.

"I'm not exactly on their speed dial these days."

"I bet you've got an idea or two." Like many Mainers, she added an *r* to the end of *idea* to make up for the *r*'s she dropped at the end of words like *supper.*

"It's what got me into trouble before, poking my nose into places it didn't belong."

"What if they don't ever catch the person who shot your friend? Then how are you going to feel?"

"I'm worried I'd just screw up the investigation."

"If it was me, I'd be more worried that the

person who shot my friend might get away with it. You're not just going to stand by and let that happen."

Aimee was right that I was fighting the urge to visit Soctomah's office and plant myself there until something happened.

"I need to schedule another visit with Billy," I said.

I wondered if he had gotten around to confessing to his wife that he'd been transferred to the Supermax. It was only a matter of time until Aimee connected the dots. In the Special Management Unit, a prisoner received a single phone call a week. What the hell had Billy done to get thrown into solitary confinement? Given that my blue-eyed, blond friend looked like Adolf Hitler's wet dream, I worried that the local chapter of the Aryan Brotherhood might have made a concerted effort to recruit him. It has been well established by history that Nazis refuse to take no for an answer.

As if I didn't already have enough mysteries hanging over me.

"Take care of yourself, Mike," she said. "I hope your friend gets better."

"Tell Billy I'll be in touch with him soon."

"He ain't going nowhere."

After we'd hung up, I tried Soctomah's number and got his voice mail. I told him I was staying at Kathy's house with her brother, knowing he would find that piece of information too tantalizing to ignore, and I left him a detailed message about our tense conversation with Littlefield. I asked that he call me back, making it sound as if it were an expectation rather than a request.

By the time I'd returned to the kitchen, Kurt had cracked open a bottle of crème de menthe and leafed his way through both newspapers. When he looked up at me with his single good eye, it looked red-rimmed and fierce.

"Listen to this quote," he said. " 'Of course we were saddened to hear that Warden Frost had been wounded, but we resist the idea that the incident is any way connected to the unprovoked murder of our son. The unsubstantiated accusation that any United States veteran—let alone a member of the 488th MP unit—might have had a hand in the shooting is offensive to us as parents and citizens. Jimmy's friends and family will not allow this sad turn of events to affect the attorney general's investigation into the unwarranted use of deadly force that ended his life. Our son deserves justice as much—or more so—than the woman who killed him.' "

I felt a nerve jump in my neck. "That's a quote from James Gammon Sr., I take it."

"That's libel! He can't just throw around words like *murder*. Why would they even allow that to be printed? Kathy's on her deathbed, for fuck's sake."

"Gammon's a powerful man," I said. "He probably goes yachting with the newspaper's owner."

"Well, he'd better shut up about Kathy, or I'm going to pay him a visit. Kathy told me he has a mansion on McLean Hill."

"I'd advise against it, Kurt." I felt in my pocket for his car keys, just to be safe.

"What the fuck do I have to lose?"

It was a valid question, I had to admit.

I should never have allowed him to start drinking again. Kathy had warned me that her brother became more unstable the more alcohol he consumed. Worse, I'd inflamed his anger by sharing those newspapers with him. I began to wonder about the firearms Kathy owned, and hoped she kept them under lock and key. That was assuming Eklund didn't have a pistol or rifle of his own stashed somewhere.

"If you're so concerned about her, you should put away the crème de menthe and take a nap," I said. "After you wake up, I'll drive you down to the hospital to see her."

"If she's unconscious, what's the point?"

"The point is that you're her brother."

"She wouldn't want to see me." He studied the newspaper in front of him. The picture showed Jimmy Gammon with his buddies, Donato and Smith. "I bet one of these assholes shot her. The father probably put them up to it. That's how these conspiracies work."

219

"Take it easy, Kurt."

"And do you know what's going to happen to them?" he said. "Nothing's going to happen to them. Even if the cops figure it out, it's going to be a cover-up. It says here that the father works with the Department of Defense. He'll just pull some strings and get the report shredded. Don't tell me it hasn't happened before, either. Agent Orange, Abu Ghraib, Haditha! It's all one god-damned lie after another."

"You need to calm down," I said.

"Don't tell me to calm down. I lost my fucking eye! And no one in the army ever apologized for it. They just gave me a Walgreen's eye patch and sent me home. 'Put the past behind you,' the shrink at Fort Knox told me. 'That's easy if you have two fucking eyes,' I said."

He rose to his feet, knocking over the chair. The bottle of crème de menthe crashed to the floor. The glass shattered and bile green liquor seeped between the floorboards. He reeled against the doorjamb and caught his body weight against the painted wood.

"The first hooker I was with couldn't even bring herself to look at me," he said, blinking. "My face was that ugly to her."

He drove his fist into the side of his face—the side with the functioning eye—so hard, I worried he might have broken his hand. It left a wine-colored mark on his cheek, as if he had managed to damage even more of the blood vessels beneath the socket. He raised his hand to strike again and then fixed me with a stare and took a staggering step in my direction.

An image flashed through my mind of Kathy and Dani Tate in that darkened barn. For a split second, I felt as if I were standing face-to-face with Jimmy Gammon.

I raised my empty hands. "Kurt," I said. "Listen to me. I want you to take a deep breath and think of Kathy."

"Kathy's not here!"

"What would she say if she were?"

He paused, wobbling back and forth on his toes, but close enough to lunge. "I don't know."

"Yes, you do. She'd tell you that she loved you and that you've got to stop hurting yourself."

"Shut up," he said, his voice choking with a sob.

"Kathy needs you, Kurt. She's your little sister, and she's in trouble."

He lowered his head, so that the tousled hair fell in his face. "I told you I was bad luck."

"Just go lay your head down for a few minutes. Don't worry about the mess in here. I'll clean it up."

He lurched away, unsteady on his feet, like an actor pretending to be a zombie. I watched him blunder around the corner, saw him stumble into the old parlor, and heard a heavy noise as he let his body fall across the sectional sofa.

I looked down at my hands. They were shaking.

I swept the glass shards into a dustpan and used a dishrag to sop up the mint-smelling liqueur.

Afterward, I sat down to read the papers. There was little in them I didn't already know, except that Jimmy had been the victim of the Taliban's weapon of choice—an improvised explosive device. I'd suspected as much.

The quote from James Gammon sounded just as vitriolic as when Kurt had read it aloud. It didn't matter that Kathy Frost had nearly died—might still die—what mattered was that his son should be avenged. There was no notice of a funeral, but the Gammons had requested that, in lieu of flowers, donations be made to the Wounded Warrior Project.

When I looked in on Kurt ten minutes later, he was lying on his belly again. His snores were softer and wetter now, as if his throat was clotted with mucus. I pulled my sleeping bag up over his long legs. I had no clue how long he'd be out. In his drunken state, I wasn't about to take him to Maine Med unless it was to drop him at the detox ward.

I needed a shower and a change of clothes. I lugged my duffel bag to the upstairs bathroom. Slowly, I peeled off the bandages and was relieved that the cuts showed signs of healing. I ran the faucet in the claw-foot tub until the water was piping hot. Then I twisted the handles and stepped inside.

The only shampoo I could find smelled of fake wild berries. The body wash was even fruitier, but I lathered myself up as much as possible, eager to strip away days of perspiration and grime. My knotted muscles eased under the heat of the showerhead.

After I was done, I had to run a hand towel across the fogged mirror to see my reflection again. I didn't see a need to apply fresh dressings to the scabs on my face. Remembering what Kathy had said about my looking like a younger version of my father, I decided to shave off my beard.

I was rooting around for a razor when I heard the sound of an engine roar to life outside the bathroom window. The glass was misted, but after I ran my palm across it, I saw Kathy's personal vehicle, the Nissan Xterra, backing away from the hay barn. I'd been so concerned about securing the keys to the Cutlass and the patrol truck that I'd forgotten all about the SUV.

Behind the wheel was Kurt.

24

As quickly as I could, I put on clean clothes and rushed downstairs. Outside, the clouds seemed thinner, gauzier—the way they do when they gather around a mountaintop. I unlocked

Kurt's Cutlass and was greeted with the smell of stale beer and Swisher Sweets cigars. He'd tried but failed to cover up the stench with one of those evergreen-shaped air fresheners. The combination of odors was noxious.

I turned the key in the ignition, and the engine made a harsh straining noise. Eventually, the rods and pistons began to churn. I backed the sedan past my Bronco and swung the wheel sharply until I was facing forward. Then I mashed the gas pedal and took off down the gravel drive in the direction of Camden.

There was no doubt in my mind where Kurt was headed. The articles in the newspaper had set off his drunken outburst. If Kurt Eklund showed up at the Gammons' door, he would be lucky if they only called the police.

Below the ridge, the road plunged into a small village that was just a cluster of old houses and a general store with a FOR SALE sign behind the dusty window. I crossed a bridge above a swollen river and then began to climb again through rolling hills that were mint green with new leaves. Most of the country had been cleared for grazing in the eighteenth century and then allowed to go back to forest after the original families had sold off their land. There were still a few hay fields teeming with dandelions, violets, and wildflowers whose names I did not know. But the people who owned the farmhouses now seemed to have little interest in tending fields or raising livestock. Occasionally, you might see a place that had a vegetable plot in the yard or a small pasture with a single horse in residence. But those homesteads were the exceptions.

Soon I found myself passing between hump-backed mountains. On either side of the road were cliffs too steep to climb, and dark rows of evergreens staggered along the ridgelines. Sometimes I could see the mountaintops, and sometimes the clouds would drift in suddenly, hiding the rocky summits from view. I was driving through the Camden Hills.

Kurt's Cutlass was the most sluggish vehicle I'd ever driven. I had to push the pedal to the floor when I came to the steeper grades. Not once did I catch sight of the Xterra.

After twenty minutes, I arrived at the turn that led to the Gammon estate. There were stone pillars at the bottom of the paved drive with black ribbons tied to the lampposts as symbols of mourning. The normally locked gates were standing open. I couldn't imagine how Kurt had managed to talk his way onto the property.

I drove through the open gates without permission and climbed a quarter mile through landscaped fields until I could see the slate roof of the house. I tried to suppress a sense of dread as I rounded the last corner, but the Xterra was nowhere in sight. If Eklund wasn't here, where had he gone?

I became conscious of my own uninvited presence on the estate. If James glanced out the window and spotted the broken-down Cutlass I was driving, I fully expected him to summon the entire Camden police force, along with the state police SWAT team. My best course of action was to turn around as discreetly as possible. With luck, the Gammons were having a late breakfast in the back of the house and would never know I had been there.

My hopes were dashed before I'd even managed to throw the gearshift into reverse. The front door opened and James Gammon stepped onto the porch. He wasn't toting a shotgun, but he was wearing an expensive-looking outfit straight out of the Orvis hunting catalog: whipcord trousers, a plaid tattersall shirt, and a matching quilted vest. The clothes gave him the appearance of the squire of a manor in the Scottish Lowlands.

I put the Cutlass into park while he came striding across the driveway. His forehead was furrowed, his chest was thrust forward, and both hands were clenched into fists. The automatic window didn't work when I pushed the button, so I had to open the door and poke my head up.

"Who are you? What are you doing here?" His voice was a rasp, as if he'd recently shouted himself hoarse.

"Mr. Gammon?" I said, giving him the warmest smile I could manage. "It's Mike Bowditch."

"Who?"

"Jimmy's friend. You had me over to hunt pheasants a few years ago, before he went to Afghanistan."

"The game warden?"

"Not anymore," I said.

"What do you want?" His dismissive tone suggested that my former occupation had tainted me and that I was not to be trusted.

"I wanted to extend my condolences." The lie was the best I could do.

He pushed a hand through his thick auburn hair. "Are you insane?"

"Excuse me?"

"You didn't anticipate that this would be awkward? One of your former colleagues just murdered our son. I'm trying to understand your thought process. You clearly lack a sense of propriety."

I'd been told that before. "I didn't mean to cause offense. I considered Jimmy to be a friend."

"Well, fine, then," he said. "Now you can take your junk car and clear off my property."

"James?" Lyla Gammon had appeared on the porch. She was dressed in her habitual riding clothes. "Who is that you're speaking with?"

"No one. A friend of Jimmy's."

"Please invite the young man inside."

He turned his head. "Lyla?"

"Please, James."

Like his son, the elder Gammon was a four-season runner, and he had the energy and stride of a man who regularly covered long distances. He approached his wife and whispered something to her, a harsh look on his face. She whispered something back and darted her eyes in my direction, causing her husband to give me the once-over again. Their discussion was heated and went back and forth for the better part of a minute.

"Come inside," he said, his voice overloud for the distance.

I closed the door of the Cutlass and followed the Gammons into their haunted house.

Our footsteps echoed off the hard granite tiles.

The couple led me into a spacious room with walls of reclaimed barn wood, a black chandelier, and linen curtains that billowed across the floor every time a gust of wind found its way through the patio doors. With a thrust of his hand, James indicated I should seat myself in a leather club chair. Before me was a rough-hewn table on which were arranged an antique set of nine pins and a bowling ball I imagined Rip van Winkle might have used. Except for a vase of yellow forsythia, there wasn't a single decorative touch I would have identified as feminine. I half-expected a uniformed servant to appear from the shadows to offer me a glass of scotch and my choice of Cuban cigars.

Lyla asked if I wanted tea.

"Only if you're having some," I said.

Her face was pale and drawn. She had unsuccessfully applied extra makeup to brighten her complexion and hide the bags beneath her eyes. "Do you have a preference?"

"Bring in a pot of Earl Grey," James said before I could answer.

After his wife had disappeared into the kitchen, James Gammon placed his hands on his legs, gripping his kneecaps the way a king grips the arms of his throne. His eyes were almost the same auburn color as his recently trimmed hair. I could smell his sandalwood aftershave from across the room.

Compared to him, I must have looked like a down-on-his luck hitchhiker. My hair was still wet along my neck. My commando sweater was fraying, there were oil spots on my tin-cloth pants, and my Bean boots were still dirty, despite my efforts to scrape away the layers of accumulated mud on the mat.

"I want you to know that I'm only humoring her," he said. "She's suffered a horrible shock, and it is my duty as her husband to offer her whatever support she needs."

"I understand."

One side of his mouth curled, suggesting he disbelieved me. "So I take it you were let go from the service since we last met."

"No, sir. I left of my own free will."

"You don't seem the better for the decision. What happened to your face?"

Reflexively, I touched the small cuts along my cheekbone. "I was shot by the same person who attacked Sergeant Frost."

He pressed his spine against the leather sofa and tilted his neck back as if to see me from a better vantage. "You were at her house that night?"

"Yes, sir. I returned fire on the assailant and then performed first aid on Sergeant Frost until the ambulance arrived."

"You returned fire? You said you'd left the Warden Service."

"I have a permit to carry a concealed weapon."

His eyes narrowed. "I hope you're not wearing a firearm in my house."

The handle of the revolver jutted against my tailbone when I shifted my position in the chair. "No, sir."

He rubbed away some moisture that had formed under his nose and around his thin lips. "Did you get a glimpse of the man who shot Sergeant Frost?"

"I'm working with state police to identify him."

I had no idea why I was lying to the grieving man. I tried to recall that I had liked James Gammon once, but now I could see the way his nostrils flared every time I mentioned Kathy's name. His hatred for my injured friend brought out an irrational meanness in me.

He lifted his chin toward the mantel above the fireplace. A framed portrait of Jimmy in his pixelated army combat uniform occupied a place of prominence. It was a different picture from the one in the newspaper. His grin had become a hard white grimace, and his dark eyes seemed empty of all emotion. I found it odd that his parents had chosen to remember their bighearted son this way.

"Did Sergeant Frost tell you about the night she and the other woman killed Jimmy?" Gammon asked.

"No, sir," I said, trying not to rise to the bait. "She's not permitted to talk about a use-of-force incident while an investigation is under way. She also knows that disclosing information would put me in line to give a deposition when you bring a civil suit against her."

"I could still depose you." He smiled without showing his teeth. "The assumption that I'm bringing a civil suit presupposes that she and the other one won't be found criminally liable. That's a fair assumption, unfortunately."

I remained silent.

He returned his hands to his knees. "Do you want to hear the statistics? They're really quite fascinating. Since 1990, Maine police have fired on one hundred and one people, many of them with mental-health, drug, or alcohol problems. And in every case, the attorney general found the use of force to be justified. Every case! What do you make of those numbers?"

My mouth had gone dry. "That Maine law-enforcement officers are well trained to deal with those situations."

"Were you well trained in crisis intervention when you were a game warden?"

My answer didn't matter, because Gammon kept on talking. "The Maine State Police deals with more of these incidents than any other agency. Do you know how many of their two hundred patrol officers they have sent to crisis-intervention training? Fourteen."

"I'm sure the situation is being remedied," I said with no great confidence.

"The irony is that Jimmy was a police officer himself. He was betrayed by the system he believed in. I've devoted my life to the law, and I've always been on the side of the good guys. Tell me who the good guys are here, because I'd very much like to know."

I hadn't noticed Lyla Gammon enter the dining room, but then her husband shifted his gaze from my face. You never would have noticed that she was shaking unless you heard the rattling of the teacups on the tray she was carrying. When she and I made eye contact, she forced her lips into a tight smile and continued into the living room.

She set the tea tray down on the table and poured me a cup from the copper kettle.

"I didn't ask what you liked with your tea, so I brought everything," she said in a soft southern accent I'd forgotten that she had.

"Thank you."

I accepted the cup and splashed some cream into it, then added two spoonfuls of sugar. I disliked tea, especially Earl Grey, but I smiled and took a sip. It tasted like a Turkish spice bazaar.

Lyla Gammon seated herself on the sofa across from me, her artificial smile still fixed in place as if with glue. Neither she nor her husband moved to touch the kettle. Instead, they both watched me drink from my cup. He was open in his disdain. Her expression, I found harder to decode. There was the barely contained anguish, the forced friendliness, but also a certain dullness in her eyes that suggested prescription medication.

After two minutes of silent observation, I was ready to thank them for their hospitality and excuse myself. I was prepared to leave without ever learning why they'd invited me inside, when Lyla blurted, "Tell us about Jimmy!"

I set my china cup down on the saucer. "We knew each other for only a short period of time."

"Yes, but you knew him beforehand."

"Beforehand?"

"You knew him when he was still Jimmy. The men from his unit, they all call him Jim. But that wasn't his name. What is it that you remember about Jimmy?" She seemed sort of moony.

I was having trouble guessing what she was after. I noticed that her husband reached for her hand.

"Well," I said. "I remember how much he loved his dog."

I must have glanced around for some sign of the spaniel. "Winnie is staying with friends," she said. "We think it's easier for him for the time being."

Easier for the dog?

"I guess what I remember most about Jimmy was his smile," I said. "Everything seemed to make him so happy. I'm not a particularly joyful person myself."

Lyla Gammon jerked her head around toward her husband. "That's exactly the word I have been looking for. *Joyful.* Jimmy was a joyful person." She turned those shrunken pupils on me. "It means so much for us to hear from his friends. It helps us to hold on to him, you see. Even before-hand, we felt like he was slipping away from us."

James Gammon tightened his grip on her hand. "Lyla, I'm not sure this is helpful."

"No, but it is." Her dreamy gaze was still focused on mine. "You didn't see him after he came back from the war, did you, Michael?"

"I hadn't heard that he was home. If I had, I would have visited. I'm very sorry that I never got to see him again."

"Don't be! It's better that you didn't come here.

People keep saying that he died in the barn, but he didn't. Jimmy died over there in Afghanistan."

"Lyla, that's enough," James Gammon said.

"Well, he did," she said. "I don't know who the person was who came back, but it wasn't Jimmy."

Her husband abruptly rose to his feet, pulling his wife up along with him by the strength of his grip.

"You need to go now," he said to me. "I knew this was a fucking mistake."

"You have my sympathies." It was all I could think to say.

I thought they might escort me out, but they remained frozen where they were, like two actors onstage before the curtain falls.

I closed the door quietly and descended the porch steps without giving a glance behind me. When I climbed inside the Cutlass, I received another blast of stale booze and cigars. The starter gave me problems again. I had a panicky thought that I might be forced to wait inside the house until roadside assistance could tow away Kurt Eklund's hunk of junk.

To my relief, the engine finally decided it was ready to start. I threw my right arm over the passenger seat and began backing out. Then a blur of motion registered in my peripheral vision. Lyla Gammon had thrown open the front door and was walking, almost jogging, toward my car. She had something in one of her hands—a small piece of paper.

Her husband was trailing fast behind her, but not fast enough. I put my foot on the brake and tried rolling down the window, having forgotten that the electric motor was busted. Lyla flattened a photograph against the glass so that I could see it. She held it there with the palm of her hand.

The image showed the face of a disfigured man. It seemed to have been taken while he was asleep. The skin had melted away like wax from a red candle. His nose and one of his ears were missing. He had no lips, either, just a slash where you'd expect to see a mouth. There was hair on only one side of his crimson skull.

Lyla Gammon's voice was distorted, muffled, coming through the window. "This is not my son," she said. "You can see it's not him."

I was glad when her husband caught up to her and wrestled her body away from the idling car. When the two of them were clear of the Cutlass, I threw the gearshift into reverse and gave the engine some gas. Lyla was still clutching the photograph in her hand the last time I saw her.

25

I'd been on the road for five minutes, maybe more, when it occurred to me that I should have warned the Gammons about Kurt. Just because he hadn't arrived at the estate yet didn't mean he wasn't on his way. The police needed to send a cruiser to watch the place.

I reached in my back pocket for my cell phone and saw that I'd missed two calls. One was from Soctomah. He hadn't left a message, which seemed typical. I didn't recognize the other number, but it was a Maine area code. This caller had left a voice mail.

The mountain road was narrow, with no shoulder, but there was a boat launch down the hill from the Gammon farm, on the south shore of Megunticook Lake. I used to stop at the ramp when I was the district warden, checking licenses and registrations. I'd chat with the local kids fishing for yellow perch and bluegills in the weedy water, trying to teach them how important it was to follow the rules when no one was watching you. The boys weren't interested in my lectures on ethical behavior. What they wanted to know about were the guns I carried and whether I'd ever shot anyone with them.

I pushed the button to listen to the message from my unknown caller. The female voice caused my breath to catch in my throat.

"Mike? It's Sarah. I heard about Kathy, and I feel absolutely devastated. You must be a wreck about it. Is she going to be all right? Can I visit her at the hospital? You know I'm back in Maine now. I'm living down in Portland, and—well, it's a long story. I got a phone call from Maddie Lawson the other day. She said you were working as a fishing guide somewhere up north! I hadn't heard that you'd left the Warden Service. I guess we both have gone through some pretty big changes. You don't have to call me back—it's fine if you don't—but I just wanted you to know I'm thinking about you. God, this must seem like the most random phone call ever."

Maddie had warned me that she planned on calling my ex-girlfriend. And Sarah knew how close I was with Kathy. If anyone could understand the agony I was going through in the aftermath of the shooting, it was the woman I considered my first love.

But our relationship had ended a long time ago by mutual consent. Sarah had resented my decision to take a low-paying job as a game warden when I was just out of college—a choice she could never understand, having come from a wealthy and ambitious family in Connecticut. She'd also seen the darkest and most self-destructive parts of my personality and had come to view me as fundamentally unsalvageable. At the time, I didn't disagree with her assessment. I was curious to hear what "big changes" she'd been through, but the last thing I needed at the moment was another distraction.

Better not to think of her, I decided. I'd call Sarah back after the state police caught the bastard. When all of this was behind me.

The thought of Eklund driving around pissed off and drunk scared me. My best bet was to enlist the state police. I punched in the number for Lieutenant Soctomah and got the detective on the first ring this time.

"It's Bowditch," I said.

"I got your message earlier. So you've taken up residence in the Frost house?"

"Her brother is living there, Kurt Eklund. The guy's a total mess. Alcoholic, unstable, probably has PTSD. I thought someone should watch out for him while Kathy's in the hospital. How is she doing? What have you heard?"

"She's in a coma."

I wasn't sure how to respond to the news.

"When there's that much trauma to the body and that much blood loss, it's always a risk," he said. "The docs have no idea when she might come out of it. There's also the likelihood of brain damage."

"You don't believe in sugarcoating things, do you?"

"Would you prefer that I did? It won't change the situation."

He was right, of course. I realized that the time had also come for me to make my confession. I told him that Kurt had gotten away from me while I was in the shower.

"So if you were watching Eklund," he said, "how did he manage to give you the slip?"

"I forgot to lock up the keys to Kathy's Nissan.

I looked out the window and saw him racing down the hill. I was afraid he might have been headed to the Gammon house."

"Why?"

"He was pissed about the quote in the paper, where Gammon called Kathy a murderer. I went over there to check, but there was no sign of him."

"You what?"

"Jimmy Gammon was sort of a friend of mine."

"You forgot to mention that detail earlier."

"I was bleeding from the head at the time. You need to find Eklund, Lieutenant. He's driving drunk, and there's no saying where he might go or what he might do."

"I'll put out an alert," he said.

"He's driving a Nissan Xterra registered to his sister." I had nothing to lose and so decided to test my luck. "Can you tell me anything about the status of your investigation?"

"You know I can't."

"What about Littlefield? It could be that whoever shot Kathy had a grudge against her and was just using the Gammon thing as cover. He wanted to make it look like retribution for what happened to Jimmy."

The phone went silent for a while. "I'm not going to spitball ideas with you."

"How about doing me a different kind of favor, then?"

"You have a pair of brass balls on you, Bowditch. I'll grant you that."

"What sort of relationship do you have with the Department of Corrections?"

"That sounds like a loaded question."

"Can you pull some strings and get me a pass to visit a friend in the Supermax? His name is Billy Cronk."

"I know who he is," Soctomah said. "He's in for a double homicide. Just swear to me this doesn't have anything to do with my investigation."

"I swear it has nothing to do with your investigation."

"You have an interesting assortment of friends, Bowditch. I still want my windbreaker back, by the way."

I hadn't been lying to Soctomah, not entirely. I wanted to see Billy because I'd promised Aimee I would.

But I had another reason to visit the jail. Jimmy's buddy from the 488th, Angelo Donato, worked as a corrections officer there. There was a decent chance Billy knew the former MP and could tell me something about the man.

When I arrived in the prison lobby half an hour later, I found that my name had magically appeared atop the visitors' list. The weasel-faced guard who had given me grief had been replaced by a tall man with coffee-colored skin and a hairless skull he had shaved smooth that morning. He glanced at my driver's license and said, "You must have a powerful friend to jump to the top of the guest list."

"You make it sound like this is a nightclub."

"A nightclub?" the lobby officer said with a chuckle. "I haven't heard that one before."

He told me to leave my keys and whatever else I had in my pockets in the coin-operated lockers across the room. I waited a few minutes on a bench, and then another guard—the visit officer—appeared. He unlocked a door and led me down a cinder-block hallway equipped with two metal detectors. The second machine had a problem with my belt buckle. The guard, a barrel-shaped man with a lazy eye, asked if he could frisk me.

"What happens if I say no?"

"Exit's back that way."

After he patted me down, he escorted me to a cubicle with a table and chairs bolted to the floor. The fluorescent lights were too bright, and a stinging chemical smell hung in the air, which made me wonder if an inmate had ever attempted suicide by guzzling the disinfectants they poured over everything inside the prison.

I waited close to twenty minutes for the guard to return with Billy. I found myself growing nervous as the minutes ticked by, afraid my brawny friend would appear diminished by his months behind bars. Eventually, the lock clicked and he came through the door, looking very much like the man I remembered. At six-four, Billy loomed over the guard assigned to restrain him. His woodsman's tan had faded, and his long blond hair had been chopped as short as Sampson's, but the guards had allowed him to keep most of his beard, which looked like it had been spun from gold and copper wire.

He was wearing a light blue shirt, darker denim pants, and the sort of sneakers you see on old people who gather at shopping malls to walk for exercise.

"Now, who could this stranger be?" he asked, cracking a broad smile I hadn't expected.

I extended my hand, but the guard intervened. "This is a no-contact visit."

Billy gave him a deadpan expression. "I guess a tug job is out of the question, then."

"Just sit the fuck down, Cronk."

We settled down across the table from each other. Now that I had a better look at his face, I could see that there were gray shadows under his eyes.

"How are you holding up in here?" I asked.

"Finestkind." The word was Down East slang for "first-rate," except when used ironically, which was most of the time. Billy spoke with one of the thicker Maine accents I'd heard among men my own age. "What happened to your face?" he asked.

"It's a long story. First I want to hear why you got transferred to the Supermax. Aimee thinks you're in the Medium Custody Unit."

At the mention of his wife's name, he hung his handsome head. When he glanced up again, his pale eyes had filled with mist. "I've been meaning to say something, but I don't want her to worry."

"What happened, Billy?"

He leaned back, but the stiff chair didn't give. It was odd seeing him without his customary blond braid. "There was a new guy who came into the prison—some bookkeeper who embezzled from a church—and I guess he was scared silly of being raped, so some wiseass told him he should find the biggest, scariest person on the block and sucker punch him, just to show the other cons to leave him alone. Guess who the biggest, scariest person was."

I had seen firsthand Billy's capacity for violence, watched him brutally kill two men in a gravel pit. To me, it had looked like self-defense, but the prosecutors claimed it was manslaughter, and the jury had unanimously agreed. At the time, I was still trying to talk Billy into appealing the verdict, if only for his family's sake, but I had discovered that when a man believes he deserves to be punished, it is nearly impossible to persuade him otherwise.

"Jesus, Billy. What did you do to the guy?"

"He's having trouble remembering things now. His name, for instance."

"How long are you in the SMU for?"

"There's going to be a trial in superior court. I could get a few more years tacked on to my sentence, I suppose."

I wanted to curse his stupidity, but what was the point? He already felt bad enough. "Can't you claim self-defense?"

"I seem to recall you offered the same advice last year." He was referring to the manslaughter trial, in which I'd been called to testify against him as a hostile witness, but the faint smile told me he wasn't harboring ill feelings. "About time you came for a visit. Thought I was going to see you here yesterday."

"Do you remember me mentioning my field training officer, Kathy Frost?"

"Course I do."

"Last week, she and another warden killed a guy. It was a case of suicide by cop. He was drunk and high and pulled a shotgun on them. He was a veteran, Billy."

"Vietnam vet or one of the younger guys?"

"Afghanistan. He was an MP at Sabalu-Harrison."

"I met a few MPs when I was at Bagram. What was this one's name?"

"Jimmy Gammon."

He shook his head to indicate he was unfamiliar

with the man. "So if your sergeant shot this guy, why are you the one who looks like you walked through a plate-glass window?"

"Two nights ago, I was at Kathy's house when someone shot her with a turkey gun, killed her dog, and took a few shots at me. Blew out the windshield on my Bronco."

"What happened to your sergeant?"

"She's in a coma."

He stroked his beard. "They get the son of a bitch who done it?"

"Not yet."

"I guess I can excuse you for missing our appointment." His voice became even deeper, which didn't seem possible. "So tell me about this dead MP."

"He was with the Four eight-eight and he was pretty badly wounded. I saw a picture of him after he came back from Afghanistan. He looked like a reject from a wax museum. He was in and out of Togus, living with his parents most recently. One night, they called for help because he was intoxicated, and when Kathy and her trainee arrived, he pulled a shotgun."

"The cops think there's a connection between the two shootings?"

"It's one of their theories."

"Like maybe one of his buddies from the Four eighty-eighth decided to get revenge on your sergeant for what she did?"

"I take it you have an opinion," I said.

Billy Cronk had one of the coldest stares on the planet. "Revenge can be a powerful motivator. In Iraq, a PV-nothing in my company got fragged for stealing another guy's iPod. The MPs could never prove it, but everyone knew what went down."

"There's a guard at the prison who was with the Four eighty-eighth," I said.

He leaned back against the plastic chair. "So that's why you're here."

"I also made Aimee a promise I'd come visit you."

Billy seemed unpersuaded. "What's the name of this guard?"

"Donato," I said.

"Yeah, I know him. He's a supervisor. Tough, but fair. He's not your guy, though."

"How can you be sure?"

"MPs are cops," he said. "They might not like what happened to their wounded friend, but they'd know your sergeant was just doing her duty in taking him down. When was the last time you heard about one cop shooting another out of revenge?"

I'd read of isolated instances, but most of those cases involved police officers who had been fired for misconduct.

"You should tell the detectives to stop barking up that tree," Billy said.

"They're not going to listen to me. You forget I'm no longer a warden."

He curled his lip. "You should be out there asking questions yourself, then. Who else might have wanted your sergeant dead? Why are you wasting your time talking with me?"

He stood up, as if he saw no point in making further pleasantries.

I followed his lead. "It's not a waste of time."

"Come back after you've caught the guy. And forget about Donato."

Easier said than done. "If you say so."

"I'm serious, Mike."

"Is there anything I can do for you?" We both knew I was in no position to improve his situation.

"Don't tell Aimee I am in the SMU," he said. "She's going to figure it out, but I don't want her worrying in the meantime."

After the guard had escorted Billy back to his cell, I realized he hadn't asked me how his wife was doing or anything about his kids. We hadn't made small talk about my guiding job or what it was like working for his old nemesis, Elizabeth Morse. I'd assumed that he would have been starved for information about the world he'd left behind. But Billy had avoided those delicate subjects. Thinking about life outside the prison walls was probably too painful for him to contemplate. I doubted he was the first inmate who had ever felt that way.

26

A guard stopped me as I was collecting my keys and other personal effects from the locker in the prison lobby. He was heavyset and had a crew cut, trimmed mustache, and a flush of color under his two chins that made me think he enjoyed tipping a bottle after his shift was done.

"Mr. Bowditch?"

"Yes."

"Can you wait here, please?" He tended to huff out his words, as if each one required its own expulsion of breath.

"What for?"

"We'd appreciate it if you'd wait here for a few minutes."

I shrugged and sat down on a bench, wondering what I had done now. Billy and I hadn't shaken hands or otherwise broken the no-contact rule. I wasn't smuggling contraband in any of my body cavities.

The fat guard stood over me, unsmiling, for a solid ten minutes, and then my phone made a buzzing sound.

"Do you mind?" I asked.

The guard frowned at me.

I rarely used the texting feature, so I was shocked to see that the message had come from

Stacey. *Bard told me your friend was the warden sergeant who was wounded. I hope she's OK. I'm sorry about the way I acted that night at Weatherby's. Sometimes I'm just a bitch.*

I was grinning from ear to ear and trying to come up with a clever response when the locked door opened and a man appeared. He was wearing a navy suit specially tailored for muscular guys, a red tie with a tie clip, and polished cap-toe shoes. He also wore his hair short, but he was growing a goatee, which so far, consisted of little more than a brown shadow under his nose and around his mouth. I recognized Angelo Donato from his speech at the televised protest outside the Maine Warden Service headquarters.

"I heard you wanted to see me," he said flatly.

It had to have been Billy, I thought. What trouble had my friend stirred up now?

"I think you've been misinformed, Sergeant."

"Then maybe you can inform me. My office is through that door."

He signaled to the admissions guard to buzz us through a locked door. I followed him down a hall to a windowless office devoid of personal items of any sort. He removed his coat and hung it from the back of his chair, revealing that his dress shirt had also been fitted to accommodate his weight lifter's physique. He took a seat and indicated that I should do the same.

"I don't know what Billy Cronk told you," I said.

"He said you were a friend of Jim Gammon. You're the game warden, right?"

"I used to be."

"Jim told us about you." His eyes had heavy dark lashes, as if he wore mascara, but they seemed to be natural features. They gave his face a feminine quality that was at odds with the rest of him. "He talked about the four of us going hunting sometime when we got home. Do you know what was funny about that?"

Obviously, there was nothing funny about it, but I let the former MP continue.

"The funny thing was that he kept talking about it," Donato said. "When I used to visit him at Togus, he'd say things like 'So when are you and Monster going hunting with me and Mike?' His face had been blown off by an IED, along with part of his brain, but he still thought we were all going to shoot pheasants together. Every time Smith and I visited him, he would talk about it— as if the plans were already in motion. 'The shooting party' is what he called it."

I could tell that Donato was going somewhere with the story and that he expected me to clear the tracks.

"Do you know when I realized he was losing it?" he said. "When he stopped talking about the shooting party."

There was a round clock on the wall that made a ticking sound as each second went by. I couldn't remember the last time I'd heard a clock do that. High school maybe—the vice principal's office.

"I have a question for you," he said after a while.

"Go ahead."

"Did you ever once visit him after he got home?"

"I never heard he'd been wounded," I said. "I didn't even know he was back in Maine."

"You don't read the papers?"

I wasn't going to divulge my own troubles with a man who didn't care to hear them. "All I can say is that I missed the news, and that I'm sorry. Jimmy was a great guy. I wish I'd gotten to know him better."

"You want to know how it happened?" he asked. "How he got injured?"

I assumed he was going to tell me in any case.

"There was this trash heap outside one of our battle positions." He waved his hand as if he wanted to strike what he'd said and start again. "It was really more of a mountain of trash. The contractors would dump all of the shit from Sabalu there, and every day crowds of Afghans would descend all over it like a bunch of vultures. They'd take every piece of plastic. Something like this pen." He held up a disposable ballpoint. "To them, it was like finding buried treasure, even if it was out of ink. Christ only knows what they used it for."

He began twirling the pen between his fingers.

"One day," he said, "there was a riot. These two guys started fighting over a bungee cord. The next thing we knew, everyone on the mountain was hitting someone. Through our scopes, we saw kids being trampled. So I decided we needed to break it up. I told Jim to drive us out there, and I ordered people to back off or we'd start shooting with our turret gun. Well, they didn't, and I wasn't going to open fire on a mob of women and children. The bottom line is, we broke the first rule and ended up getting out of the truck. Smith and I went one way, and Jim went another. It turned out the whole thing had been a set up by the terrorists. Jim was helping one of the kids who'd been trampled when the boy's body exploded. They'd cut the kid open and planted an IED inside his stomach. Then they'd sewn him up again."

He opened his desk drawer and found a roll of Life Savers and popped one in his mouth. He didn't offer me one. I heard it crack between his teeth when he bit down on it.

"And that was how I gave the order that got Jim Gammon wounded," he said.

"I'm sorry."

"You keep saying that. I might even believe you if it wasn't for the smear campaign."

"What smear campaign?"

"The one against Jim," he said. "It wasn't

enough that two of your people had to kill him in cold blood. You also had to ruin his reputation. The guy was a fucking hero."

I measured my words carefully. "So is Kathy Frost."

He leaned across the desk, giving me a whiff of the peppermint on his breath. "And that's another thing. Do you know how *offensive* it is to me as an MP to be accused of shooting a fellow officer? It's beyond offensive. It's fucking vile is what it is. I fought for my country. How'd you like to have state police detectives show up at your house one night and start interrogating you—in front of your wife and kids—about your whereabouts on the night a game warden was shot? Are you people that desperate to close ranks?"

"I'm not even a warden anymore, Donato. I have nothing to do with Lieutenant Soctomah's investigation."

He laughed at what he took to be a pretty brazen lie. "So you were just here to visit your scumbag murdering friend? Because from where I'm sitting it looks like you came here to yank my chain."

Billy could be such a well-meaning fool. He thought the detectives were making a mistake by questioning members of the 488th in the shooting of Kathy Frost. He believed that Donato was a brave and honorable man who didn't deserve to have his own integrity called into question. And so, to prove his point to me, Billy had said something stupid to a guard, and that comment had led to a pointless confrontation. Who knew what grief my friend had caused himself by instigating this meeting?

"I have no idea why Billy Cronk told you I was here," I said calmly. "He gets odd ideas in his head sometimes. I just think he wanted us to meet because he respects your service to our country. Please don't take your anger out on him."

He laughed again and leaned back in his chair hard enough that his suit jacket dropped to the floor. "You're afraid I'm going to have him punished?"

"He doesn't even belong in the SMU."

"That's good, because we value your opinion."

I stood up. "It's probably best if I leave now."

"In that we agree," he said. "I'd tell you to let yourself out, but you can't."

He bent over and gathered his coat from the floor. He wrestled his big arms into the sleeves and brushed off the dust from the pockets. He walked me back down the hall and through the locking door that led to the lobby. I didn't expect to hear another word from him, but he surprised me again.

"You're probably thinking I'm going to have your name removed from the visitors' list now," he said.

"The thought crossed my mind."

"That shows how little men like you understand men like me."

I left the prison thinking that Donato was undoubtedly right. The values by which a soldier lived his life were a mystery to me and always would be.

27

Kurt Eklund's Oldsmobile guzzled gasoline the way its owner consumed alcohol. I burned through the better part of a tank driving the eighty miles to Portland. I tried not to think of the boy with the bomb inside his stomach, but it was a hard image to get out of my head.

I turned my mind to other things. Donato had interrupted my texting conversation with Stacey. I had never replied when I had the chance. And now my window of opportunity had slammed shut.

All in all, it seemed to be a fitting reflection of how badly my day was going.

I parked in the hillside garage on Congress Street, the one attached to the hospital. To find a space, I had to drive all the way to the top. Fat-chested pigeons swooped through the openings between the levels, looking for hidden ledges on which to roost. The iridescent birds scattered when I slammed the car door, but they flapped back as I headed for the elevators connecting the garage with the ER admitting desk. The pigeons were accustomed to the comings and goings of the sick and the grieving.

I am not a superstitious person. Nor do I enjoy visiting places where hundreds of people have died. However, Kathy Frost had stayed by my side on the night my mother had passed away in this very place. At the information desk, I identified myself to the receptionist as a colleague of the injured warden and asked if she was permitted to have visitors yet. The kind-faced woman made a call to the Special Care Unit. She lowered her voice so I couldn't hear her questions.

"You should speak with your major," she said.

"Is he here?"

"I wouldn't know. Maybe you can give him a call?"

I started to walk away, then returned. "Can you do me another favor? Sergeant Frost's brother might be on his way here to see her. Will you alert security that he is intoxicated and unstable? His name is Kurt Eklund, and you might have a problem with him if he demands to see his sister."

The receptionist appraised me with clear brown eyes that had seen hundreds of people in every emotional and pharmacological state imaginable. My tired, scab-covered face couldn't have offered her many assurances.

"I'll let them know," she said.

I decided to buy myself a cup of coffee in the cafeteria while I tried Major Malcomb's cell.

I was looking for a private table when I caught sight of Dani Tate. As usual, she was seated by herself, and she'd already spotted me wandering around with my coffee and Danish. Her expression hardened.

Without being invited, I took the chair across from her. She was wearing the same clothes she'd been wearing the last time we'd met: flannel shirt in a Black Watch pattern, carpenter's pants, scuffed-toed work boots. Her blond hair had acquired a greasy sheen. I wondered if she'd even left the hospital. How long could she have been here? Close to forty hours? She was holding an empty plastic water bottle.

"What do you want?" Her throat sounded in need of more water.

"I'm hoping to see Kathy."

"She's in a coma, if you haven't heard."

"Lieutenant Soctomah told me." I knew she'd find the comment provocative.

A dent appeared in her chin when she made a certain contemptuous expression. "So what are you? Part of the investigation now?"

"Not exactly."

"What does that mean?"

"Did you know that Kathy's brother, Kurt, was living with her?"

Looking at Tate up close, I could tell that her

nose wasn't naturally flat; she had broken it some time ago. Maybe those rumors about her Brazilian jiu jitsu matches were true. "She never mentioned having a brother."

"So you wouldn't know where he was the night she was shot?"

"I told you: She never mentioned him." She stood up from the table. "Excuse me."

"You and I have more in common than you think, Tate."

"That's doubtful."

"I used to have your district. Maybe we should have lunch sometime, and I can fill you in on the local hooligans."

"What makes you think I need your help? There's a reason you're sitting there looking like a homeless person. Good-bye."

She began making her way through the narrow, knee-knocking spaces between the tables.

I called after her: "For someone who acts so sure of herself, you get defensive pretty fast."

"What the fuck is that supposed to mean?"

I pointed at the chair she had just vacated. She sat down at the edge of the seat, as if she was prepared to spring at any second.

"Tell me what Kathy has been up to lately," I said. "Has she been looking into anything unusual?"

"Like what?"

"I don't know," I said. "Anything out of the ordinary."

She crossed her arms under breasts that were pretty much invisible beneath her man-sized shirt. "Interfering with a criminal investigation is obstruction of justice under state law."

"All I'm doing is giving the state police a list of names to check out. Does the name Marta Jepson meaning anything to you?"

"Should it?"

"She's an old woman who died on Saturday up in Aroostook County. She fell down a flight of stairs. Kathy printed out a newspaper article about her death. I found it in a waste basket inside her house."

"You're amazing," she said. "Everything I've heard about you is true."

"The rule book is only going to get you so far, Tate. You're going to make your arrests and be in line for promotions. But sooner or later, you're going to realize that the best wardens aren't the ones who can quote you Title Twelve, chapter and verse. The best wardens catch bad guys and make a difference in people's lives."

She rose to her feet again, this time with force. "Kathy was totally right about you."

"About what?"

"Being an arrogant asshole."

Dani Tate's intent had been to insult me, but I was past that point. Even if Kathy had used those exact words to describe me—probably in exasperation, after I'd given my notice—it didn't change the fact that she was lying in a hospital bed while somewhere a violent man was still at large. If "arrogant" meant that I trusted my own intelligence over the collective wisdom of the state police, then I would have to plead guilty. If "asshole" meant I didn't care whose feelings I hurt to achieve my goal, then I would accept that label as well.

One positive aspect of not having a career anymore was that I no longer needed to worry about it.

I drank my coffee, chewed on my pastry, and thought about what I could do next. Not much, unfortunately. Without Dani Tate's help, I would have a hard time identifying alternate suspects—unless I could enlist the aid of one of Kathy's other district wardens. Tommy Volk was a hothead. Maybe he'd share information with me about some bombshell case Kathy had been quietly pursuing.

My mind kept coming back to the fact that Kathy had been shot with a turkey gun, loaded with ball bearings, rather than by a high-powered rifle firing a hollow-tipped bullet. Snipers almost never use shotguns. It was an odd detail, and in my experience odd details often proved significant. Was her neighbor Littlefield that big of a fool as to parade through her yard with the same weapon he'd used to slaughter Pluto hours earlier?

If only I could figure out where Kurt was hiding.

What had he meant when he cried, "It's all my fault"? I'd assumed he'd been lapsing into alcoholic self-pity again. He seemed to have this fucked-up idea of himself as a bringer of misfortune—someone so cursed that he infected other people with bad luck. But what if he'd been speaking literally? What if the shooter's target that night had been Kurt Eklund?

I was readying myself to call Major Malcomb, hoping I could persuade him to let me in to see Kathy, when the man himself appeared at my table in the hospital cafeteria.

He looked like he'd lost fifteen pounds since I'd last seen him. He badly needed a shave, and the smell of cigarettes emanated from his green uniform. The Maine Medical Center complex—from the hospital building to the parking garage—was off-limits to smokers. I wasn't sure where he'd been sneaking off to satisfy his craving.

Out of habit, I stood at attention. "Major."

"Tate told me you were here." His voice was rough and raspy, as if his vocal cords had been scarred by some corrosive chemical.

"Oh, yeah? What else did she tell you?"

"That you were meddling with Soctomah's investigation. She said you were grilling her about Kathy's recent cases."

"Curiosity wasn't a crime the last time I looked."

He frowned at me. "Don't be a wiseass, Bowditch. You have no idea what I've been dealing with over the past few days."

"Colonel Harkavy?"

He stared at me with bleary eyes that didn't give away his thoughts. "Where'd you hear about it?"

I had no intention of narcing on the Warden Service's chaplain. "The grapevine."

"Don't believe everything you hear through the grapevine."

"Maybe you shouldn't believe everything Dani Tate tells you, either."

"She's not the one with the lengthy history of insubordination."

I could hardly take issue with that statement. "Can you get me in to see Kathy?"

"I don't make those decisions," he said. "The doctors do."

"Have other people been allowed to see her?"

"Some."

"Her parents?"

"Yes."

"What about other wardens?"

"She's in serious condition, Bowditch. If someone sneezes, she could come down with an infection."

"Look, Major," I said. "You know what happened at Kathy's house. The last thing I remember is sticking my hands into her wounds to stop the bleeding. I'd rather not carry that image around in my head as the last time I saw her."

He blinked his tired eyes at me. "Let me see what I can do."

I sat back down again at the table and waited.

He returned about fifteen minutes later with a brown-skinned, black-eyed woman in doctor's scrubs. She had three surgical masks dangling from her hand.

"Come this way," she said in an accent that had a Caribbean cadence.

The doctor guided us through a series of doors into the nerve center of the Special Care Unit. Men and women were seated at a central desk, monitoring computer screens while machines beeped and buzzed. The door to Kathy's room was wide enough for a bed to be wheeled in and out should the patient require emergency surgery.

The doctor gave us our masks and then slid open the door. "Hands in pockets, please."

Kathy lay on her back in a pale sleeveless shift. There was a mask clasped to her nose and mouth. She had a monitor attached to her wrist and an IV unit pumping fluids into the crook of her uninjured arm. The doctors had been forced to shave her head above her left ear in order to suture a wound I hadn't noticed the night she was shot. A pellet must have grazed the skin above her ear. Except for her many freckles, her skin had turned a bleached-bone color, as if all of the blood the doctors had pumped back into her heart hadn't yet made its way to the surface.

"Did they get all the pellets out?" I asked the doctor.

"She will need other operations to remove them."

"Are there any near her heart or arteries?" I asked.

A foreign object embedded in the body can move over time for a variety of reasons, and I knew that a tungsten alloy shotgun pellet would be subject to magnetic fields. Walking through a metal detector could kill a person with a ball bearing close to a major blood vessel.

"No," said the doctor. "But she suffered hemorrhagic shock from the loss of blood. We don't know how that affected her brain."

"So she might have brain damage?"

"It is too early to say."

I remembered the wounds to her torso. I'd stuck my dirty hands in them. "What are the chances of her suffering an infection?"

"Sepsis remains a concern."

I couldn't really see Kathy's face with the mask over her nose and mouth; she might have been anyone underneath that contraption. I wanted to pull the thing off and give her a kiss on the cheek. I had a premonition that this would be my one and only chance to say good-bye.

"Hands in pockets, please," said the doctor again.

I was unaware of having removed them.

28

The major returned to his vigil outside Kathy's room while the doctor escorted me from the Special Care Unit back to the cafeteria. She studied me with coal black eyes, the irises as dark as the pupils. She was older than I'd first guessed. There were wrinkles etched in parallel lines across her forehead.

"Have you studied emergency medicine?" she asked me in her charming accent.

"Just wilderness first aid," I said.

"You must have been a good student."

"I realized someone's life might depend on my knowing all I could."

"Someone's did," she said.

She had intended the kind words to make me feel better, but I couldn't shake the feelings of rage I'd experienced seeing Kathy in such a fragile and unrecognizable condition. I went into the washroom and splashed cold water on my face and rubbed it fiercely along the back of my neck until I felt it running down my spine. I had hoped the shock might cool the blood pulsing in my temples.

I studied my dripping face in the mirror above the sink. The cuts on my head would heal in time. I peeled up a few strands of wet hair to inspect the old scar on my forehead, remembering the night I'd gotten it. I had been twenty-two years old, meeting my father in his favorite North Woods roadhouse after a long estrangement. I'd wanted to introduce him to Sarah—to show off my beautiful girlfriend and tell him that I had decided to become a game warden. He'd laughed at my plan, which he recognized, even then, as a cheap bid for his attention. Later that night, a biker had cracked a beer bottle across my skull in a fight. My old man had nearly cut the man's throat in retribution.

My mom had always worried that I would inherit my dad's predisposition for violence. She seemed to think it was attached to the Y chromosome in certain unfortunate individuals. I might be carrying some genetic abnormality, but it didn't give me "license" (that was the word she used). My mother had raised me to be a good Catholic and believed that God would grant men the strength to transcend "their animal selves" if we asked for His help. If she were still alive, she would have said that I owed it to Kathy to master my emotions and not lash out merely because I was feeling dull-headed and impotent.

I could start by finding Kurt, I decided.

Deb Davies had told me that the Eklunds had driven from northern Maine to be with their daughter. When parents have a sick child in the hospital, even an adult child, they don't pack up their car and go home. They stay as close as possible, because you never know. The Warden Service would have arranged to get them a hotel room in the neighborhood.

Kathy's parents were somewhere in or near the hospital.

In the hallway, I found a posted map showing all the usual visitor destinations in a hospital: the cafeteria, the gift shop, the florist. The chapel was located at the south end of the building, near the central courtyard. I made my way through the maze of corridors.

I'd expected to find pews in the chapel, but there were only chairs, arranged at the edges of a rectangular space. A red Muslim prayer rug was folded over a stand in the corner, and at the far end of the room was a lectern with a heavy Bible. There were several people seated in the room, all of them gray-haired: two women and a single gentleman. The man was tall and lanky, with a full head of white hair, and he was sitting next to the lectern, while the others held back, as if daunted by the elevated dais and the power it represented. As a retired minister, Kathy's father would feel no timidity in approaching God.

I was surprised to find myself genuflecting before the lectern. My mother's Catholicism had deep roots.

The old man had his head bowed and his hands clasped. I couldn't get a good look at him, but he must have sensed that I was watching him. When he raised his eyes, I saw an older version of Kurt Eklund's face, but one free of the ravages of alcohol.

"Pardon me," I said in a whisper. "Are you Kathy Frost's father?"

"I am."

"You don't know me, Reverend, but I am a friend of your daughter's. My name is Mike Bowditch."

He straightened his shoulders as if they had been hunched so long that the muscles had cramped. "I know who you are, Mr. Bowditch. Kathy has told us about you." He extended his liver-spotted hand to me. His grip was strong for a man in his eighties. "I also know what you did for my daughter the night she was shot. Alice and I owe you a debt we can never repay."

I glanced behind me, wondering whether I'd missed seeing his wife when I entered the chapel.

"Alice is resting," he explained.

"There's something I'd like to speak with you about, Reverend," I said in a hushed tone.

"Erik." He stood up, using the top of the next chair for assistance. "Let's talk outside."

I watched him push open the chapel door with his long arms. As he did, the commotion from the hospital flooded into the quiet room the way water rushes through a crack in a dam. A praying woman, clutching rosary beads between her thumbs, looked at us with an annoyed expression.

Erik Eklund pointed a knobby finger at the big

269

window that faced the courtyard. "Would you mind? I could use some fresh air."

The courtyard was a well-kept green space with beds of multicolored tulips and concrete sidewalks designed with wheelchairs and walkers in mind. A red-eyed vireo was singing from the branches of a cherry tree whose blossoms had mostly fallen and lay scattered like unmelted snowflakes on the newly cut grass.

The old man reached into his back pocket and removed a farmer's bandanna, which he opened and spread on the nearest bench. The seat was damp from the fog and rain that had bedeviled the state for the past week. I didn't see what difference a handkerchief would make in keeping his backside dry, but lacking one of my own, I had no choice but to settle down beside him on the wet cedar.

"How did you know where to find me?" He spoke with the same flat, almost Midwestern accent as his children.

"Kathy told me you used to be a minister, so it made sense to look for you in the chapel."

When he grinned, he resembled his daughter more than his son. He had pale eyelashes, crusted from lack of sleep. "Our daughter told us you were a good investigator, Mr. Bowditch."

"Please call me Mike."

"You are searching for information about who might have done this to her?"

"How did you know?"

"Because you are a good investigator," he said. "I have no special insights. Kathy spoke with us on the phone every Sunday, but she didn't discuss her cases. She's dealt with many dangerous men over the years. Some she sent to prison. There are many who might wish to do her harm."

"Did she mention the death threats she received after the incident involving Jimmy Gammon?"

He cleared his throat. "She wouldn't have wanted us to worry. Kathy always felt protective of us, even when she was a little girl."

"Did you know that Kurt was living with her?"

"Yes, she told us." A breeze rustled the leaves of the cherry tree over our heads. "We couldn't have him in the house anymore. It was too painful for Alice. He was stealing money from her purse. And then her jewelry box went missing. We assumed it was to take to a pawnshop. My son claimed not to know anything about it."

"He had gambling debts," I said.

"Our phone would sometimes ring, and there would be a man on the other end, asking for him. Kurt would pretend not to be home. He seemed frightened."

"He never mentioned the name of someone he owed money to? Someone who might have wanted to hurt him?"

"You have to understand that my son is an alcoholic," Erik Eklund said. "He lies about so many things. Alice and I stopped trying to determine what was true and false a long time ago. We did our best to love him. But it was hard when he hated himself so much."

The man had a calmness about him that made me feel as if I'd known him forever. "He told me that he didn't want to see Kathy because of all the bad luck he's had in his life. It was like he was carrying around an infection and was afraid she might catch it."

"Did he tell you the story of how he was wounded?"

"No."

"He told us he was injured by a mortar," Erik said. "Alice and I flew with Kathy to Fort Knox to visit him when he was in the hospital there. He was in complete despair because of his eye, but he said he was lucky, because two of his friends had been killed in the same explosion."

I could feel the dampness of the bench seeping through my pants. "That's not what happened, though."

"The doctors told us he was running away from a firefight, and he ran into a broken branch. That is how Kurt lost his eye. That was more than thirty years ago, and he has never confessed the truth to us."

"Thirty years is a long time to keep repeating a lie."

"We never cared if he was a hero. We were only

glad that he was alive." He sighed. "The war didn't make him an alcoholic, but his actions seemed to justify some bad opinion he already had of himself. No one has ever been able to convince him he is worthy of God's love. I have tried many times. Have you read the Pauline Epistles?"

He must have interpreted the expression on my face as a no.

"There is a verse in Ephesians: 'Let all bitterness and wrath and anger and clamor and slander be put away from you, along with all malice. Be kind to one another, tenderhearted, forgiving one another, as God in Christ forgave you.'"

"I haven't known many people who were capable of that kind of forgiveness," I said. "I'm having trouble putting away my own bitterness and wrath and anger."

"You need to have faith."

"In God or the state police?"

He smiled, as if the distinction were meaningless. "I should look in on Alice. She wanted me to wake her after two hours." The top of his head brushed the lower branches of the cherry tree, sending more petals floating down onto his shoulders.

"Kurt took off with Kathy's SUV," I said. "No one knows where he went."

"With any luck, the police will find him already in a jail somewhere. At least he would be safe there."

"Do you mind me asking one more question?"

"Go ahead."

"Does the name Marta Jepson mean anything to you?"

He closed his eyes, as if to peer back through a lifetime of memories. "There are a number of Jepsons in Aroostook County," he said. "But I don't recall a woman with that first name."

"She died in her home last week in Lyndon. I found an article about her on Kathy's desk."

"Oh, yes. I remember reading the story. I was surprised I didn't know her, since she lived so close to us. I will ask Alice about her if it would help."

"Thank you," I said. "I wish Kathy and I had talked more. Maybe there would be fewer mysteries now."

"My daughter has always been a private person."

"I've known her for three years, and she barely even mentioned her ex-husband."

"Darren? He was such a kind man. You remind me of him a little."

"Why did they get divorced?"

"They didn't," he said. "Darren was killed in a car accident. His car went off the road during a snowstorm during the first year Kathy became a warden. She always said it was the worst year of her life. I think she was glad to be transferred south. But her mother and I have missed having her in our lives."

We shook hands again, and I watched him cross the courtyard, an upright and dignified man who was facing the possibility of losing both of his children in a span of days. Erik Eklund had resigned himself to the knowledge that eventually he would receive a phone call telling him that his son was dead in a car wreck or had blown his brains out after a drinking binge. Kathy's death would be another matter; it would devastate the old man.

Why hadn't she told me about Darren? At the very least, the revelation helped to explain why she had devoted herself to her career at the expense of a social life. Kathy had never struck me as someone haunted by the past. But what made me think I was the only person who heard ghosts?

The afternoon was fading, and the events of the day had left my nerves feeling overtightened. I wandered back through the hospital building to the parking garage, pausing to watch the anonymous cars passing below on Congress Street. We live alone in a world surrounded by strangers, I thought.

The lights in the parking garage were so dim, they might have been designed to give muggers better shadows in which to hide. I found Kurt Eklund's Oldsmobile where I had left it near the top floor, undisturbed, because what thief in his right mind would choose such a vehicle to rob?

When I opened the door again, I considered making my next stop the nearest car wash: anyplace where I could dispose of the accumulated trash and run a vacuum nozzle across the seats and carpets.

My cell phone rang as I was negotiating the twisting ramps to the ground floor. I pulled it from my pocket and peeked at the screen. There was no name associated with the number, but I recognized it immediately as belonging to Sarah.

29

I pulled over to the side of the street and took a deep breath.

"Hi, Sarah."

"Mike! I thought I was going to have to leave you another embarrassing voice mail."

The sound of her pretty voice after all these years made my heartbeat quicken.

"I'm sorry I didn't get back to you before. I've been at the hospital with Kathy."

"How is she doing? When I read the news, I wanted to throw up."

"She's in a coma. She lost a lot of blood when she was shot. The doctors still don't know if it caused brain damage. I guess they won't know until she wakes up."

"Oh, Mike, you must be a wreck."

"It's easier when I'm the one in the hospital bed and not someone I care about."

I didn't mean to divert the conversation from Kathy, but Sarah interpreted the remark in a way I hadn't intended. "I was so sorry to hear about your mom. Did you get my card?"

I hadn't followed up any of the condolences I had received. Social niceties had never been my strong suit, as Sarah knew better than anyone. "Thank you, yes. I haven't been back down here since she died."

"Wait a minute," she said. "Are you in Portland?"

"I just left the hospital. I'm parked on Congress Street."

"I'm downtown, too!"

"Maddie told me you were living here."

"Are you free? Do you want to get together?"

She didn't mean "free" in the sense of having no romantic attachments, but that was where my mind immediately went. I had abandoned my sentimental ideas about Sarah Harris a long time ago, but the thought of seeing her again intrigued me. And it wasn't as if Stacey cared what I did, text or no text.

"Sure."

"Can you meet me for a drink? I'd love to catch up."

I had expected she would invite me to her office at the charter school. A drink came with certain implications. Maddie Lawson had told me Sarah was involved with the school founder. How would he feel about his young girlfriend having a cocktail with an old flame? Other people's romantic relationships were so mysterious. For all I knew, the guy was immune to jealousy. The same could not be said of me.

I ran my hand along my face, feeling the tiny scabs and the whiskers that I had meant to shave the night before. I realized that I didn't care if Sarah saw me looking grungy. What was past was past.

"When and where?" I asked.

"How about five o'clock at the Top of the East?"

It was a rooftop lounge at a luxury hotel where we had once spent a wild New Year's Eve. We were just college seniors, but we had splurged on a room so we wouldn't have to drive back to Waterville after a night of bar hopping. One of us (probably me) had gotten the idea to have sex on every piece of furniture in the room. I woke up the next morning with cold sunlight streaming through the window, hungover, and sore in every part of my body. I had never been happier in my life.

There were dozens of bars Sarah could have suggested. I was astonished she'd picked one that came with so many suggestive memories attached.

"I'll see you there," I said.

I arrived fifteen minutes early and found a parking spot in front of the Immanuel Baptist Church on

High Street. It was a great granite building with stained-glass clerestory windows and a towering bell tower. I'd never thought of the Baptists going in for Gothic architecture.

I entered the hotel and crossed the gilt-tinted lobby. I rode the elevator to the twelfth floor and asked the hostess for a table with a view of Portland harbor. The bar wouldn't fill up until after five, but there were a handful of tourists seated on the couches and random guys in business suits with loose neckties getting a head start on their boozing. A woman dressed smartly in a black shirt and black pants came over to take my drink order, and I asked for a double bourbon on the rocks.

The view from the Top of the East was the best in Portland. I wasn't remotely an urban person, but looking down on the brick buildings and the cobblestone streets, and then the port of Portland itself, bustling with fishing boats and island ferries, with the forts and lighthouses of Casco Bay in the distance, I could understand why Sarah had decided to make her home here. David DiPietro was the game warden whose district included the city. I could never imagine what sorts of calls he received. *Help, there's a raccoon in my trash cans! An owl just flew off with my house cat!* The whole appeal to me of joining the Warden Service had been of making a life for myself in the woods. But maybe if I'd been assigned to Portland after graduation, Sarah and I would still be together.

There was no point in dreaming up alternate realities when I was having a hard enough time coming to grips with my actual life.

Sarah arrived late, as usual. Late enough for me to be halfway through my second bourbon, and feeling the warmth of the first one entering my bloodstream.

I watched her negotiate the tables between us, smiling, waving, and I thought she looked even better than the last time I'd seen her. She'd grown out her blond hair to shoulder length, and she was wearing a pinstriped gray suit that I never would have described as sexy until I saw her in it. Sarah had always been athletic. She'd been a competitive diver at Choate.

When I stood up, she gave me a hug—not too tight—and then held me at arm's length, her hands squeezing my shoulders, smiling as she studied my face. "Maddie was right. Look at you."

"I need a haircut and a shave."

"You look good with actual hair."

She'd never been a fan of my biweekly crew cuts. "What about the beard, though?"

"I don't usually like them. I'm not sure I would have recognized you if we'd passed on the street. It's so great to see you again, Mike."

She took a seat, and I did the same. She was wearing lipstick and eye shadow, heavier than before. She brought her elbows up on the tabletop, intertwined her fingers, and smiled at me. I didn't notice a ring.

"You look beautiful, by the way," I said.

"Even with long hair? I thought you liked it short."

"I think we had plenty of misconceptions about each other."

She let her gaze turn toward the window and the cityscape below. "I'm not sure what made me think of meeting you here."

"We had a nice time in this hotel."

She glanced back at me with one corner of her mouth turned up. "*Nice* isn't the word I'd use. It was room two twenty-seven, I seem to remember."

The server reappeared, and Sarah asked for a Dark and Stormy, a cocktail she never used to order. She was looking at me with wide blue eyes, as if I were a strange new creature she had never encountered before.

"Your beard makes you look like your father," she said.

"People keep telling me," I said.

"He was a good-looking guy for someone his age. What happened to your face, though?"

"I was shot the same night as Kathy."

"Wait. You were there?"

"The guy blew out my windshield as I was driving up to her house."

The skin tightened above her eyebrows. "I thought you weren't a warden anymore."

"I was just visiting."

She leaned across the table, giving me a whiff of her perfume, which smelled expensive. "Are you allowed to tell me what happened?"

"I can do whatever I want now," I said with a smile. "I'm a civilian."

"I still can't believe you quit the Warden Service. Never in a million years would I have imagined that happening."

"People change," I said.

"That's no explanation."

The waitress returned with Sarah's drink and asked if I wanted another Jack Daniel's. I was tempted—something about being with Sarah again in this place made me want to let myself go—but I passed. I had a long drive back to Appleton.

I thought I had gotten away with not answering Sarah's question, but as soon as the server left the table, she returned to the topic. "What happened to you, Mike? On the one hand, you seem like the same guy I lived with in Sennebec. And yet you're totally different, too."

"It's just the beard. It makes me appear older and wiser than I really am."

"That's what I mean," she said, tapping my chest with her painted fingernail. "Where did that guy come from?"

"Which guy?"

"The funny one."

"I was always funny."

"Trust me," she said. "You weren't. Look, it's OK if you don't want to talk about it."

I threw back my head and laughed.

"What?" she asked, genuinely perplexed.

"You're not going to stop asking me questions until your curiosity is satisfied. That's one thing that hasn't changed about you, Sarah."

"I always thought we were mutually curious," she said with a sly grin. "It was something we had in common."

"One of the only things we had in common."

"I don't know about that."

"I'll make you a deal," I said. "Let's talk about you for a while and then we can return to the subject of my radical transformation. Tell me about this school you're working for."

She took a long sip of her fizzy rum drink. "I'm afraid I'll just bore you."

"I need a diversion from the past few days."

She set the glass on the table. "Well, it's called the Coracle School, and it's for kids ages two to six. Do you know what a coracle is?"

"Like the Welsh boat?" I didn't understand the connection but didn't want to interrupt her by saying so.

"It's circular in shape," she said. "The philosophy behind Coracle is just so progressive and revolutionary. When I talk about it, people say, 'Oh, it sounds like the Montessori approach,' but it's totally leading edge. Maria Montessori died seventy years ago, and we've learned so much about neuroscience since then. The Coracle curriculum comes out of proven discoveries in how a child's brain develops. I mean, we now know that three-year-olds become more interested in structured activities." She had been speaking faster and faster. Suddenly, she caught herself. "I just realized I was giving you my fund-raising pitch. It's the curse of being a development director."

"Tell me about the man you work for, then," I said.

She flared her nostrils. "Maddie told you about Jon."

"She said you were involved."

"It's complicated," she said. "Jon is a genius. He's literally the smartest human being I've ever met. He's so charismatic and kind and wise. When you talk to him, it's like there's no one else in the room. He just has this magnetism about him."

I drained my glass. "How old is he?"

A shadow fell across her face. "That's a rude question. I thought you were genuinely interested in my work. I haven't asked who you're seeing now."

"I apologize," I said. "I guess it proves I'm not as grown-up as my beard."

The waitress must have been watching us closely. When she noticed me finish my drink, she came back to see if I wanted another now. I said no, but Sarah did something that surprised me: She downed the remainder of her Dark and Stormy in one big gulp and ordered a second cocktail.

"Wow," I said.

"It's been a long week." She began absently fiddling with the top button of her blouse, buttoning and unbuttoning it. "So, who are you seeing?"

"At the moment, I am single," I said.

"There's got to be someone."

In my mind's eye, I saw Stacey's face, but it was the laughing, blueberry-lipped version I had seen in my dream, not the real person; just a figment of my imagination. "The dating options in Washington County are not what you'd call optimal."

"Maddie said there was a woman at the lodge that you were staring at all night."

"That's just someone I know from the department. She's a wildlife biologist."

The waitress returned with the Dark and Stormy. She set a bowl of miniature pretzels between us and then departed. Once again, Sarah took a serious pull from the cocktail glass.

"You might want to slow down," I said.

"Listen to you," she said. "The voice of moderation. You really have changed. I live in the West End, so you don't need to worry about me driving. Maddie said that you and this woman got into a pretty passionate argument at one point."

I couldn't stop myself from laughing. "Maddie thought Stacey and I were involved because we were arguing?"

"You and I used to argue."

"I'm not dating Stacey Stevens," I said, trying to sound insistent.

She gripped the glass by the bottom and had it halfway to her mouth. Her hand hovered in midair. "This woman is Charley and Ora's daughter?"

Sarah and I had been living together when I first met the Stevenses, and she knew what a mentor Charley had been to me as a rookie warden.

"Yes."

She took a drink and then set the glass down again on the circle of condensation it had left on the mat.

"Huh," she said.

We talked as the shadows lengthened. The setting sun turned the western sides of the buildings below us to gold. Across the mouth of the harbor, the lighthouses began to wink on, one after the other: Bug Light, then Spring Point Ledge Light, and finally Portland Head Light, commissioned by George Washington himself, at the far entrance to Casco Bay.

Sarah's mood was erratic. She pulled information out of me about Jimmy Gammon's death and then the night Kathy was shot. She listened with tears in her eyes. After a while, I returned to the subject of the Coracle School in an attempt to show her that I was genuinely interested in her new life. I also wanted to dodge the many questions she still had about about my decision to leave the Warden Service. Her spirits rebounded— assisted by a third cocktail I didn't stop her from ordering but probably should have—and she began to speak with animation about the exciting work she was doing: how she could see positive changes in the kids from week to week, and that her belief in the school's mission and practices made her even more passionate about raising money to support it.

She referred to the school founder, Jon Hogarth, repeatedly, but always in terms of admiration and awe rather than affection. If I hadn't known from Maddie that they were a couple, I might have mistaken their relationship as platonic—a father figure mentoring an enthusiastic young believer. I'd met charismatic older men who used their "wisdom" to charm impressionable women into bed. Even though I wanted to wish Sarah the best, I found myself instinctively distrusting this man Hogarth.

"I'm glad you found such meaningful work," I said, trying to conceal my misgivings. "It was always so important for you to have a sense of purpose."

"You, too," she said. "Are you missing it? The job, I mean."

"It's not the worst thing to wander in the wilderness for a while."

She reached across the table and touched the injured side of my face. "You seem so lost, Mike."

"It's a bad time is all."

"I wish there was something I could do for you."

The suggestion wasn't so subtle that I missed it. And I couldn't deny that I still desired her. She was the most gorgeous woman I'd ever been with. But I could hear the alcohol in her voice. I removed her hand and gave it a squeeze. "You and I had our time together. I'll always be grateful for that."

She lowered her chin and looked up at me through her lashes. "You've always been so damned chivalrous. I'd forgotten how sexy it is."

"You're mistaking cluelessness for chivalry. There's a reason I'm not seeing anyone."

She stared steadily into my eyes for a long time. "Can you excuse me for a few minutes?"

"Sure."

I watched her beautiful backside as she crossed the room, feeling less like a noble knight than a self-flagellating monk. What had I just passed up? And for what reason?

I let my gaze wander back to the window. A flock of herring gulls was gathered on one of the rooftops below, lined up along the edge, looking down expectantly at the street. Among them was a great black-backed gull. It was the largest species of gull in the world and a natural bully. When one of the smaller birds found a baguette someone must have tossed into a Dumpster, the big gull attacked until the other gull was forced to drop its prize.

The natural world had always been so much easier for me to comprehend than my fellow human beings. Amid all the bricks and concrete, the crowds and the cars, I found comfort in watching gulls, knowing I could understand their motivations. The great black-backed gull acted with aggression because it was hungry and because it was large enough to take what it wanted. There were no hidden reasons for its behavior. If only people were so easy to decipher.

Sarah was gone for ten minutes. I was beginning to wonder if she'd walked out on me for some unknowable reason, when my phone rang.

"Hello?"

"I'm in room two twenty-seven," she said, and hung up.

30

I knocked on the door. My stomach had been doing flip-flops in the elevator. A voice had told me to hit the button for the ground floor and make a dash through the lobby. And yet here I was, staring at the peephole of room 227.

Sarah opened the door. She was wearing one of the hotel's plush robes and she was barefoot. Her lips were parted in a smile.

I remained in the hall, as if paralyzed from the waist down. "What are you doing?" I asked.

"It's not obvious?"

I stepped through the door. It closed behind me on account of its own weight.

She reached under my sweater and pressed her palm over my heart. "I decided I like the beard."

"What about Jon?" I asked.

"He doesn't have one."

"You know what I mean."

She tightened her fingers in my chest hair. I grabbed the back of her neck and pulled her head up until our eyes were locked together. Then I brought my mouth down to hers and we began to kiss, not lovingly, but with lips parted, using our tongues. I reached inside her robe, found her breast, and I squeezed the hardened nipple. I let her neck go and wrapped my other arm around the

290

small of her back. Her robe was open and her flat stomach was pressed against my groin. I wanted her to feel how much I wanted her.

She began pulling at the hem of my sweater, trying to work it and my T-shirt up over my head at the same time, but my arms got tangled in the sleeves.

"Wait a second," I said. "Let me."

I managed to get my shirt and sweater off with a minimal amount of fumbling. She dropped to her knees and reached for my belt. I found myself looking down at the uneven part in her blond hair. This was happening fast, and I was trying hard not to think about it, preferring just to let my body do what it wanted to do. She took the tip of my cock in her mouth but wouldn't take any more of it at first. I wanted her to slide the rest down her throat as far as it could go, but she remem-bered how much I enjoyed being teased. When she finally did, it was almost more than I could stand.

"Wait," I said. "Wait."

I was worried about coming too fast.

"Lie down on the bed," I said.

She glanced up and gave me a wicked smile that would have scandalized the parents of the students at Coracle. Then she let the terry-cloth robe slide from her shoulders and stood up, naked, in front of me. She took a step backward and flopped back on the bed with her arms and legs open. The sight of her bare body wasn't helping me regain control of myself. She had recently had a wax.

She was lying there, waiting for me to work my feet out of my pants, when a phone rang. It wasn't mine.

Sarah glanced at the nightstand. Her phone wiggled across the tabletop as it rang. The ringtone was a snippet of a pop song I didn't recognize, something a teenaged girl might listen to.

After thirty seconds or so, the phone stopped ringing. The call had gone to voice mail.

The interruption had made us lose our rhythm.

Sarah returned to work on me, and I reached both hands down to hold her head, but something had been lost. My mind had started working again. The ringtone had sounded customized, signifying that the call was coming from a specific person.

After a few awkward silent seconds, the phone rang again. It was the same bubbly little song.

Sarah looked up at me. "Sorry. I should get that."

She rose from her knees, reached for her robe, and knotted the belt around her waist.

I stood awkwardly in place. My pants were down around my knees.

"Hi, Abbie," Sarah said. "What's going on? Is everything OK?"

I could perceive a high-pitched female voice coming through the receiver but couldn't make out the words.

Sarah saw me watching and turned away.

"Why were you using the washing machine?" she asked.

She waited for an answer. I bent over and pulled up my pants.

A guilty feeling had come over me that I was being unfaithful to Stacey. It was a ridiculous notion, because we had never been romantic. But emotions are not reasonable. They simply are what they are.

"It's probably just the circuit breaker," Sarah said in a motherly tone of voice. "The circuit breaker goes off when you have too many appliances running at the same time. All you need to do is reset the switch. There's a panel in the basement near the furnace—"

She was speaking with Jon Hogarth's daughter, I realized. Sarah hadn't mentioned anything about where she was living or with whom, but I saw the situation clearly in my head.

"No, you didn't actually *break* anything," Sarah told the girl. "It's just a name for the electrical box."

In the bar, I had intuited her lack of fulfillment. Whatever her relationship was with Hogarth, it wasn't a romance. I had formed a negative image of the man as a late middle-aged Svengali, and the stereotype had allowed me to shove my conscience aside for a few minutes.

Sarah walked toward the opposite end of the

room, trying to explain to Abbie Hogarth how to reset the switch on the circuit breaker. There was a faint chill in the hotel room, as if the heat hadn't been on before she rented it. I retrieved my T-shirt and sweater from the floor.

I knew nothing about Sarah's relationship with Jon Hogarth. I only knew that I didn't want to be complicit in someone else's betrayal. As the son of a man who had wrecked more than a few marriages, I could say that much about myself.

Sarah kept her back to me until she was finished with the call. She seemed surprised to find me fully dressed again. "That was awkward," she said.

"Was it his daughter?"

"How did you—" She clutched her robe around her throat. "Her name is Abigail. She's twelve."

I dug my hands into my pockets. "I can't do this."

"Because of Abbie?"

"I heard the way you talked to her," I said. "It's like you're her big sister. You're part of her life."

"It doesn't have anything to do with the way I feel about you. I wish you wouldn't judge me without hearing my side of things."

"I'm not judging you."

"If you leave like this, it's the same thing as judging me."

I removed my wallet from my pocket. "I'll pay for the room."

"That just makes it worse! It makes me feel like a prostitute." She plopped down on the bed and leaned her head forward, so her hair was covering her face. "Are you seriously going to run off?"

"Do you want to talk about what's going on between you and Jon?"

She shook her head. "No. Fine. Leave."

"I'll stay if you do."

"How chivalrous of you." When she glanced up, her eyes flashed with anger. "You're right. This was a mistake. I had too much to drink. I don't know what I was thinking."

"You weren't thinking," I said. "Neither of us was."

"Don't be so sure about that."

She gathered up her clothes and went into the bathroom. I hung around to say good-bye, until it became obvious that she wasn't coming out until I left, so that is what I did.

It hadn't been my intention to make Sarah feel ashamed of herself. I only knew that I had needed to stop myself before I had a reason to regret my actions. I had so much practice in my life doing the wrong things; I hadn't realized I could feel just as lousy when I did something right for a change.

The traffic was heavy leaving Portland, and there was night construction along Route 1 that forced me to stop periodically.

I had given in to temptation with Sarah because

I was lonely and because things had ended badly with us the first time. Like everyone, I fantasized about rewriting my past. To have had sex with her one more time—after she'd been the one to reject me and the family I'd hoped to have with her—would have recast our relationship in terms that made me feel less self-pitying. But mostly I had been acting out of a pent-up frustration with the wayward man I'd become.

"I can do whatever I want now," I had told Sarah. "I'm a civilian." In fact, I had never felt more powerless.

The moon had climbed above the Camden Hills and was lighting up the eastern slopes of the blueberry barrens when I turned off the Ridge Road and began my cautious approach to Kathy's house. The windows were all dark, and I didn't see the Xterra parked among the assorted boats and motorized vehicles. I could call the VFW Hall in Sennebec and ask if Kurt Eklund had showed up, but my gut told me that he hadn't raced off in such a hurry just to play Texas Hold 'Em.

I searched under the seat until I found Deb Davies's pink LadySmith revolver, then tucked the gun into my pants at the small of my back.

When I stepped out of the car and closed the door, I heard a toad trilling nearby. The air was crisp but dry and the aroma of a blooming shadbush was drifting down the hill. I hadn't remembered

296

seeing one of the shrubs, but the sweet smell of serviceberry was unmistakable. There were still shreds of police tape hanging from bushes around the property, and in the light of the moon, they looked like festive decorations from a recent party.

As I approached the front door, I noticed a piece of paper that had been affixed with a heavy-duty staple gun at eye level. I tore the paper loose and held it up in the moonlight to read it. NOTICE OF PROPERTY LIEN, it said. For an instant, I thought it might be a legitimate legal document. The fine print was so small as to be almost unreadable. Then I remembered Kurt's comments about the crackpot neighbor. When I peered closely, I located LITTLEFIELD in block letters halfway down the page, listed as the lien holder. His first name, evidently, was Lawrence.

He must have downloaded the bogus form off of the Web and trudged across the barrens to post it in the event Kathy expired without a will. He wanted dibs on his damn right-of-way, and so, like a modern-day Martin Luther, he had decided to nail his grievances to her door. I fought against the impulse to pay the man a surprise visit. I wondered how much he might enjoy eating this piece of paper.

I entered the unlocked house and made my way from room to room, turning on lights as I went, searching for signs that Littlefield or someone else had been inside, but everything seemed to be in the same shape as when I'd rushed off that morning. The newspapers were spread across the kitchen table and, upstairs in the bathroom, my still-damp towel was wadded in a ball where I'd dropped it on the floor.

I returned to the living room and sat down on the sectional sofa, stretching my legs across the coffee table. In the process, I nearly dislodged the mug I'd filled with rum after I'd tucked Kurt into bed. I played with the idea of pouring myself a nightcap, but the two double bourbons I'd consumed at the Top of the East—followed by the sexual fiasco that had followed—had soured my stomach.

A fleeting impression came to me that something about the room was different, but I couldn't identify a single item that had been moved. I let my gaze wander up the wall to the big-screen TV hanging there and saw my silhouette reflected in the obsidian-dark glass. It felt as if I was looking not at myself but at the featureless shadow of the man I was searching for. The synapses in my brain were as tangled as a ball of rubber bands. After a while, I gave up trying to unravel them.

31

S tacey's father, Charley, had once told me, "Don't mistake action for progress," but I had reached the emotional state where the distinction no longer mattered. I needed to take action even if it led me nowhere.

The next morning, I took a quick look around the house, but Kurt had not returned during the night. I took a hot shower and dug out the last clean underwear and socks I had from my duffel. When I left the bathroom, I found a voice mail on my phone from Jeff Jordan at Weatherby's, telling me he had a fishing party arriving the next day and to call him back if I wanted the guiding job. I deleted the message. Instead, I sat down at Kathy's desk and opened the binder that listed the names, home addresses, and phone and pager numbers of every game warden in the state. I flipped through until I found Danielle Tate's information. She lived twenty minutes south of Appleton, in the old German township of Waldoboro. I tucked Deb Davies's revolver into the back of my pants and set off.

The weather seemed to have taken a decided turn for the better. The sun was bright and the sky was the cornflower blue you expect to see in Maine during the last weeks of May. I drove with the back windows of the Cutlass rolled down, letting the breeze dry my wet hair. I passed an old man on a John Deere tractor. He was mowing an overgrown lawn he'd been unable to tend during the many days of rain. He waved at me as if we were old friends. The pleasant smell of freshly cut grass drifted to my nose as I rounded the curve.

Dani Tate lived in a smallish modular home in a clearing in the trees along the Friendship Road. The property looked as if a team of professional landscapers had recently visited; there wasn't a single weed sprouting from the tulip beds. The black patrol truck and the silver Toyota Tacoma parked side by side in the drive had both recently been washed and waxed. The woman was a neat freak.

I parked Eklund's beater on the side of the road. I made a bet with myself how quickly Tate would slam the door in my face. Thirty seconds, I decided.

The doorbell glowed orange. I heard electronic chimes, followed by quick footsteps descending a staircase. I waited with my hands plunged deep into my pockets and a dopey smile on my face. I wanted to appear clueless enough that she would at least open the door when she saw me through the spy hole.

The door opened, but she held her sturdy arm across the opening to bar me from entering. She had been exercising when I had arrived. Her compression T-shirt was drenched with sweat, and her forehead and cheeks were pink and glistening. She was barefoot and her feet were raw-looking. She had been practicing her martial arts, I concluded.

Her expression was openly hostile. "How did you know where I live?"

"Warden Service roster."

"So what do you want?"

"I thought I might buy you breakfast," I said, never once dropping the grin I'd put on for her benefit.

"You've got to be joking."

"Come on. It's healthier than smoking a peace pipe."

She started to close the door. "Thanks, but no thanks."

I stuck my Bean boot into the crack and nearly got my metatarsals crushed. She yanked the door wide.

"What the fuck, Bowditch?"

"Kathy would want us to be friends."

"Not gonna happen."

"She wouldn't want us to hate each other, at least."

She narrowed her eyes. "You're serious about this? You drove all the way out here to buy me an Egg McMuffin?"

"I was thinking more like a bowl of oatmeal at

the Square Deal. You strike me as an oatmeal person."

She hung in the doorway, studying me with the same open suspicion with which she probably approached every hunter or fishermen she met in the field. Her facial features weren't unattractive. It was her attitude that made her appear so mean and unapproachable.

"If this is some lame ploy to get information out of me, I swear to God I'm going to punch you in the heart."

"Duly noted," I said.

Without another word, she closed the door, leaving me standing on a welcome mat that was the dictionary definition of false advertising. I wandered back across the road, leaned against the side of the Cutlass, and raised my face to the sun. A wave of excited magnolia warblers had descended into the crab apple tree behind me. A soft hum at my feet made me look down. A low-flying bumblebee was scouting for a mouse hole in which to nest.

I wasn't sure if Tate would accept my invitation or not. But after five minutes, she emerged from the house, having taken the world's fastest shower. She was wearing a denim jacket over a baggy sweatshirt with the Unity College insignia on the front, Carhartt carpenter pants, and scuffed work boots that looked like she'd done real work in them.

She waved me across the road, heading toward her silver Toyota.

"Are you afraid of being seen in the Cutlass?" I asked.

"I don't trust your driving," she said, putting on a pair of aviator sunglasses. "Besides, this way I can kick you out anytime you start pissing me off."

The humorless tone of her voice let me know I should take it as a very real threat.

The inside of the vehicle made it appear as if she'd just driven it straight from the dealer's showroom. There were no stains on the graphite fabric, no trace of dust on any plastic surface. I secured my shoulder belt while she switched on the Bearcat police scanner she'd installed on the dash.

"I thought you were suspended," I said.

She fired me a look. "I still want to know what's going on."

She backed out of the driveway quickly but with the expertise of a professional race car driver. She kept her hands at nine and three o'clock on the wheel—the way we'd been taught on the Criminal Justice Academy's practice course—and never crossed them when making turns. She was a better driver than I was.

She didn't say a word to me for the first few minutes. Instead, we listened to the almost incomprehensible burbling of the police radio.

Kathy had compared driving with her taciturn rookie to being alone in the truck with her dog. I was coming to appreciate the comparison.

"So, where did you grow up?" I asked finally.

"Pennacook."

It was a papermaking town in the western Maine foothills. "Did your dad work at the mill?"

Her gaze never veered from the road. "What's this? Twenty Questions?"

"Just pretend I'm someone you don't despise."

"He's a shift supervisor. At least for now. The mill's been laying off people right and left."

It was the familiar story of the Maine North Woods. The state had been the logging capital of the world in the late 1800s, but by the twenty-first century, most of the paper mills had been shuttered and the jobs shipped off to countries like China, Indonesia, and Brazil. There were too many communities in northern Maine that were just another economic downturn from becoming ghost towns.

"Let me guess," I said. "You're the only girl in the family."

"Why? Because I'm a tomboy?"

"Am I right?"

"Yeah, you're right." We crossed the town line into Sennebec, where I had lived when I had patrolled this coastal district. "But it would be more polite to ask me direct questions rather than pretend you're Sherlock Holmes."

"What made you decide to become a warden?"

"I grew up hunting and fishing. My grandfather was a warden in New Hampshire. He took me on ride-alongs before he retired. I liked the idea of catching bad guys. The usual stuff."

"You ever consider becoming a regular cop?"

"Nah. I like the woods too much. And I prefer to work alone."

Dani Tate's motivations for joining the Warden Service weren't so different from my own. The difference was that she believed in following the policy manual as if it were holy Scripture. I had always been a heretic.

"Rumor is you have a black belt in Brazilian jiu jitsu," I said.

"Jesus, you are nosy."

"True or false?"

"I wanted to be an Ultimate Fighter for a while when I was in high school. Then I decided it was too much about performing for the cameras. I never gave a shit about being famous like Gina Carano. If I could live my whole life without anyone knowing my name, I'd be happy."

Her involvement in the Gammon shooting had quashed those hopes.

I was desperately curious to hear her account of what had happened that night at the Gammons' farm, but the attorney general had sworn her to secrecy during the investigation, and I already knew enough about Danielle Tate to realize I had zero chance of persuading her to break a vow of silence.

The Maine woods in springtime are as pretty as pastel paintings. The formerly dull hillsides were now vibrant with colors I hadn't seen since fall. The road dipped and passed through a cluster of old houses along a slow-flowing brown river. Locals still referred to the area as Sennebec Village, even though the only commercial enterprise left was the old Sennebec Grocery. The market had gone from offering butchered meat and fresh vegetables in its heyday to selling cartons of cigarettes, cases of cheap beer, and spools of scratch lottery tickets. I doubted that when its current owner, Hank Varnum, decided to retire he would find a buyer for the business.

Seeing my former district from the passenger seat of Tate's truck put me in a nostalgic mood. I'd endured some of the most dangerous and difficult experiences in my life here, and yet I found myself feeling an abiding affection for the salt marshes and spruce-fir forests of the Midcoast. The passage of time erases the rough edges of memories.

We climbed the steep hill that led up to the main road and the Square Deal Diner and Motel.

"I've been asking you a lot of questions," I said.

"No shit."

"I figured you might have some for me. You don't want to know about my mysterious past?"

She gave what sounded like a snort. "No need."

"Why's that?"

"I already know all about you, Bowditch. You're a living legend."

I grinned. "Is that so?"

"But not in a good way."

Faces turned toward the door when we entered the Square Deal, and the whispering started just as fast. Dani Tate and I had both become infamous personalities in Sennebec. She kept a blank look on her face as we settled into a booth, but I could tell from the rigid way she was holding her shoulders that she already regretted her decision to accompany me here.

There were paper place mats on the lacquered wooden table, featuring boxed advertisements for a variety of local businesses and organizations. The Shear Perfection Beauty Salon ("Because you deserve nothing less"); the Lighthouse Pentecostal Church ("Sin sees the bait but is blind to the hook!"); Big Al's Gun Shop ("Offering 10 percent off all muzzle-loader supplies").

God, how I missed this place.

I'd looked for Dot Libby when I'd come in but hadn't seen her. The talkative plumber I'd spoken to a few days ago, Pulkinnen, was hunched at the counter. He'd been the one complaining about Dani Tate to me. He'd said the local poachers were unafraid of her, but I'd come to the conclusion that the rookie was facing much bigger challenges if she was ever going to be a successful warden.

The new waitress, Destiny, came over with a pot of coffee. She must have just received a perm at Shear Perfection; her hair was twisted into ringlets tighter than any I'd ever seen on a poodle. She filled our coffee cups without asking.

"How are you two doing today?"

"Fine," said Tate. "I'll have the oatmeal."

"You want any raisins or brown sugar on top?"

"No."

"I'll have a molasses doughnut," I said.

"Healthy choice," said Dani Tate.

I leaned back against the creaking booth and spread my arms along the top. "My body is a temple."

She kept her mouth clamped shut as she surveyed the room, so she seemed to have no lips at all. She made fierce eye contact with every person who tried to sneak a peek at our booth. The woman might have been antisocial, but she was hardly a shrinking violet.

"Can I give you some advice?" I said.

"This is going to be good."

"Stop trying to intimidate everyone you meet. Giving people the stink eye won't make them afraid of you."

"I'm a woman, and I'm five-four. How do you expect me to intimidate anybody?"

"By knowing their secrets."

308

"The arrogant asshole returns," she said.

"It's not arrogance," I said. "It's experience. You need to talk to people if you're going to be an effective warden. Cultivate a few informants. There are dozens of feuds going on around here —neighbors who hate their neighbors—and they'll happily rat each other out if they trust you with their secrets."

She made a penciling motion with her empty hand on the place mat. "Should I be taking notes?"

"There's an old woman named Reetha Gee who lives with her clan on Maple Grove Cove," I said. "She has something like twenty teenaged grandkids. The boys all have rap sheets and the girls are all dating guys with rap sheets. You should pay Reetha a visit someday and give her some deer meat as a bribe."

"I know who Reetha Gee is. She's basically the matriarch of a heroin-dealing organization."

"She's also a useful informant. If you're nice to her, she'll call you with incriminating evidence you can use to make a bust. It's how she gets rid of her enemies."

"You don't have a problem doing business with someone like her?"

"Not if I bust some bad guys along the way."

She threw her elbows on the table and tried the alpha-dog thing with me, staring hard into my eyes.

"You know what?" she said. "I do have a question about your 'mysterious past.'"

Her irises were the color of shale fragments, I decided. The woman was made entirely of stone.

"Fire away."

"If you were such a kick-ass warden, why did you quit?"

An answer came out without my being able to stop it. "I've been asking myself that question every day."

The frankness of my response seemed to surprise her. She slunk back into the booth but kept the muscles in her jaw clenched. "I still don't understand why the colonel didn't fire you a long time ago."

"Maybe it was because I had the highest conviction rate in the service two years in a row."

She crossed her short, strong arms. "Big whoop."

"I also had Kathy Frost looking out for me for a while. She seemed to think I was worth holding on to."

"I don't know why."

"When she wakes up, you can ask her."

My comment was an unwelcome reminder that a woman we both respected was still in a coma. Tate's face flushed red. She pushed herself violently out of the booth.

"I need to take a piss," she said.

The other diners stopped what they were doing in order to watch her. I wasn't sure what I'd hoped

310

to learn from Dani Tate, but I had blown any chance of getting her to open up. When she returned, she would tell me it was time to go, breakfast or no breakfast.

Destiny returned with our orders. The last time I'd been to the diner, she'd mentioned something to me about the Gammon shooting; she'd used an unusual phrase. But my mind was drawing a blank. She set the doughnut down on its little plate in front of me and the bowl of oatmeal on Tate's place mat. She said, "That woman you're with, she's the one who shot that wounded soldier in Camden?"

"She and another warden," I said.

"They couldn't have just wounded the poor guy or something?"

"He pointed a shotgun at them. They were in fear for their lives."

"It's all people are talking about here. Some people think they should've shot him, and some people don't. There ain't many on the fence."

Suddenly, the previous conversation I'd had with Destiny came back word by word.

"Do you remember me?" I asked. "I was in here the other day, talking to Dot."

She gave me a coquettish smile and raised her left hand to show me that there was no ring on her finger. "I absolutely remember you, dear."

"You said there was a big guy in here asking questions about Kathy. The word you used to

311

describe him was 'Neanderthal.' What did he look like, exactly?"

"I don't have a memory for names and faces." She leaned in close enough for me to smell the cinnamon chewing gum she was snapping between her teeth. "Unless a guy is wicked cute, I mean."

I tried to play dumb and pretend she wasn't flirting with me. "Why did you call him a Neanderthal?"

"He was just wicked big, and he had gross hair all over his arms and neck. I remember thinking he looked like he should have been dressed like Fred Flintstone, you know, in a tiger skin."

Kathy's neighbor Littlefield was a large man, but I hadn't seen his face. One of Jimmy's buddies from the 488th was also a big dude, the guy who lived up in Aroostook County: Ethan Smith. Even Kurt was a sizable human being. Maybe if Destiny described the mystery man to Dani Tate, the warden could tell if the description fit any of the local lawbreakers Kathy had been investigating.

More likely, Take would just punch me in the heart, as she'd already threatened to do.

"What sort of questions was this Neanderthal guy asking?" I said.

"Like if that warden sergeant was a regular. If she came in every morning. He wondered if she lived nearby. Someone at the counter said, 'No, she lives in Appleton.' "

"Do you remember who it was at the counter who told the guy where Sergeant Frost lived?"

"Sorry, honey. Like I said, I don't have a memory for names and faces."

I dug out my cell phone and typed the address of the *Portland Press Herald* into the browser bar. The site came up and I searched for the name Ethan Smith. The article appeared, along with a miniature version of the picture of Jimmy Gammon, Angelo Donato, and Ethan Smith horsing around at Camp Sabalu-Harrison. I held the phone up so Destiny could view the tiny screen.

"Could this be the Neanderthal?"

She squinted her already squinty eyes. "Maybe if he had longer hair now?"

I'd missed seeing Dani Tate return. She'd taken a circuitous route to avoid a busboy who was clearing one of the tables. She loomed over my shoulder, seeming taller than five-four.

"What the hell, Bowditch?" she said.

"Destiny may have talked to the guy who shot Kathy. He came in here the day of the shooting, trying to find out where she lived."

Tate scowled at me. "You just can't help yourself, can you?"

"She said he looked like a Neanderthal—big and hairy, with a unibrow. Does that describe anyone you and Kathy were investigating? A poacher or a pot grower? Someone dangerous?"

Tate reached into the kangaroo pocket of her sweatshirt to find her key fob. She pushed the button to unlock the truck.

"I think this is significant," I said.

"And I think you can hitchhike back to my house."

She turned on her heel and made for the door.

I barely had time to pay for our uneaten breakfast. The bell rang loudly as Dani slammed the door. As I passed Pulkinnen on his stool by the door, I thought I heard him mutter "Bitch" beneath his breath. I glared at him, but the Finnish plumber spun away to face the pie case.

32

I honestly thought she was going to drive off without me. As it was, I had to chase her truck halfway across the parking lot. She stopped long enough for me to open the Tacoma's passenger door. I started to climb onto the nerf bar, using the interior handle to pull myself up into the cab.

"I'll take you back to your car under one condition," she said.

"What is it?"

"Don't say a fucking word to me until we get back to my house."

I slid silently into the passenger seat and fastened the belt buckle.

Leaving the parking lot, Tate gunned the engine, raising a spray of sand and gravel behind the rear wheels. She cranked up the police scanner the way a teenager listening to the radio might if her favorite song suddenly started playing. I leaned my head against the padded headrest and watched the blur of green scenery. Deb Davies's revolver pressed uncomfortably against my tailbone.

I figured that maybe I would drive back to the Square Deal and ask around at the counter to see if someone else there remembered Destiny's Neanderthal. I could also prod Soctomah again. I no longer felt the need to be respectful of the detective's seemingly stalled investigation.

We hadn't driven more than half a mile when a call came over the radio. The Knox County dispatcher was reporting a 10-55—a vehicle accident—on the Old County Road in Rockland. "All available units please respond," she said. "A car went into one of the quarries."

"We need to take that," I said.

Tate looked at me with disbelief. "What do you mean, 'we'? I'm suspended, and you're not even a warden."

"You know those quarries. The cliffs are fifty feet high, and the water is who knows how deep. We're only a few minutes away. The people inside could drown by the time first responders arrive."

She didn't slow down or turn the wheel.

"What's more important to you, Tate," I said,

"keeping your nose clean or saving someone's life?"

Tate braked so hard, I nearly got whiplash. She threw the truck into reverse and executed a perfect three-point turn. In ten seconds, we were speeding back up the hill in the opposite direction.

I had passed through Rockland's stinking quarry land on my drive south, and the image of a car crashing through the guardrail had been vivid in my mind. I might have taken it as a premonition, but vehicles were going off that winding road all the time. Coincidence is a master of disguise.

It took us less than five minutes to reach the accident scene. There was no question we'd found the right quarry. The gaping gash in the steel barrier would have been hard to miss. Other vehicles had stopped where they could—the road was narrow, with few places to pull over—and bystanders were gathered along the cliff, gazing down into the pit. As I had predicted, Tate and I were the first responders to arrive.

Tate slowed, looking for a place to park her truck without it being sideswiped by rubber-neckers. I took the opportunity to unfasten my shoulder belt and jump from the idling Tacoma.

"Jesus Christ, Bowditch!"

I ran up the road until I was shoulder-to-shoulder with the other people who had stopped. There was an old couple and a woman with a baby in her arms and a group of teenagers, some with cell phones pressed to their ears, others crying hysterically. I looked down at my boots and saw a steeply sloping limestone cliff. At the bottom of the quarry was a man-made pond filled with water as blue as the Caribbean, and in that water, twenty feet from the shore, was an overturned car. The undercarriage and wheels were completely exposed, and it was clearly sinking.

"Help her! Somebody, please!"

I hadn't noticed the soaking-wet girl at the bottom of the cliff face. She was clinging to the rocks with bloody hands, trying to pull herself out of the water. Her upturned face was a white oval, framed by strands of dark hair.

I didn't pause to remove my boots. I just took three running steps and hurled myself off the cliff wall. I seemed to hang in the air for half a second like a cartoon character who has just walked off a precipice, and then gravity grabbed me by the ankles. I fell fast and hit the water hard. I felt the impact all the way up my legs and spine. If the cliff had been any higher, I would have broken a dozen bones and spent the rest of my life in a wheelchair—assuming I'd even survived.

My body had somehow remembered that my arms should be folded across my chest, so I went in like a missile. The force of the drop plunged me deep into the aquamarine water. It was much colder than it looked. The shock caused my heart to clench tighter than a fist.

I found myself staring up at a blur of blue light, which I knew to be the surface but which seemed to be receding faster and faster. I thrust my arms out to stop my descent and gave two powerful kicks. My Bean boots weren't heavy enough to pull me down, but they didn't make swimming any easier, especially as my clothes became waterlogged.

My head popped up like a fishing bobber. I splashed around, gulping air and trying to get my bearings. My ears were stuffed up, but the injured girl's screams were loud enough to grab my attention. I followed the line from her pointing finger to the roiling rectangle of water where the overturned car was going under. All that remained above the surface were the rear wheels, and they were disappearing fast.

I put my face back in the foul-tasting water and began kicking my legs and pulling myself ahead with my arms. I tried to pretend I was back in the lukewarm pool at the Criminal Justice Academy, but my mind wasn't so easily tricked. Someone was in that sinking car, and that person was dying.

I reached the frothy spot where the car had been moments ago and ducked my head, squinting into the depths. There was a dark rectangular shape beneath me. I did a half somersault and began swimming for the vehicle. It seemed like I'd never catch up to it, that the car would disappear into a bottomless abyss, but it must have caught on something—an outcropping, a submerged tree, maybe even a junk vehicle someone had pushed over the edge—because it came to rest abruptly. A cloud of gray sediment rose around me.

The light was murky. I couldn't see more than a few feet, especially with the billowing mud, but I found the back bumper and was able to pull myself along the vehicle by moving from the exhaust pipe to the rear wheel to the handle of the back door and finally to the driver's window.

Inside was a thrashing girl.

She was stuck, her body upside down in the seat. I wasn't sure if she was just panicked or unable to release the buckle of her seat belt. The blobby air bag was pulsating in the water like a cuttlefish that had wrapped its tentacles around her chest. It was hard to see inside the vehicle itself, but I had a thought that the other girl must have squeezed out the passenger window, which was why there was no air left inside the car.

The girl had long reddish hair that was moving around in the water. When she saw me, her eyes widened and she made a yelling motion with her mouth, which only filled her lungs with more water. She reached with both hands for the window, flattening her palms against the glass. I tried the door handle, but it was locked. When I looked at the girl again, her eyelids had begun to flutter. I held on to the side mirror with one hand, feeling a nerve pinch in my brain as my own oxygen supply started to run out.

I needed a hammer, something to break the glass. When I'd been a warden, I'd bought myself a special emergency tool designed for that purpose. It was in a box back in Elizabeth Morse's cabin now.

I had my pocket jackknife, but it wasn't big enough to use as an awl. What else?

Deb Davies's revolver.

I reached around my back, worried the gun had fallen out during my jump into the water, but I found the handle pushed down into the ass of my jeans. I drew the revolver out and pressed the barrel against the corner of the window, well clear of the girl. Most people think a gun won't fire underwater, but gunpowder contains its own oxidizer and a bullet casing is waterproof. The slug won't travel far pushing H_2O instead of air. I just needed it to crack the glass.

When I pulled the trigger, the gun leaped in my hand, stinging it so hard, I lost hold of the grip. I saw the pink handle dropping away into the murk and had an impulse to swim after it, then looked up again and saw a hole in the window at which I had been aiming. I punched at the fractured glass and kept punching until blood was streaming from my knuckles. When the hole was large enough, I reached in and tried to unlock the door, but nothing happened, so I kept working at the glass until the opening seemed big enough for me to pull the girl through.

She was unconscious when I grabbed her by the shoulders. I braced my knees against the door and pulled. Nothing happened. Her shoulder belt was still fastened. I was running out of air and could feel a panicking sensation rising in my lungs. I fumbled inside the car for the seat belt and located the clasp. I pushed the button with my thumb. To my utter amazement, it sprang free. There was nothing wrong with the belt. She had just been too terrified to remember how to unlatch it.

I grabbed the girl by the shoulders again and pulled. This time she came through the window. I hugged her with one arm and used the car for leverage, bracing my foot against it and kicking hard for the surface.

I hadn't realized how close I'd come to blacking out until I tasted air. I turned the girl so her face was pointed at the sky and gripped her around the chest. I began doing the backstroke toward the cliff face. My eyes and nose were burning from whatever filth was in that deceptively blue water, and the taste in my mouth was like I'd been sucking on a rotten egg.

The shore was closer than I'd expected. I whacked my outstretched arm on a rock as I tried to take one more stroke. I felt two hands close around my wrist. I looked up into Dani Tate's gray eyes and found myself being pulled to the rock where the injured girl was crouched, crying and shivering.

"Is she dead?" the girl shrieked. "Oh my God, she's dead!"

I didn't have the strength to push the unconscious girl onto the ledge, but Tate was able to get her by the armpits. I held on to the lip of the rock with my bleeding hands while Dani used her back to hoist the teenager onto dry land.

The other girl tried to reach for her friend, but Tate shoved her out of the way. She placed the driver on the ledge and began giving her chest compressions. Frothy water gushed from the senseless girl's mouth every time Dani leaned on her chest.

I made another effort to push myself onto the ledge, and this time I had the strength. I couldn't have spoken if I'd tried. It was all I could do to catch my breath.

"She wasn't texting!" the other girl kept saying.

Bright mountain-climbing ropes fell down around us. I saw men's boots, legs, and rear ends overhead. Rockland firemen were rappelling toward us.

I heard coughing. Dani Tate leaned back on her heels as the driver vomited water from her lungs. I had no idea how Tate had managed to get herself down that cliff, but the front of her sweatshirt and pants were gray with limestone dust.

My hands were a bloody mess. When I glanced

up again, I found Dani Tate staring at me over the prone body of the coughing girl. "Has anyone ever told you you're fucking insane?"

It was the first time I'd ever seen her smile. She actually had very pretty teeth.

33

An EMT bandaged my hands. Then Tate and I both gave statements to the Rockland police. We watched firemen help both girls into an ambulance that had arrived belatedly at the scene. And then we were free to go.

I turned to Tate as she started the engine. "I swallowed about a gallon of that toxic water. I feel like I should have my stomach pumped."

"You'll live," she said.

"Good job with the rescue breathing."

"You saved her as much as I did."

She should have smiled more often. It made you feel like there was a real person under all that hardness, one who might be worth getting to know.

I had poured the water out of my boots and wrung out my socks, and one of the fireman had given me a towel, but I was still soaked to the skin. I turned up the heater, and the dampness my hair gave off caused the passenger window to mist over.

"When you jumped in, how did you know you wouldn't land on a rock?" she asked.

"I didn't think about it. I just acted. People say I have a reckless streak."

"You could have killed yourself."

"There are worse ways to go than trying to rescue someone."

She fell silent until we reached her house. She idled the truck in the driveway. I reached for the door handle, but she grabbed my wrist. For a small woman with little hands, she had a surprisingly firm grip.

"Kathy told me you were involved in two use-of-force investigations," she said.

"That's right."

She let go of my wrist. "Cleared both times?"

"Yes."

"Did the inquiry panel treat you like you were guilty of negligence when they brought you in for questioning?"

"That's just their standard approach," I said. "The process seems more prosecutorial than it is. Jimmy Gammon didn't give you and Kathy any choice when he raised his shotgun. The AG's panel will decide you acted in self-defense."

"How can you say we did the right thing? You weren't even there."

"I know Kathy. If she says she acted in self-defense, then she did."

She brought her fingers to her mouth, and I

noticed for the first time that Dani Tate was a nail chewer.

"Did she ever talk with you about the first guy she shot?" she asked.

"Decoster?" I settled back against the seat. "Kathy said it was a domestic violence call. I guess the guy had been beating his wife with the buckle end of his belt. When Kathy arrived, he grabbed a butcher's knife from the kitchen and came after her with it."

"Nothing else?"

"Only that he weighed three hundred pounds."

"She told me that, too."

Kathy had always been closemouthed about that particular incident. In general, she didn't tend to spend much time talking about the past—hers or anyone else's—and seemed to grow annoyed whenever I waxed nostalgic in her presence. "What's past is past," she used to say. "Why worry about what you can't change?"

To which I'd respond with a maxim of my own: "Just because you're done with the past doesn't mean it's done with you."

Dani Tate stopped her nibbling. "She was my age when it happened. Right out of warden school."

"She probably wanted to reassure you."

"I guess so."

She turned off the ignition, and I took it as a signal that she considered the conversation to be over. I opened the door and slid out, leaving a wet stain on the newly vacuumed fabric.

"Don't be intimidated by the Gammons' money and political connections," I said.

Her face hardened again into its less appealing aspect. "That's easy for you to say."

She didn't say good-bye, just clicked the automatic garage opener and drove inside. I found myself staring at a closed door and thinking that she might well be right. The review board was unlikely to hang Kathy out to dry, given that she'd just been wounded in the line of duty. But you couldn't have asked for a better scapegoat than Danielle Tate.

My boots made a squishing sound as I crossed the road to Eklund's car. I needed to change clothes yet again, which meant heading back to Kathy's house and doing some laundry. I should also craft an apology to the Reverend Davies for losing her revolver. All things considered, I doubted she would mind my carelessness.

My phone buzzed on the drive back to Appleton. The text befit the person who had sent it to me: blunt and to the point.

> Seacoast Security informs me that you have not been in residence at Moose-horn for the past four days, putting you in breach of our contracted agreement. Please remove your possessions from

my buildings by end of business Friday. Combination locks will be changed on that date and you will not be permitted on the grounds w/o escort.

Billy had been right about my foolishness in accepting Elizabeth Morse's job offer. I had never been more to her than a replaceable drone in a hive that was already buzzing with impotent worker bees.

I was officially homeless, I realized.

Maybe I could share the guest room with Kurt Eklund—if he ever reappeared.

Ten minutes later, I found myself passing the VFW Hall in Sennebec and noticed a single car in the lot: a Ford Taurus with two American flags, one protruding from the top of each front window. Kurt said he'd been playing poker at the hall the night his sister was attacked. I'd never thought to follow up on the story.

The front door was locked, but inside I heard what sounded like a vacuum cleaner. It hurt my knuckles to knock, so I resorted to kicking with my still-wet boot.

After a minute, I heard the vacuum stop. The door opened, and a short man peered out. He was dressed in chinos, a button-down shirt, and sneakers, and he was wearing bifocals and one of those U. S. Navy baseball hats that displays the name of the veteran's signature ship. Evidently, this old gent had served aboard the USS *Philippine Sea* (CV-47).

With my longish hair and beard, scabbed face, and bandaged hands, I must have appeared to him as a wandering beggar who had just fallen into a lake. "Are you trying to kick down the door, young man?" he asked.

"You'll have to excuse me, sir," I said, showing him my bloodstained knuckles. "I have trouble knocking."

"You been in a fight?"

"Not exactly."

My answers weren't doing much to reassure him of my character or intentions. "We don't do handouts here, if you're looking for money," he said, glancing at the puddle of water forming around my feet.

"Actually, I'm looking for a man. His name is Kurt Eklund."

His wrinkles deepened when he frowned. "Does he owe you money, too?"

"You haven't seen him recently, have you?"

"Not for the past week. He wore out his welcome here pretty fast. You can't run up a drink tab and have people spotting you chips and then sneak off without paying."

I massaged my injured knuckles with my fingers. "So Eklund wasn't here three nights ago, playing cards?"

"Is that his alibi?"

"His alibi for what?"

"He strikes me as someone who can't keep his stories straight. The man has a problem with alcohol."

I gave a nod. "You wouldn't know if he has any particular enemies? Maybe there's a club member he owes a wad of cash?"

He narrowed his eyes at me through his bifocals. "What did you say your name was again?"

"I didn't."

"That's what I thought." He took a step back into the unlighted building and closed the door.

It would have been easy to read too much into Kurt's story not checking out. When I'd found him lying dead to the world in his sister's bed, he'd been coming off a bender. It was just as likely he had no memory of what he had done over the previous days and had concocted an alibi to cover up the fact that he'd suffered a blackout. The question remained where he'd been during those crucial hours, however. The man had clearly pissed off more than a few people in his life.

My head was aching when I arrived at Kathy's house and noticed that the formerly dented mailbox had been pushed over entirely and that letters and catalogs lay scattered about the road. Littlefield or some other local vandal had used Kathy's hospitalization as an occasion for mischief. I stopped and picked up the dirty mail. It was just a collection of bills and leaflets, the usual stuff, except for an unstamped envelope with no address or name other than the word *DYKE* scrawled on the front. I tore it open.

> Gammon was an AMERICAN hero and not some bull dyke who thinks wearing a gun makes her a man when really she's just a scared pussy. I would throw a pillow over your ugly head and toss you down the stairs and whip you up with an electric cord until you start screaming like a bitch. I wouldn't even bother to fuck you first.

At least the penmanship was good. The anonymous writer seemed to have missed the news that the object of his hatred had already been attacked by someone using a weapon more lethal than an electrical cord. I tended to forget that most unsigned death threats didn't come from Mensa members.

I tucked the letter in my pocket.

Kurt still hadn't returned.

I took another shower to wash away the filth from the quarry and found a pair of sweatpants, too long in the legs, in the guest bedroom. I stripped off my damp clothes and gathered all the other shirts, pants, and socks I'd dirtied over the past days. While my clothes were washing, I microwaved some chicken and rice dish I found in the freezer. Kathy shopped at health-food stores that sold quinoa in plastic bins and had coolers filled with expensive organic vegetables that weren't as bright and leafy as the ones in the supermarkets. She used to drag me into these co-ops at lunchtime.

"Better than variety store pizza," she used to say.

"Says you."

"Someday your arteries are going to thank me, Grasshopper."

I sat in the living room, leaning over the coffee table, and scarfed down my unknown lunch. I had to admit it was tasty. She'd used a lot of curry to give it some zing. The large-screen television taunted me from the wall; I couldn't figure out how to operate the remote control. After I'd finished eating, I stretched out my bare feet on the sofa, leaned back, and closed my eyes, trying to think.

Where had Kurt Eklund gone in such a hurry? Maybe he'd gathered up a few of Kathy's more valuable possessions to pawn. I wouldn't have put it past him.

I moved my eyes about the room, looking for empty places on shelves and tables where I could remember having seen some family heirloom. Earlier, I'd had the impression that the scene had been disturbed. I had the same feeling again, but I couldn't put my finger on what was different about the room.

I nearly tripped over one of Pluto's rawhide chews on my way to the kitchen. The house was full of reminders of the dead dog: rubber balls Kathy had stuffed with peanut butter, soft beds for him to sleep on in just about every room, dried puddles of drool, and hair everywhere. Coonhounds are heavy shedders. I hadn't asked Malcomb what he'd done with Pluto's body. Knowing the major, he'd probably arranged to stash the cadaver in the state police morgue so Kathy could give the dog a hero's burial.

That, of course, was assuming Kathy would recover. The prospect of suffering brain damage had always scared me more than death. What if Kathy awoke and she was no longer Kathy? I found myself empathizing with Lyla Gammon. The military had given her back a head-injured person it claimed was Jimmy, but whoever that disfigured man had been, he hadn't behaved like her son.

My cell phone was ringing on the coffee table. It was Lieutenant Soctomah. "Where are you?" he asked.

"Back at Kathy's house. What's going on?"

"You wanted me to call you if we found any trace of Kurt Eklund."

"So where is he?"

"We're not sure. A trooper found Sergeant Frost's

332

Nissan abandoned at a scenic turnout on I-Ninety-five. It's the rest area at Mile two fifty-two. The keys were still in the ignition, but there was no sign of Eklund anywhere."

34

Interstate 95 is Maine's central artery. It runs more than three hundred miles from New Hampshire to the Canadian border, east of Houlton. Mile 252 was a long ways north of Appleton. Had Kurt Eklund been heading home to Aroostook County when he decided to ditch the vehicle?

"Is that the rest area north of Medway?" I asked Soctomah.

"It's the one with the view of Mount Katahdin."

I knew the place. There was a small parking lot on a hillside above the highway where travelers could snap pictures of the tallest and most majestic mountain in Maine.

"Was the vehicle unlocked?" I said.

"Yes."

"Was it out of gas?"

"No."

"So why did he abandon it?"

The detective paused and I heard a phone ring in the background, then a garbled voice. It sounded as if he was in a crowded office. "I was hoping you might have an idea. You were the last person to talk with him—as far as we can tell."

Kurt had been drunk and distraught when he'd left Appleton. Somehow he'd managed to travel more than a hundred miles through the population centers of central Maine without crashing the SUV or being pulled over. It was a dirty secret among cops that some people—especially those with years of practice—could drive drunk without giving themselves away on the road.

"Have you searched the woods nearby?" I asked.

"You're thinking suicide?"

"He told me he had cirrhosis," I said. "He was definitely acting in a self-destructive manner. Or he might have just fallen down a hill while taking a leak."

"I'll have the wardens take a look around," he said. "But the trooper said there was no evidence of a crime. Eklund never dropped a clue where he might be going?"

"His parents live in New Sweden, but they're in Portland now with Kathy. Their house is still Kurt's legal address. It could be he was headed back up there for some reason."

"Unfortunately, we have no grounds to search for Eklund, since he's not technically a missing person. He's an adult who can go wherever he wants. It's not our business unless we can connect his disappearance to a crime."

In the legal sense, that was true. But I had

a bad feeling about the abandoned Xterra.

"One of Jimmy Gammon's buddies from the Four eighty-eighth is a potato farmer in Aroostook County," I said. "Kurt saw his picture in the newspaper. Maybe you should try calling this Ethan Smith to see if Eklund contacted him."

He paused, as if he were writing a note to himself. "Anything else?"

"I don't know what other leads you've been following, but Kathy had printed out an article about a woman who died a few days ago named Marta Jepson. The newspaper said she fell down her basement stairs in Lyndon, near Caribou. Kathy must have known the woman."

"Where did you find this piece of paper?" Soctomah sounded angry.

"In the wastebasket under Kathy's desk."

"Why didn't you tell me about it sooner?" The forensic techs who had searched the house had failed to identify the paper in the trash as potential evidence and that was why the lieutenant was upset. I couldn't remember what I'd done with the clipping. Had I left it on Kathy's desk?

"I thought you knew about it. It doesn't seem like you're making much progress with the investigation."

"With all due respect, you don't have a clue what we're doing."

"I haven't heard that you've identified any suspects."

"You need to trust that we're going to find the son of a bitch."

That was easy for him to say. "What are you going to do with Kathy's vehicle?"

"We'll have it towed back to her house. If we find any sign of Eklund, we'll let you know."

After he'd hung up, I took a look in Kathy's office. The story about Martha Jepson wasn't there. I dug out the wastebasket and found only that weird doodle. I couldn't make heads or tails out of the sketch. It looked like a toddler's drawing of stick men.

I went downstairs to the basement and stood over the dryer, feeling its heat rising against my bare chest, until my clothes were done. Then I got dressed and packed the extra clothes in my duffel.

Before I left the house, I paused for a few minutes at Kathy's locked gun safe, trying to imagine what the combination might be. The numbers wouldn't be simple to guess, and she was too crafty to leave a slip of paper lying around. I'd gotten used to carrying a firearm again over the past few days and felt naked without one.

Soctomah had said that I needed to trust him to find the shooter.

The problem was, I didn't.

In the dooryard, I paused to inspect my Bronco. I'd been telling myself that the damage might be fixable, but now I had to acknowledge the truth. It wouldn't take my insurance agent more than ten seconds to declare the truck to be a total loss. As best I could recall, my auto coverage didn't include a rider covering damage done by a shotgun-wielding assassin.

I rooted around the back of the Bronco for anything I might need on my trip: my hiker's tent, portable stove, butane container, wilderness first-aid kit, and a hatchet that I'd never thought of using for self-defense.

I stopped for gas at the first station I came to. I would need a full tank and a refill to go where I planned on going. It felt strange to be headed north again—but in a different direction from Grand Lake Stream. Ahead of me lay a series of millpond villages and dairy farms, the pastoral heart of Maine. Eventually, the winding country road would intersect with I-95, south of Bangor, and then it would be a straight shot into the deep woods. The sun doesn't set in May until after eight P.M., but I had miles to go, and I would need every minute of daylight once I reached the rest area outside Medway.

I'd been trying in vain to track down Kurt Eklund. Now I had a place to start looking.

Soctomah had asked if I considered Kathy's brother to be a suicide risk. The honest answer was that I didn't know, but it seemed unlikely to me that he would have killed himself quietly. Eklund wasn't a wounded animal that would slink into a hole to die. He was too melodramatic for such a quiet end. Blow his head off in a public place? Yes. Throw himself off a bridge in front of a speeding truck? Sure. Wander off into the woods to slit his wrists? I didn't think so.

If he had left the Xterra with the keys in the ignition and gas in the tank, he had done so for a reason. Given the twisted way his brain worked, the reason might not make any sense on the surface. But I had confidence I could decode whatever clues he might have left behind.

The larger question was where he had been going and why.

My best ideas usually found me when I wasn't looking for them, so I decided to focus on my driving and the ever-changing scenery outside my window. Maine combines aspects of all the New England states: Portland's affluent suburbs were Connecticut in miniature; the sand beaches of the southern coast were dead ringers for the Rhode Island seashore. The villages clustered along the swift-flowing rivers of central Maine—with their Civil War monuments dedicated to the Union dead—were right out of Norman Rockwell's paintings of western Massachusetts. The open fields where enormous flocks of crows gathered at dusk reminded me of Vermont's green dairy farms. And the massif around Katahdin, which I finally glimpsed after hours on the road, was as snowy as the White Mountains of New Hampshire.

Katahdin came into view when I was still miles to the south on Interstate 95, rising higher and higher as I approached, until the highway dog-legged to the east and I lost sight of it for a while. I passed the exit to the Golden Road and Baxter State Park and continued north until a blue sign appeared ahead: SCENIC VIEW OF MT. KATAHDIN. OPEN MAY–OCT. NO FACILITIES. I took a right and climbed a hillside to the lot.

The Wabanaki Indians, who had been the inhabitants of this land when the first Europeans bumped their boats against the shore, believed a capricious and vengeful deity lived on the peak of Mount Katahdin. His name was Pamola, and he had the body of a man, the horns of a moose, and the beak and wings of an eagle. Pamola was a violent thunder god who forbade humans from climbing his mountain. He was known to snatch away anyone who dared and imprison them in a place called Alomkik: a cold and windswept hell only slightly more hospitable than Maine's contemporary Supermax.

The rest area was accessible only via the north-bound lane of I-95. So Kurt had been heading north when he stopped here. But there was still gas in the tank.

There were several cars and trucks parked at the turnout, their noses facing to the west. The view, across an old rail fence, of Salmon Lake in the foreground and then the multiple jagged summits of Katahdin in the distance was worth stopping for. No police cruisers were to be seen. The cops had come and gone.

As promised, the state police had towed away Kathy's Nissan. It was en route back to her house after a short detour to the forensics garage at the state police headquarters in Augusta. The circumstances of the Xterra's abandonment were such that Soctomah, even if he wasn't treating Kurt Eklund as a missing person in the legal sense of the word, would be curious enough to want his technicians to have a look inside the vehicle.

I climbed out of the Cutlass and felt a stiffness in my limbs that was an aftereffect of my morning swim at the quarry. The wind was blowing out of the southwest, carrying warm air across the evergreen forests and up from the electric blue waters of the Salmon River watershed. I took a deep breath and fancied I could actually smell the fish in the lake. After my days in the city, it felt good to be back in the North Woods again.

"Excuse me, mister," said a woman behind me.

I turned around and saw a tattooed couple in their twenties.

"Can you take our picture?"

She offered me a smartphone the size of a paperback novel.

"Sure."

The couple sat atop the rail fence with the mountain behind them. I took their picture with

Mount Katahdin gleaming over their shoulders. The woman thanked me. Her boyfriend lit a cigarette and slouched back toward his Camaro.

"You didn't see any police cars here when you arrived?" I asked the young woman.

"Why? Are you on the run?" she asked.

After they had left, I wandered around the parking lot, looking for something, although I wasn't sure what. I knelt in the grass and poked a stick in the fine dust under the picnic tables, hoping to turn up the filter end of one of Kurt's Swisher Sweets. A mourning cloak butterfly fluttered up from a patch of sunshine where it had been basking. I made loops through the adjacent trees, finding many paths that dead-ended behind walls of evergreens: places where men had anonymous sexual encounters with each other. I found nothing to indicate that Kurt Eklund had ever been at this place.

Eventually, I found myself back behind the steering wheel of the Cutlass, staring at Katahdin's several peaks. From this vantage, none of the surrounding mountains could be seen. I thought of one of my favorite books from childhood, *The Hobbit*, and the Lonely Mountain, where lived the dragon Smaug.

As a boy enchanted with fantasy novels, I had dreamed of a life full of adventure. As a man, I had learned that placing yourself constantly in life-and-death situations was a mug's game.

Sooner or later, you were going to lose your bet.

Sitting in Kurt's dirty car, gazing at that beautiful vista, I felt the chilling conviction that its owner had lost everything a man had to lose.

35

The farther north you go in Maine, the more disoriented you become. Start with the distances. Aroostook County, which juts into New Brunswick and Quebec, is the largest county east of the Mississippi—about the size of Connecticut and Rhode Island combined. Glance at a map and the drive to Canada seems manageable, as if you could knock if off in no time—until you find yourself on the road for more hours than you ever dreamed.

Then there is the geographic and cultural dislocation. People who have never been to northern Maine think that everything just becomes wilder and wilder once you cross the forty-sixth parallel. They enter the big woods outside Bangor, spend hours traveling through seemingly endless forests of spruce and fir, and are stunned when the road finally spits them out into farm fields that are nearly as spacious as those of the Great Plains. Soon the unprepared travelers are cruising through tidy towns lined up with geometrical precision along Route 1: bustling communities that defy anyone's idea of a remote borderland. Americans have trouble processing the idea that Canada exists at all, let alone that most of its population centers should be pressed up against its southern border (which just so happens to be our northern border). And so the concept that there should be split-level houses and wide lawns —those defining characteristics of suburbia—in a place as far from "civilization" as northernmost Maine seems unimaginable.

I'd made the trip on many occasions, and even I found the road stretching before me like a piece of rubber being pulled taut beneath my wheels. Miles were clicking on the odometer, but I seemed to be making no progress. I found myself being worn down by the never-ending journey. I'd hoped to reach New Sweden before dark, but more and more of the cars passing me in the opposite direction had their headlights on. I stopped for coffee at a truck stop in Houlton and drank three cups without feeling any effect on my central nervous system. I ordered a BLT, hoping that food might do the trick, but if anything, it just made me sleepier.

Route 1 took me through Presque Isle, the largest town in the county, with close to ten thousand inhabitants. Anywhere else, it might have been considered a hamlet, but there was a feeling of life on the streets that came from the steady flow of traffic between two (mostly) friendly nations.

There were as many cars and trucks with New Brunswick plates as Maine tags. Leaving town, an eighteen-wheeler passed me with the McCain's Potatoes logo splashed on the side. Jimmy Gammon's and Angelo Donato's buddy lived nearby: Ethan Smith, the man the MP's Pashtun interpreter nicknamed "Monster." He owned a potato farm somewhere in these rolling fields.

I found a tractor-supply company just as it was closing up shop for the day. The lot was jam-packed with brightly painted machines; back-hoes, tillers, bulldozers, and garden-variety farm tractors like giant versions of the ones I'd played with as a kid. A bell sounded as I came through the door, and a middle-aged man wearing a short-sleeve dress shirt and green Dickies sought me out. He had a flat-top hair cut, a name tag with TRAVIS on it, and the same excellent posture as Erik Eklund.

He gave me a big smile, as if I was an old friend he hadn't seen in years. "Can I help you?"

"I'm not sure," I said. "I'm trying to find someone who lives near here, but I don't have his address. He's a potato farmer named Ethan Smith."

If I had asked that question most other places, even in Maine, I would have received a scowl, but Travis, the tractor salesman, treated it as an innocent inquiry and not suspicious in the least. "Oh, sure. I know Ethan. He lives out on the Alder

Brook Road, outside Mapleton. Are you a friend of his?"

The lie came easily. "Yes."

"From the National Guard, I bet."

"How did you know?"

"I'm ex–Air Force myself. Came up here with the wife to work at Loring and liked Limestone so much, we decided to stay and raise a family. If you want to hang on a minute, I'll get you directions."

People in Aroostook County were so damned nice. I felt guilty for misleading such a helpful man. He disappeared for a few minutes, leaving me to wander around the brightly lighted showroom. I hadn't planned on showing up unannounced at Smith's doorstep, but I was bothered by Destiny's inability to say for certain whether he was the Neanderthal who had shown up at the diner, asking about Kathy.

Travis returned, still smiling, holding a wireless phone. He handed it to me. "I decided it would just be easier if you spoke with Ethan directly and he told you how to get there."

I had no choice but to accept the phone. "Thanks."

I held the speaker to my ear. There was no dial tone. Someone was already on the line.

"Hello?"

"Who is this?" The man sounded like a bullmastiff that had been taught human speech.

"Is this Ethan Smith?"

"Who is this?"

I turned my back on Travis and took a few steps toward the nearest display of rototillers. "A friend of Jimmy Gammon."

"I know who you are. Donato told me about you. What the hell are you doing in Presque Isle?"

"Heading north."

"I think you mean south. You're turning around and getting the hell out of here before I come kick your ass."

"I'm just looking to have a conversation."

"That's the last thing you want, asshole. Take my word for it."

"I don't suppose you've received a call from a guy named Kurt Eklund recently?"

There was a click, and he was gone.

When I turned around, the tractor salesman was scowling. Travis was a polite and friendly fellow, but not above eavesdropping. "We're closing up here, and I think you should go."

I handed him back his phone and thanked him for his assistance, but he didn't say another word as he locked the door behind my back.

Except for a few wisps of clouds, the night sky above New Sweden was almost completely clear. Jupiter hung above the treetops to the northwest, bright white and unblinking. The planet seemed like a hopeful beacon until it slowly began to descend and then disappeared from view below the horizon.

Deer had come out to the edges of the fields to nibble the first green shoots poking up through the soil. Their eyes were luminescent in my headlights, and they were very shy. Kathy had told me that when she was a rookie warden in the county, her district had been "Night Hunter Central." If that was still true, the local deer had a right to be jumpy after dark.

I passed a cheery blue-and-yellow sign by the side of the road. It lit up in the glow of my high beams:

It was illustrated with the U.S. and Swedish flags. I truly felt like I had crossed into a foreign land.

I didn't need a helpful tractor salesman to find the Eklund place. As I neared the village of New Sweden, I passed a mailbox with that name on the side. There were probably more than a few Eklunds in town, but this house was located across from the volunteer fire department's building, and Kathy had told me her father had been the fire chief for many years.

The house was white, with clapboard siding, blue shutters and trim, and a blue metal roof that looked like a recent addition. In a part of the world that averages nine or ten feet of snow a winter, it pays to have a roof that snow and ice can slide off. The windows were dark, with the shades pulled, and there were no vehicles in the driveway. I parked along the road and reached for the small flashlight I'd packed in my duffel.

It wouldn't have surprised me if the Eklunds' neighbors were peeking through their curtains, trying to decide whether to call the police. People in these villages tended to watch out for one another's properties, and everyone in New Sweden would have known that the Eklunds were in Portland, at the hospital bedside of their beloved Katarina. Even if they recognized Kurt's Oldsmobile, they probably knew better than to trust him.

I pulled on the navy blue windbreaker Soctomah had loaned me. I wondered how I would explain to a responding officer why I was roaming around a house that didn't belong to me, wearing a jacket with police on the back. I decided I would deal with that problem if and when it presented itself. No one answered the bell, but that didn't mean anything. For all I knew, Kurt was passed out inside, just as I had found him at Kathy's house.

The door was locked, and there was no key under the *Valkommen* mat. I stepped quickly around the side of the building.

I felt a pang of disappointment when I found the back door intact. I'd had the notion that Kurt might have punched out a pane of glass to let himself in. Despite the evidence of my own eyes, I was growing more and more certain that he had visited the house. I almost left without doing the obvious thing and trying the doorknob. To my surprise, it turned. Someone had left the house unlocked.

Instead of switching on the lights, I pushed the button on my SureFire and moved the beam around the room. The Eklunds' house had been laid out in the same plan as their daughter's: The back door admitted you to a mudroom, which opened onto the kitchen. The first thing I noticed was the subtropical warmth. The oil furnace was laboring away in the basement. I didn't imagine for a second that Erik and Alice Eklund would have left their house with the thermostat cranked.

There was also an odor in the air that didn't belong. It was smoky and cloying—the smell I'd come to associate with the Cutlass: Swisher Sweets cigarillos. I switched on the overhead kitchen lights.

"Kurt? It's Mike Bowditch." I didn't want him mistaking me for an intruder and rushing me in the dark.

There was no answer.

The kitchen showed no sign of having recently been used. There were no plates or cups in the old porcelain sink. The chairs were tucked carefully beneath the breakfast table.

"Kurt?"

I passed through the formal dining room. Wooden display cabinets held wineglasses and china plates. On the wall hung a framed family photograph taken decades earlier. Erik and Alice looked to be in their thirties; both blond, they were fit and ruddy-cheeked, as if they had just returned from a day spent cross-country skiing. The adult Eklunds were dressed in matching Nordic sweaters. Kurt appeared to be twelve or thirteen and was wearing a flower-patterned shirt and bell-bottom pants. His hair was feathered around his shoulders. It was heartbreaking to see him with two functional eyes and a complexion not yet ruined by alcohol. Kathy was just an anonymous-looking baby.

The front parlor in the Eklund's house was still a sitting room where the family entertained visitors. There was no television or reclining furniture, only rocking chairs and a stiff-backed love seat. The coffee table was a mess. There were three empty liquor bottles: one of vodka, one of aquavit, and one of coffee brandy, which Kurt had no doubt bought on the road. He'd used a tea saucer as an ashtray but must have dropped one of his smokes on the love seat, because it showed a black spot where the fabric had burned.

I raised my voice. "Kurt? Where are you?"

Again, there was no answer.

I found his old room down the hall from his parents'. The bed had been slept in. He hadn't bothered to flush the toilet after using it. I checked every room, including the basement, but there was no trace of him. After five fruitless minutes, I returned to the parlor and sat down on the love seat, imagining him there, boozing it up and nearly setting the house on fire.

I'd had a suspicion that he might have come here to loot the place, looking for items he could pawn for cash. I'd thought he'd been looking to settle his gambling debts. But there were no indications that he'd rifled his mother's chest of drawers again. So why had Kurt returned home to New Sweden?

Kurt was on a mission, and my gut told me it had to do with Kathy. Maybe he had some suspicion about who had shot her—something he hadn't shared with me. But if he was set on coming back to Aroostook County, why had he abandoned his sister's SUV at a scenic turnout a hundred-plus miles away?

Something about that rest area was bothering me. I tried to imagine myself back there. I saw the rail fence, the glistening lake, and the mountain in the distance. I heard the rush of traffic moving on the highway below.

So had he driven here from the overlook, gotten drunk, and then turned around and headed south again? But if that was the case, why was Kathy's Nissan found at a rest stop you could only access via the *northbound* lane? The only reason that would make sense was if someone had wanted it to appear that Kurt Eklund had never made it to New Sweden.

And at the root of that question was another: What had compelled him to return to Maine's Swedish Colony?

The last time I'd seen him was through Kathy's bathroom window. I'd looked outside and seen him speeding off in his sister's SUV. I'd assumed he was racing away to confront James Gammon, because of his infuriating quote in the paper. It hadn't occurred to me that he might've had another reason to be angry.

Kurt had been downstairs in Kathy's woman cave when I'd gone upstairs to take a shower. Later, I'd had the gnawing feeling that something wasn't quite right about the room. Now I realized what had been missing. I had left the article about Marta Jepson's death on the coffee table. Kurt had taken it with him.

36

The dead woman had lived in the neighboring village of Lyndon. I had originally thought she might have been a friend of the family, maybe one of Kathy's former teachers. But Erik Eklund had shot down that theory when he said he'd never heard of her.

Somehow Kurt knew who Marta Jepson was. Otherwise, he wouldn't have snatched the article from Kathy's coffee table. And he wouldn't have raced off in his sister's vehicle for reasons I still couldn't comprehend. Why had he been in such a hurry? The old woman had fallen down a flight of stairs five nights earlier. According to the article in the *Aroostook Republican*, the authorities didn't consider the death suspicious.

I needed to read the story again. I tried my iPhone, but there was only a single bar, and I couldn't get the browser window to open. Northern Maine might not be the wooded wilderness people assume it is, but like the rest of the state, it has lousy cell coverage.

I turned off the lights and made sure to lock the back door. I didn't want the Eklunds returning home to find that they had been robbed. Aroostook County was generally a safe place to live, but it was also a border region that had seen a spike in drug-related offenses as more and more illegal prescription medications had been smuggled into the state from Canada. Burglaries, home invasions, and drugstore stickups were on the rise here—as they were back in Washington County— as addicts resorted to desperate measures to pay for their habits.

I drove southeast along the Caribou Road. It had been named for an animal that hunters had eradicated from these parts generations ago. Human beings love to commemorate the things they destroy. Building memorials to the dead and naming places in their honor is our way of recasting the past in terms that don't hold us accountable.

At the crossroads outside Lyndon, I pulled over and tried my phone again. This time, I was able to pull up the Web site for the local paper and read the article about Marta Jepson. I'd forgotten that the Aroostook sheriff had hedged in his statement about the old woman's fall clearly having been an accident. There weren't any follow-up stories suggesting police had discovered reasons to continue investigating her death. Nor was there a formal obituary discussing funeral arrangements, which seemed unusual. Did she have no family?

The article said that Marta Jepson had lived alone in a house on the Svensson Road. My phone's GPS worked long enough for me to find it on a map. Then my car rounded a bend and the signal dropped. I turned north at the crossroads and began poking along, watching for a road sign.

I drove into Lyndon village, past the post office, and crossed the bridge above the flooded St. John River. The rain from the previous week was still gushing down out of the highlands, and in the starlight I saw whitewater where there were standing waves in the river. As I neared the town center, I saw two big-wheeled all-terrain vehicles race across the paved road, traveling west along the local rail trail. If I had been the district warden, I would have felt obliged to chase down the riders and ticket them for speeding.

Kathy had missed the ATV craze when she had worked this district; the vehicles hadn't been widely popular two decades ago. Now four-wheelers were as common in rural Maine as cars. It wasn't uncommon to see them parked outside the local churches on sunny Sunday mornings or outside the local roadhouses after dark on Saturdays. Most of the veteran wardens I knew waxed rhapsodic about the days before wheelers, when your primary duties were catching poachers and finding lost hunters.

In truth, the warden's job had always been dangerous. According to her own father, Kathy's year here had been the worst in her life (until now), or she never would have requested a transfer to the southern part of the state. Her new husband, Darren, had died in a car crash. And she'd had to fire her weapon at a man who intended to carve her into pieces.

Marta Jepson's home was a ranch house situated under a stand of tall pines. There were no neighboring homes within a quarter of a mile. At first glance, it reminded me of the rental property in Sennebec I had shared with Sarah. Our place had also been set back from the road and shaded by evergreen boughs. The difference was that we had lived in a drafty lobsterman's shack that spouted a new leak every time it rained. This was a neatly kept residence with flower boxes under the windows and a flagstone walk swept clean of pine needles.

On one of the trees near the road someone had tacked a FOR SALE BY OWNER sign. A phone number was scrawled on it with a permanent marker. It was unclear to me in the darkness if the sign was old or new. Had Marta Jepson put it up herself, or had someone else?

I parked along the road and shined my flashlight on the dirt driveway leading to the house. At the Advanced Warden Academy, our instructors had taught us the obscure art of decoding tire treads. We learned automotive forensic terms—*contact patch, noise treatment,* and *stress cycle.* In the field, we measured tire widths to determine wheel-base dimensions by recording the turning diameter of a vehicle's rear wheels. By examining the wear and tear, we could tell whether the tires were old or new, whether they were factory originals or retreads. And we could ascertain how recently the tracks had been made by using simple meteorology. Mud is Mother Nature's gift to game wardens.

Many vehicles had been to the Jepson house in the past week, but one had visited more recently than the others. Glancing at the set of tracks, I couldn't swear that they belonged to a Nissan Xterra, only that the width indicated an SUV or a truck. What I could say for certain was that there was no standing water in the tread marks. This particular vehicle had left the property after the rain had stopped and the dirt had begun to harden again.

Kurt had been here. He'd come to this house, guessing that there was a connection between Martha Jepson and the person who had shot his sister. If so, he had almost certainly seen the FOR SALE sign nailed to that maple, and there was no doubt in my mind that he'd called the phone number.

I removed my cell from my pocket and checked the signal. Two bars. I keyed in the seller's number.

A woman answered. "Hello?"

"Hello, I'm calling about the house for sale."

"Can you repeat that? You're not coming through."

"I'm calling about the house in Lyndon."

"OK?"

"I drove past and saw the sign. I was wondering if you'd mind showing it to me."

"Now? It's kind of late."

Northern Maine didn't exactly have the hottest real estate market in the nation. Aroostook County had seen its population decrease in the last census. There were simply too few good-paying jobs to be had north of Bangor, especially after the Air Force had closed Loring Air Force Base in the 1990s. Perfectly nice houses tended to stay on the market now for months, sometimes years. And those that did sell were rarely purchased by some random guy calling from a darkened roadside.

"I thought you might live nearby," I said.

"No, we're down in Presque Isle."

That was where Ethan Smith lived. The man jokingly called "the Monster."

"It doesn't have to be tonight," I said, not wanting to spook the young woman. "So I take it you've gotten other calls about the property?"

She was silent long enough that I thought the call might have been dropped. "You need to talk to my husband. It's his mom's house."

His mom? I'd been under the impression that Marta Jepson had no immediate family.

"Is he there?" I asked.

"Hang on a second."

While I waited, I weighed my options. If I obeyed the speed limit, I could be back in Presque

Isle in half an hour. Travis, the tractor salesman, had told me that Ethan Smith lived on the Alder Brook Road, outside Mapleton. That should be easy enough to find.

But there was a problem: As soon as his wife told him that a man was on the phone asking about his mother's house, Smith would realize I was on his trail. He'd already gotten one suspicious call from me earlier that evening, and now here was some stranger on the line claiming he was shopping for houses by the light of the crescent moon. Smith knew from Donato that I used to be a game warden. Five minutes from now, he'd be taking off for the nearest crossing into New Brunswick. Unless I found a way to convince the Canadian Border Services Agency to stop him, the customs agents would probably just wave him through the checkpoint. Maybe if I could get through to Soctomah, he could alert the CBSA.

My mind was racing through the options when the line went dead. I checked the signal. One bar. Had she hung up on me, or had I lost the signal?

I sprinted for the Cutlass and slid behind the wheel. I turned the sedan around in Jepson's drive and floored the gas pedal. At that moment, I would have traded my soul for the V-6 engine in my old patrol truck.

I picked up a cell tower again when I hit the Caribou Road. Three bars showed on my screen. I braked hard and pulled onto the gravel shoulder. It was lucky I didn't slide into a ditch.

I was scrolling through the recent numbers for Soctomah's direct line when a realization came to me. The woman I'd spoken with had never said she was married to Ethan Smith. She only said that she and her husband lived in Presque Isle. Nearly ten thousand other people did, as well. I opened the browser on my cell and found a reverse White Pages site. I typed the number from the FOR SALE sign into the search bar.

Please, God, I thought, let it be a landline—one with a name and address attached to it.

The screen instantly showed a map of Presque Isle with a street address, but it wasn't Alder Brook Road. The name associated with the number wasn't Ethan Smith, either.

It was Jason Decoster.

37

The name of the first man Kathy had shot and killed was Jacques Decoster.

Jason Decoster had to be his son.

That meant Marta Jepson had been the abused woman whom Kathy had saved from being beaten to death so many years ago. She must have changed her last name after her husband died. And then, five days ago, she'd taken a mysterious fall

360

down her basement stairs. The timing of her so-called accident—the day after Jimmy Gammon was shot, when Kathy's face was everywhere in the news—couldn't have been a coincidence.

A fat little boy had been at the house on the night Jacques Decoster died. Kathy had told me that the son had witnessed the event, seen her shoot a hole in his father's chest. Jason had carried the horrible memory inside his heart, until one day he had turned on the TV, and there was the woman who had gunned down his father. It must have seemed like a ghost from his past had appeared with another man's blood on her hands.

"Revenge can be a powerful motivator," Billy Cronk had told me back at the prison.

But why would Jason Decoster kill his mom? You would have thought the child of a wife beater would side with his mother, but sons can have sentimental fantasies about their absent fathers, as I well knew. Maybe he blamed Marta for everything that had gone wrong in his life ever since. And seeing Kathy Frost on television might have been like throwing gasoline on coals that had been smoldering a very long time.

Erik Eklund hadn't recognized Marta Jepson's name, but Kurt knew who she was. Maybe Kathy had talked with her brother about the old woman. He'd told me how guilty his sister had felt about killing Jacques Decoster. When Kurt saw that clipping on the coffee table, that keen brain of his had made the connection: Jepson had died suspiciously just two days before his sister herself was attacked. What were the odds of something like that happening? Kurt was a gambler, and he would know.

And so Kurt Eklund had raced off to his own death. Because what other explanation could there be for the abandoned vehicle? Kurt had found Marta Jepson's son, and he had paid the price for his own reckless desire for revenge.

That, at least, was how I imagined the events might have unfolded. I had no evidence to prove my theory, but it turned what seemed like random puzzle pieces into a completed picture inside my brain. I knew I was right, just as surely as Kurt had known as he drove to that fateful meeting with Decoster.

The question remained whether I could convince anyone else.

The problem I faced was time. The Canadian border was only miles away, and Jason Decoster could slip across it as easily as I had imagined Ethan Smith might. When this was over, I'd owe the MP an apology for suspecting him.

I tried Soctomah's number and landed, as usual, in his voice mail.

"Lieutenant, it's Mike Bowditch. I'm up in Aroostook County, and I think I know who shot Kathy Frost. If I'm right, it's the son of the man she killed twenty-something years ago. His name is Jason Decoster, and he lives on the Lake Josephine Road in Presque Isle. His mother, Marta Jepson, fell down her basement steps five days ago. I think her son might have pushed her. There's a good chance that he killed Kurt Eklund, too. Kurt was up here snooping around before he disappeared. I know this probably sounds crazy, but you need to alert the Canadians to stop Decoster if he tries to cross the border. I'm afraid I might have spooked him into running. Call me back, and I'll try to explain this better."

I hung up in despair. How could I expect Soctomah to take me seriously? For all I knew, the state police had already looked into Jason Decoster and dismissed him as a suspect for legitimate reasons. There wasn't anyone else I could call who might believe me, and every minute I sat in my car, the odds increased that Decoster would get away.

There was no choice but to drive down to Presque Isle. I had the grim feeling I might be following in the same steps that had led Kurt Eklund to his death. My only hope was that Soctomah would get my message in time and that he would believe my ravings.

My GPS showed the Lake Josephine Road as being on the southeast side of Presque Isle. It seemed to run through an open expanse of what I assumed were potato fields, given the absence of intersecting roads on the map. The house was less than seven miles from the New Brunswick border if a man had an ATV and was willing to drive it cross-country.

I pushed the Cutlass as hard as it would go, clutching the wheel tightly with my bandaged hands, waiting for a return call from Soctomah that never came. I kept expecting to be stopped by a deputy or state trooper as I raced down Route 1 at seventy miles per hour.

As I neared Presque Isle, I was forced to hit the brakes suddenly when a huge bird rocketed across both lanes of traffic, just feet in front of my windshield. At first, I thought the dark, flapping thing was an owl—but it wasn't. Some predator had frightened a hen turkey out of her roost.

Three decades ago, there were no wild turkeys at all in Maine. The species had been wiped out by hunters as thoroughly as the woodland caribou. Then wildlife biologists had brought a couple of dozen birds back from Vermont and let them loose in the woods of southernmost Maine. The turkeys bred and spread, until they were considered such an agricultural pest that farmers were given permits to shoot them almost on sight. The department estimated that there were now sixty thousand of them running wild in the state of Maine.

Kathy had been shot by a gun loaded with metal pellets designed to kill turkeys. I kept telling myself that I wasn't superstitious, but how could I not view the freak appearance of this bird in my headlights as anything but an omen? I drove a little more cautiously the rest of the way.

In Presque Isle, I took a left at the stoplight on Academy Street and soon found myself leaving a suburban neighborhood of neo-colonial homes and ranch houses for the wide-open agricultural fields at the edge of town. There was a thin sliver of moon dangling like an ornament in the night sky. It wasn't bright enough to obscure the wheeling constellations overhead: Hercules and Scorpius and Leo. There were no streetlights along the Lake Josephine Road, and it felt like I was driving across the High Plains.

The homes stood far apart from one another here, as if the people who owned them were standoffish and didn't want anyone to know their business. I glanced at the GPS and saw that the address given for Decoster indicated the house should be coming up soon. I topped a small rise and found myself looking across a bowl-shaped expanse. On the far side of the bowl was a lighted building.

The lot had been carved out of the still-brown fields, with only a line of trees in the back to serve as a windbreak. The house itself—a feature-less two-story structure, big enough for a large family—appeared to be new. In the yard were several young evergreens that might have been dropped into waiting holes that very morning. There was an attached garage, also lighted, with open doors revealing two big pickups parked inside, one of which had a raised suspension for mudding. There was a separate shed for the owner's snowmobiles and ATVs.

I rolled slowly to a stop about a hundred feet down the road. There was no traffic out here in the middle of nowhere, and I saw no obvious way to approach the home on foot and unseen. The only option I could see was to sit and wait. Either Soctomah would call me back or Decoster would take off in his truck and I would give chase, hoping that the poky little Cutlass could keep up with his big V-8 engine. I thought longingly of my Walther PPK/S in a locker at the state police headquarters and of Deb Davies's LadySmith revolver lying in toxic muck at the bottom of a quarry. I had never felt so frustrated.

Although the moon wasn't that bright, I found that I could see quite a distance under the stars. From this vantage, I had a view of the backyard, which was outfitted with one of those elaborate wooden play sets that had replaced the metal jungle gyms of my childhood in backwoods Maine. For a moment, I thought I saw two bobbing lights flickering in the tree line, and then they were gone. They had looked like the headlights of an all-terrain vehicle.

I peered over the steering wheel to survey the

road ahead. Several hundred yards in the distance there seemed to be another rise. If I parked beyond the ridge, I might be able to get down to the line of trees and move in secret to the spot where I'd glimpsed the four-wheeler.

I was reaching for the keys when the front door of the house opened and a woman stepped outside and stared intently in the direction of the Cutlass. She seemed to pose in the glow of the floodlights mounted above her head, as if she wanted me to see her watching the car. She was short, dark-haired, a little overweight. She was wearing a puffy pink jacket and acid-washed jeans tucked into farmer's boots. Her hands were in her coat pockets. I had no doubt it was the woman I'd spoken to on the phone: Decoster's wife.

She took her hand out of her jacket, and I saw she was holding something. It was a phone. Was she calling the cops about the suspicious vehicle parked down the road from her house? Was she giving the license plate number to the dispatcher?

The woman nodded, then put the phone back in her pocket and started down the concrete steps, headed in my direction. She didn't seem in any hurry to approach the car. In fact, she seemed to be almost literally dragging her feet. I couldn't blame her for being cautious.

She hardly looked threatening, but I felt an urge to restart the car and hit the gas. Instead, I stuck my phone in my pocket and rolled down the back window, since the driver's was still stuck. A chilly breeze blew the smell of newly turned earth into the car. I shivered and waited for the woman to come closer. She paused a while in my blind spot and then came near the vehicle, approaching it via the middle of the road, right where the snowplows had shaved the center line down to nothing. She stopped just behind the rear door. Eklund had managed to knock the side mirror a-kilter, so I couldn't see her there. I was forced to turn my head.

"Are you OK, mister?" She had a tremor in her voice that hadn't been there when I called about the house.

"Sorry. I didn't mean to make you nervous. I just pulled over to talk on my phone."

"We didn't know what you were doing out here."

"Just taking a call."

"You're the guy who called about the house, ain't you?"

In the faint starlight, I couldn't make out her features clearly, but I could tell that she had a fat lip. One corner of her mouth was as purple as a crushed plum.

Like father, like son, I thought. I had been angry before, but now my heart was burning, as if it had been tossed onto a fire. The son of a bitch. The murdering, wife-beating son of a bitch.

"I'm the one who called," I said.

She started to tremble. It was as if a cold wind had come up, causing her to shiver. But there was no wind.

"Fuck, fuck, fuck, fuck."

She seemed so scared. I wanted to help her. "It's OK."

She reached into the pocket of her jacket again, and this time she drew out a small black pistol. She pointed it at my head.

"No, it's not."

38

G et out of the car," she said. "I'm a good shot. Don't think I won't shoot you."

I had let my anger make me stupid. Driving here unarmed. Allowing this woman to approach the car. And then dropping my guard while I indulged my sympathy for an abused wife. I would deserve whatever happened to me.

Her hands were shaking. That was not good. Being terrified made her more likely to pull the trigger. I needed to calm her nerves while I came up with an escape plan.

I raised my hands from the wheel so she could see them. "Easy."

"Get out of the car." Her words didn't have any force behind them. She seemed to be acting on someone else's orders.

"I need to reach down to open the door," I said.

"No! I'll do it."

She lunged for the door handle with one hand, keeping the other gripped tightly on the pistol. I believed her when she said she was a good shot. She lifted the door latch and jumped back as if a firecracker had been thrown at her feet.

Keeping my bandaged hands raised, I slid my knees out from beneath the steering wheel, placed my feet firmly on the asphalt, and rose to a standing position with my back to the car.

"You don't have to do this," I said.

"Do what?"

"Follow Jason's orders."

Her sorrowful laugh told me all I needed to know about how she viewed this suggestion.

"Walk around the front of the car," she said.

"Where are we going?"

"Walk out into the field and keep walking until I tell you to stop."

I was bigger and stronger than she was. It occurred to me that my chances would be fair if I spun around and threw myself at her without warning. But I wasn't yet willing to risk my life on one desperate gamble, not when I still had time to assess the situation without getting my head blown off.

I took a step onto the sandy shoulder and then another into the salt-killed weeds along the irrigation ditch.

"Stop!" she said.

I turned my head slowly and saw that she was staring at my back. I was wearing Soctomah's windbreaker. I had forgotten that there was a word stenciled in white across the shoulders.

"You're a cop?"

I felt that I had play now but wasn't sure how to use it. "I am."

"Where's your gun?"

"I'm not wearing one."

"Stop right there!"

I was hesitant to turn my neck to see what she was doing. I stood as motionless as a mannequin. There was a long moment when I wasn't sure what was happening.

"He says he's a cop," she said into her cell phone.

The overloud mumble of a man's voice carried through the speaker.

"Where's your badge?" she asked, repeating the phrase like a parrot.

"Back in the car. Do you want me to get it for you?"

"He says it's in the car." She paused, listening to her husband's instructions.

She directed her next words at me: "Just keep walking."

The ATV lights snapped on again in the distance, directly in front of us. I took another step into the furrowed potato field, heading for the tree line.

"What's your name, ma'am?" I asked.

"It doesn't matter."

"The state police are on their way here now. They know what you and your husband did."

"I didn't do nothing!"

I could hear her footsteps behind me and judged that she was following at a distance of ten to fifteen feet. The soil had soaked up a lot of rain and was tacky beneath my boots.

"You helped your husband kill a man name Kurt Eklund. He went to Marta Jepson's house because he suspected her death was connected to the shooting of a game warden named Kathy Frost, and he was grasping at straws. He saw the phone number on the 'For Sale' sign and called here, but he didn't realize he was talking to the son of Jacques Decoster. You and Jason lured Kurt out here, and you killed him. Then you helped your husband dispose of the SUV."

"I don't know what you're talking about."

"We found the abandoned vehicle in the rest stop where you two left it. I'm guessing your husband drove down to Medway in the Nissan, with you following in one of your trucks. You turned around there and started north again to that parking lot. Then your husband jumped into your pickup and you headed back to Presque Isle. Jason wanted the police to think that Kurt Eklund never made it up to Aroostook County. That's how we know you were his accomplice."

I was trying to walk as slowly as possible to let my words settle in.

"Did you help to dispose of the body, too?" I asked.

"Shut up!"

"Kurt Eklund is buried in this field, isn't he? After I called you, Jason got scared. That's what he's doing down there, digging up the body of the man you two killed."

"I didn't kill no one!"

She was so pumped full of adrenaline now that even the slightest flinch might cause her to pull the trigger. I was taking a big risk, getting her so worked up.

"But your husband did," I said. "He killed Kurt Eklund. And he pushed his own mother down her stairs. Her death wasn't an accident, was it?"

She remained silent

I decided that the time had come to take a gamble. I stopped in my tracks but kept my hands raised.

"Keep walking!" she said.

I needed to find what the self-defense instructors called a "break state": a split second where her mind was diverted from pulling the trigger. "What kind of man murders his own mother?"

"She shouldn't have called the cops on her husband. That's what Jason always says to me."

"He says that when he hits you?"

Her voice went soft. "Jason doesn't know his own strength sometimes."

I saw her shadow grow larger beside me on the ground. She was almost within reach. I pivoted toward her, keeping my hands raised.

"Don't turn around!"

"How many children do you have?" I asked.

She didn't answer, but the frown on her face told me the Decosters had a family.

"What do you think's going to happen to your kids when the state police get here?"

She glanced at the house but kept the pistol barrel leveled at my chest.

"If you kill me—or if Jason does—you're never going to see them again. Do you think they let cop killers see their babies in prison? You're going to die inside the Supermax without even seeing their faces one last time."

"Stop it!"

I heard an engine roar to life in the distance. Jason Decoster was getting nervous about his wife. I was running out of time.

"It doesn't have to be that way," I said. "If you surrender, the prosecutor will take it into account. You still have a chance to watch your babies grow up."

The roar of the ATV grew louder and louder. I moved my head toward the line of trees and saw the headlights—like the close-set eyes of a mechanical monster—bearing down on me. I had hoped to distract Jason's wife long enough to grab the pistol away from her, but now I saw her stumbling away, nearly falling backward to get herself clear of what she knew was about to happen.

I turned and planted my feet as the four-wheeler barreled down on me. I held my arms out and lowered my center of gravity. The trick was to time my leap to the last-possible second.

Jason Decoster revved the engine and charged me like a bull driven to madness in the bullring. The man riding it was nothing but a huge shadow. I could see the outline of his humpbacked shoulders and his enormous head. Then the machine was upon me.

The ATV had a winch and a metal cargo rack on the front. I must have struck my foot on it as I threw myself clear of the vehicle. Pain shivered up the nerves of my leg from my ankle to my thigh. And I landed face-first in the dirt.

Decoster was an experienced rider. He pulled the handlebars around sharply, causing the rear wheels to spin out, like a hot rodder doing a doughnut on a darkened stretch of highway. In seconds, he managed to turn the machine in a complete circle, but now he was only yards away, and I was lying prone on the ground with a barking ankle.

As he accelerated, I somehow managed to roll to one side. I saw his front wheel pass, and then his motorcycle boot resting on the footrest. The back tire spit mud in my face as he missed me for the second time.

He braked hard and turned the handlebars as far as they would go. I knew this was my last chance. As the four-wheeler swung around broadside, I pushed myself up onto my arms, raised one of my knees, and used the leverage of the earth to hurl myself at him. He hadn't expected the attack, because he barely had time to raise his elbow to protect his head. I grabbed him around both shoulders and we toppled over the ATV.

The man was enormous. If he hadn't been standing on the footrests with his ass hanging over the seat, I doubt I could have unhorsed him. Both of us landed awkwardly: Decoster on his shoulder and bent arm, me with half of my body on top of him and my legs dragging in the dirt. My forehead knocked the side of his skull, hard enough that a phosphorous flash exploded in my eyes.

Decoster didn't seem to have had any self-defense training; he was probably too big to have ever needed any. From a young age, he had learned that all he had to do was use his considerable size and weight to maneuver his opponent around beneath him. Just pin the poor kid's arms down with his knees and start whaling away with both of his rocklike fists.

My body registered what he was trying to do without the recognition even traveling through the neurons of my brain. It was all muscle memory on my part, gained through hours of practice. My body still belonged to a cop, and that was how I reacted.

Decoster pushed with his free arm into my chest, trying to flip himself on top of me. Rather than get pinned under his weight, I moved my arms from his shoulders to his neck. I pushed myself up onto my knees so that we were facing each other. For a split second, I found myself staring into the eyes of a living caveman who had stepped out of a museum diorama. He had greasy hair, a heavy brow that could shatter your knuckles if you threw a punch against it, deep-set brown eyes full of rage, and a huge stubbled jaw.

I reared up on my knees, wrapped my left arm around his neck, and grabbed my left hand with my right. He drove himself into me until I was flat on my back, but that was what I'd wanted. I had my arm against his windpipe now. I brought my legs up around his fat ass, crossed my ankles together, and extended my thighs. The move is called a guillotine choke. Slowly, I was stopping the flow of air to his brain. He tried using his fat chest to crush my rib cage, but the angle was wrong. Then he began clawing at my face with his clumsy fingers. I turned my head away, craning my neck as far as it would go, and kept pushing my arm against his trachea, hoping to hear the cartilage crack.

Decoster was growing desperate. No one had taught him how to escape this chokehold. He should have been pushing my legs away from his hips, not fumbling for my face. Eventually, he began clutching at my right hand, hoping to break the grip, but by then it was too late. He could no longer breathe at all.

He thrashed and flailed his arms and tried to roll over, but the guillotine works whether the attacker is lying on his side or on his back. I never heard a crack—his windpipe was too well protected by the blubber in his neck—but his movements began to slow, as if he had lost conviction. I didn't know if he knew was dying, but I wanted the thought to pass through his brain before it ran out of oxygen.

Eventually, he stopped moving altogether. I wanted to kill him. The desire to strangle him to death was nearly overwhelming.

But I couldn't. It was as if some gentle hand was pulling me off the man and a soft voice was whispering "Enough" in my ear. When Decoster had finally stopped struggling and I was sure he wasn't playing possum, I found myself releasing my grip and letting my legs fall loose.

I'd had my eyes squeezed shut through most of our wrestling match, afraid he might gore them out. When I opened them, I saw his wife standing over us with her hand over her mouth and a look of shock on her face. The pistol hung at her side.

"Did you . . . Did you kill him?"

As out of breath as I was, I had difficulty spitting out the word *no*.

I became aware of the sound of the idling ATV

engine. She was standing in the glow of its head-lights, so that half of her face was illuminated and half was a black mask. She raised her arm until the barrel was weaving back and forth between my exhausted body and her husband's unconscious one.

"People deserve the bad things that happen to them," she said, more to herself than to me. "Yeah, they do."

I took a breath, trying frantically to think what I could say to stop her.

In the end, it didn't matter. She dropped the gun in the mud and then turned and walked in silence back to the house, where her children were sleeping.

39

I sat on the ATV and waited for Decoster to wake up. It was a Yamaha Grizzly: the high-end 700 FI model, painted in stealth black. I had no handcuffs or plastic cable ties to secure the big man's wrists. There was some rope stowed with my gear in the back of the car, but I didn't like the idea of leaving him alone until the state police arrived.

Not having heard from Soctomah, I called the dispatcher in Houlton. It took a while to explain what had happened. I started in the wrong place, talking about how Kathy had been shot, when I should just have said, "There is a dead body here, and I'm holding a gun on the man who killed him." I didn't know for certain that Kurt's corpse was in a hole down along the tree line, but I was willing to wager on it.

I had maneuvered the Yamaha around so that the headlights would shine in Decoster's eyes if he lifted his head. He was lying on his back, with his arms and legs spread, as if enjoying a snooze. I leaned over the handlebars and looked at him. Destiny had been right about the unibrow and about the hair that sprouted from his unbuttoned shirt and ran all the way around his neck. He was wearing dark brown Carhartt bib coveralls over a tan chamois shirt. I estimated his weight to be about 250 pounds.

The thought occurred to me that I could simply rev the engine and crush his spine under the saw-toothed tires, but I had already called the police and committed myself to a different course of action. There would be no vigilante justice tonight, not unless he forced me to use the pistol. It was a Glock 17. The magazine was fully loaded with hollow-tipped 9mm cartridges. I had made certain of it.

Jason Decoster began coming around in a few minutes. It was a slow, strange process, which I observed with the detachment of a scientist. His chest began to rise and fall, and then his limbs went rigid, almost as if he were undergoing rigor mortis before my eyes. It took a few more minutes for him to groan and raise his mud-smeared head. He squinted into the blinding beams of his own four-wheeler.

"Huh?" he said.

"Stay down, or I'm going to put seventeen bullets in you."

"What?"

I couldn't tell if his synapses were having trouble flickering back to life after I'd put out his fuse box, or if he was just a moron. The possibilities weren't mutually exclusive.

"Just don't move."

His head slumped back into the damp soil and he crossed his hands over his heart the way you see corpses arranged in coffins. I found myself hoping he'd try something so I would have an excuse to shoot him. I was having a hard time ridding myself of the murderous impulse.

"Why did you do it?" I asked.

"Do what?" His voice sounded peaceful. He seemed content to lie on the cold ground.

"Murder your mother, shoot Kathy Frost, kill Kurt Eklund."

"No idea what you're talking about."

Every cop learns not to trust appearances. Jason Decoster might have looked like an extra who had walked off the set of *Quest for Fire*, but he was no idiot.

"I'm guessing that you ditched the shotgun you used on Kathy," I said. "But they're going to find Kurt Eklund's body down at the end of your field. Too bad you didn't have time to move it after I called your wife."

He kept his eyes closed and a faint smile spread across his ugly face, as if he were asleep and enjoying a pleasant dream. He had no plans of saying a word to me. I could only keep goading him and hope for a slip.

"So what's the story? You wanted vengeance for your old man. The same guy who used to beat your mom with a belt. I'm betting he beat you, too. But you forgot all about the whippings after the nasty game warden put a hole in him. Poor Jason. It must have made you so angry to think about all those women who deserved to be punished—your mother, the warden, your wife. I bet you had all sorts of dark fantasies. You thought about what you'd do if you ever had a chance to get back at that bitch warden."

He yawned.

My ankle throbbed from where I'd knocked it against the side of the all-terrain vehicle. "And then one day, you hear on the news that she's shot another guy. And you think to yourself, My chance has come. Because the police are going to assume her death was an act of revenge over the soldier she'd just killed. They won't look back twenty-five years—"

"Twenty-eight years," he said.

"What?"

"My dad was murdered twenty-eight years ago."

I sat up on the padded ATV seat. "You blamed your mom for what happened to him, didn't you? That's why you killed her."

"My dad was tough on us, but so what? That's what fathers are supposed to be. And that stupid old bitch took him away from me. If she hadn't called the cops—" Decoster seemed to catch himself. "My mother was an old woman. She fell down the stairs."

It wasn't the full confession I needed. "We'll see if your wife tells the same story."

The threat amused him. "She can't testify against me."

"What's her name, by the way?" I asked. "Your wife, I mean."

"Trisha."

"How many kids do you have?"

"Three."

"The Supermax doesn't allow contact visits, even from family members, so don't plan on holding them for a while. You're never going to fuck another woman again, by the way. Why don't you lie there in the mud and let those facts sink in."

"When are the real cops getting here?"

I'd thought that because he had anger issues, it wouldn't take much to work him into a violent rage. But Jason Decoster reserved his fury for the people in his life who had hurt him personally. I was nobody to him, just a voice in the dark.

"I was there that night, you know? I was the guy who drove up in the Bronco, the one who shot at you."

He opened his eyes.

"If it wasn't for me, you would've finished the job. But I scared you off and saved Kathy Frost's life. You'll see her when she testifies at your trial. I'll be there, too. It'll be a grand reunion."

He rolled over, lifted himself onto his shoulder, and squinted back into the headlights. "Go fuck yourself."

Blue lights were twirling up on the road. The state police had finally decided to show up.

I gave my statement to a trooper named O'Keefe. He said he was a sergeant at the Houlton barracks. We stood in the potato field, talking, while other officers appeared on the scene. We watched two deputies lead Decoster in handcuffs to a waiting cruiser. Another local cop escorted Trisha out the front door with her hands behind her back. The woman screamed back at the house, words directed at the children inside, who would soon be in the custody of social workers from the Department of Human Services.

"I love you!"

I doubted the kids even heard her.

Sergeant O'Keefe asked me where I'd first seen the headlights of the ATV, and I pointed at the line of trees across the field.

"I think he was trying to dig up the body and move it off the property," I said. "My call from his mother's house had rattled him. I haven't been down there yet."

He looked like most of the troopers I'd met: tall, wide-shouldered, hair barbered down to bare skin. "I heard you used to be a warden."

"Until two months ago."

He motioned for me to accompany him.

It was a beautiful evening. Overhead, chip notes sounded in the sky at random intervals—a flight of warblers was migrating on the southwest breeze. I almost forgot about my sprained ankle.

We followed the tire tracks down to the tree line. A tumbled old wall of stones ran away from us into the darkness. It reminded me of the rock walls on Kathy's land. The two farms had a similar feel to them.

"I shouldn't be letting you down here," he said, making sure I understood the courtesy he was extending me.

"I appreciate it."

On the far side of the newly green oaks an oblong hole had been dug into the ground. Nearby, a shovel stood upright in a mound of damp soil. The trooper shined his flashlight into the shallow grave. Decoster had worked fast. He had gotten all the way down to the black trash bags in which he had wrapped Kurt Eklund's corpse.

"You think that's him?" O'Keefe asked.

"I don't know who else it would be."

"We have to wait for the evidence techs to open it up."

I wasn't particularly certain my stomach could stand seeing Kurt's one-eyed face again.

Another trooper came across the field, holding a flashlight in one hand and a BlackBerry in the other.

"It's for you," he said.

I took the phone. "Hello?"

"Bowditch? It's Soctomah."

"I thought you might have gone on vacation or something."

"I was at Maine Med."

I held my breath, realizing he had news.

"She's awake," he said.

"And?"

"She's having a little trouble speaking, but the neurologist says it could just be a side effect of the coma. They need to do some testing. She doesn't remember much of anything about that night."

"What have you told her?"

"As little as possible. I heard you found a body. Is it definitely Eklund?"

"We're waiting for the forensic guys to unwrap the trash bags. But yeah, I'm pretty sure."

"How the hell did he know about Jason Decoster?"

"I don't think he did," I said. "He drove out to Marta Jepson's house because Kathy had said something to him about her death sounding suspicious. He called a phone number on a sign, hoping it might lead him somewhere. He was a bright guy, but he was drunk and not thinking rationally. It was easy for Jason and Trisha to lure him down to Presque Isle and then ambush him. Tell me something: Was Jason Decoster even on your list of suspects?"

"We were looking into Kathy's entire history."

In other words, no. "That's what I thought."

"I'll be there soon—I'm flying up in an hour—and you can pick apart our investigation to your heart's delight."

I wasn't pissed off at the lieutenant so much as angry and sad about the entire sequence of events. "So who's going to break the news to the Eklunds about their son?"

"Once we have a positive ID on the body, Malcomb will do it."

"Did he tell Kathy about her dog yet?"

"She was asking about him. I think she sensed something."

I didn't need to ask how that scene had gone. "What do you want me to do until you get here?"

"There's a room booked for you at the

387

Northeastland in Presque Isle. Go get some sleep. You and I can talk in the morning."

By Aroostook standards, the hotel was an expensive place to spend the night. "Who paid for my room?"

"The wardens chipped in on it when they heard you'd caught the son of a bitch."

40

The next morning, Soctomah met me in the breakfast room at the Northeastland Hotel. He put a tape recorder on the plate beside my eggs and asked me to go through the series of decisions that had led me to Aroostook County. He'd been up all night, flying under the stars to the Northern Maine Regional Airport, then watched quietly while his forensics team removed Kurt Eklund's plastic-wrapped body from the grave. The techs had scanned the corpse's fingers and pulled the prints off the database to make a positive ID. Kurt had been arrested on multiple occasions for drunk driving and public intoxication. His biometric data was just a click away in the system.

"How do you feel about flying back to Augusta in the same plane with the body?" Soctomah asked. He looked weary.

"As long as I get the window seat."

What was there left for me to do but joke about it?

He stared at me over the rim of his coffee mug. "What do you think we should have done that we didn't do?"

I pushed my scrambled eggs aside. "Nothing. Kurt Eklund had a death wish."

"It sounds like he wanted one last chance to be a hero."

"I'm not going to begrudge him that." I took a sip of my own coffee and found it had grown cold. "Has Malcomb told his parents yet?"

"Yes."

"What about Kathy?"

"They asked to break the news to her." He glanced at his wristwatch. "You'd better finish eating. You have a plane to catch."

"What are you going to do?"

"Knock on a bunch of doors around here that I should've tried a few days ago."

I reached into the duffel at my feet and handed him back the windbreaker he had loaned me. In return, he gave me back my Walther. I hefted the pistol in my palm, feeling its familiar weight, and tucked it in the back of my pants.

The plane was a propeller-driven Cessna 182. I stood aside while an evidence technician and a deputy medical examiner manhandled the body bag from the wheeled gurney into the space behind the rear seats. The plane was small, and it was a tight squeeze. Because of the weight of the load (four bodies, three living), the tech stayed behind while the coroner and I clambered into the available seats. The pilot put me up front. It didn't bother me, having some distance from the dead man.

The 182 had a bigger engine than the 172 Skyhawk that Stacey Stevens flew. I hadn't thought of her in a few days, but now I found myself wishing that she was the one flying this plane and not some middle-aged dude with a cheek stuffed full of Black Jack chewing gum. I hadn't been this lonely in days.

At first, the pilot tried to make conversation over the intercom, but the deputy medical examiner—a graying woman with tightly bound hair and even a tighter face—was in less of a talkative mood than I was.

At least Kurt had died in a heroic attempt to find his sister's assailant. All of his adult life, he'd been searching for some opportunity to atone for one bad night in Vietnam. It might have been a foolish quest—but so what? The only difference between his efforts and mine was that he was lying cold in the rear of the plane and my heart was bruised but still beating.

Mostly, I found myself worrying about Kathy. I had witnessed the effects of brain injuries in too many people to count. Nearly every family I'd met in the boonies had a brother who'd crashed his snowmobile into a tree or an uncle who'd wrapped his Mustang around a telephone pole. Some of these invalids were near vegetables. The others were even scarier. They reminded me of zombies: shambling, unreasoning creatures who were no longer recognizable as the self-directed human beings they once had been.

Jimmy Gammon had suffered a traumatic injury when the IED had exploded in that pile of garbage. His mother had no longer been able to identify his personality as belonging to her son. I was terrified of finding Kathy similarly altered beyond recognition.

Flying from Houlton to Augusta, we covered most of the state of Maine. The land turned greener and greener beneath us, from a pale, almost yellowish tone that reminded me of the pea soup my French-Canadian relatives used to serve us when I was a kid to a deep, almost jungle-green color down south. There were still a few threadbare hillsides and valleys that the sun hadn't yet warmed—where you could see winter hanging around in the shadows—but those chilly corners would be gone in a matter of weeks.

We passed from the potato fields of Aroostook County over the commercial timberland east of Baxter State Park. It was a clear day and the summit of Katahdin was bright white with unmelted snow, which caught the glare of the rising run. Then we were flying over fields again: hardscrabble farms carved out of the second-growth forest and great fenced pastures full of white dairy cows. My window faced west, not east, so I had no view of Appleton Ridge or the Camden Hills. Mine was an inland perspective.

I did see a great many turkeys bobbing along at the weedy edges of the cow and sheep farms. Hunters, too, although they were inevitably set up in blinds far from the nearest flocks. The season would be over in a few days, and, as usual, most of the big toms would survive to service their harems. Next year, there would be even more poults.

We landed at the Augusta State Airport, where we were met by another emergency vehicle, this one owned by the state medical examiner's office. Men were waiting to remove Kurt Eklund's body from the plane. I started to unhook my headset, but the pilot reached over and gripped my left wrist.

"This is just a pit stop," he said over the intercom. "You and I are headed for Portland."

It always amazed me how quickly a small plane could get up and down. We weren't more than ten minutes on the tarmac in Augusta, and then we were zipping along the runway again, my stomach pressed against my spine. The next thing I knew, I was looking up at a cloud as the nose of the Cessna pointed skyward.

"This won't take more than fifteen minutes," the pilot assured me. "Are you feeling airsick?"

"I have a pretty strong stomach."

"That's what they all say!"

He waggled the wings to be funny, but my mood was too heavy for him to lift.

We landed at the Portland International Jetport exactly fifteen minutes later and taxied to one of the private hangars on the east side of the terminal. I saw a teal-blue GMC Sierra parked in the lot. I recognized it as one of the Warden Service's unmarked patrol trucks.

Major Malcomb was waiting for me inside the hangar. The cavernous space smelled of petroleum products, and a radio was blasting classic country for the mechanics' listening pleasure. I couldn't remember the last time I'd heard Hank Williams.

"Thank you for flying with us," the pilot said as I handed him my headset. "We hope you enjoy your stay in Portland or wherever your final destination may take you."

I felt a little sorry for him. He had tried so hard to coax a smile out of me.

The only luggage I was carrying was my waxed canvas duffel. I'd packed it with all the personal items I thought were worth keeping—my tent, my Snow & Nealley kindling ax. I'd left the rest in the trunk of Kurt Eklund's Cutlass.

The more you know, the less you carry. That was a saying they used in wilderness-survival schools, but it applied to more than just bushcraft.

Malcomb grabbed the bag away from me before I had a chance to resist. He tossed it into the backseat, beside the locked case in which he kept his AR-15 rifle. He'd done a lot of vacuuming, but the stale smell of cigarettes lingered. Regulations said he wasn't permitted to smoke inside the state-owned vehicle, but who was there to punish him now?

"How was your flight?" His throat sounded as cracked as a waterless arroyo.

"Faster than driving."

He spun the wheel in the direction of outer Congress Street and pressed the accelerator. I'd seen Maine Med standing like a citadel on the Western Promenade as the plane had turned and banked over the city.

"I heard she's awake," I said. "Soctomah said you were going to break the news to the family. How did it go?"

"It didn't come as much of a shock."

"Kurt told me he had cirrhosis. I'm guessing they'd given him up for dead a long time ago."

He'd put on his mirrored sunglasses, but I felt him glancing at me out of the corner of his eye. "How old are you again, Bowditch?"

"Twenty-seven."

"That's what I thought. Parents don't give up on their kids until they see them in a casket. Doesn't matter how old the kids are."

I leaned back against the seat, feeling properly chastened. "How did Kathy react when you told her about Pluto?"

"I think you know the answer to that question."

The major seemed unaccountably hostile. I hadn't expected a hero's welcome, but when Soctomah told me that wardens had paid for my hotel room, I'd experienced a brief period of forgiveness, as if I might be welcomed back into the fold.

We crossed the Stroudwater bridge, headed toward downtown Portland. A snowy egret was standing in the tidal muck, one leg tucked beneath its tail feathers. I saw its bright yellow foot. I unrolled the automatic window and let the salt air clear away some of the tobacco reek.

Malcomb pushed a button on his door and my window rolled back up.

"I suppose you heard the latest about the colonel," he said.

"No."

"Harkavy announced his resignation last night."

Colonel Duane Harkavy had been both my commanding officer and my personal nemesis for as long as I could remember. In my mind, he'd represented everything wrong with the Warden Service—the resistance to new ideas, the cronyism that rewarded political savvy over experience in the field, the sexism toward female officers. I had a hard time imagining the department without him. I should have been hopeful about the future, but Malcomb's sourness suggested he wasn't planning on throwing his hat in the ring.

"Does that make you the acting colonel?" I asked.

"Until the commissioner replaces me, it does."

We paused at a stoplight. Malcomb wasn't upset because he had inherited the job; he was upset because he would never be allowed to keep it. His new boss, the current commissioner, was an incompetent bureaucrat who didn't give a shit about protecting the state's natural resources. She was just a shill appointed by a governor who cared even less about Maine's environment.

"You did a good job up there," Malcomb said out of the blue.

"Thanks."

"I don't think I could have stopped myself from shooting the guy, but you did the right thing."

"I'm still not convinced."

His eyes never left the road as we crossed the busy intersection at St. John Street. "I read Tate's report about that incident at the quarry, too."

It didn't sound like a question, so I didn't reply.

"You did an exit interview when you resigned from the service," he said. "Who did it? Peasely?"

"Yes."

"Did he mention that you had a year to rethink the decision? If there's an opening, you don't need to formally reapply."

"He said the provision was applicable only if a warden left under good circumstances."

"Did he say you were fired?"

"No."

"That means you left under good circumstances."

I had never imagined that returning to the Warden Service was a possibility. I had too many enemies in the Augusta headquarters. My resignation had felt irrevocable from the moment I'd offered it.

The hospital loomed ahead.

"So I could just come back?" I said.

We entered the darkened interior of the Congress Street parking garage. "At the colonel's discretion," he said.

Or the acting colonel's, I realized.

Malcomb escorted me as far as Kathy's private room. "I'm going to get myself a cup of coffee. Do you want anything?"

"I'm good," I said.

I knocked and heard a man's voice tell me to come in. I braced myself before turning the doorknob.

Kathy's parents were seated in chairs they'd pulled up beside the bed. They both rose to their feet as I entered. The father I knew from the chapel, but the mother I recognized only as an older version of the woman I'd seen in the family photograph hanging in their dining room. Alice Eklund was as tall as her husband. Her hair had faded but still had a slightly blondish tint. There were deep folds of skin along her neck, and the blue veins were prominent in her hands. But she seemed fit and healthy for a woman in her eighties.

The hospital bed was adjustable, and Kathy had raised it so that her head and shoulders were only slightly elevated, as if sitting upright might be a step too far in her recovery. Her skin was no longer gray, but there was no other word to describe her complexion except *sickly*. Her hair hung close to her scalp, as if she'd recently been wearing a cap; the sutured wound above her ear looked painful. She was wearing actual pajamas rather than a hospital Johnny. They were white, patterned with images of Walt Disney's cartoon character Pluto.

"Hey, Grasshopper," she said in a hoarse voice.

"Hey, yourself."

Kathy raised a hand weakly to indicate her parents. "Did you meet my folks?"

"Reverend Eklund." I extended my hand to the old man.

"Erik," he reminded me. "Alice, this is the warden we were telling you about, Kathy's friend Mike."

The old woman stepped forward and pressed both of her wrinkled hands around mine. They were ice-cold. Her eyes welled up with tears so fast that they were running down her cheeks before she could lift a tissue. "Thank you."

Erik Eklund put an arm around his wife's shoulders. "We can never repay you for what you've done for us."

"Papa," said Kathy from the bed.

"What?" asked her father.

"You're embarrassing him." She was having a hard time getting her words out, but her tongue didn't have the swollen sound of a person with a speech impediment. "Can you leave us alone? Just for a little while?"

"Of course," said her father.

Her mother wouldn't let go of me. It became a bit awkward. Her husband nearly had to pry her fingers loose.

After the door closed behind them, I remained standing at the foot of the bed, as if Kathy had a contagious disease.

"You've looked better," she said to me.

I smiled and raised my hand to the side of my face. "You should see the other guy."

"Decoster, huh?"

"It's sad about Marta Jepson."

"She asked me what she should tell Jason about that night, and I said she could blame me. I'm sure he grew up hating my guts. But he held it against Marta, too. I think he wanted to kill her his whole life."

"It doesn't make much sense, does it? The son avenging his abusive father."

"I think I heard that story before."

She gave me a faint smile to indicate that it was a joke. My own father had been a bastard, and no one had been quicker to defend him than yours truly. She waved me forward. I took a seat beside the bed. Her arm was connected to all sorts of tubes and wires, but she held out her hand to me. Her grip was so light, it was barely there.

"I'm sorry about Kurt," I said.

"You can't save someone who doesn't want to be saved."

I had learned that lesson before. But it's one you keep forgetting. "So, how are you feeling?"

"Like a pincushion. Or a piñata. Both, I guess."

I was trying to gauge from her speech how her mind was working. "You'd lost a lot of blood when I found you."

"They put it back. Now they're afraid I've got brain damage. The docs keep testing me. 'Count backward from twenty. Remember these three things.'"

She seemed dehydrated and more exhausted than I had ever seen her, but her thinking seemed sound enough. Whatever the doctors were giving her for the pain had left her a little loopy, though. It seemed to have the same effect as truth serum.

"You don't remember anything about that night?" I asked.

"I remember arguing with you. Did I forgive you?"

"Yes."

Her laugh was as soft as a sigh. "Of course I did."

We sat there gazing at each other. She really looked horrible with her sunken eyes and flat hair—almost as bad as my mom had on that last night of her life. I was afraid I might choke up if I didn't distract myself.

"Do you want to hear some gossip?" I asked.

"Harkavy? Yeah, I know."

"It's good for the major, though."

"He won't get the job. Doesn't kiss enough ass."

"The wardens chipped in for me to stay at the Northeastland last night."

"Fancy."

"Maybe after you get out of here, you can show me around Aroostook County. I'd like to see all your old stomping grounds."

She shook her head. "Too many memories."

The reference might have been to Jacques and Jason Decoster or to the tragic life of Marta Jepson, but my gut told me she was talking about her late husband, Darren.

She seemed eager to change the subject. "Guess who was just in here? Tate."

"I thought you two weren't supposed to communicate until the investigation is complete."

"She broke the rules."

"I don't believe it."

"You're a bad influence, Grasshopper."

I studied her smiling face, and I realized that

there was something I needed to tell her. The attorney general's investigation was still proceeding. Kathy had time to come clean.

"Kathy," I said, lowering my voice. "I know you didn't shoot Jimmy Gammon in that barn. It was Tate who killed him, but you took the blame."

Her bloodshot eyes widened. "How?"

"You kept saying to me that it wouldn't have happened if I'd been there. At first, I thought you meant it wouldn't have happened because I was more experienced. But you were speaking literally. Then, later, I found a diagram in your wastebasket. I thought it was just a doodle until I realized you were plotting out the trajectories of the two bullets. You lied in your report, Kathy. You could be prosecuted for obstructing justice."

It took her some effort, but she rolled her eyes. "Who's going to tell?"

Not me, obviously. "Tate might confess if she figures it out."

"She thinks it was me who hit him. I told her I did it, and she believes me."

"What about the ballistics investigators?"

"The bullet went through his neck. No way to tell which one hit him. But I know I missed. I plotted it out, and there was no way I could have hit him in the carotid from where I was standing."

The confession left me feeling like I'd gotten the wind knocked out of me. "Why did you lie to protect her?"

"She's a good warden. I thought she deserved more than a few second chances."

"Like me, you mean."

"Yeah."

Why should it have surprised me that the woman who had spent years stopping me from throwing away my career—who had sacrificed so much on my behalf—would do the same for another promising young warden?

"Jesus Christ, Kathy."

Her lip curled on one side, the way it did when she was being a smart aleck. "I think she has a crush on you."

"Tate?" The woman disapproved of everything I did.

"I told her you were taken, though."

I leaned back in the chair and frowned. "I'm taken? Tell that to Stacey Stevens."

"She's an idiot. She's going to end up with a dog if she isn't careful."

Without meaning to, she'd brought up a topic I'd been avoiding. "I'm sorry about Pluto."

"He was a good dog."

"The best."

A tear slid down her pale cheek.

I squeezed her hand as gently as I could, afraid of injuring her. Her eyelids lowered. "Are you getting tired?" I asked.

"A little."

"I'll come back when you have more energy."

"No. Stay."

She shut her eyes. I thought she might be falling asleep, but then she opened them again.

"When are you going to shave that fucking beard?"

41

My new vehicle was a shiny black GMC Sierra, the crew cab version with the standard box. The bed was spacious enough to carry a snowmobile or an all-terrain vehicle. The truck came with a set of tires so rugged, I felt like I could have driven it up the side of Katahdin, right into Pamola's living room. I cruised from Augusta up I-95 through Bangor, enjoying the smoothness of the acceleration, and turned east when I saw the billowing smokestacks of the Lincoln Paper and Tissue mill rising above the eastern treetops.

May had turned to June. Where there had been only dandelions before, there were now lupines growing wild in the fields: pink, blue, and white. Now you could walk through the forest and identify every tree by the shape of its newly formed leaves. Jeff Jordan had told me that the salmon were biting on Pale Evening Duns in Grand Lake Stream, which was where I was headed.

I followed Route 6 east to the crossroads, where I paused at the stop sign, thinking about the past few months. If I turned left on Route 1, the road would lead me north to Houlton, Presque Isle, and the outskirts of Maine's Swedish Colony. The Eklunds, I'd heard, were back home after a somber trip to Arlington National Cemetery. They had wanted to bury their son in the town cemetery, but Kathy had convinced them that—whatever lies Kurt might have told to win his Purple Heart—he deserved to rest in the company of heroes.

Kathy hadn't been well enough to make the trip herself; the doctors said it would take months for her wounds to heal, and even then she shouldn't expect to return to her former routines. In short, she would never be the same. The initial neurological tests showed no signs of traumatic brain injury, but she had lost her spleen, which meant that she would be more susceptible to the bacteria that cause pneumonia, meningitis, and other dangerous infections. She had survived her brush with death, but at a significant cost.

There might be additional costs yet to come. After burying their own son in the hallowed ground of Arlington, the Gammons had returned home to read the official report on the circumstances surrounding his death. The report was titled "Findings of the Attorney General in the Shooting Death of James P. Gammon by State

405

Game Wardens in Camden," and it declared that Sgt. Katarina Frost and Wdn. Danielle Tate had been justified in their use of deadly force to protect themselves from physical harm. An independent review conducted by the Maine Warden Service had arrived at the same conclusion. There was no definitive ballistic evidence to indicate which officer had killed Jimmy Gammon, but the investigators had accepted the wardens' independent statements that Sergeant Frost had fired the fatal shot.

Only two people in the world would ever know otherwise.

The newspapers said that the Gammons were still contemplating a suit against the department and the warden sergeant who'd killed their boy. The burden of proof was lower in civil cases, so it wasn't a foregone conclusion that a jury would excuse Kathy's actions. At the very least, James Gammon had the resources and connections to make her life difficult. Maine's intemperate governor had condemned the AG's report as a "whitewash" upon its release. Later I saw that the Gammons were listed as major donors to his reelection campaign.

Revenge is a powerful motivator.

I'd received a voice mail from Aimee saying that her husband had been moved back to Medium Custody for good behavior and asking why the heck I hadn't told her he'd been in the frigging

Supermax. I owed her a personal apology, especially now that I would have less time for household repairs.

Jason Decoster was being held in the Aroostook County Jail in Houlton, pending his trial for the murder of Kurt Eklund and the attempted murders of Sgt. Kathy Frost and Michael Bowditch. The investigators from the attorney general's office had been unable to prove that Marta Jepson's death had been anything but an unfortunate accident.

The Neanderthal was proving to be a most intelligent sociopath. If I hadn't caught Decoster attempting to move Kurt Eklund's corpse off his property, he might well have escaped justice. His lawyer would need to get creative to explain the dead body with the 9mm bullet in its head.

Eventually, Jason Decoster was going to find himself behind the walls of the Maine State Prison, where I had a dangerous friend who was inclined to do me favors. The truth was, though, I would never ask Billy Cronk to bloody his hands on my behalf, not when he needed to keep his nose clean to keep his sentence from being extended. I'd already had an opportunity to take revenge, and I'd been unable to pull the trigger. One of the other things I'd learned about myself over the past months was that I was no vigilante.

I gave a honk on the horn as I passed by Weatherby's. Jeff Jordan was out mowing his steep lawn, but his sweaty back was turned to the street, and he was wearing ear protectors against the noise of the engine, so he didn't hear me. I'd have to catch up with him at dinner.

I crossed the bridge over the stream and saw fishermen on both sides. Word must have gotten out about the big salmon being caught in the river. I'd come back here with Charley some evening to try our luck.

West of town, I passed the roadside memorial to the young woman who had died in the car crash. There were fresh flowers to mark the spot. White roses signified remembrance.

I could have continued on to Moosehorn Lodge and my former cabin, but I'd already hauled away the cardboard boxes containing my life's possessions, carted them off to my temporary home in southern Maine. And I hardly expected a warm welcome from Elizabeth Morse, if she even happened to be in residence. I wondered if I would ever see the lodge again, then caught myself being naive. Just because you close a chapter in a book doesn't mean you won't ever reopen it. That was another life lesson I was trying to absorb.

I made a turn onto the woods road leading to Little Wabassus. The light had a greenish quality from the sun filtering through the bunched leaves overhead. The cinnamon ferns in the ditches had unrolled their tight little fists since my last visit. As the summer progressed, some of their fronds would turn reddish brown, but on this day in early June, everything around me looked lush and full of life.

The Stevenses' house was an old lakeside camp that Charley had thoroughly overhauled. He had added ramps in the front and back for Ora's wheelchair and paved a path down to the boathouse, where he kept his floatplane and wide-beamed Grand Laker. My heart sped up when I saw that Stacey's Outback was parked beside the van with the wheelchair lift. I'd been gambling that she would be home this afternoon.

Charley was sitting in the screened-in section of the porch, enjoying a cup of coffee and the breeze lifting off the lake. When he saw my truck roll up, he sprang to his feet and hurried to the mesh door. His German shorthaired pointer, Nimrod, pushed at his knee.

"Come in quick!" said the retired pilot. "And don't bring any of them skeeters with you. This time of year, a man can lose a pint of blood going to the danged outhouse."

Charley had a colorful way of speaking, which he'd learned in the lumber camps as a boy, but I'd noticed that he saved his best bons mots for me.

"Thank God for indoor plumbing," I said.

He clapped me hard on the back, hard enough to rattle my teeth. "It's good to see you, young feller. You cleaned yourself up a dite since your last visit."

Charley Stevens had a lantern jaw, laugh wrinkles that radiated from his eyes, and a thick head of white hair that his wife trimmed for him with sewing scissors out in the yard.

"How was your Canadian vacation?" I asked.

"Just grand. The folks up in Newfoundland are the salt of the earth. I don't think I ever met a merrier bunch. There was this one pub we liked in St. John's. When Ora rolled up in her wheelchair, everyone inside would rush out to lift her through the door. And they've got the same rocky cliffs and highlands as in Scotland. It's a damn beautiful place. You need to get yourself up there, pronto."

"I'm not going to have vacation days for a while," I said.

"I expect you won't!"

"Is Ora here?"

"She's trying to teach Stacey to pickle fiddleheads. Can you believe it? I didn't think my daughter had a domestic bone in her body. 'Every day brings a new surprise,' my mother used to say." He peered into the darkened interior of the building, holding his hand flat above his eyes in imitation of a Hollywood Indian. "Where are those girls? They know we have company."

"I'm not in a rush."

"But you're not here to see a slide show of our vacation, either."

"Maybe some other time."

Charley pulled on his chin. "So Harkavy is out and Malcomb is in down in Augusta. I hope Tim is in the job long enough to make some overdue changes. The Warden Service could use a good spring cleaning."

"He's made a few changes already," I said.

Before I could say anything more, Stacey and Ora appeared in the doorway. The daughter was pushing her mother's wheelchair. They were both wearing aprons. Ora's was pristine white, while Stacey's was smeared with handprints.

"Mike!" said Ora. She had the same high cheekbones as her daughter and the same jade-green eyes. She'd pulled her hair back from her beautiful face and secured it in a small ponytail. "It's so nice to see you."

"And in uniform," said Stacey with enough of a barb to sting. "You look like a new man."

I rubbed my hand over my buzz cut. "I was getting tired of combing my hair."

"Charley told us you'd rejoined the Warden Service," said Ora. "What good news."

"I wasn't sure they'd take me back."

"After what you did for Kathy Frost? I don't see how they could have said no. How is she doing? Have you seen her?"

"She's recovering, but it's going to take a while. She's already thinking about coming back to work, but she's worried they'll put her behind a desk until she retires."

"She shouldn't hurry things," said Ora in her most motherly tone.

"Have they given you your old district back?" Charley asked.

"They offered it to me," I said. "But I said it belongs to Dani Tate now. For the time being, they're moving me around to cover vacant districts. I'm not sure where I'll end up."

Stacey untied her apron from her neck, as if she'd suddenly gotten self-conscious about it. She was wearing a waffled long underwear shirt, which clung to her chest and shoulders, and her usual blue jeans. "So what brings you back Down East?"

"I thought I might take you to dinner."

"What?"

"I have a reservation for us at Weatherby's."

"This is a joke, right?"

"We can drive around awhile, and I can show off the fancy new truck they gave me."

Charley put his hand on his wife's shoulder.

Stacey touched a loose strand of brown hair that had fallen onto her forehead. "You're asking me out on a date? In front of my parents?"

I'd had misgivings about the timing because I didn't want to put her on the spot. But I already knew I was rolling the dice. It would be a gamble however I played it.

"They're welcome to join us. But I made the reservation for two."

"That's nice of you, but we have other plans," said Ora.

Stacey glared down at her mother. "You do not!"

"So what'll it be?" I said.

"This is too weird." She gave that snorting sound she made when she was in disbelief. Then she rolled her eyes and shook her head. "I've got to take a shower."

Without another word, she stepped around the wheelchair and me and pushed open the screen door. The three of us watched her cross the pine-needled yard to her cabin.

I turned to Charley with my eyebrows raised. "Was that a yes or a no?"

"It was a yes," said Ora. Her husband's big hand was still on her shoulders. She looked up at Charley with a smile. "A man in uniform is always hard to resist."

"I always said you'd regret leaving the service," Charley said.

"You were right, as usual."

"What made you decide to come back?"

The question had been turning in my mind for weeks. Colonel Malcomb had asked me the same thing in his new office when I'd taken the oath again. I'd fumbled for an answer then, but now the words came to me clearly, as if someone else was whispering them into my ears.

"I realized it was the best job in the world."

AUTHOR'S NOTE

This book is a work of fiction, but it contains references to actual places and organizations. Among these is the 488th Military Police Company of the Maine Army National Guard, which served with distinction in the War in Afghanistan. I am grateful to Specialist Erick Helpin for educating me about the mission, equipment, and daily challenges that the "Guardians" faced at Bagram Air Base—and I honor his service and that of his company. The character of Jimmy Gammon has no real-life counterpart among the MPs of the 488th, but his troubles reflect the difficulties many wounded warriors are dealing with in the aftermath of the longest armed conflict in this nation's history.

I am indebted to Corporal John MacDonald of the Maine Warden Service for answering my questions about the protocols wardens use to manage crises in the field. Maine Today Media's investigative series "Deadly Force: Police and the Mentally Ill" provided me with a solid bedrock of information about police shootings in Maine. To those who would learn more about conditions in Maine's prison system, I would recommend the many articles that award-winning journalist Lance Tapley has written for the

Portland Phoenix since 2005. Thank you, Lance.

Many friends, relatives, and colleagues assisted me during the research, writing, and publication of this book. First and foremost is my wife, Kristen Lindquist, who also happens to be my best critic as well as my best friend. CB Anderson helped me make the writing better. Jeff McEvoy treated me like a celebrity at Weatherby's in Grand Lake Stream (and showed me some guiding tricks). Tom Judge and Eric Hopkins shared their stories about LifeFlight of Maine and the indispensable role its helicopters play in saving lives in the most rural state in the country. My father, Richard Doiron, formerly Director of Psychology at Maine Medical Center, gave me a tour of the fast-growing hospital.

Thanks to the people in the Flatiron Building: Charlie Spicer, Andrew Martin, Sally Richardson, the late Matthew Shear, Hector DeJean, Sarah Melnyk, Paul Hochman, and my unsung team at Macmillan Audio.

Ann Rittenberg, I am so grateful for all you do on my behalf—especially the work behind the scenes.

Last but not least, thanks to the many booksellers and librarians who have pressed one of my novels into the hands of a new reader and said, "Here's a book I know you're going to like."

Center Point Large Print
600 Brooks Road / PO Box 1
Thorndike, ME 04986-0001 USA

(207) 568-3717

US & Canada:
1 800 929-9108
www.centerpointlargeprint.com

$37.00
8/18

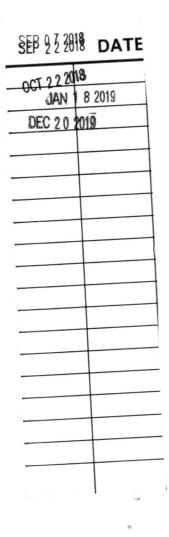

SEP 07 2018 **DATE**
SEP 22 2018

OCT 22 2018
JAN 1 8 2019
DEC 20 2019